D0961006

DAW titles by John Marco

The Books of the Bronze Knight:

The Eyes of God
The Devil's Armor
The Sword of Angels

The Forever Knight

* * *

The Skylords:

Starfinder

THE FOREVER KNIGHT

JOHN MARCO

DAW BOOKS, INC.
DONALD A. WOLLHEIM, FOUNDER
375 Hudson Street, New York, NY 10014
ELIZABETH R. WOLLHEIM
SHEILA E. GILBERT
PUBLISHERS
http://www.dawbooks.com

Jacket art by Todd Lockwood.

Jacket design by G-Force Design.

DAW Books Collector's No. 1605.

DAW Books are distributed by Penguin Group (USA) Inc.

First Hardcover Printing, April 2013
1 2 3 4 5 6 7 8 9

DAW TRADEMARK REGISTERED
U.S. PAT. AND TM. OFF. AND FOREIGN COUNTRIES
—MARCA REGISTRADA
HECHO EN U.S.A.

PRINTED IN THE U.S.A.

With heartfelt thanks for her encouragement and faith, this book is deservedly dedicated to my good friend, Janîce Leotti.

THE STORY

My father was the kind of man who never taught me anything. This is not because he abandoned me when I was young, or because he worked in the foundry each day until his face was sooty black. It is simply because he showed no interest in me, not even enough to strike me. Most men have strong memories of their fathers, even if they were tyrants. My father was a ghost, no more memorable than a day when nothing happens.

Without a father's love, a man might still become many things. I have seen people pray to all manner of gods, and I have seen genuine magic, but I don't account my fortune to anything of heaven. I've learned to place faith only in myself. It was merely good luck that plucked me from the streets as a boy. I grew up in the house of a king and became a man there, with the king's own son for a brother. You could say I didn't deserve any of this, and you'd be right. But in those years I endured jealous stares.

Then, one day before I knew it, I was no longer a bastard. I was a knight, one of Liiria's Royal Chargers. They say that our gifts are the things we are best at, and if that is so then killing is my gift. My real home, I discovered, was the battlefield, and I proudly carried the standard of my king to war; to make our country great only to see it fall. In my lifetime I've spilled much blood, but I have paid for these sins dearly. All the things I touch seem to wither just for being close to me. To be honest, I think I'm owed some solace now. In some parts of the world I am called a legend, a hero, a traitor, a myth. But the only thing I want to be is forgotten.

I remember a story from when I was a boy, about a knight who spent his whole life protecting his city from a monster that lived in the hills. Every year, when the monster came to find a maiden, the knight would ride out from the city and fight the beast, and every year he would win his battle and send the monster back to the hills. Then, one year when the knight was very old, a little boy asked him why he never killed the monster and wouldn't that make much more sense, instead of having to fight the monster every year.

The next day, the knight rode out to the monster's lair and killed it while it slept. When the city people heard the news, they rejoiced. The little boy asked the knight if he was happy now.

"No," the knight told the boy. "Now I have no reason to live."

For years I wondered what the story meant. Now, I think I understand.

My father told me that story. So perhaps he taught me something after all.

1

Easy . . .

The sand, still warm from the day, clung to my lips as I slithered. My one remaining eye blinked away the burning. Head down, chin scraping the sand, I pulled myself with bloody fingers closer to the lair. Whenever I stalk a rass I get the same sick feeling of excitement. My guts churn. My brain turns to fire. I wanted to leap but I calmed myself. I told myself to wait, but the voice in my head wasn't my own.

Easy, Lukien . . .

I know, I answered back.

Malator fell silent, but I could feel his unrest. He's like a second skin on me, impossible to get away from. I laid my face down flat in the sand and cursed him. His home, the sword, pulsed against my thigh.

Stay out of my head, I said. I wondered if the rass could hear my heartbeat. *Let me do this alone.*

Malator retreated. I spread my fingers in the sand, took the smallest breath, and lifted my face to see. The moonlight had turned the desert into a shimmering sea, the dunes like waves. The sun had gone down an hour ago and the temperature was dropping quickly. Rass love the first, cool hours of the night, when they come awake to feed. I spied the lair, surrounded by bones. The scarlet markings of the creature's hood writhed as it awoke.

The sight of a rass can make a man's heart shrivel like a dead flower. In Torlis, where I found the Sword of Angels, the rass are worshiped. I can almost understand that, but here in the real world we hate them for a reason. This one is old, a scarlet monster that kills for pleasure. Not many travelers come through the desert any more, not since the war with Ganjor, but this rass has made sport of them. He's a hunter.

So am I.

I should have killed it in its lair. One stab through the brain and I could have walked away. Instead I tracked it and stopped, giving it every chance to taste me in the air. Finally, I pushed myself up just a little too quickly, just loud enough for it to sense the tremor in the sand. Its hood rose up and its red eyes opened wide. Across the sand, it gazed at me.

I was amazed by the thing. How easily it saw me in the darkness! With no more reason to hide, I stood up. The sand fell like rain from my white robes. Curious, the rass uncoiled from its lair, swaying high against the moon. I must have looked like a mouse to it, a stupid rodent who had stumbled into its own death, because the thing seemed to smile.

"You think this was an accident?" I asked it. "You think I made a mistake?" I hooked my thumb over my sword pommel and felt the instant surge of strength. "I've been watching you and asking myself the same question. It's your nature to kill. Maybe I should just have accepted that and stayed in Jador."

Malator had enough. *Lukien! Stop talking and do it!*

If I moved quickly the rass would strike. Very slowly I unsheathed the sword. The Sword of Angels isn't a beautiful weapon, but now it glowed like starlight. It was my talisman, the only thing keeping me alive. I held it out in both fists and looked up into the serpent's shining eyes.

"Don't think you can kill me," I said. It wasn't a warning. I'd been out in the desert for more than a week. I should have been dead from lack of food, or at least too exhausted to stand, but I wasn't. I was still alive and always would be, and for that I hated Malator. "You should run," I warned my prey.

We both chose that instant to strike. I thrust out the sword and saw the fanged mouth coming down at me. A rass doesn't fight like a regular snake. It's whole body moves at once. I leapt and watched the tail fling out from the lair, trying to snare me. My blade caught its throat as I twisted away, rolling quickly through the sand. Without a sound the rass encircled me. The patterns of its body, like tattoos, rose up around me like a prison.

There's no time to think in battle. Strategy is for the night before. Every plan you make just disappears, and all you have is instinct.

Draw it closer, said Malator.

In his own life he had been a soldier too. Instead of hurdling over the snake's body, I let the noose close around me. I squatted on my haunches, held the sword down low, and waited for the monster's face to block the moonlight. As I felt its scaly flesh press against me, the burning eyes appeared above.

I jumped, screaming, both arms thrusting up. I felt the sword puncture skin. Hot blood and saliva struck my face. I drew the blade deeper, not really sure what I had struck. But I was still in the creature's coils. For a moment the rass opened its grasp in shock, only to tighten up quickly around me. The thing hissed and spat, its dripping venom popping on my skin. I pulled out the blade then stabbed it again.

"Malator!" I summoned. "Strengthen me!"

The snake's muscled body wrapped around my own, crushing out my air. I thought about the mouse again. Red eyes flashed before me. I worked the sword, slicing through the creature's jaw. It reared back its bloodied head, half its mouth hanging from fibers of flesh. It would die from the wound, but not quickly. Not before I did. And still Malator's magic strength didn't come. My voice was gurgled as I shouted his name.

"Malator!"

Where was he? *I'm dying,* I thought. *This time for real!*

And then I heard his voice, so calm it enraged me.

Do you want to die?

"No!" I screamed.

Are you sure? You seem to be trying hard.

The rass constricted around my chest. My rib cage groaned, ready to crack. "Stop . . . it!"

As I screamed I felt the Akari's power flood my bones and blood, scalding me. My fingers stopped shaking. I could grip the sword again, and this time sent it charging up into that grinning, reptilian face. The tip slammed into the creature's eye and kept on going. With all the might Malator could give, I pushed and pushed the Sword of Angels deep into the rass's brain. Its coiling body fell away, dropping me to my knees. The rass thrashed, blinded and bleeding, its tail whipping me aside. I spun as if struck by a club. Stunned, I lay in the dirt, unable to move. The dying rass made for its lair. Half its body disappeared into the ground . . . then the thing fell dead.

I was bleeding, my shoulder torn open by the beast's spiky tail. Every breath made my ribs cry out. The sword lay just feet away. I turned my head and stared at the enormous, twitching snake. Malator's burst of strength had left me.

Pick it up, said Malator.

I could hardly hear him through the fog of pain.

Pick it up!

The blade seemed so far away. I made a claw of my hand and stretched for it with my wounded shoulder. Breathing was almost too difficult.

You said you didn't want to die, the spirit chided. *Prove it.*

Some Akari were gentle, but mine was a taskmaster. "Eat shit!" I growled even as I rolled to reach the sword. My fingers touched its worn out hilt, wrapping around it. Suddenly, I could breathe again. I dragged the sword over my chest as I rolled onto my back. The fog in my mind began to lift. The pain in my shoulder subsided.

The stars in the desert are like no other place in the world, and I remember how many stars were out that night and how close they felt to me, as if my spirit could just rise up and join them in the heavens. I felt sleepy. I wanted to let go of the sword, but I had promises to keep. Or maybe I was just too afraid to let it go. I shut my eye and felt my body healing. When I opened it again he was kneeling next to me. To anyone else he would have been invisible. Even to me he seemed a ghost, his boyish face shimmering. He shook his head with a scowl and a loud, motherly sigh.

"My shoulder," I sneered. "Fix it."

"Rest. In the morning you'll be fine." He glanced over the at the dead rass. "What will you do when there are no more rass to kill, Lukien?"

I thought about his question as I lay there. It's impossible to hide your thoughts from an Akari. That's the hardest part about having one. They're not like little angels on your shoulder. I wanted to tell him that the world would never run out of monsters to kill, but none of this was about the rass. I was testing myself, and Malator knew it.

"I can heal you this time," he warned. "But if you make me go along with this much longer . . ."

"What?" I asked. "What will you do? Leave me?"

"You could be so much more."

"You keep telling me."

I didn't want to talk, so I looked into the sky again and pretended not to care. I—we—had been gone from Jador too long. We were irritating each other, bored with each other. I was supposed to spend the rest of my life with Malator—a life that really had no end—and the thought frightened me more than any monster. I tried to ignore him, but he kept staring at me, waiting for an answer.

"Malator, a friend would let me sleep."

"I am your friend, Lukien. I'm the only friend you need." He bent forward, and his eerie light around me made me stronger still. "You keep looking for something that's right in front of you."

"I miss her," I said. "You don't know what it's like."

"I feel everything you feel, Lukien. I know precisely what it's like. I was a man once, remember?"

Malator had died when he was young, so his ghost looks young too. His smile is more like a smirk, charming and maddening. He wanted me to go home to Jador; he'd been pushing me to go back for days. Now I was out of excuses. The sword sat across my chest, rising and falling as I breathed. And the stars kept calling to me.

If I died, I thought, *I could see her again.*

Malator didn't even pretend my thoughts were private. "But then you'd never know what lies ahead for us."

"True," I nodded. But did I want to know? Not really. Not then. All I wanted was to look up at the stars and imagine I was all alone.

2

A day and a half later, I was back in Jador.

Nothing had changed in my absence, which is why I took my time getting back, loping through the desert and stopping even when I wasn't tired. I had taken what I needed from the dead rass, stuffing my prize into the leather bag I carried on my back. I spent the first night of my trip home at the hidden oasis I'd discovered on one of my earliest jaunts into the desert. By noon the next day I could see Jador on the horizon, its towers gleaming in the powerful sun.

Even the quickest caravans take days to reach Jador from the continent. By then the sun has burned your body raw and swelled your tongue with thirst. People die crossing the desert, killed by rass or lack of water, and yet they've come by the hundreds to Jador. There's a great white wall around the city, and around that is a dismal shanty town, filled with throngs of uninvited, desperate foreigners. From the shacks and shrana houses it's easy to see the palace where I live. And yet nobody seems to begrudge the Jadori their fabulous home. They're safe in their shacks, protected by those inside the walls.

These people are light-skinned like me. I drink and dice with them when I have time, but today I headed straight for the palace gates. With the hood of my gaka drawn around my face, I tucked the sword under my robe and walked casually through the narrow avenues. Children and dogs roamed the stalls and the men and women from a dozen different countries went about their chores. Some were lame, some were blind, and some had ailments deep within their brains, but they'd all come to Jador with the same futile hope: to get an Akari of their own.

To be healed.

The noise of the crowd maddened me. After so long in the desert I'd become used to hearing only Malator's voice. I kept my head down as I hurried toward the gate. Jadori warriors stood guard, casually shooing away the kids that came to gawk at their kreel. The enormous lizard made a show of flicking its tongue through the bars. The children laughed and pretended to be afraid, but when the kreel tasted the air again it paused and looked straight at me. The warriors followed its gaze.

"Shalafein?" asked one of the guards.

I stood taller and peeled my hood away. When they saw my eye patch, the children cheered. They surrounded me as the Jadori opened the gate, tugging at my robes, asking for a glimpse of the sword.

"No!" I said as gently as I could.

The kids—four boys and a girl—backed off. A Jadori scolded them, waving them away. I didn't have time for their hurt feelings. They were glad to see me, that was all, but I'd been in the desert too long, and the thought of dealing with them wearied me.

Later, I told myself. After I rested awhile I could leave the palace and be with them, my own kind. I rushed inside the gate. Once it clanged behind me, the whole world changed.

Suddenly, there were gardens. Pools of cool water with spraying fountains. Birds picking at berry bushes. I looked up to the palace, a small city really, sprawling within the white wall. Dark toned men and women—and some of the Akari-gifted Inhumans from Grimhold—moved along the avenues. I hid from them all.

My room would be waiting for me, I knew. Every day the girls had come and put flowers in it for me. They'd changed the water in the basin, too, because Gilwyn and White-Eye told them to and because they knew—like everyone knew—that I'd be back eventually. The thought of my clean bed weakened me a little, but I'd been rude enough already. Before I even washed my hands, I had to see Gilwyn.

Even with my filthy clothes and bearded face, my size let them recognize me instantly. I know enough Jadori now to speak clearly, so when they greeted me I hugged them and smiled and told them briefly of my time in the desert. Before I could make it up the first flight of stairs I ran into Monster, the hunch-backed Inhuman who looks after White-Eye. He was overjoyed to see me and told me that White-Eye would be, too, but I explained that I was just back from my sojourn and wanted to see Gilwyn first.

"In his study," said Monster, pointing a bony finger up the staircase. "As usual."

Monster smiled like he was hiding something. A crowd began to gather. I would need to see White-Eye soon, and in truth I longed to do so. She was the one who'd made me *Shalafein*, Jador's "protector," and it was really she I was sworn to protect. That she had married Gilwyn was really just his good luck. I nodded politely at everyone who'd gathered, apologized, then went quickly up the twisting staircase.

You're becoming a hermit, I heard Malator chide.

"I am not," I shot back. "Gilwyn should know I'm back, that's all."

Malator said nothing more, and I was glad for that. I ran my fingers through my tangled hair as I climbed the stairs. My time in the desert had turned my skin the same bronze as my well-worn armor. Grit dirtied my hair and fingernails. I smiled as I thought of Gilwyn, sure I would find him buried in his books.

His study, as he called it, was really just a tiny room with a spectacular view. I reached the top of the stairs and noted the study at the end of the quiet hall. The door was open, but no one ever disturbed Gilwyn while he worked. I grinned as I headed that way, expecting my heavy boots to rouse him. But he didn't call out to me, not even when I reached the door. Surprised, I peered inside and saw him behind his desk. Bent over his papers, bright light flooding through the window, his thoughts deafened him. His cane sat propped up against his chair. Books and scrolls lined the shelves and littered the floor in unsteady piles. An orrery sat at the edge of his wooden desk, ready to fall off. Gilwyn scribbled madly in a book, the pen gripped tightly in his one good hand.

"Gilwyn?"

He snapped back in his chair, wild-eyed with surprise. The pen spun from his hand. "Lukien!"

Forgetting his cane, he kicked aside the books to reach me. It was a real hug, the kind brothers give each other. I stooped to tuck my face against his own and felt his kiss on my cheek.

"Look at you!" he laughed, stepping back to see all of me. "You look . . . horrible!"

He steadied himself against his desk, favoring his clubbed foot. He still wore the special boot Figgis had made for him years ago. I stared back, smiling. He wasn't a boy anymore, I realized. He hadn't been a boy for years, really, and I don't know why I only saw the change in him that moment. He even seemed a little taller. I went to his chair and pulled it out for him.

"Clear that junk away," he said as he sat down, gesturing to another chair covered with papers. "You just get back?"

"Just now," I said as I set the papers aside. I dragged the chair across the floor and sat down. Behind him, white towers and sand twinkled through the window. The room was warm but not unbearable, and Gilwyn's hair fell into his eyes, damp with sweat. Like all of us from the continent he'd gotten used to the desert heat. I took the pack off my shoulder and dropped it to the floor. That's when I noticed Gilwyn smiling, the same way Monster had.

"What?" I asked.

"I'm glad you're back, Lukien."

"And? You're hiding something."

Gilwyn shrugged. "White-Eye's with child," he said. Then he laughed. "I'm going to be a father!"

This was news I didn't expect. Gilwyn had married White-Eye less than a year ago, not long after the war with Ganjor. Suddenly, I felt angry at myself for having gone away.

"Ah, good work!" I crowed. "When did you find out?"

"Just before you left. White-Eye wanted to be sure."

"What do you call a little Kahan? A Kahanette?"

"Or a Kahanarina," joked Gilwyn. "If it's a girl."

"Where's White-Eye?" I said, getting out of my chair. "I have to see her."

"Who knows?" Gilwyn shrugged. "I've been up here all day going through petitions. They still come in, new ones every day." The joy in his face went away. "Just sit, okay?"

It's easy to know when something's on Gilwyn's mind. His eyes sort of dance all over your face without really looking. He glanced at my sword, and that's when I noticed the Eye of God around his neck, bulging out from under his shirt. Both of us were immortal now, or very nearly so. I had tried to die a dozen times since finding the sword, and the amulet Gilwyn wore had once been mine as well. I had cursed him with it just to save his life. It had stopped his aging, mostly, but not the havoc of worry. Since Minikin's death he wasn't only the Kahan of Jador—he was also Master of Grimhold now.

Gilwyn leaned back, bracing me for what was coming. "Twenty-nine days."

"Yeah," I nodded. "But you knew I'd be back."

"That's the longest you've ever stayed away."

"You're already sounding like a father, Gilwyn. I'm fine. Look at me."

"I am looking, Lukien. When was the last time you ate anything? Besides snake meat, I mean? Maybe that's how you plan to kill yourself—starvation."

"Whoa," I said, surprised. "Being a ruler has made you bold, Gilwyn. I'm a big boy, all right? Let's talk about the baby."

He shook his head. "I want to know what's going on with you. You said you were okay with keeping the sword. But all you've done since you found it is try to find new ways to hurt yourself. And you're never here more than a couple of weeks at a time."

I got up and headed for the window. "You're as bad as Malator. I thought you'd give me a day at least before badgering me." I looked over the city, then beyond it to the desert. I had just returned from there and already I wanted to go back. "Fate above, I'm out of my mind with boredom," I confessed.

"You're restless," said Gilwyn.

He sounded like a physician. I turned and gestured to all the books and papers tumbling off his desk.

"Look at all this stuff you have to keep you busy," I said. "Good thing you have the amulet—you'll need eternity just to get through all these letters! The Inhumans need you, the refugees need you . . . but none of them need me. Jador doesn't need Shalafein anymore. Who am I protecting us from?"

"Lukien," said Gilwyn calmly, "you're absolutely right."

I stopped raving. "I am?"

"The baby isn't the only news I wanted to tell you, Lukien. I've been talking with White-Eye. She agrees with me." Gilwyn stood up and leaned on the edge of his desk. "It's time you left Jador."

That staggered me. "You *want* me to go?"

"Yeah," he said. "I mean, I've been thinking about it, all those things you said. It's all true. Ganjor isn't a threat any more, and there's only a trickle of Seekers coming to the city now. Malator's right, Lukien—you're powerful. You can do a lot more good somewhere else."

"You want me to leave," I said again. I was almost struck dumb. No one likes to be told they're not wanted, and even though I knew that's not what Gilwyn meant it still hurt a little. "I'm pledged to White-Eye," I argued. "And to Jador. It's not something I can just walk away from you know."

"You wouldn't have to," said Gilwyn. He shuffled over to my leather bag and poked it curiously with his cane. "You could be a knight-errant."

"What, a mercenary?" I'd already been one of those and lost my eye in the bargain. "Forget it."

Gilwyn looked annoyed. "Didn't you read stories growing up? A knight-errant isn't a mercenary. He's like a champion. He goes from place to place looking for people to help. You know, in the name of someone, like a lady or a queen. You could do it in the name of Jador. That way you'd still be Shalafein. You'd still be keeping your vow."

"That's crazy," I scoffed. I didn't want to admit it appealed to me. "I'm just supposed to wander around like some tramp?"

"No, Lukien," said Gilwyn sharply. "That's what you have been doing. Clean yourself up, give your life some purpose. You're like a caged animal here in Jador. This is a chance to find out what Malator means about your future."

He'd already thought it through, tying up his argument in a neat little bundle. Just the thought of leaving Jador was dreamy. I was glad when he looked at my bag again, trying to see inside it.

"What is that?" he asked, lifting it partially with the tip of his cane and squinting inside.

"Go ahead, look."

"I don't trust you," said Gilwyn. "Probably a bag of scorpions or . . ."

His eyes went wide when he saw the prize I'd brought back. He set aside his cane and opened the bag, pulling out the snake skin. Twice as wide as Gilwyn, he held it up like a sheet. The scarlet patterns of the rass's hood looked fiery in the sunlight.

"You did this yourself?" he asked.

"Like pulling off a sock. Scaled it, too. Feel how smooth."

The skin was as supple as the leather bag and hadn't even been tanned yet. I'd left most of it behind of course, but had carefully removed the most interesting part, the best part—the rass's giant hood.

"Beautiful," said Gilwyn. "But what am I supposed to do with it?"

"It's not for you," I told him. "It's for Cricket."

"Oh." Gilwyn looked relieved and handed the skin back to me. "So what'll she do with it?"

"I thought we'd make a cape for her. More than big enough for that." I smiled as I tucked the skin back into the bag, knowing she would love it. I was always bringing things back from the desert for Cricket. Trinkets usually brightened her mood.

"Good," pronounced Gilwyn as he dropped into his chair again. "It'll give her something to do. Maybe she'll stop stealing chickens."

"What?"

"She stole a chicken from the kitchen. Said she needed to set it free. Oh, and she painted one of the walls of the cistern, too. Stripes. She says it wasn't her, but . . . come on." Gilwyn gave a big sigh and looked at me. "She misses Minikin. It gets worse when you go away."

I wasn't sure what he expected me to do about it. I knew Cricket was attached to me, but she was fourteen years old and barely in control of herself. "I'll talk to her," I promised. "Where is she?"

"Grimhold." Gilwyn saw my surprise. "I needed to get her out from underfoot, Lukien. She likes going there. It's good for her."

"No, it isn't," I huffed. "It reminds her of Minikin, and it depresses her." I cinched up my bag, making to leave. "Let me go see White-Eye."

"Are you angry about Cricket or are you angry about my idea?" asked Gilwyn as I headed out.

"When's she coming back?"

"I don't know; a day or two. Go see her if you want. She'd like that. And Lukien? Think about my idea, all right?"

"Right."

"It's a good idea. You know it!"

"Congratulations on the baby, Gilwyn." I waved as I started down the hall.

But I did think about his idea. I was worried about Cricket and worried about Jador and Grimhold and everything else, and I was *sick* of worrying. I imagined disappearing, going back home to Liiria or wandering around Norvor, or maybe going to a place where no one had ever heard of me. I could be a new person, I figured. I could forget about everything.

Just like Cricket had.

I bathed before going to see White-Eye. She was the Kahana and I was a tramp, and although she was blind and wouldn't have minded my filth, it would have been an insult to her beauty. I took my time to ready myself, soaking the sand out of my fingernails and shaving the beard that had sprouted from my days in the desert. I let the serving girls comb my hair and convince me to perfume it. I was nervous about seeing White-Eye, and it irked me that I should feel so.

Not everyone in Jador has an Akari. They are rare things, gifted to those in dire need. They are immortal but not indestructible, and White-Eye had learned that in the most horrible way, having her own Akari ripped from her by a demon. After years of being able to see through her Akari's eyes, she was once again blind. But she was not bumbling or stupid, and most of all she wasn't helpless.

I found White-Eye that evening, looking after a group of playing children. There she sat in the middle of the garden, her delicate fingers macraméing as the boys and girls climbed trees and chased each other around a foaming fountain. I stopped at the edge of the garden, my face hidden by a trellis of vines as I studied White-Eye, looking at her belly for a hint of her growing baby. A contented smile warmed her dark face, working the knots of the fabric she was making, her head tilted slightly as she listened to the children frolicking around her. They were Jadori children mostly, with the same dark skin as her. Some of them I recognized, others I'd never seen before. As I took my first step toward them, only one of them noticed me at all—a sightless boy named Alik.

He stopped midway up the tree he was climbing, turning his blind eyes toward me, seeing me in his mind the way White-Eye once could. I could easily imagine his Akari, Dianis, whispering my arrival in his ear. Before I could put a finger to my lips to silence him, Alik sprang down from the tree.

"Lukien!"

Some of the children turned to see me; others played their games. But White-Eye lowered her macramé at once. "Lukien?" She stood up, cocking an ear to locate me. Alik rushed to take her hand.

"He's here!" cried the boy, pointing at me as though White-Eye could follow. The green landscape between us was no obstacle at all to him. Everything, every plant and stone, was revealed in his mind by his Akari. Discovered, I laughed.

"It's me, White-Eye," I said, going toward her and the boy. "I'm back."

A gaggle of children gathered around me, except for Alik, who protectively held his Kahana's hand. I greeted them as best I could, pretending I knew them all. A girl with a clubbed foot like Gilwyn's bounded toward me with ease. A deaf boy smiled when I said his name, understanding me perfectly. These were the children of Grimhold.

"All right, let me talk to White-Eye now," I told them gently. "Go back to playing—I'll be around."

White-Eye kindly waited for me near the fountain. She had no need of young Alik's help but held his hand anyway. The boy beamed at me.

"We were wondering when you'd come," said Alik. "Me and Kahana White-Eye was just saying that!"

"Well I'm back now," I said brightly. I leaned down and looked into Alik's blank eyes, knowing he could see my face precisely. "Thank you for taking care of White-Eye while I was gone. Maybe I should call you 'little Shalafein,' eh?"

"Alik likes to touch my belly. He says he can feel the baby inside me," said White-Eye. She managed to grin at the silly notion so only I could see it. "Will you let me talk with Lukien, Alik?" she asked him. "Go and play—you can see him later."

Alik ran off without offense, the other children following his lead. When it was only us two, she gave me her prized smile.

"Have you come to touch my belly?" she joked.

But the offer was irresistible. I gently placed the palm of my hand on her stomach, feeling the flatness of it but knowing that inside it grew the offspring of my two closest friends. White-Eye sighed and closed her own hand over mine.

"You will be the finest mother any child ever had," I whispered to her. White-Eye chuckled. She'd been brave when her father died and brave when her eyesight was stolen. Having a child seemed not to trouble her at all.

"And you must stay here to help us raise this child, Lukien!"

"I'm here now," I said without commitment. "Let's sit."

We lowered each other to the edge of the fountain. Around us the children played and laughed. The great, white wall of Jador loomed in the distance, separating us from the throngs of foreigners that had come to White-Eye's home. Foreigners like me. I had washed and scented myself, but White-Eye could tell I was troubled, and there was no point at all in hiding it from her.

"I saw Gilwyn. Did he tell you?"

"He told me. I expected you to come sooner, Lukien."

"I needed a bath first."

"No. I meant I thought you'd come home to Jador sooner. You were gone a very long while this time."

I nodded. "It is nice to be missed, though."

"You won't find what you're looking for in the desert. There is nothing in the desert. Only Jador." She looked sad. "Jador won't make you happy."

"And this scheme of Gilwyn's? Do you think that will help me?" I asked sincerely. "I have been an adventurer most of my life, White-Eye."

"Adventure? You don't understand, then. Purpose is what you need, Lukien. Find a cause and give yourself to it. And when you're done, return here to us. That's all we're saying."

I looked down at her belly, imagining the child growing within. "I need to see your child," I said. "I can't be gone for that."

"Of course," said White-Eye. "You must be here for that. I told you—I'll need your help with this bundle! But there's many months before the baby comes. Just go and then return. You can do that, can't you?"

Her words baffled me. Not her question but her statement. I kept staring down at her unborn child. "White-Eye, I'm a fighter. A killer. You want a child who lives in peace. What can I possibly teach your baby?" I thought about it. "A boy should learn how to use a weapon, I suppose. And I'm a good horseman . . . I could teach your baby that."

"Lukien, no," said White-Eye. "Anyone could teach our baby those things."

"What, then?"

White-Eye grew unusually serious. "You make me say this? You saved this city from invasion. You destroyed the demon that took away my Akari and made me blind. You are the hero of everyone in Jador. Lukien, boy or girl, you will teach my child the most difficult things of all. Things that cannot be learned from scrolls or stories: bravery and honor. But most of all, you will teach my baby goodness. Because even if you don't think so, you are a good man, Lukien."

I sat there. I nodded. But I didn't argue with her because I could not even speak.

Ever gracious, she allowed my silence. She went back to her macramé, diligently making knots as I sat there beside her and watched the children play.

3

How can I describe Cricket? She's like a mirror image, the opposite of what you think you see. She's pretty but doesn't care at all about looks. She hordes trinkets till they're spilling out of her pockets. She complains about her chores but does them to perfection, and she loves to be alone but clings to me like bark. Near as we can tell she's fourteen years old. Sometimes she acts half that age, sometimes twice it. She'll talk for an hour then shut up tight for days, and no one—not even Minikin when she was alive—can ever figure out what's going on inside her impish head.

The day we left Grimhold, Cricket was in the mood to talk. She wore the cape we'd made together out of the rass skin, proudly primping it over her little shoulders as her pony sauntered through the canyon. I'd gone to Grimhold myself so we could work on the cape together. When she saw me arrive, Cricket circled me like a child searching for sweets, wondering what I'd brought her. The sun was hot on the black cape as we rode, but Cricket didn't care. She was full of questions and eager to get back to Jador. I was happy just to see her smiling.

A decent road winds from Grimhold to Jador, through a canyon of sheer, red rock. Inhumans and Jadori have used the road for decades, keeping their alliance secret. Before Gilwyn took over, Minikin was Grimhold's mistress. She'd spent her vast lifetime searching for the kind of kids Gilwyn had been once. Blind kids or crippled, she brought them all to Jador for an Akari, for the chance to live a normal life. I'm an Inhuman now, too, in a way, because Malator keeps me alive. Without him, my old wounds would quickly kill me.

Cricket isn't one of us. She has no Akari, and no use for one. She's not blind or lame or deaf. She's normal in every way—except for her broken memory—and it's only because Minikin loved and pitied her that she has such access to our world. Seekers from the Bitter Kingdoms had found her in Akyre. She'd been wandering, they said, starved and alone. No family and no memory of one either. All she knew for sure was her name. Cricket.

I rode beside her on my horse, listening to her explanations. Ahead of us, the two Jadori warriors Gilwyn assigned as escorts bobbed on the backs of their green-scaled kreels.

"It was like a dream," Cricket exclaimed. "Like it was talking to me. It was screaming, and no one else could hear it." She turned, imploring me. "That must have happened to you once, right Lukien?"

"No, Cricket. I've never had a chicken talk to me."

"With its *eyes,*" she stressed. "It knew I would help. I had to!"

"Uh huh." I nodded, bored with her horseshit. "What about all the chickens you actually eat? Can't they talk to you? And what about the cistern?"

"He told you that?" Cricket frowned. "Gilwyn's an ass."

"Hey!" I reined in my horse.

She kept riding for a while, then stopped. "Sorry."

The warriors turned around to look at us. "Go," I told them, waving them on. "It's all right."

I rode up close to Cricket. "You want to go live with the other Seekers in the shanties?"

"I'm not a Seeker."

"Anyone who comes across the desert to Jador is a Seeker, Cricket. And any one of them would trade places with you. You live in the palace because Gilwyn lets you. So show him some respect."

"I said I was sorry." She sighed as she got her pony going. "You ain't been in such a great mood either, you know. Like you got an itch or something."

"Yes, I've got an itch. And I don't need you making it worse. I come back from the desert and all I hear about is how worried everyone is about you. I'm not your mother, Cricket."

"What's itchin' you, Lukien?"

I still hadn't told her about Gilwyn's idea. I'd meant to, but the days just sort of slipped away. "Nothing," I said, "forget it," and reached up to scratch beneath my eye patch. Cricket stared, trying to see under it.

"You got an eyeball under there?"

"Of course I do. It's gone white, that's all. Sometimes I get a grain of sand in there. Makes me crazy."

"How'd that happen to you? You're a handsome man, Lukien. Bet you were pretty to look at when you were younger."

I smiled, because she was so good at changing subjects. "You're dodging, Cricket. We're not done talking about the cistern."

"I'll paint it back to normal," she groaned. "So what happened?"

"A Norvan scimitar."

"From when you were a mercenary?"

"That's right."

"Must make it hard to fight, having one eye."

"Two would be better," I admitted. "Doesn't hurt any more, though. Malator sees to that. Nothing hurts me anymore. Not for long, anyway."

We both got quiet, the horse hooves echoing around the canyon. The claws of the kreels clicked on the sandy road as their tongues flicked in and out. Cricket looked at me. She wanted a story.

"Norvor's a lot like Akyre, I guess. Just a bunch of barons fighting for territory now. No real king or queen any more. There's been fighting in that part of the world since I can remember."

"Yup," nodded Cricket. That much she already knew. Everyone figured it was the fighting that took her family away, but Cricket couldn't remember.

"I had to be a freelance," I continued. "Didn't want to be, but I was exiled from Liiria then. Not much else to do but hire out my sword. The Diamond Queen was rich enough to pay, so I took it. Got a lot of cuts and scrapes working for her, but this was the worst of 'em." I gestured to my blind eye.

"Norvor," she echoed. "The people who brought me here talked about Norvor, thought I might have come from there. I told them I was sure Akyre was my home. Don't know why, though."

"You'll remember one day," I told her. "If you want to."

"Of course I want to! It's all in my head, waiting for me to discover it. Maybe it'll come to me in a dream someday."

"Or maybe a chicken will tell you where you came from."

We laughed, which was good because neither of us liked the way the conversation had gone. The sun was warm and the sky was crystal clear, and all of a sudden I just started talking.

"Gilwyn thinks I should go away," I told her. "He says Jador doesn't really need me right now. Says it's time for me to find out about myself, just like you."

Cricket's round face tightened. "Huh?"

"I'm thinking he's right. I've been restless here. That's the itch. I need to see what's out there for me, maybe do some good in the world. Like a knight-errant. Try to find my mission."

"You've got a mission, Lukien. You're Shalafein!"

"Yeah, well, I'll still be Shalafein. I'll just be doing it somewhere else. Don't you know how a knight-errant works? He rides around helping people. I'd be doing that in the name of Jador."

Cricket looked puzzled. "Sounds like being a mercenary to me. You're the Bronze Knight, Lukien. Why do you need to go around proving yourself all the time? Why can't you just stay here?"

"Because I'm going mad here, Cricket." I slowed down, letting the Jadori get further ahead. "You remember when you told me how you like to keep doing things, how sometimes you can't control yourself because the stuff in your head drives you crazy, because you're trying to remember so hard that you can't stop your mind from buzzing? That's what it's like for me. You need to remember things . . . but I need to forget."

Cricket lifted her chin. "You mean Cassandra."

"Yeah. Cassandra." I touched my sword, thinking its power would make me feel better. "Maybe we're the same, you and me. Always looking for trouble. Sometimes I have to fight just to feel something besides sorry for myself." I looked at her. "You understand. I know you do."

Cricket nodded. "I do. Just thinking about myself, I guess. With Minikin gone, and now you . . . What'll happen to me, Lukien?"

"Oh, you'll be fine," I said. It was all I could think to say, the kind of thing no one ever wants to hear. "If it wasn't safe here I wouldn't be going."

"But what'll I *do*? I don't even know who I am. And Gilwyn's always too busy for me. He'll just shovel me under with chores."

She looked genuinely scared. Not about the chores, which was nonsense, but about being alone. And that's when I had my idea. At first I just smiled as it came over me, then I chuckled. Cricket grimaced.

"It's not funny." Her face got gloomy. "I don't want to stay here without you."

"Well," I said, taking a deep breath, "a knight should have a squire. What about that?"

"A squire?"

"Someone to look after my armor, my horse. You think you could do those things?"

"Me?" She looked as startled as I was by my idea. "But what about your mission?"

"You could be my mission, Cricket. You want to find out about yourself? So do I. We can go to Akyre together, try to find something to knock loose your memories."

"Akyre." Cricket's gloominess returned even darker. "Isn't that dangerous?"

Before I could answer, Malator screamed in my ear, *Yes!*

I patted my sword to show them both I wasn't afraid. "There's no safer place than at my side. I'll have a squire, and you'll have your own bodyguard—one that can't get himself killed."

That's idiotic. You can *be killed! You're not immortal!*

I said to Cricket, "Gilwyn'll try to talk us out of it, but I'll make him understand. It was his idea in the first place. Why should he begrudge me some friendly company?"

Because she's just a kid!

Cricket thought about it, then gave me her little grin. "I want to do it," she said. "It's like I'm out there, wandering around somewhere. I want to go find myself."

"It's a long way," I warned. "Hard travel."

"I know it; I already did it once. I can make it," she promised.

"Good," I declared, pleased with her passion. For the first time in months I felt happy.

We rode on, Malator chattering at me the whole while. Out of spite I ignored him. Malator didn't control me, I told myself. Let him rant and rave. I was a man, not a boy. I'd go wherever I damn well pleased.

When I get an itch, I scratch till it's bloody.

4

I was right about Gilwyn not being happy, and I was right about him not trying to stop us. I had my arguments prepared and the determination to make them stick, and in the end he relented. Cricket couldn't stay in Jador forever. She wasn't an Inhuman either, so living in Grimhold was out of the question. She was, Gilwyn admitted, a mystery to everyone. It made sense that she should try to discover who she really was.

We didn't leave Jador quickly, though. I had affairs to get in order and friends to say good-bye to, and crossing the Desert of Tears took planning. We needed water, mostly, and mules to carry it. Food would be a problem, too. I had made the passage several times and had a good map that I'd drawn of the resting spots along the way. I knew every hidden oasis, every cave, every stand of fruit trees. If we found a rass I would kill it, I promised Cricket, and make her a necklace of its teeth. I was excited about leaving but also swore to Gilwyn and White-Eye that I'd return before their baby was born. I figured that gave me at least six months.

Eventually, everyone got used to the idea of us leaving, except for Malator. For days he brooded, not even bothering to talk to me. I refused to care. He'd played that game before with me, and in truth I liked the quiet. Having an Akari constantly in your mind can drive you crazy, so I didn't bother calling to him either, not even the night before our journey.

It was one of Jador's perfect nights, totally cloudless, where every star demanded to be counted. I was outside the paddock with my horse, standing in the cut grass strewn over the dirt, enjoying the night air while I brushed the burrs and sand from his coat. Inside the stable the other animals were resting. Not the kreels, though. Kreels are always kept far from horses, and need to be trained not to attack them. I've seen kreels rip the bellies out of horses. Zephyr—my horse—was used to kreels, though, as was Cricket's pony. I'd already brushed the pony for the trip, but I took my time with Zephyr.

"First we'll get your coat all shined up, then we'll dig that slop out of your hooves. How's that sound, boy?"

Zephyr loved the dandy brush. His gray eyelids drooped with relaxation as I ran it down his side. He'd been a gift from King Baralosus of Ganjor, a kind of peace offering after the war. I didn't much like Baralosus but didn't mind having such a fine horse, either. I babied Zephyr whenever we were at home in the palace, because out in the desert I demanded so much of him.

"It's going to be a long one this time, Zephyr," I warned. "We won't be back here for months. No telling what we'll find in the Bitter Kingdoms. Don't be scared, though. Don't be scared . . ."

Zephyr nodded his big head as I spoke. I swear that horse could understand me. I stepped back to look him over, startled by a ghostly figure crouching just outside the paddock's gate. I stared for a moment, shocked to realize it was Malator. He had his back turned to me, kneeling as he drew in the sand with his finger. Stupidly I looked down at my sword. It was still there, of course, but Malator had left the magic weapon.

"Hey," I called. We were alone, and no one else could see him anyway. He ignored me, not even lifting his head, absorbed in what he was doing. "Malator?"

"Come look at this, Lukien," he said. I put down my brush and left the paddock, going to stand over his shoulder. He had drawn what looked vaguely like a dragon in the sand.

"Nice," I commented. "So you're talking to me again?"

"Look at the dragon, Lukien," he told me, then passed his ghostly hand over it. The moonlight went through his fingers, striking the image and bringing it to life. The drawing twitched, the mouth and wings suddenly moved. It was a grotesque looking thing, changing quickly as I watched it, sometimes barely resembling a dragon at all. The trick made me smile.

"I didn't know you could do that," I said. "What is it?"

"I'm not sure," said Malator. He leaned over to study it, the moonlight passing through his body. "Something I've been seeing lately in my mind."

Now I was really interested. "What? Like the future?" Minikin had been able to glimpse the future and so could some Akari. But then I said, "There's no such things as dragons."

"The dragon could be anything," said Malator. "A symbol maybe."

"A symbol for what?"

Malator shook his head and would not answer. He watched the drawing change from a jumbled mass, then to something that looked like bones, and then at last back to a dragon. His unease made me nervous.

"What's it telling you?" I asked.

Slowly he reached out and wiped the thing away.

"Come on, Malator," I said. "What was that? What'd you see?"

Malator stood up to face me. Though he'd been kneeling, not a single grain of sand clung to him. "We need to talk about Cricket," he said, "and the stupid decision you've made."

"Now?" I turned back toward the paddock. "It's too late. We're leaving in the morning."

"You need to listen to me, Lukien. Cricket can't go with you."

"Why?" I looked at him again. "What aren't you telling me, Malator?" I gestured toward the sand where he'd made his picture. "Did you see something about Cricket?"

"No," he said flatly.

"No. And if you did, would you tell me?"

"You're letting her come between us, Lukien." His face was earnest, even sincere. "You're special. But I can't teach you what you need to know if you're distracted."

"Special," I scoffed. "Are you ever going to tell me what that means?"

"You'll know in time," said Malator. "But not if you take the girl with you."

None of it made sense to me. I was sick of trying to figure out his riddles. "I'm going, Malator. And Cricket's going with me." I returned to Zephyr, picked up my brush, and continued grooming. Malator floated up behind me.

"Go to Akyre, Lukien," he said. "It's important that you do. But go alone."

"Nope."

Malator growled, "Stop blaming me for keeping you alive! *You* chose to stay alive, Lukien. *You* made the promise to Gilwyn and White-Eye. Cassandra's dead. Cricket can't replace her."

I lowered the brush but didn't turn to face him. "No one can replace her," I said. "Why would you ever begrudge me something as simple as a friend?"

"I'm your friend, Lukien," said Malator. "The only friend you need. Cricket can't help you find peace. Neither can Gilwyn or anyone else. Only I can do that, but you need to listen to me. Learn from me. You have a destiny."

"Which you won't tell me about, right?" I threw the brush to the ground. "It's always riddles with the Akari! If it's my destiny then it's *mine*. Who are you to keep it from me?"

"I'm not a fortune teller," said Malator. "I can only be a guide."

"Right," I sneered. "What was that thing you drew? And why's it important for me to go to Akyre all of a sudden? That was my idea, Malator. You had nothing to do with it."

"I see things, Lukien. I don't always know what they mean." Malator folded his arms over his chest with an imperious, irritating expression. "But a host needs to trust his Akari."

"Give me a reason to trust you," I pleaded. "Tell me what this great destiny is you've got planned, and I won't take Cricket to Akyre. Just once tell me the truth without wrapping it in riddles."

Malator refused to budge. "The future cannot be revealed. You know that."

"Then I'm going. I'm going, and I'm taking Cricket with me, and to hell with my destiny!" I pulled the sword halfway from its sheath. "You can keep me alive, Malator, but that's all I want from you. From now on you serve me—not the other way around."

"I'm an Akari, not a slave," he bristled. "Let me be a friend to you. Trust me—and leave the girl here."

"Why? Is she in danger? Because I can protect her, Malator. You of all people should know that."

"You're not immortal, Lukien. How many times must I tell you?"

"I know what I can do."

"Leave the girl here."

"No deal." I determined to meet his stubbornness with my own. "Cricket comes with me. You'll just have to live with your jealousy, Malator."

"I could leave you," he warned.

"No, you can't, because I have the sword, and you're bound to it. You leave when I decide it's time for you to go. That may be in a day or two or a decade or two, but it'll always be my choosing."

His impish smile returned. "Your path could be wondrous, Lukien. If you let me help you."

"Then let it be my path, Malator. That's all I want from you."

He said nothing more, simply disappearing, leaving me alone in the moonlight. I sheathed my sword and felt his quiet energy within it. He had frightened me. As accustomed as I was to talking with a ghost, I was rattled. If he had something wondrous in store, why couldn't he tell me? Why did the Akari always couch their words in puzzles?

Curious, I went back to the spot where he'd drawn in the sand. Most of the picture was gone, except for a bit of the creature's head. It was inanimate now, no better than something a child might draw. But I swear I saw nothing wondrous in it, and the word that gripped me wasn't destiny.

It was death.

5

The worst part about crossing a desert isn't the heat. It's not the way the flies eat your skin or the fear of running out of water, either. The problem is how small it makes you feel. Anyone who's done it knows what I mean. Once you've traveled for just a few hours, you look back and see nothing. And when you look ahead you see nothing, and you keep looking and looking and there's nothing. There's just sand and dunes and the horizon. There's a fever that sets in when all you see is desert. If a man isn't careful, it can madden him.

I had made the crossing more than once, and wasn't afraid for myself. I knew how to guard against the desert's bewitchments. We had our mounts and our mules loaded with everything we'd need, and I had my map. Still, I worried about Cricket. All that first day I watched her for signs of trouble, careful to measure the look in her eyes. We were just two people, infinitely small with an ocean of sand around us and nowhere to turn if trouble arose.

But Cricket was better than her word. She rode without complaint, quietly studying the dunes on the horizon, glancing up occasionally to marvel at the sun. She drank only sparingly and only when I said so, and she quickly adopted the habit of desert people of not speaking too often, a way of saving both strength and body moisture. I knew as I watched her that I'd made the right choice.

Our journey, though, would be a long one, because I had mapped out a route that looped south beneath Ganjor, avoiding it entirely. Almost everyone who came through the desert did so through Ganjor, especially if they were from the continent. We could have rested there for days, refreshed our animals and gotten new supplies, but only if I wasn't recognized. King Baralosus might have given me Zephyr as a peace offering, but I doubted he'd be happy to see me.

So we rode south for one day then another and spent our nights beneath the stars. I took watch at night, afraid a rass might find us, and in the morning slept for just an hour. "Tomorrow night we'll sleep somewhere special," I promised Cricket.

"Where?" she insisted. She had taken off the cape of rass skin, deciding wisely to wear it only at night. Now we both wore clothing from the continent—good, plain shirts and trousers instead of gakas. We did, however, cover our heads with hoods. Cricket's hood swallowed most of her face, but her eyes danced excitedly as she looked at me.

"A spring," I told her. "A Seeker from Norvor told me about it. Said he came across this way himself. He told me right where to find it."

"You sure he wasn't lying, Lukien? No one from Norvor goes around Ganjor . . . unless they're criminals or something."

"Norvor's full of criminals," I said, not really caring. Mostly the shanties around Jador were filled with decent folks, but some shady types had come across the desert, too. "No reason for him to lie. I know the desert well enough. What he described sounded right to me."

"We'll make it there by tomorrow night? You're sure?"

"Tomorrow night we'll be sleeping under palm trees, slurping up fruit. That sound all right to you?"

Cricket's face turned dreamy. "Sure does. You know what I'm gonna do? I'm going to soak my feet in that spring."

"We'll take our time there, dawdle a bit the next morning. Can't say we're in a real hurry."

As soon as I said it, I was sorry. Cricket grimaced and faced forward again. She *was* in a hurry. I didn't apologize because there was no sense to it. We just kept on riding.

We did find the oasis the next day, right where the Norvan said it would be. By the time we reached it, dusk was settling over the desert. The wearying journey showed on Cricket's face now, but when she saw the spring—surrounded by trees and grasses and tucked against a shading ridge—she beamed.

"Please, please, tell me that's not a mirage, Lukien," she said, and charged toward it on her pony. I let her go, laughing, understanding her almost delirious happiness. The Desert of Tears was blessed with very few spots like this one, a greenish island in an ocean of sand. Fruit hung heavily off the ancient trees, trees so worn and weather-beaten their roots erupted from the soil. I heard insects chirping in the grasses, felt a coolness strike my face. My parched mouth longed for water.

"Can I drink?" called Cricket. She quickly dismounted and eyed the spring, bubbling up into a river that stretched out into the desert, where it died.

"If it smells right, drink it," I answered, watching her as I led Zephyr and the mules into the shade of the ridge. Cricket knelt down near the spring and cupped her hands full of water. She took one sniff and smiled.

"I don't smell anything. That's good, right?"

"Right," I said and dropped down from Zephyr's back. The water was just as the Norvan described it—clear as rain. Cricket poured it into her mouth, then splashed her whole face with it. Then she looked deep into the bubbling pool.

"There's no end to it!" she crowed. "We can have as much as we want!"

I led Zephyr and the mules toward the water. "Get your mount. A squire always waters his horse first."

Cricket looked chastened. "Sorry." She got up quickly and retrieved her pony, letting it drink with the other animals. "There's a lot to being a squire."

"You'll learn it," I said. "Now, though . . . we rest."

It was easy to lose track of time at the oasis. We unburdened the animals, rolled out our sleeping blankets to flatten the tall grass, and soaked our feet in the spring water. Cricket was careful to pay attention to the mounts, making sure they were settled and comfortable. She even went through our supplies to give me an accounting of what we brought with us. But when she came to the case carrying my bronze armor, she paused.

I watched her as I leaned back, opening a fruit with my dagger. The leather case had traveled with me from Liiria to Norvor and then to Jador. It contained the only precious things I owned, save for the Sword of Angels. The case wasn't locked, and I could tell Cricket wanted to look inside.

"Go on," I told her. "You're my squire. You should check it from time to time."

Cricket knelt over the case like it was a treasure chest. As she opened it, the bronze armor reflected yellow on her face. Unlike my sword, there was nothing magical about my armor. Still, people who saw it always got a strange look in their eyes, like they were seeing something priceless. I pried open my fruit and drank its sweet nectar.

"Here," I said, offering her the bigger half. "Sit with me and talk."

Cricket softly closed the case. "Will you wear it when we get to Akyre?" she asked. "You should. You should announce to everyone that a hero has come."

Her adoration made me uncomfortable. "That armor's for fighting, not for showing off. I'll wear it if I need to. Otherwise it stays in the box."

"Oh, there'll be fighting," she said. She scraped her top teeth over the fruit meat. Her brown eyes darted up toward the moon.

"What makes you so certain?"

"'Cause we're heading to the Bitter Kingdoms."

"Are you remembering something, Cricket?"

She shook her head. "Nothing new. I just know it, is all. Trouble made me lose my memory. That I know for sure."

I didn't know much about the Bitter Kingdoms back then, but I knew Cricket was right. They were little kingdoms, ruled—if you could call it that—by blood-soaked barons. Mostly folks just passed on through the Bitter Kingdoms on their way east for spices. That made the Bitter Kingdoms poor, and that made them covetous. Cricket was lucky to have escaped.

"Tell me what you do remember," I said.

"What? Nothing's changed."

"They found you wandering around Akyre, Borlis and the others. You were alone. Starving, they said."

"I remember," said Cricket sharply. "*Before* that's the problem."

For a long moment I didn't say anything. I hoped the peace of the night would loosen her tongue and maybe her memory too. "Look at that moon. You ever see one so big? They say the heat here makes it look like that, all pink and shimmery. I like to watch it."

I stared at the moon, and Cricket stared too. Then she let out a big, relaxing sigh.

"What will we do when we get to Akyre, Lukien?" she asked. "How are we going to find out about me?"

"I'm not really sure," I told her honestly. "Look around. See if you recognize anyone, or anyone recognizes you. Ask some questions. First we have to find out what's going on in Akyre. The things I hear don't make me happy."

Cricket nodded, because she knew the stories too. War stories, mostly. Atrocities and all the things that come with war. Cricket gazed blankly at the moon.

"Cricket . . ." I said it softly. "How do you know your name's Cricket? How can you remember that, if you can't remember anything else?"

She shrugged. "How do you know your name's Lukien? I just do is all. I haven't forgotten how to talk or walk either. It's just some things I can't remember. Sometimes it's on the tip of my tongue and I can't get it out . . ." She closed her eyes and grumbled, "It makes me crazy! I try to remember. I have dreams sometimes and can't remember them."

"Don't force it. You have to come at this thing from the side, not head on. It'll all fall in place eventually. Maybe when we get to Akyre."

Cricket put down the fruit and drew her rass skin cape around her shoulders. She looked tired but restless too, like she wanted to keep talking.

"There's one thing I remember," she said. Her eyes narrowed as she focused on the memory. "A waterfall. Maybe a river, but I think it's a waterfall. I can see myself there."

"In Akyre?" I asked.

She closed her eyes completely. "Yes. Definitely Akyre. I can see it, kind of."

"What else do you see? Are you alone?"

"I'm . . ."

She struggled, holding her breath. And then she opened her eyes and looked at me.

"Can we go there, Lukien?"

"Where? You don't even know if it's a river or a waterfall."

"We can find it. Akyre's not a big country. We could ask around. We could do that, right?"

She was fixated suddenly, and I didn't understand it. "Sure," I told her. "We could do that."

Like a charm, the promise calmed her. She leaned back against the ridge. "Now it's your turn," she said. "Tell me something you remember."

"You're an imp. It's late. I don't feel like talking."

"Ah, you're always making excuses. You have as many secrets as I do, Lukien." Cricket smiled at me. "I just want to know about you, that's all. Not just the stories everybody says about you. Not just how you lost your eye. Before that."

"Oh. When I was your age, you mean."

Her brown eyes blinked at me. I couldn't escape. So I settled back and told her what life was like for me before becoming "the Bronze Knight." I told her about growing up in the streets of Liiria, about how I lived by breaking into stores to keep warm at night and by stealing food. My mother had died before I was old enough to have memories of her. But when it came time to tell Cricket about my father, I had to stop. What could I say about a man who left me to fend for myself? Who one day decided that life was too tough for him?

"There's only one way a man should leave his family," I said finally. "By dying."

Cricket looked baffled. "He just left you? Out there on the street?"

I couldn't look at her. I stared at the moon. "Right."

"Didn't you wonder what happened to him? Didn't you try to find him?"

"You mean beg? You can't beg someone to love you, Cricket. I decided it was easier to hate him. Now . . ." I stood up and brushed the sand from my trousers. "It's late and I'm tired. More next time, all right?"

As I walked toward my bedroll, Cricket said, "Lukien? You think I'll ever be able to remember stuff like that?"

All of a sudden she sounded like a little girl. And I was the closest thing she had to a father.

"Yes, I do," I told her. "When you're in a stronger, safer place, you'll be able to remember. That's why I'm here. So we can find that place together."

6

Malator had been strangely quiet since we left Jador. For the first two days I felt him hovering just out of reach, like a child peeking around a corner. Within the sword I could feel his presence, stoic but solid, but by our fifth day I could barely sense him at all. He had stopped speaking to me entirely, and when I touched the sword it was almost like a normal blade at my side.

Perhaps I had been hard on Malator, and perhaps his silence was just childish payback, but I was determined that he should be my servant now and not the other way around. Akari are kind and generous with their powers, but they aren't angels, and they aren't selfless. They see the world from a mountain peak none of us can ever reach, but there's one thing they forget—they need us, we poor humans. I intended to remind Malator of that.

Our fifth day in the desert was blazing hot. By noon the sun felt like fire on our hoods. The sand, which was everywhere now, blinded us as we tried to look ahead. We had already skirted south of Ganjor, making good progress east. Maybe two more days of riding and we'd be out of the desert. That alone was enough to give us confidence. With the sun mighty on our backs, I let Cricket drink her fill from our canteens. Head down, I rode without thinking.

"Lukien?"

Cricket's voice took me out of my daydream.

"Look at that," she said, pointing north. A caravan of drowa riders were heading east as well, their path slowly crossing our own. They were still far away, but I knew they had seen us; the gait of their hairy mounts slowed a little.

"Ganjeese," I said.

Cricket's voice rose. "Really? How do you know that?"

"First, because no one else would be traveling east. And look how they ride—like an arrowhead, you see?"

"Uh huh."

"They ride like that to keep the rass away," I said. "It doesn't work."

We had gone all this way without seeing another soul. We were practically knocking on the door of the Bitter Kingdoms. And now Ganjeese. My hand went fast to my sword.

"Malator? You still here?"

I don't know why I doubted it, because Malator barreled into my mind.

Company?

"Maybe trouble, maybe not," I said. Cricket looked at me, but she knew who I was talking to. "We can't avoid them."

"They're coming this way," said Cricket.

"Hospitality of the desert. They'll ask if we need anything, maybe try to trade."

"But they're gonna know we're from Jador."

"No way to hide it. Keep riding," I said, "and don't be afraid."

As we closed the distance I could see their expensive looking clothes, the kind of colored silks and dyed skins the wealthy of the city wore. There were four men, with a big, well-fed fellow leading them. He rode at the tip of the arrow, bouncing on his drowa with a scimitar strapped across his chest. A jet mustache glistened against his dark face. When we were finally close enough, he raised his hand in greeting.

"Aman da Vala," he called.

The words mean 'Vala watches us.' Even Cricket understood, but as a girl she wasn't supposed to return the greeting. I lifted my own hand and called back the response.

"Vala kabar shahan."

'The great god Vala blesses us,' I said, and didn't believe a word of it. I brought my horse abreast with Cricket's pony. The big man puzzled over my accent, looking at our clothes.

"North," he said. "You come from Ganjor?"

"From Jador," I answered and pulled back my hood.

All of them—the big man and the younger ones behind him—fixed on my eye patch. The big man's hand twitched like he might go for his weapon.

"A one-eyed man from Jador," he said, effortlessly using my own language. Instead of reaching for his scimitar he twirled his oiled mustache. "You are like I see when I have dreams of you, Bronze Knight of Liiria."

We'd all stopped dead in front of each other, and no one moved an inch closer. "Do you know me, *azizi*?" I asked, using the Ganjeese word for friend. Cricket was so quiet next to me that I thought she'd stopped breathing.

"The desert is too hot for games," said the big man. "I am Sariyah of Ganjor, and these are my sons . . ." He gestured to the others. "And you are Lukien of Liiria. How many sons do you see, please?"

His question startled me. "I see three sons."

Sariyah nodded. "You see three sons. You do not see a fourth son because my fourth son is dead. Killed by Jadori."

Sariyah looked at me without flinching. I tried to read his face but couldn't.

"Your son was a warrior for Baralosus," I guessed. "A lot of men died that day. Many *azizi*. Many Jadori."

Sariyah leaned over and spat into the sand to his right. "Baralosus is a pig."

"We agree." Quickly I offered him honors. "The warriors of Ganjor were brave that day. I am told they died like heroes. In Jador we grieve all your sons."

Sariyah's dark face softened. He turned to his sons and ordered them to reveal their faces, a sign of respect. All shared their father's sharp, handsome nose, especially the youngest one, who looked barely Cricket's age.

"Many in Ganjor blame you for that battle, Shalafein," said Sariyah. He wasn't at all afraid, though he clearly knew my reputation. "But I am wiser."

"I was far away from that battle," I said.

"And now you are far from Jador again."

He looked inquisitive, too polite to ask directly what was on his mind.

"We go east," I told him. I turned to Cricket. "It's all right. Show yourself."

She pulled back her hood, shaking out her brown hair to the astonishment of the Ganjeese. Sariyah's mouth fell open, but he closed it quickly, inclining his head. His sons just stared.

"We go east, too," said Sariyah. "To Zura for spices."

"Our business is in Akyre," I replied.

Sariyah hid his surprise poorly but said, "We have bread to share and good drink from Ganjor. And I have heard you are talented at killing rass, Bronze Knight. We can ride together as far as Arad. Is it a bargain?"

Cricket glanced a warning at me, but Sariyah was right—it was too hot for games.

"We welcome the company," I told Sariyah. In Ganjeese, I said, *"Our water is yours."*

We ate and drank with Sariyah and his sons, spending the hottest part of the day beneath a tent while trading stories about the desert. Sariyah was good at telling stories. Cricket and I both relaxed quickly around him. He told us about sleeping in the sand with scorpions and how to pit stone fruit with your teeth and how the stars and moon follow *him* when he rides at night but not the others with him. He told us about Ganjor and about the wife and daughters waiting for him there, and how his spice business had grown, so that now he and his family had everything they needed. And like a true man of the desert, he asked few questions, careful to walk the thin line between his code and curiosity.

I learned quickly that Sariyah wasn't a man to be feared, though he did look fearsome to me. He kept his scimitar as close to him as I kept my sword, and he was at least as tall as me and probably twice as heavy. They talk in the desert about men who are lions, and Sariyah was surely one of them. His voice was a quiet roar, his manners commanding. His sons didn't just respect him but, rather, did his bidding with something like reverence. Even Cricket warmed to him, laughing at his tales. In Ganjor a girl her age had almost no rights at all, and yet Sariyah and his sons treated her with respect.

I didn't want our time beneath the tent to end, but the day was still young and we had many miles left to go.

We rode into the desert night, refreshed by the cool air and the brightest moon I'd ever seen.

"You see?" Sariyah laughed as it he pointed at the sky. "It follows me!"

We all followed Sariyah, even me, riding beside him at the front of our arrowhead. Cricket rode a few paces back, while Sariyah's youngest son, Asadel, eyed her the way boys that age naturally do. Cricket blushed at the attention but not enough to say she minded it, and that's when I realized I didn't have a girl with me, but a young woman. Sariyah glanced at them, then leaned over and spoke to me softly.

"I have three daughters," he whispered. "Never would I bring one to the Bitter Kingdoms."

"Three daughters *and* three sons? You're quite a man, Sariyah," I joked.

Sariyah grinned. "My wife likes to be busy," he said. But I had my opening and took it.

"What can you tell me about the Bitter Kingdoms?" I asked. "I've never been to that part of the world. I only know what I hear."

"Then you should know it's not a place to take a girl. The kings there are lawless. They do nothing but fight and kill. I would not be going myself if there was a better way to Zura." Sariyah looked down at his big knuckles. "I wonder if this trip will be my last."

"If it's so dangerous why are you going?"

"Because that's where the spices are, Lukien. Your world lives on spices! They are like gold. Many men get rich sending spices to the continent. If Vala wills it, I will be one of them." Sariyah's smile filled his face. "My sons have families to feed. We are together in this. One day we will be rich. Like Anton Fallon."

"Fallon? I know that name." I thought about it a moment, sure I'd heard of him once in Norvor. "A spice trader, right?"

"He is the prince of spices," said Sariyah. "Anton Fallon is the most powerful man in the Bitter Kingdoms. And not a drop of royal blood! They say he has a palace as big as a sea. The most beautiful women in the world serve him." He wagged a finger in the air. "Spices, Lukien."

"And you want to be like that? Wealthy?"

"I *will* be like that," Sariyah declared. "Anton Fallon is just a man like me. Two hands and a brain is all any man needs. *If* he has the will of Vala."

I tried to smile, but to me Vala was a superstition, just like the Fate I'd grown up with in Liiria.

"Lukien, ride with me," said Sariyah. He urged his drowa on more quickly, breaking away from the rest of us. I looked back at Cricket, who looked puzzled.

"It's just to talk," I assured her, spurring my horse to catch up with Sariyah. Sariyah did not speak until he was sure no one could hear us.

"Don't go to Akyre, Lukien," he said. "Nothing good there. Only trouble. I cannot speak these things in front of the girl." His voice dropped lower. "There is death magic in Akyre."

Now that was a phrase I'd never heard before. I sidled closer to him. "Tell me."

"Do they talk about Diriel in Jador?"

I shook my head.

"Diriel is King in Akyre. Calls himself Emperor now, of all the Bitter Kingdoms. An army of dead men serve him. Men without souls."

"Dead men?" I must have grinned, because Sariyah looked annoyed. "You've seen them?" I asked.

"No. And Vala willing I will not. I will ride straight to Zura with my sons, far from Akyre. You must do the same, Lukien. Whatever you seek in Akyre cannot be so important."

"It's more important than wealth, Sariyah, and yet you'll risk yourself for that."

"You do not believe me?" asked Sariyah. "Men I trust have told me this, Lukien. Diriel commands death itself. His army without souls marches."

I was glad Cricket couldn't hear us. "Sariyah," I said, "I'm not going to turn around because of some stories. You say you've heard about me. If so, you know what I can do. If there's trouble in Akyre, I can handle it."

Sariyah looked down at my sword. "It is enchanted?"

"It has . . . power."

"A spirit?"

I nodded. "An Akari. An ancient being, like a ghost."

Sariyah frowned. "Like death."

I thought about that a moment. Then I thought about that picture Malator drew in the sand. Death was following me, and I didn't know why.

Or maybe I was riding toward it.

"I'm not a superstitious man, Sariyah," I said. "I've seen a lot of things that make little sense. If you tell me there's an army of dead people waiting for me in Akyre, I believe you. One thing, though—maybe someone should warn *them* about what's coming, too."

7

Sariyah described Arad a day before we arrived. When I finally saw the city for myself, I realized he had lied by calling it a 'cesspit.' Like most desert people, Sariyah was too polite.

There are places in the world where laws are meaningless and human life holds no regard. I had seen those kinds of places in Norvor, a fractured country where I'd spent far too much of my life, and as I rode into Arad I smelled that same stink of debauchery. Arad, a city just beyond the borders of both the continent and the desert, was how the Bitter Kingdoms greeted new comers, where all the effluence of those places sloshed together in a pool of human vices. We were no more than a minute past the city outskirts when I saw the crowded slave market.

"Cricket," I said, trying to get her attention, but it was too late. She gaped at the men and women on the rickety stage, surrounded by onlookers. A naked woman stood before the crowd, sucking the finger of a prospective buyer as he roughly checked her teeth. Men from the continent and men from the desert leered at the woman, their pockets bulging with money.

Sariyah brought his drowa up quickly, blocking the market from Cricket's view. She looked stunned and frightened.

"Never mind it," I told her.

"But that woman—"

"Never mind it."

Sariyah's son Asadel rode up as if to protect her, and suddenly Cricket was surrounded. She craned her neck to see between us. The gambling halls spilled drunks into the streets. Stray dogs ran through the crowded market. There were children, too, some of them playing barefoot among the stalls, others skulking like orphans in the alleys. Men in unremarkable uniforms laughed as they wandered aimlessly through the streets. I knew at once they were mercenaries. The city had no tall buildings or great cathedrals, nothing that would draw a traveler other than its prostitutes.

"Any vice can be brought in Arad," Sariyah had told me, confiding it to me as we fell asleep in the desert the night before. He was afraid for Cricket, that was plain, and now I knew why. I kept one hand low toward my sword as we rode, aware of Malator's presence in my mind. There were no quips from him this time. Instead, I could feel his vigilance.

Sariyah spoke in a low voice to his sons, his Ganjeese words too soft for me to understand. Cricket kept her pony close as we rode past the markets of the city's main road, watching with disgust as an old man pissed against a house. Chickens screamed in a nearby stall while a crusty-looking butcher cut their heads off with a cleaver. I glanced ahead of us, hoping to find a spot to stop. I wanted a bed with a real pillow. I wanted food that didn't come out of a saddlebag. Mostly, though, I wanted to get Cricket somewhere safe. I looked at her. She seemed mesmerized.

"This look familiar to you?" I asked. "Any of it?"

She didn't answer right away. Her dark eyes studied everything. Her face had a hardness a girl her age should never have.

"No," she said finally.

"No? You sure?"

She looked at me sharply. "I'm sure, Lukien. I'm sorry, no."

Sariyah talked to his sons while Cricket and I rode ahead. A crowd was gathered on the side of the street, where a barker called them to attention. A boy moved quickly through the throng collecting bets. A patchy spot of grass had been cleared away on the roadside.

That's when I first saw him. His shaved, shining head.

Sometimes you see a thing and just have to stare. I once saw a cat choking on a lizard, with just the tail and hind legs sticking out of its mouth. This man was like that—an obscenity. Stripped to the waist, big hands resting on his hips, chest puffed out like a robin's. Taller than me, taller than Sariyah, he taunted the crowd, his nostrils flaring as the barker sought a challenger. Ropey sinew bulged on the back of his neck. His hairless body flexed one muscle at a time, like some sideshow freak. I couldn't imagine what had given him such a physique, both mountainous and willowy, and when he looked at me his eyes got wide and curious. His smile seemed to call me down from my horse.

"A wrestler," said Sariyah, coming up beside me on his drowa. "They are all criminals here. Bodyguards mostly. Come, Lukien . . ."

But my gaze wouldn't leave the man.

"Hey." Sariyah reached out and tapped my face. "He goads you. Enough now."

I don't know why I wanted to fight the wrestler, but I did. You only had to look at him once to hate him. When another man stepped out of the crowd—someone dumb enough to take the barker's bet—Sariyah looked relieved. He turned his drowa toward the road, his sons quickly following. Cricket waited for me, her eyes glazed.

"We'll find a place," I told her. "Someplace safe and away from all this noise."

"We need water, at least. And a place for the horses."

"And beds for us and good food," I added with a smile. "We made it across the desert. We should be happy for that."

My words put a little bounce into her as we followed after Sariyah. We rode out into the middle of the street, away from the crowds and shouting. Sariyah came to a stop and looked around, a long bead of spit dribbling from the mouth of his drowa.

"It needs rest," I said. Drowas are hearty beasts but not indestructible.

"She'll rest when we are ready," said Sariyah. His sons remained quiet. Sariyah sighed. "Akyre is north and east. South and east is Mosvar, and the road to Zura. Beyond Arad is scrub land, then forest in all directions."

"The Bitter Kingdoms," I said, unimpressed with what I'd seen so far. "Let's stop now. Then we'll talk."

"We do not stop, not here. Not us," said Sariyah. "We go south and east."

"What, now? Sariyah, we need to rest, get fresh supplies . . ."

"Lukien, we are people of Vala. We cannot stop here, not even for a sip of water."

"Sariyah, look at your animals," said Cricket. "They won't make it."

"We'll camp beyond the city tonight. The drowa can rest there, and rest is all they need for now." Sariyah looked at me. "*Azizi,* I will ask you this, though I know you will refuse me—come with us to Zura. Come with us and forget whatever it is you came here for."

"He came here for me," said Cricket.

"No, I didn't," I said quickly. "I came because I wanted to, Sariyah. I didn't come for spices or riches or anything like that." I put my hand out for him. "I'm sorry."

Sariyah took my hand with a powerful squeeze. "Good-bye Bronze Knight."

I knew how badly I would miss him. "North and east, right?"

He nodded sadly. "North and east." Then he looked straight at Cricket. "And you, girl—mind yourself here, always. The men of these nations have no honor."

"I'm not afraid, Sariyah," Cricket told him. "But I'll be careful."

Then, after days and days in the desert, Sariyah and his sons rode away from the food and shelter of Arad.

"Now that's dignity," I whispered.

I wondered if I would see him again. Cricket looked sad, staring after them. The world seemed to shrink, growing silent as Sariyah disappeared.

"Now what?" asked Cricket.

"A bath," I declared. "And food and a proper place to rest. How's that sound?"

She smiled. "Let me pick the house. Men don't know how to pick clean places to stay."

She started off on her pony toward a square of buildings up ahead, some of them tidy, others dilapidated, each with a colorful, steepled roof. This, I supposed, was the best part of town. A building with a scarlet façade and a sign reading 'Central House' caught Cricket's eye. She studied it, nodding approvingly.

"That one."

I looked it over. The house was near some useful shops and the well in the center of the square, and there were enough women and children around to set me at ease. Certainly it was good enough for a night or two. I got off my horse for the first time in hours and handed the reins to Cricket.

"Take them to the trough by the well and let them drink. We'll hire a boy to brush them once we're settled."

Cricket dismounted and almost stumbled on her wobbly legs. Eagerly she led the horses into the square. I pretended not to watch her as I headed for the house, but when I reached the door I turned to steal a glance. No trouble. And no one around to bother her. I headed in to the house where the proprietor took his time renting us a room.

But young girls in places like Arad are never safe for long, and why I didn't listen to that little voice in my head . . .

I stepped outside and looked for Cricket. She wasn't near the well. It took only a moment for dread to hit me. I opened my mouth to shout her name, then heard her shouting from around the corner. I ran toward her cry, and when I rounded the alleyway I saw her panicked eyes, looking out from behind a giant body pinning her to the wall. Her hand shot out to reach me.

"Lukien!"

The big, bald wrestler had his fist around her collar. She was like a little bird in his grasp, terrified and fluttering to get away. Still half naked, I knew what he wanted even before his lust-filled eyes turned toward me. Like an angry bull, all I saw was red.

"You ugly gargoyle," I hissed. "You shit-eating goat fucker. I'm gonna kill you."

I wanted him to toss Cricket aside, to come at me and let her flee. But he held her as he came, dragging her by the collar to face me.

"One-eye, you own this girl?" he croaked. I could smell his drunken breath.

"I don't own her. Nobody owns her." My hand went to my sword. "Let her go."

He stood up even taller. "I want to buy her. I have gold."

A crowd gathered behind me, but no one moved to help. Somehow I had to get Cricket free of him.

"Let her go, and you'll die in one piece," I warned. "Otherwise you'll just be a lot of little bits."

His eyes were the color of stone. "Are you afraid of me, One-eye? You look afraid. Where's your fat friend?" He look around for Sariyah. "That black-skinned hyena's not around to save you?"

"You'll have to let her go to fight me."

"Not fair, little man. Your sword."

All my life, my anger has made me stupid. Right then, all I thought about was my hands on his throat and how good it would feel to strangle him. As I undid my sword belt, Malator screamed at me.

No!

But I didn't want his help. The wrestler gave a smarmy smile as he hurled Cricket toward me. She stumbled then bolted up again like a cat, spitting at the man. I pushed her aside.

"Take my sword."

"No, Lukien, just kill him with it! Just—"

"Take it!"

I shoved the sword into her arms. Malator shouted in my head as I stepped forward. The crowd behind us swelled. I faced the wrestler, feeling my muscles coil. In a lawless place like this, no one would care if I killed him.

Faster . . .

Big men move like syrup. I struck like lightning. My boot smashed his groin, my fist his shattered nose. His face came down, gushing blood. His arms encircled me. Beneath the fat of his neck, I targeted the vertebrae. My elbow a hammer, I struck. The wrestler faltered . . . and held on.

Faster!

He lifted me, a doll on his shoulder, spinning me toward the ground. I reached back and found his face, clawing his eyes, holding him and sliding head-first down his back. I didn't let go, dragging him, tugging his huge bulk back with me, sure he would tumble. My face smacked the street.

And still he had me.

On the ground he was an octopus, pulling me, his arms and legs like tentacles. I scrambled, rolling to avoid his hold, driving my fists wherever I could find him. But I was in a puzzle box, and the more I moved the more he tightened. Staring at the sky, I summoned my strength as his calves closed around my neck. Cricket was screaming. Malator tried to reach me. My throat closed up, and my sight went black, and I knew the wrestler's next move would kill me.

He twisted, and my neck snapped. I heard it without feeling it.

And I was gone.

8

Gone.

To a place I couldn't see or feel or comprehend. Floating in a space that terrified me. Blind, without a body or pain.

Alone.

I was dead, or very nearly dead, and I knew that my mind had left the rest of me behind. But my soul, if that's what it was, didn't drift freely up to heaven. I was trapped, suffocating in a blackness that went on forever. I searched the darkness but saw nothing, horrified that I had no eyes at all now.

But I could remember. I knew who I was and what had happened to me. I wondered where Cricket was, if she was dead like me. Or worse.

"Malator?"

My voice carried through the void. I tried to feel Malator, hoping he was somewhere in the darkness.

"Malator, I need you!"

He was gone. Like me, he didn't exist any more. If I had eyes, I might have cried.

"Malator. Help me."

After a while—after forever, maybe—I realized I wasn't dead. I couldn't be dead. The dead were like the Akari. Once the spirit leaves the body it dwells forever in its special place. Like Cassandra in her apple orchard. She wasn't floating mutely through eternity. She had another life beyond her mortal one. She had a world around her.

I had only darkness, and that's when I knew I was still alive somewhere. Barely, yes, but alive, although I couldn't imagine what kept me from death. The wrestler had broken my neck. No one could have survived it. He might as well have decapitated me.

Yet here I was.

"I can't stay here forever!" I screamed. "I'm alive!"

That's when I felt him. Just a tremor at first, far away, invisible out there in the blackness.

"Malator!"

I put everything I could into my cry. All of it, all of *me*. Anything to reach him. Suddenly he was there with me, like a mother over the bed of a sick child. Still invisible, but I could feel him.

"Malator, where am I?" I pleaded. "What happened?"

"Wait. Not now."

"Where's Cricket? Is she all right?"

"Lukien, you're almost dead."

"My neck . . ." I understood. "Can you save me?"

"I *will* save you, Lukien," he insisted. "No matter what it takes of me."

"You can let me die, Malator. It's all right."

I heard him laugh, and it cheered me. "Same old Lukien. You have a mission, remember?"

"Now can you tell me what it is?"

"I can't talk, Lukien. I need my strength. You have to fight, too."

I imagined reaching out for him, but he was already gone.

Except for Malator, I thought I was alone in the void. I thought I could just wait—until I realized something was in there with me.

It was the first thing I had seen in however long I was trapped there. A shadow among the shadows, moving across my consciousness. I had no body, no flesh to grow cold, but it chilled me. Suddenly I felt it everywhere, and I couldn't run from it or fight. So I watched, and for a moment it appeared like a pile of bones, then bloody rags of skin, and then as just a pair of horns. Finally it looked at me through the eyes of a dozen decayed faces.

Human faces.

"Leave me!" I cried.

It fled so quickly it stunned me. But I knew what I had seen.

Time passed, more and more, until at last Malator returned. This time I could see him. He brought light with him. His weary face nodded at me, and I knew he was too tired to speak. But he had saved me. I would be alive again.

"Malator," I said. "I saw the monster in the sand."

9

Malator told me to wake up, and I did. I imagined myself being born, struggling through the tunnel of my mother's womb. I imagined a light beckoning me out, out, into the world. My hands reached for the light. My one eye blinked open.

I was alive again.

Above me twinkled the night sky, fretted by tree branches. I could *feel* the air in my lungs. I was afraid but not panicked, and knew I was in a forest somewhere. Somehow. My ears perked awake at the sound of insects chirping. Weight pressed upon my chest. I glanced down and saw it was Cricket. She lay over me, slumped with sleep, my chest her pillow.

"Malator," I whispered. "Thank you . . ."

Cricket heard me and stirred. She sat up groggily, her eyes struggling with the darkness.

"Hello," I rasped.

"Lukien?" She leaned closer. "Lukien!" She flung herself at me then stopped in horror. "Oh, I'm sorry! You—are you all right? Can you move? I thought you were dead!"

My mind was so cloudy I could hardly grasp her questions. "I'm alive. Malator . . ."

That's when I noticed the sword in my hand. It had been placed there, tied into my palms with rags so I couldn't let go. I flexed my fingers around the hilt. Inside the sword stirred Malator, unmistakable but slighter than I'd ever felt him before. Barely there. Whatever he'd done to save me had exhausted him.

"I can move a little," I told Cricket, but couldn't raise the sword or do more than flex my arm. I remembered the horror of my neck breaking. To my amazement, I could turn my head. "But I'm all right. I *am*."

Cricket's expression melted. I had never seen her cry before, but now tears dampened her cheeks. "God damn it, you scared me, Lukien! That man killed you!"

"He didn't, Cricket." I wanted to sit up. "I told you," I joked, "nothing can kill me. Look!"

Cricket swallowed and smeared the tears with her sleeve. She touched my face. "Yeah," she nodded. "Okay."

"What about you? You weren't hurt?"

She shook her head. "No. He didn't touch me after . . . what happened."

I hoped she wasn't lying. "Where are we? Arad?"

"We left Arad, Lukien. Three days ago." Cricket shrugged. "I don't really know where this is."

"How?"

Cricket's voice dropped low. "Marilius."

"Who?"

She cocked her chin toward the trees at my left. "Over there."

Surprised, I turned my head, struggling to see over my nose with my one eye. A man was huddled among the leaves, slumbering in the darkness.

"Who's that?"

Cricket put a finger to her lips. "Easy. He helped us, Lukien. He saved us. His name's Marilius. He's a captain."

"Of a ship?"

"He's a soldier." Cricket looked over to make sure the man was still asleep. "I couldn't get you out of there alone, Lukien. After what happened to you I . . ." Her eyes pleaded with me. "I started screaming. The wrestler left me there, left us both there, right in the street. No one came to help. Just Marilius. He put you over your horse and got us out of there. We rode for a day, then we came here. You can be mad if you want, but I did my best."

"You did good," I told her. "You were brave. I'm proud of you." I looked over at the stranger again. "I want to talk to him."

"What, now?"

"Yes," I said, trying not to sound angry. I thought again and sighed. "No. I'll be stronger in the morning. I'll talk to him then."

"Why are you mad, Lukien? I told you—he saved us."

"I know." I smiled at her. "I do, Cricket. I'm obliged to him. And that's what I'm going to tell him when he wakes up."

Cricket looked relieved. She beamed suddenly, brushing the hair out of her eyes. "I swear I thought you were dead."

"Me, too," I admitted. "I guess it'll take more than a broken neck to kill me."

When I woke the next morning it was the stranger, not Cricket, sitting next to me. Cross-legged, disinterested, he whittled aimlessly with a dagger, and when I grunted awake he glanced my way.

"Cricket told me you wanted to speak to me," he said.

I looked around but couldn't find her. "Where is she?"

"Gone for water. It'll give us a chance to talk."

I tested my sword arm, feeling stronger than the night before. I even raised my head a little. "You're Marilius?" I took a good look at him. Dirty hair. Young, too. Hardly more than twenty. His muddy boots were the kind worn in Norvor, his crestless coat more like a Marnan's. He'd let his beard get out of control. "Cricket said you were a captain," I said, not hiding my disbelief. "You're a mercenary."

"I'm both."

"I know about mercenaries. You don't look much like one."

His eyes sharpened on me, shifting quickly to my sword and back again. "You think you can do the job, old man? You think I'm here to rob you?"

"I'm obliged to you for saving me," I said. "But make no mistake. I'm as rigid as a timber, so if you're planning anything do it now. You won't get another chance."

Marilius frowned with offense. "Didn't the girl tell you about me?"

"She told me. But if I find out you laid a hand on her, or that she's too afraid to tell me the truth, or that she's protecting me by lying, I'm going to kill you. And not quick either. I'm going to chop off bits of you and make you eat 'em."

Marilius expertly flicked his dagger into the dirt by my sword hand. "It ain't a lie."

"Tell me what happened. And it better match Cricket's story or—"

"Yeah, I know, I know, you'll kill me." He smiled wildly. "That big man who broke your neck? His name's Wrestler. That's it, nothing else. Just Wrestler. He's a bodyguard for King Diriel."

"Diriel. From Akyre." I began to remember what Sariyah had told me about Diriel. And about the 'death magic.' "Why was he in Arad?"

"Same reason all soldiers go there. Booze and whores."

"Is that why you were there?"

Marilius picked up his dagger. "It doesn't matter why I was there. Just lucky for you that I was." He began twirling the dagger, threading it through his fingers without thinking. "Wrestler's like a lot of us these days. You take a job where you can find it. Guess he figured he'd put his talents to better use, breaking necks for a king. He still puts on those sideshows, though. And he ain't never been beat." Marilius studied my sword. "You should have kept that instead of giving it off to the girl. You might have had a chance against him."

"I won't make that mistake again. Next time, Wrestler's head's going home with me in a sack. You saw the fight?"

"Oh yeah," grinned Marilius. "Heard your neck snap and everything. Made a sound like popping corn. You should be dead. You nearly were. I tossed you over your horse and rode you out of there, and that didn't kill you either. I wondered about that. Then you started mumbling to yourself, like you were talking to someone. And then I figured everything out."

He smiled like a card player with an unbeatable hand.

"What did Cricket tell you?"

"Nothing. She didn't have to. Maybe you think we don't hear news all the way out in the Bitter Kingdoms, but I'm from Norvor. I heard all about you. Heard how you went across the desert and got that sword of yours, heard how you got a ghost that makes you a hard man. I figure there's only one person in the world you could be. Only person who could have his neck broken and be talking about it two days later." Marilius stopped twirling his dagger. "Tell me I'm wrong . . . Lukien."

Maybe he was challenging me, but I didn't see challenge in his eyes, just curiosity. I was about to ask him what he wanted when Cricket returned. She broke through the trees with our canteens strapped around her waist like cowbells. When she saw me talking to Marilius she stopped.

"Everything all right?" she asked.

"Everything's fine," chirped Marilius like a bird. "Lukien and me are just getting to know each other."

Cricket's face fell. "Lukien, I didn't tell him anything about you."

"That's right, she didn't," nodded Marilius. "See? You don't have to kill either of us." He waved Cricket closer. "Sit yourself down, little girl."

Cricket came over but sat down on my other side, away from Marilius. She wore the rass skin cape, using part of it to cover my chilled body. I lifted my hand, brushing the back of it against her leg, a way of showing her I could move better now.

"Untie the sword now, Cricket," I told her, sure I could hold it by myself. When she was done I managed to prop myself up onto an elbow. Cricket and Marilius both grinned like it was some great feat. "I've got questions for you," I told Marilius. "How long have you been gone from Norvor?"

"Less than a year," said Marilius.

"Who you working for? Diriel?"

"Diriel?" Marilius laughed then spit on the ground. "Never. Diriel's turned Akyre into a pit. Not that it was anything to brag about before, mind you."

Cricket bristled, "Akyre's my home."

"Oh?" Marilius shrugged. "Sorry to hear that. You already know what's happened to it, then."

"We don't," I confessed. "We came here to find out." The more I talked the more my head cleared. My instincts were getting sharper, too, telling me Marilius was hiding something. "You didn't answer my question—who'd make a kid like you a captain?"

Just as if I'd squeezed a trigger, Marilius started getting nervous again. The dagger flipped quickly between his fingers. "His name's Anton Fallon. Heard of him?"

Now it was my turn to smile. "That explains a lot. Anton Fallon's got just about all the money in this part of the world. Probably has nothing better to spend it on than a bunch of wet-behind-the-ears mercs. So why'd you come to Arad? Why are you alone?"

"Well, that's my business now, isn't it? I didn't expect to have to rescue you two. Now I'm heading back there. I want you to come with me."

"Why?" asked Cricket.

"Cause it's safe there," said Marilius. "Akyre's no place for you, girl. If you come with me south to Fallon's palace, your champion here can mend a bit."

"Uh-huh. That's a real nice offer," I said. "And Anton Fallon just happens to have a desperate need for more mercenaries, I bet."

"You've got special talents," said Marilius. "He'll pay you well, better than any other swording job you'll find around here."

"I'm not a mercenary," I said. "Not anymore."

"He's a knight-errant," declared Cricket.

"Ah, so you're a principled man," said Marilius. "What if I told you that Fallon really needs you. People are dying and you can help stop it. Would that interest you?"

"Not unless you tell me the whole story."

"Can't," said Marilius. His lips tightened behind his beard. "That's for Fallon to say. Anyway, where else you gonna go? There's nothing worth your time in Akyre, and if you head up there, Wrestler will just snap your neck again. At least if you come with me you'll get a chance to do some good."

I thought about it, then shook my head. "No reason for us to go all the way to some palace to rest. Seems pretty quiet here. By tomorrow I'll be able to ride. So thanks for the offer, but no."

Marilius stood up. "I thought knight-errants were supposed to have honor." He sniffed and put his dagger into his belt. "Guess you don't think much of paying your debts. Seems to me you'd still be laid out in Arad if I hadn't come along. And Cricket? Who knows. Wrestler might have come back for her."

I wished he hadn't said that. I still wish it. Before I was a mercenary I was a real knight. A Royal Charger. The word 'honor' didn't seem to mean much in the Bitter Kingdoms, but it did to me.

"Lukien, I don't want to go with him. We got our own mission, you and me."

"We do," I sighed, but I hadn't told Cricket of the monster I'd seen. That thing was death itself coming at us. Coming, I supposed, for Cricket. That was the truth Malator wouldn't tell me. Suddenly, a detour from our mission seemed like a fine precaution.

"How far is it to Fallon's palace?" I asked.

"Just a couple of days, on the southern coast," said Marilius. "I'm telling you, you've never seen anything like it."

10

"So Lukien, tell me what it's like to be immortal."

The question came at me like an arrow, too fast to duck. I glared at Marilius. "Why would you ask a question like that?"

"Look at you—you're already riding like nothing happened." Marilius studied me as if I was faking. "Does it hurt?"

"No," I told him, a fact that surprised me. I turned my head from side to side. After just four days, I felt completely healed.

"Lukien doesn't like talking about his powers," said Cricket. She rode up closer, wedging her pony between our horses.

"They're not powers," I said. "But she's right—I don't talk about it."

"Oh, come on. I've heard you talking to Cricket, mumbling behind my back. And I saw the way you went after Wrestler. You're not afraid of anything, huh?"

"Some things," I said. "But they're none of your business."

Marilius shrugged. "We still have a full day ahead of us. Nothing to do but talk. Fallon's going to ask you about your powers anyway."

"Because you can't keep a secret, right?"

"He needs a man like you, Lukien. But he'll be curious. Can't blame him for that. Hell, *I'm* curious. You've got the one thing money can't buy, and I'm not talking about love."

"A deal then," I proposed. "You tell us why Fallon needs me so badly, and I'll tell you what it's like to be immortal."

"Ooh, tempting," smacked Marilius. "But no."

"Why not?" asked Cricket. "We're gonna find out once we get there. Just tell us now and save us the bother."

"Nah, he won't do that, Cricket," I said. "He's gotta keep his secret, otherwise we might not go with him. Must be something pretty bad, though, since he's not willing to tell us."

"Is it bad, Marilius?" asked Cricket.

Marilius shrugged. "Let's just say it's interesting."

"Yeah, but you want to tell us," pressed Cricket. "I can tell you do."

"But I won't," Marilius snorted. "Now can we be quiet?"

"What's the problem? Seriously, what's Fallon need us for?"

"He needs Lukien," Marilius corrected her. "You're just along for the ride."

"So are you, apparently," I said. "Whatever it is, it's something you can't handle . . . *Captain*."

This time Marilius didn't answer. He pretended to scan the scrubby horizon. We were in the flat lands now, in the very heart of the Bitter Kingdoms. An occasional, dilapidated farm appeared as we rode, crops struggling in the hardscrabble earth. To the east loomed Zura, Sariyah's dreamed-of spice lands. Near the mountains up north waited Akyre. Isowon was a day's ride south and east, an isthmus of land Fallon's fortune had turned into a garden, or so Marilius claimed. I dreamed of its promised water, so clear and turquoise you could see a rainbow of coral at its bottom.

"Okay," Cricket said finally. "Just tell us about Fallon, then. What's he like?"

"Rich," said Marilius.

"We know that already. What else? Why's he got so many men?"

"Why shouldn't he? He can afford them."

"Seems to me they're not doing him much good," I said. "I've got a feeling your employer isn't so innocent around here, Marilius. If you're bringing us to help him make war, you're wasting your time."

"Oh right, I forgot," said Marilius. "You're not a mercenary anymore."

"That's right."

"Look around, Lukien. You're in the Bitter Kingdoms now. War's a way of life here. Tell him, Cricket."

Cricket grimaced. "I can't."

Marilius looked at her. "What's that mean?"

"It means she can't remember," I said. "She's forgotten everything. What do you think can make someone forget everything they know, Marilius?"

"Damned if I know," said Marilius.

"Damned sounds about right to me," I said, and kept on riding.

The rest of that day we met not a single traveler on the road. We stopped as needed but made steady progress through the afternoon, all of us keeping our questions to ourselves. Malator continued to ignore my efforts to rouse him. I didn't know if Akari ever got sick, but now I was worried. It wasn't just a foul mood keeping him quiet this time. This time, he'd pushed himself too far. Both Cricket and Marilius rode in a sort of bored trance. I fixed my mind on Malator.

I can feel you, Malator, I said, imagining myself deep inside the sword. *Just tell me you're all right, and I'll let you sleep.*

For a long moment there was nothing. Then, at last, he stirred.

Sleep . . .

I chuckled to myself. "Good!"

Cricket perked up. "What's good?"

"Malator. He's . . ." I stopped myself. Marilius stared at me, puzzled. "Nothing."

"Talking to your ghost friend, Lukien?" he asked.

"Keep riding, Norvan," I replied. Then, quietly in my head, I said to Malator, *Just sleep now. We'll talk soon.*

He slipped away like a drowsy child. The sun disappeared behind incoming clouds. I peered at the darkening horizon, surprised to see another group traveling toward us.

"Look," said Cricket. "People!"

Next to me, Marilius stiffened. His gaze narrowed as they came into view.

"Soldiers?" I ventured.

"No," said Marilius. He dropped his guard with a sigh. "Refugees."

Next to me, Cricket went white. A single ox-drawn wagon shambled toward us, piled high with furniture, bundles of clothing, dilapidated crates—all manner of belongings. A dozen people trudged alongside it, thick with the dust of the road. Atop the wagon, teetering at the pinnacle of their possessions, sat a single, lonely child.

"Where are they from?" asked Cricket. She looked at Marilius. "Do you know?"

Marilius shrugged. "Could be anywhere. Maybe Drin. Or Kasse."

"Maybe Akyre?"

"Sure, maybe."

"No sense in wondering," I said and rode forward.

The refugees stopped as we approached, bringing their pair of oxen to a halt. Three men gathered to greet me, shielding the others. I counted thirteen in all, at least four of them women. The boy—I could tell now he was a boy—was the only child among them. His blank eyes studied me behind a mask of grime. I raised a hand in greeting.

"Heading west?"

The group looked me over. A single man in a torn brown hat stepped forward, his grizzled face flaked with sunburn. He had farmer's hands, hammy with great big knuckles.

"You coming from that way?" he asked.

"That's right," I replied. No matter where they come from, refugees only want to know one thing. "No troubles on the road. Should be safe for you."

His forehead crinkled. "You from Norvor? You sound like a Norvan."

"I've spent some time there," I answered. "We're bound for Zura. You?"

The man wilted at the question. "Anywhere safe that'll take us. It's good you're heading east. Stay clear of the north. Diriel's soldiers crossed the border. Took over both our farms, took our livestock 'cept for these two." The man's face twitched, on the verge of tears. "Torched the house."

Now I could see these were two different families. Neighbors, probably, who'd taken everything they could with them.

"Are you from Akyre?" asked Cricket. She didn't address the men, though. Instead she spoke directly to the boy. The man with the hat answered for him.

"We're from Kasse."

"Southeast of Akyre," Marilius explained. "On the border. They've been warring with King Diriel for a year."

"No more," said the man. "Diriel's taken Kasse. Calls himself 'Emperor' now. Almost all the old provinces have fallen. Not Drin, though."

I didn't know much about Akyre or its history, just whatever bits Cricket could remember. "How's that possible?" I asked. "It's always been a stalemate down here. How'd Diriel get so powerful?"

The man looked at his cohorts, but none of them answered. A woman in the background whispered a warning to him. The man scratched his sunburned cheek.

"Can't say," he said.

"Can't?" I worked to hide my annoyance. "A friend of mine told me about Diriel. Told me about his army. Told me they were dead men. Is that what's got you scared?"

Marilius shifted in his saddle. "Lukien, don't."

The man took off his hat to fan his face. "We gotta move on."

"No," Cricket insisted. "Just wait. We need to know what you saw. Please!"

They all fell silent.

"They won't tell you," said Marilius. "Just let 'em go."

"What about you?" asked Cricket, looking up at the boy. "Will you tell me what you saw?"

The boy—maybe seven years old—nodded. "The legion of the lost."

"Tomas!" shrieked one of the woman.

I looked at the man with the brown hat. "You can be a big help if you'd tell us. Anything about Diriel, Akyre . . ."

"Can't!" barked the man. "I warned you off the north. That's all. Have the sense to turn around. Go back to Norvor. Or stay in Zura when you get there. Just keep clear of Akyre. All of it."

He yanked the oxen forward and the wagon waddled past us. Cricket called after them, begging them to wait. Marilius looked at me, his expression cross.

"Will you take some advice?" he asked. "Nobody here's going to tell you about Diriel, Lukien. Nobody. So just stop asking."

Finally that night, I saw Malator again.

We rode until the sun went down, finding a campsite far enough from the road so no one would see us while we slept. I helped Cricket clear the brush and make a fire, and Marilius took care of the animals. None of us spoke as we worked. Cricket was in a particularly foul mood. Spooked by the refugee boy, she kicked away the branches with clenched teeth. When we sat around the fire to eat, Marilius helped himself to our food, while

Cricket picked at her own. My appetite had flown as well. All I wanted was rest.

But when I tried to sleep I couldn't. Images flashed through my mind—of Cassandra, Cricket, even Wrestler's ugly face. I looked up at the stars, counting them to quiet my mind, but the constellations taunted me, forming monstrous patterns in the sky. I listened to Cricket's breathing next to me, using the cape I'd made her for a blanket, her peaceful face turned toward me.

She was safe, for now, but where was I taking her? I sat up, anxious to get away, needing a place to scream. In the shadows of the dying fire I tiptoed away, the Sword of Angels still—forever—belted to my waist. The darkness trapped me like a cage. I took a moment to let my vision adjust, then prowled through the trees like a restless tiger until at last I reached the road.

Silence.

I walked out into the center of the road, awash with moonlight. I looked east toward Zura and thought of Sariyah. I looked west toward home and thought of Gilwyn. When my sight cocked north, I heard Cassandra in my head. I closed my eye to hear her voice, imagining it precisely. Just a year before I had heard that voice for real, in the Story Garden. I had summoned her from the world of the dead just to see her one more time. She alone had convinced me to live, when all I wanted was to join her.

"You can always go back there, you know," said a voice. "The Story Garden remains."

I looked down and saw Malator sitting cross-legged in the middle of the road. He smiled up at me, his impish face weary. He seemed substantial this time, as if the moonlight had made flesh of him. But he was a spirit, and I wondered if I had conjured him the way I'd conjured Cass's voice.

"I'm all alone, Malator," I whispered. The desolation and empty road felt unbearable. "Why am I here? Why'd I come? I miss her so much. I *should* be with her. Really with her."

"She doesn't want that, Lukien. She told you that. She wants you to live and find your destiny."

Malator didn't understand. He'd spent his whole life fighting, back when he was alive. He'd never been in love. Not really. I sat down beside him in the dusty road, laying the sword across my lap. "Shouldn't you be in here resting?" I asked, tapping the blade.

"I'm all right now," he said in a reedy voice. "Your loneliness woke me. I'm very angry with you."

"Angry? Why?"

"For making me save you—again. You shouldn't even be here talking to me. You should be floating around somewhere like a ghost. You know where you'd be if I let you die? In Arad. That would be your death place."

Like Cassandra in the apple orchard, a death place is where a soul resides when the body finally expires. But Cassandra's orchard was a far better place to spend eternity than Arad.

"That's not what's bothering you," I said. "You're angry because you think I tried to kill myself."

"Didn't you? I thought I had you figured out, Lukien. I thought you wanted to die just to be with Cassandra again. Now I can't tell if you're trying to die or just trying to prove yourself."

"You saw what he did to Cricket, Malator. You know what he wanted. Wrestler deserved to die. And when I see him again he will."

"You mean when you go to Akyre?"

"That's what you want, isn't it? You told me to come to the Bitter Kingdoms, remember? Well, here I am! I don't see a whole lot of answers! What's the point of me coming to this shithole? What am I supposed to find here?"

Malator grinned. "Why ask, Lukien? You know I'm not going to tell you."

"You make me want to strangle you, Malator. But . . ." I leaned back. "Thank you for saving me. I was afraid when I was dying. Just floating in that darkness." I looked at him. "What was that thing I saw, Malator? Tell me that at least."

"I still don't know," said Malator. "Maybe nothing. Maybe just a symbol."

"No, it was real. I saw it. It was dead like me, only it wasn't."

"Just like you."

"That's right. It was dead, and it wasn't dead. What could be like that, Malator? You must know."

"I know a lot of things, Lukien. Some of them I can tell you, some of them I can't."

"You drew that thing in the sand, then told me not to take Cricket with me. Is that thing after Cricket?"

"I can't answer. I told you that already."

"All right," I said, "then what's this Legion of the Lost that boy mentioned? Diriel's death army?"

Malator looked around, then up at the stars. "It's dark. How is your vision, Lukien?"

"No, don't do that. Don't ignore me."

"I'm not. How is your eye?"

"My eye is fine, damn-it. Better than fine."

"And you feel good? Your neck feels good? You feel strong?"

"Yes, I feel strong! Why?"

Malator shrugged. "I give you what I can, Lukien. I give you *everything* I can. Do you realize how dark it is out here? The moon seems bright because you're more than just a man now. I made you that way. Cricket or Marilius wouldn't be able to find their shoes in this darkness. They'd have never made it to the road. So don't ask me for answers I can't give you, please. Just take what I offer." He stood and glared down at me. "You can go on or you can turn back. It's up to you. Or you can just go back to Torlis and spend your days babbling to Cassandra in the Story Garden. I don't manipulate you, Lukien. It's always been up to you."

"I know," I grumbled.

Malator held out an upturned palm, summoning a tiny yellow flame. He blew on the flame, making it grow until it was the size of an apple, lighting the road around us.

"Put out your hand," he said, and when I did so he placed the flame into my palm. It wriggled there, soft and alive but did not burn me. "This will keep you company," he said.

I laughed in delight. "What is this? A pet?"

"A gift. So you won't feel so lonely."

With my other hand I caressed the ball of flame like it was a baby bird. "I didn't know you could do that, Malator."

"I can do a lot of things, Lukien," Malator answered, then quickly disappeared.

11

As Marilius predicted, we reached Isowon the very next day.

Gradually, the ground beneath us turned from sun-baked rock to sandy soil. The heat abated, becoming almost bearable, and the tang of salt in the air told me we were nearing the sea. Our horses and mules picked up their pace, eager for water and rest. A single pomegranate tree greeted us along the roadside. Cricket reached up from horseback to fill her pockets with fruit.

"Don't stop now," said Marilius. "We're almost there."

An hour later, Cricket's lips were purple with pomegranate juice. Her pockets were empty, but we still hadn't reached Isowon. Then, like a mirage, we saw it. And all of us, even Marilius, mewed.

Isowon was just as Marilius described it, a finger of gardens and architecture poking out into the sea. There were no dilapidated homesteads, no broken-down shops, none of the sewage-stained streets I'd seen all my life. Isowon's avenues were plump with flowers, all the buildings painted shades of white and sand. Watermills churned slowly by the docks where silver boats waited. People walked the sloping streets, watched by handsome statues of gods and goddesses.

Cricket's eyes swelled at the sight. "Paradise . . ."

"Did I tell you?" smirked Marilius.

I nodded. "Just like Sariyah said."

Cricket pointed at one, vast structure standing out from all the others. "Is that his *house*?"

"Breathtaking, I know," said Marilius. "I told you—the palace is unbelievable."

I had spent my life around wonders: the Library of Koth, Hanging Man, even the Story Garden where Cassandra waited. Yet I'd seen nothing compared to Fallon's palace. He was not a king or prince, but he had built himself an enormous home of golden limestone, clinging to the shore as the sea flowed into it. Palm trees spotted its courtyards. Fountains spouted crystal blue water. Brick lanes looped through gardens and manicured lawns, while alabaster stairways and coral bridges threaded the buildings together like pearls.

"Come." Marilius sped his horse onward, cheered by the sight of home. Cricket looked at me with a twinkle in her eyes.

"See Lukien? I told you we could trust him."

She dashed her pony after him, leaving me with the mules. But a lifetime of soldiering had made me distrustful, and Marilius still perplexed me. Surely a peach so perfect had a blemish somewhere. I decided to take a bite and find out for myself.

The streets of Isowon were emptier than they should have been. I tucked that bit of knowledge away as we rode up to the palace. Two tall, golden spirals flanked the garden leading to the gates. A perfume of spices hung in the courtyard. The mercenaries in the towers watched as we approached. Behind the gates, more eyes spied through the iron bars.

"Open up," ordered Marilius. He got down from his horse and stood before the gates. The men looked shocked.

"Marilius?" said one of them.

"Open the gates, Dorik. I need to see Fallon."

Dorik pointed at Cricket and me with his chin. "Who are they?"

"Friends," said Marilius. "For Fallon."

"Friends!" Dorik's laughter boomed. "You mean like you, Marilius?"

The others laughed too, jeering us. I got down off my horse, about to say something when Marilius stopped me. He glared at Dorik.

"You think Fallon doesn't want to see me?" he hissed. "He'll find out I came back, because one of you apes won't be able to keep it secret. Then he'll find out *you* sent me away, Dorik. And then you know what he'll do?"

Dorik didn't answer the question. Like the rest of them he was unshaven, unkempt, and at least a little dim-witted, but I could see his mind working behind his thick skull.

"Open it," he relented.

The others pulled the chains from the bars and swung the gate open for us. As we stepped inside, Dorik bumped Marilius's shoulder.

"You should have stayed gone," he whispered.

I pretended not to hear as I helped Cricket down from her pony. Marilius thrust the reins of his horse toward Dorik.

"Take care of the animals," he sneered.

By now others had gathered to watch us arrive. Some were mercenaries, some civilians from the town. Now I could see Fallon's riches close-up. Silvery sidewalks led through the gardens and archways toward fountains and reflecting pools and stands of fruit trees where children played among the flowers. On the giant lawn, every emerald blade of glass stood at attention. Marilius walked lock-jawed, humiliated. He led us out of the powerful sun into a great, open hall with a view of the sea and a ceiling alive with frescos. Here, handmaidens in white tunics carried jugs and trays of food, their legs so creamy I could barely look away.

Cricket caught me staring and grinned. "Nice place, huh?"

"Beautiful," I agreed.

Every step took us deeper into Fallon's paradise, until there were no more mercenaries, no one at all to challenge us, just the well-fed merchants and the doting, compliant servants. The smell of spices was everywhere, piping up from burning sconces on the walls and crystal bowls suspended from the ceiling. It got so thick I had to hold my nose.

"Lavender," said Marilius. "His favorite."

There was a bit of contempt in Marilius's voice that I hadn't heard before. When at last we came to a pair of golden doors, he stopped.

"Is Fallon in there?" I asked.

Marilius nodded.

"How do you know?" asked Cricket.

"Because he's always in there at this time of day. Wait here. I'll be back in a minute."

He opened a single golden door, just enough to slip inside. A sudden silence swallowed the hall. Cricket blinked at me. I looked around, surprised we were alone in such a vast space. Cricket smoothed down her cape and shirt, then wet a finger to paste down her hair.

"Look at this place! What do you think he's like, Lukien?"

Now I was getting nervous, too. "Wealthy," I said. "And wealthy men can't be trusted. Full of sweet talk and bullshit, I bet. Watch yourself, Cricket. All those girls you saw back there? Probably slaves."

"I don't think so, Lukien. They looked happy."

"Of course they do. Imagine being whipped for not smiling like an idiot all the time." I took a deep breath, regretting it at once as the stink of lavender filled my nose. "Ugh! What kind of man—"

"Shh, he'll hear you," scolded Cricket.

I rolled my eyes at her. "Under his spell already."

And yet I was happy, mostly because Cricket was happy. The palace had sparked a brightness in her eyes I hadn't seen in weeks. Once again, I let myself believe I'd done the right thing by taking her with me. If there was war in the Bitter Kingdoms, it seemed far away from Fallon's extraordinary home.

Finally, the golden door opened again, this time wide enough for us to see. Marilius stepped aside for us to enter, but Cricket and I just stood there, too awestruck to move. Sunlight struck our faces, streaming in off the sea. A pool of blue water washed slowly in and out of the palace. The chamber, if that's truly what it was, hugged the water like two great arms, wrapping it in fantastical architecture. Inside were tiny palm trees and orchids the size of coconuts. Half-nude servants—men and women both—waited at the edge of the pool near a table heavy with food and silverware. A figure swam alone in the water, naked, twirling and backstroking. Cricket's mouth fell open at the sight of him.

"Oh . . . my."

I scowled at Marilius, offended even if Cricket wasn't. "Fate above, Marilius, what is this?"

Marilius shrugged. "It's noontime. This is where he takes his meals."

"Marilius, he's naked."

"You'll get used to it. Come in."

Cricket didn't need to be asked twice, bolting for a better look. Song birds twittered in the miniature trees, and a perfect breeze blew off the sea. I caught up to Cricket as I approached the pool, putting my hand on her shoulder to stop her from diving in. She stared at Fallon, wide-eyed as he swam. Embarrassed, I tried to look away yet couldn't somehow. He was, I admit, an amazing looking man. His strong physique moved effortlessly through the water, his longish copper-colored hair streaking behind him. He was thin like a woman but muscled like a man, like the palace statues. His skin was strange too, not white like mine or black like Sariyah's, but a deep, tawny tone I'd never seen before. He rolled onto his back, spouted water from his mouth like a porpoise, then swam toward us, emerging from the water smiling and dripping wet.

Marilius stepped forward. "Anton, here they are—Lukien and his squire."

Fallon's emerald eyes flashed. In the center of his forehead a black tattoo caught my attention. A serving girl offered him a robe. Fallon waved if off as he looked us over, appraising us like pieces of art.

"Sir Lukien," he said, "you don't look like a monster slayer." He glanced at Marilius. "Are you sure about him?"

"He can do it," assured Marilius. "Trust me."

"He's not too old?"

"Hey," I barked, hooking my thumb over my sword. "Talk to *us*. We're standing right here."

Fallon smirked. "A one-eyed knight and a peasant girl? I'm skeptical."

"It's rude to ignore us," said Cricket.

"And to stand there naked," I added. "Put that robe on, please."

"Westerners." Fallon folded his arms. "Where I come from whole families bathe together." He smiled at Cricket and said, "Would you like to try that?"

"That's enough," I erupted. Marilius quickly got between us.

"Lukien, no. It's nothing. It's just how he is."

Fallon laughed and took the robe from the servant. "If it makes you more comfortable . . ." He slipped on the garment. I studied the tattoo between his eyes, but couldn't make out the symbol, like an upside down Y with a cross through it. A Zuran letter, I supposed. As Fallon took a seat at the head of the table, a bare-chested boy began brushing his long, wet hair.

"It's all right," Marilius whispered. "He's just . . . different."

"Different? Marilius, he's out of his mind. Why'd you bring us—"

"Enough muttering, please," said Fallon. His long fingers plucked a grape from a bowl. He sucked on it as he regarded me. "Marilius tells me you got in a tangle with Wrestler. He says he broke your neck. I find that remarkable." He glanced at Cricket. "What's your name, child?"

"Cricket," she replied.

"Cricket? Ugly name for a pretty girl. Are you from these lands?"

Cricket nodded. "I think so."

"Uh, excuse me, Lord Fallon," I began.

"Anton." He smiled at me.

"Exactly how much do you know about us?"

"Sir Lukien, five minutes ago I'd never even heard of you. Marilius seems to think you're well known. Among mercenaries I suppose. Will you sit?"

The servants held out chairs for us. Marilius took a seat close to Fallon. I held Cricket back.

"Marilius hasn't told us why he brought us here," I said. "Did you say 'monster slayer'?"

"That's right." Fallon chose a strawberry this time. His eyes fell upon my sword. "That sword you carry—that's your magic?"

"Something like that."

"May I see it?"

Malator said nothing. I unsheathed the sword, laying it out in both hands. Fallon seemed disappointed.

"Boring. But if it's as powerful as Marilius says I could sell it for you, Lukien. Maybe make you a very rich man. After you do what I need of you, obviously."

"And what would that be, exactly?" I sheathed the sword. "I should tell you I'm not for sale. We're only here because of Marilius."

"He saved us," said Cricket.

"Did he?" Fallon patted Marilius's arm. "So brave."

Marilius bristled. "He can help, Anton. That's why I brought him."

"You brought him here to redeem yourself," said Fallon. His nostrils flared, and I wondered—were he and Marilius *lovers*?

"Please," I said, "just tell us why we're here."

Fallon flicked a wrist toward one of the servants, a girl with honey-blonde hair and one perfect breast exposed. The girl gently took my arm, smiling as she led me to a chair across from Fallon. Another servant—a male—gingerly took Cricket's hand and did the same. My servant, however, sat down in my lap.

"Her name is Druan," said Fallon. "She's yours for the night. Try eating grapes from between her legs. Heaven!"

I let the girl kiss my cheek. Her naked breast brushed against me. I could feel the heat rising in my face.

"No." I gently pushed Druan away. I swear she looked dejected.

"All right," said Fallon, "just business, then. Druan is only part of my offer. I can pay you whatever you want, Lukien. If you're the man to rid me of my problem, it'll be worth it. Isowon isn't just my home, you see. She's my child, my dream. I built her with nothing, and I'll not have her taken from me."

"Too fast," I said. "Who's trying to take Isowon from you?"

"That *thing*," said Fallon. "Diriel's monster, whatever it is. He sent it to kill me."

"Diriel? From Akyre? Why would he do that?"

"To take what's mine, obviously! Look around, Sir Lukien. Isowon is incomparable. There's nothing like it in all the Bitter Kingdoms and certainly not in that ash heap, Akyre. I built this whole place with spices. My routes, my contacts—they're worth more than all the provinces of Akyre put together."

"Akyre's already at war with Kasse and Drin," I said. "We saw the refugees on the road. I doubt he'd try to attack Isowon as well."

"You don't know Diriel, then," said Fallon. "He wants everything, all the Bitter Kingdoms. This was all part of the Akyren empire once. That's Diriel's goal—to remake the empire. My spice routes would make that a lot easier for him."

Cricket grimaced at the news. "I don't remember any of this. Not even Diriel. How can that be, Lukien?"

"She's from Akyre, Anton," explained Marilius, "but she can't remember more than that."

Fallon's delicate face grew tender. "Then you're a refugee too, girl. Like the others. I promise you: when this deed is done and the monster is killed, we will find your lost memories."

"Don't get ahead of yourself," I warned. "I never said I'd help you. I don't even know what this thing is." Suddenly all I could think of was the monster I'd seen when I'd nearly died. "Describe it."

"It isn't human, that's for sure," said Fallon. "It comes at night, looking for me, prowling outside the palace. Nine feet tall at least."

"You've seen it?"

Fallon shook his head. "No. But Marilius has."

"So?" I looked at Marilius. "What's it like?"

"Like Anton said, Lukien—a monster. I barely even got a look at it."

"When was that?"

Marilius shrugged. "About a week ago."

"Right before he left me," sneered Fallon. "After the worst attack."

"Mercenaries don't stick around when things get too tough," I said. "Now I know why you left, Marilius. The only thing I don't understand is why you came back."

"And that's none of your concern, Lukien. Are you going to help us or not?"

"I still haven't heard a good reason why I should."

"Because I'm rich," said Fallon. "And I can make you rich, too."

"Not interested. Marilius should have told you I'm not a mercenary anymore."

"He's a knight-errant," said Marilius sarcastically. "Lukien wants to do good, Anton."

"Well then, it's killed people," said Fallon, dangling that fact like a treat. "Not just soldiers but townspeople too. Almost a dozen now."

I tried to look unmoved. "Maybe the townsfolk should leave."

Fallon grinned. "Or maybe you're afraid, Sir Lukien?"

"I'm not afraid of anything, Fallon. Not dying and certainly not your monster. I just don't want us involved."

"Bullshit," said Marilius. "You wouldn't be here if you didn't want to get involved. You came to the Bitter Kingdoms looking for trouble, Lukien, you and that sword of yours. You want to prove what a big man you are? Here's your chance."

"Marilius, I don't think I'm the one trying to prove himself here," I said with a wink. "Besides . . . my business is in Akyre."

"Oh, right," said Marilius. "Time for a rematch with Wrestler. Go ahead, take Cricket to Akyre. Get your neck broken again. But just remember those people you saw on the road, Lukien. That's what Diriel is like. That's what you'll be riding into if you leave here."

"Or you can stay!" said Fallon brightly. He reached a hand across the table toward Cricket. "Let me help you figure out who you are, child. You'll be safe here."

"*If* you help us beat this monster, Lukien," said Marilius.

Now they had me stumped. Fallon, Marilius, even the servants—they all waited, staring like helpless kittens. But the only one I really cared about was Cricket.

"Cricket, walk with me."

I got out of my chair and started toward the other side of the pool, where the sea lapped into the palace. Cricket quickly followed. Out of earshot I said, "I'm lost here, squire. I can't make this decision without you."

"What about Malator?" she asked. "What's he think you should do?"

"I haven't asked him, and I'm not going to. These are our lives, Cricket. We can leave right now. We can head back toward Akyre and take our chances, maybe try to find that waterfall of yours, shake lose some of your memories."

"We could," agreed Cricket. "But I know you, Lukien. You want to fight this thing because no one else can beat it. And you want to pay your debt to Marilius for saving us."

"Cricket, Fallon is out of his mind. And I can't be sure, but I think he and Marilius are lovers."

"What?" Cricket stifled her laugh with her hand. "Honestly!"

I just shook my head. "This is madness. Malator showed me a monster before we left Jador. And I saw a monster in my dreams. It's all connected, Cricket—the monster, the Legion of the Lost, everything."

"Then that's your answer, Lukien. You found your mission."

"I already have a mission, Cricket. You."

"Oh, I'm not going anywhere, Lukien, don't you worry. I'm your squire. I want to see this beasty for myself!"

I didn't tell Cricket why I really wanted to find this monster. I didn't tell her that day or any other day. This monster stalking Anton Fallon, this unnamed, unseen thing—how could it not be the same beast Malator had drawn? It wasn't just after Fallon, it was after Cricket, too. And if it was after Cricket, that meant it had to die.

12

We rode out from Isowon at dawn the next morning, the new day's sunlight gleaming off my old bronze armor. Cricket had spent much of the night making it ready, insisting I wear it to battle the beast. She had polished the breast plate into a satiny mirror, removing every bit of grime. She worked proudly, like a real squire, and rode at my side on her well-groomed pony, her cape of rass skin on her shoulders like a trophy.

Marilius rode at point, leading us east along the coast. Before he'd fled Isowon for Arad, other of Fallon's men had tracked a trail of blood this same way. They never found the monster, just the skeletal remains of their fellow mercenaries. Still, they suspected the creature made its lair in the hills at the mouth of the Dovra River—almost a day's ride from Fallon's palace.

No one seemed to know why the creature only attacked at night, or why it made its home so far from its intended prey. I puzzled over this as we rode.

Before long we were out of Isowon's shadow, leaving the protection of the palace far behind. For the first time in months—maybe even years—I felt like a knight again, like a Royal Charger, confident and ready to face Fallon's monster. I'd made a terrible mistake when fighting Wrestler—I had left my sword behind. This time, Malator and all his magic would be with me. Whatever the creature might be, it was mortal, and I was not, and that meant I could kill it. I made the link with Malator as we rode, speaking to him wordlessly while Cricket and Marilius made small talk of their own.

You've been quiet, I told him. *Any advice?*

I expected Malator to be petulant over being excluded. Instead he was pensive. *This is why you came here, Lukien,* he said. *Maybe now we'll have some answers.*

You still don't know what the monster is?

I do not.

But you've been thinking about it, right? I sighed out loud. *Come on, Malator—you saw death when you drew that picture in the sand.*

You saw death, Lukien. I saw a monster.

But you told me not to take Cricket with me! Why? Because of the monster?

Lukien, I can only tell you what I know. And I can't know everything, remember?

His answer unnerved me. *This will be our fight, Malator,* I said. *We'll face this thing together. Whatever it is.*

I'll do my best.

Hey . . . your best? I stared ahead as I rode, but my mind's eye fixed on him. *Malator, are you afraid?*

It's always wise to be a little afraid before battle. You know that.

"Lukien?"

I awoke as if from a trance. Cricket was bouncing along next to me, excited. "Huh?"

"I told Marilius about the waterfall. He knows it, Lukien!"

"Waterfall?"

"The place with the *stream,*" she said, annoyed. "The place I dreamt about, remember? I dreamt about it again last night."

"It's Sky Falls," said Marilius. Then he shrugged. "Probably."

"Sky Falls . . ." Cricket's eyes went dreamy. "Yes."

"Yes, you remember it?" I asked.

"No, but that must be it. I can feel it, Lukien. Marilius described it just like I picture it. Tell him, Marilius."

"Not much to tell," said Marilius. "It's up in Akyre near the border with Kasse. Part of the Dovra River. People go there to see it. Or they used to before the war. It's well known."

I wasn't convinced. "That's not much to go on. There could be a hundred waterfalls up there, right?"

"Maybe, but why would Cricket know about any of them? She's just a kid. I figure the only one she could have seen is Sky Falls."

"It is Sky Falls," Cricket insisted. "Lukien, can we go?"

I looked at Marilius. "How safe is it?"

"To swim? It's a waterfall."

"Not the waterfall, idiot—what about the area? Can we get there safely?"

"No chance. Diriel's men are on the march all around there."

"But that's the place," said Cricket desperately. "I remember the ferns, the boulders—everything Marilius described."

"And the caves," said Marilius. "There's little caves around the cliff—remember?"

Cricket blinked quickly. "I don't remember caves. Oh, but that's the place. We have to go, Lukien!"

"We'll try, Cricket."

"When?"

"As soon as we can."

Her dark eyes grew skeptical. "When, Lukien?"

I didn't want to tell her how much I mistrusted her memories. "When we're done with this mission. We'll kill this monster, then we'll ride for Sky Falls."

"Promise?"

"Cricket, you're my squire. Everything I say to you is a promise."

"Look at that," said Cricket. She pointed up ahead toward a sparkling lake, circled in shade by a vanguard of trees. "What do you say, Lukien?"

It had been hours since our last rest. Marilius was sure we'd reach the mouth of the river by dusk. Finally, I saw the chance I'd been waiting for.

"Yeah, good idea," I told Cricket. "Ride up ahead. Make sure it's clear."

"Really?" Cricket studied the way ahead. The flat road led clearly to the lake. "Why?"

"Because I said so. Ride on, squire."

With a shrug Cricket drove her pony forward, leaving me with Marilius. Marilius watched her go without saying a word. When she was far enough ahead, he let out a heavy breath.

"All right, she's gone," he said. "What's on your mind?"

He'd been waiting for it.

"Anton Fallon," I kept my one eye straight ahead as we rode. "I'm guessing you're more than just his hireling. Now listen: it makes no difference to me what a man does for his pleasures. I just want to know what I'm getting into with you both. Tell me I'm wrong, and I'll say no more about it."

"You're not wrong," said Marilius. "It's obvious."

"Uh-huh. Is that why he made you a captain?"

Marilius nodded. He looked ashamed and very, very young. "I shouldn't have let him. But it was a place for me to stay. Anton knew what I was and didn't care. You show me one other man who would have kept me on as a soldier after knowing what I am."

"I can't," I admitted. "I spent my whole life soldiering. Men like you don't usually last too long. How long have you been with him?"

"Two months. I came down from Norvor to hire on as a free-lance. I heard Anton Fallon had all the money so I went to him first. He liked me, and I liked him. The rest just happened."

"So I was right about you trying to prove yourself. And I bet that's why you took up soldiering in the first place."

"How'd you know that?"

"I see it all the time. Men are always running away from things and thinking that becoming a soldier can fix it. Fix *them.*" As soon as I said it I thought about my own life. "Seen it all before."

Marilius and I slowed our horses. I turned my head to look at him—really look at him. I knew his story. Somewhere there was a father that disapproved, or a brother, maybe. Somewhere, someone important to him had made up their minds and decided he wasn't good enough.

"I ran, Lukien," he said suddenly. His face turned ashen. "I was scared. I'm scared right now. I don't want to see that thing again. If not for you I wouldn't even be here."

"Everyone gets scared, Marilius. Being scared isn't the problem. Running away and staying away—that's the problem."

"But you don't get scared. I saw the way you went after Wrestler. And when Anton told you about the monster you didn't even think twice. That's the way I want to be. But I'll never be that way because I'm a—"

He stopped himself.

"What?" I pressed. "What are you, Marilius? A boy-lover?" I laughed. "Stupid. It's so stupid! Listen, you know the worst kinds of men to have in battle? Men that don't give a damn. You have to love men to be a soldier. You're not a coward, Marilius. If you were a coward you wouldn't be here. If you were a coward you never would have come back."

Marilius let a tiny smile supplant his frown. "Did you ever love a man, Lukien?"

"Yes," I admitted. "Not in the way you mean, maybe, but yes. There once was a man I loved almost more than my own life."

"Who?" wondered Marilius. "King Akeela?"

I turned in surprise. "How'd you know about Akeela?"

"I told you—I know a lot about you, Lukien."

"Yeah, well . . ." I rode on, uncomfortable. "I don't talk much about Akeela these days. I'm the one that killed him, after all."

"His madness killed him," said Marilius. "That's what I heard."

"I drove him to that madness. Make no mistake about that, Marilius. Whatever else you hear about me, know this: I am a king-slayer. I'll bear that guilt all the way to whatever hell awaits me. You're a better lover of men than I am."

"Ah, now you mock me."

"No, I do not," I said seriously. "Whatever you are, you're no coward. Don't let a father label you a failure. Don't let any man. You've got courage inside you. I see it. I promise—when the time comes, you'll know what to do."

13

The Bitter Kingdoms were nothing like my old home in Liiria. They were rocky and harsh and wholly ugly, and I had never thought to feel at ease there until the end of that day's ride, when we finally reached the river valley. There, with dusk just touching us, we saw the hills with the pine trees Marilius had promised, the land sloping gently downward toward a hidden dell. I could smell the river too, the musk of it like the River Kryss where I'd fought so long ago. It felt like I had stumbled again into one of Malator's made-up dreamscapes, with birds chirping in the trees and long shadows touching the land. I took a breath, shocked by the sweetness of the air. How could this be the place?

"Here?" I looked around, slowing Zephyr, my exhausted horse. "You're sure your monster isn't a bear, maybe?"

Marilius seemed more nervous than usual. Instead of just slowing his horse, he brought it completely to a stop. "Let's wait here," he said. "It'll be dark by the time we get deep enough into the valley."

"Wait?" said Cricket. "For what?"

"For it to find us," said Marilius. "It comes out at night, remember? It probably already knows we're here."

I looked ahead, studying the dell and surrounding hills. "We'll find its lair," I told Marilius. "Better to kill it while it sleeps than have it find us first."

"The valley's full of caves, Lukien. We'll be groping around like blind men. Better to wait till morning, when it's light."

"There's enough sunlight to get started," I said. I looked at

Marilius, not wanting to embarrass him. Yes, he was afraid, but there was something else, too. "We should go on . . . don't you think?"

"Let's go," said Cricket anxiously. "Before it wakes up!"

"Look at those cliffs," said Marilius, pointing ahead. "If we enter the dell it'll be able to trap us. It may already know we're here. We should stay where there's room to fight."

It was worth considering. The hills did indeed close in around the dell, but I wanted to see it for myself. "Fallon said it only comes at night, right?"

Reluctantly, Marilius nodded.

"Then maybe it only *can* come out at night. Maybe it sleeps during the day, like a rass."

"The day's almost over, Lukien. If the monster hasn't wakened yet then it soon will. I say we stay and wait for it here, out in the open."

"Oh, let's decide!" said Cricket. "Before it finds us!"

"Easy, squire. The last time I went off without thinking I got my neck broken, remember?" I looked west toward the setting sun, then ahead toward the dell. Bare minutes of sunlight remained. We could strike a camp, I thought . . . But no.

"We go on," I decided. "If this thing does have a lair we should find it."

Cricket bounced in her saddle. "I'm ready."

Marilius frowned. "Me first, then," he said. At his side hung the beat-up sword he'd spent the night sharpening. He drew the blade as he urged his horse slowly forward, his eyes lighting up like embers. I didn't need to tell Cricket to stay close. She stuck beside me as I followed Marilius, my ears alert to every breeze and chirping bird. I sensed Malator inside my sword, felt his essence searching out in front of me.

Malator? Anything?

Yes.

His certainty startled me. *Where? Do you see it?*

This place . . . He paused as if looking around. *This is where it comes from.*

Is it awake?

It's . . . alive.

Where is it, Malator? Does it see us?

Malator fell silent. I could almost feel him putting up a hand to quiet me. I thought of slowing down, maybe stopping until he answered, but Marilius was already far ahead. Cricket rode next to me, stiff with fear.

"Breathe," I whispered.

With one giant sigh she let out the air she'd been holding.

It's hiding, said Malator finally.

I nodded. *A trap. What is it, Malator?*

A monster, Lukien. Just like they said.

"Marilius," I called out. "It's up ahead."

Marilius snapped his head around. "How do you know?"

"I just do. It's not sleeping. It's waiting for us in the dell."

"Waiting for the darkness, I bet." Marilius reined in his horse. "What do you want to do?"

"Find it," I said. "Let it think it has us trapped." At last I drew my sword, angered at the thought of being stalked. Marilius brought his horse around again, about to continue. He sniffed the air.

"Ugh! What the hell is that?"

The shifting breeze carried the smell over to Cricket and me. Cricket hurried a hand over her mouth.

"Fate above!" She turned away, shutting her eyes and clamping shut her nose.

I barely had to inhale—the stench struck me all at once. The smell of rot, like an open grave. Marilius strained to control his dancing horse. The breeze rolled out of the dell, bearing with it the unimaginable stink. Cricket pulled up her cape to shield her face. I held my breath as I wondered what it was.

"The monster?" Cricket guessed.

"No, it didn't stink," said Marilius. "Only corpses smell like that!"

I'd trudged through enough battlefields to know he was right. "Malator," I said out loud, "What else do you see?"

Malator was quiet, but I could feel his confusion. *Find it, Lukien.*

"But what is it?"

I cannot say.

"Cannot?" I spat. "Or won't?"

I'm not a god, Lukien. I don't know everything. Find it for yourself.

His answer wasn't angry, just matter of fact, and I was too confused to argue. I drove my horse forward, catching up to Marilius and urging him onward. Together with Cricket we rode for the dell, staring at the long-faced hills. The trees tightened around us, funneling us forward, the stench growing more unbearable. A fly flittered past me, then another and more, until I spotted a swarm of them ahead, and the heap of flesh they feasted on.

"God's death!" screeched Marilius. He moved to block Cricket's way, but she'd already seen it. Her face flashed purple, then up came her breakfast, right over the side of her pony.

I left them behind, moving up slowly, forgetting the monster as I spied the hill of body parts. Bones and rags of skin sat rotting in a pile, withers-high to my horse. I stared, disgusted and confounded, watched by the dead eye of a half-chewed human skull. An outstretched arm beckoned me with rigored fingers. Blood-crusted fur and bits of people wriggled with maggots. I saw an antler in the pile sticking up like a flag, the scrap of a uniform caught in its tines. Decaying entrails dripped watery bile into the soil. I choked down a rush of vomit.

"Cricket, don't come closer," I shouted.

"Oh, don't!" She turned away from the heap completely, wiping the puke from her mouth. She waved at me with her free hand. "Just get away from it!"

But I was too shocked to look away. Blood never bothered me but this did. I stared, watching the maggots bring the mass to life, the squirming of old bowels and shit. Behind me Marilius was saying something. Cricket kept puking, and Malator . . .

Lukien!

Why didn't I hear him? It was only when the mound started moving that I realized Malator was shouting. My horse wheeled beneath me, ready to bolt. The mound of bones and bodies shivered, shedding flesh and scurrying the flies. Malator hollered in my brain, warning me back. I just stared like a dullard. Slowly, impossibly, the hill tumbled toward me, surrounding the hooves of my snorting horse as the creature emerged, rising up out of the limbs and cast-off bones.

No good gods had created the thing I saw. It was wholly unnatural, made from the very skeletons and skins it had burrowed beneath. It climbed into the sky, towering over me astride my horse, its bony head the stolen skull of an ox. A ladder of broken spines made its backbone, the ribs of its varied victims forming its chest. Four legs protruded from its vaguely human shape, the two in front capped at the knees by mismatched skulls, the other pair dangling behind it. It made its arms from borrowed bones, using goat horns for fingers. In fact the thing was armored in bones, human and otherwise, an absurd and ghastly mishmash of corpses hung with rags of flesh.

This was the thing stalking my dreams. Nine feet over the

ground, its dead-eyed ox head looked at me. I searched for a heart inside its ribs but saw instead a glowing darkness. Nothing alive seemed within it. I spun Zephyr free of the filth around his hooves, out where I could fight. Cricket and Marilius started toward me.

"Back!" I cried.

They reined in their mounts. The creature, whatever it was, pulled free of the stinking mound, then stopped as if guarding the dell.

"It's different now," said Marilius. "It was just skins when I saw it."

"But what is it?" asked Cricket. "What *is* it?"

"A monster, I told you!"

I quickly rubbed Zephyr's neck to calm him. I needed him now. And Malator.

Malator? Are you with me? I asked, gripping the sword tighter.

I felt him pour into me. *Like thunder, Lukien.*

Rage is all I know in battle, and rage was all I felt. I silenced the others with a wave, raised the Sword of Angels, then cried out and charged. Zephyr shot forward, straight for the beast. The sockets of its two dead eyes turned against us. I drew back my sword, turning my arm to steel, spying the heartless chest of the thing, the pulsing darkness behind its stolen ribs. It hunched to meet the blow, unafraid. Zephyr galloped forward, splashing through the gore. A single bony arm came up, big as a tree limb. I ducked beneath it easily, saw my mark . . .

I swung the sword. I hit the mark. And then like fire it struck me. Unimaginable, burning pain, turning my arm to water in my armor. I think I screamed. I know I fell from horseback. The sword tumbled out of my hand, over and over my head until it hit the ground beside me. I tasted dirt in my mouth. I rolled to recover, but my arm felt broken, almost useless. Cricket ran to me, grabbing my breastplate. Marilius was over her, still on horseback.

"The horse!" he cried, and I didn't know why.

I staggered to my feet, felt the shadow of the creature, and shoved Cricket away.

"Move!" I shouted, and turned to see Marilius. His horse bucked wildly, fighting him. My own horse had tangled in the bones of the beast, its slapping reins wrapped around a pair of elk ribs. Marilius whirled his mount around to push me backward.

"Lukien, run!"

My sword! I scrambled to find it. Cricket rushed it into my hand.

"Come on!" she cried, tugging at my hair. Marilius was still in front of me. I shouldered past him to get to Zephyr, watching as my horse—my brave and beautiful horse—kicked its way free of the beast and ran.

"Zephyr, go!"

I ran forward, screaming, as the monster came at me, its ox skull animated, the four legs coming alive beneath it. Again it met my sword, and again that icy fire surged up my arm. This time I managed to keep the sword in hand, spinning for another blow. Pain roared up my arm, rattling the bones and burning the skin. Malator cloaked me in his magic. Up went the creature's enormous hand, slapping hard against my breastplate, sending me tumbling. I shook off the pain and rose again.

"Cricket, Marilius, run now! Run!"

Marilius galloped toward me. He raised his sword, charging past me like a mad man. His blade glanced the monster's hide and shattered. Marilius screamed, holding up his hand. I could see the red and blistered skin, already charred. He managed his horse, turning it back toward Cricket, who once again was coming for me.

"You stay there, god-damn it!" I shouted.

Marilius brought his horse in front of her, guarding her. I looked up into the monster's eyes, those two black holes crawling with insects, and summoned the rest of my strength.

"Whatever you are, demon, whatever hell you came from, hear me—I am forever! Cursed and immortal!"

It lowered its head, its uneven horns twisting in thought, as though pondering what I was. I braced myself, holding the sword in both hands now, my sword arm still shrieking in pain. It took one hulking step, its fleshless nostrils sniffing me. Then like a dog it sprang, its goat horn fingers seizing my shoulders, forcing me down and pinning me to the dirt. I struggled, trying to drive the sword into it, but all its weight and fire pressed on me, cooking me inside my armor.

"Malator! Strengthen me!"

The great ox skull hovered over my face, and I looked into those maggoty eyes, hypnotized by the living emptiness. I swear, whatever soul I had fled my body. The monster was inside me, searching me, raging in my mind even as Malator fought to free me. The breath spilled from my lungs, filling with fire instead. I wanted to scream but couldn't. Darkness soaked my brain, and I felt my one eye closing, closing . . .

And then it was off me. It rose up, retracting its bony limbs, and with one last questioning look regarded me. Then the thing turned and stalked toward the dell. I sputtered, coughing blood from my seared lungs, fighting unconsciousness. My fingers coiled around the sword, hungry for its power.

It's gone, spoke Malator. *Hold on.*

"After it," I choked. "Marilius, help me."

Cricket hovered over me, wiping the blood from my mouth with her sleeve. Marilius swooped down from his horse.

"We're getting out of here," he said. "Cricket, help me with him."

"It's escaping . . ."

"Lukien, my shoulder," ordered Cricket, burrowing under my arm to lift me. "Come on, onto the horse."

I could barely feel my arm. Words bubbled from my bloody lips. "Why'd it go? It let me live."

"Stop talking," snapped Marilius. With Cricket's help he hoisted me into the saddle. "Hold on to that damn sword. Go, Cricket!"

Cricket snatched the reins. Quickly she pulled the horse back the way we'd come. I don't remember much of anything after that. My vision dimmed as I surrendered to nothingness, but I wasn't afraid. I couldn't die, no matter what the creature dealt me. As sleep took me I heard Marilius's voice, at once taunting and sweet.

"Hang on, Lukien . . . I'm gonna save your ass again."

14

I opened my eyes but was still asleep, and I knew immediately that I was still dreaming. I was back in Anton Fallon's palace, in the room I shared with Cricket. Only it wasn't really our room anymore. Now it was much, much bigger, like a throne room, with a hall at the end where a door had once been. Moonlight pierced the window over my bed, and when I sat up I thought for a moment I had left my body behind. My head swam with magic, and I felt no pain, even when I glanced at my badly burned arm. Someone had taken off my armor and bandaged my arm and chest, and when I remembered what had happened I looked around in fear.

"Cricket?"

She was in her bed, not far from my own. Relieved, I tossed my bare feet over the bedside, then saw that she was in the grip of her own nightmare. Her body shook with fits, her eyes dancing madly beneath their lids. She was saying something, but I couldn't tell what, gasping as she wrestled her dream. I walked across the ornate carpet, hovering over her, my hand dangling above her forehead.

"Cricket?"

I touched her shoulder, gently at first. She felt cold. I brushed her clammy forehead. Her hand shot up and grabbed my wrist, pulling me. I let her drag me down, almost to face to face, and when I looked into her terrified expression her eyes shot open.

"Cricket, wake up! It's me."

For a moment my voice calmed her. She released me and closed her eyes but then slipped quickly back into her shivering dream. I was confused and annoyed because I knew who had dragged me here, to this place between the worlds.

"Malator! Where are you?"

I looked around the chamber then heard his voice coming from the hallway.

"You can't wake her, Lukien."

My eye scanned the room. Mostly it was how I'd left it. I saw my armor tucked neatly in a pile, my boots beside it, gleaming and polished once again. The Sword of Angels rested against my wooden bed, not far from where I was—or had been—sleeping.

"Am I awake?" I asked.

"Partly," said Malator. "Come out to the hall."

"Why the theater?" I groaned. "Just answer me—what's happened? What's wrong with Cricket?"

"Just a dream, that's all."

"Why won't she wake?"

"It's her dream, Lukien, not yours. She'll wake when it's over."

I drifted toward the hallway. "But it's a nightmare. She's afraid."

"She dreams this way all the time. Haven't you noticed? She's told you about it. Tomorrow she'll tell you again. Maybe this time you'll listen. Come on, I want to show you something."

His voice was almost playful. I followed it like a dog whistle. I had been in Malator's dreamscapes before. He loves drama, my Akari. This felt different, though. He was right about me not really being asleep, but neither was I awake. The body was mine, plainly, but now I was in a different realm. I was irritated, but excited, too.

"How are you doing this?" It took me forever to cross the chamber. "This is new."

"Someday you'll be able to do this on your own," said Malator. "Maybe."

"What? Sleepwalk? I can do that without your help."

"Cross between the worlds," said Malator. "If you let me teach you."

"Really?" I had almost reached the dark hallway, but still I couldn't see him. "What world is this, then?"

Finally he stepped out of the hall, emerging from the darkness with his wavy smile. I never know for sure how Malator will appear to me. His body never changes but he loves to play dress up, like a little kid. I've seen him in Akari garb, and in the armor he once wore. I've seen him in priestly robes and in rags and in kingly finery, but I never once saw him dressed the way he appeared that night. I recognized the uniform at once. A Liirian soldier. An elite, like I had been before my fall. A Royal Charger.

"Why are you dressed like that?" I asked.

"I'm a soldier, remember?"

"An Akari warrior," I said. "And that was a long time ago. Never a Liirian. Never a Charger."

He held out a ghostly hand without apology. "Come. You'll like this, I think."

I wanted to talk about the monster. I wanted to know what happened, not just to me but to Cricket and Marilius. When I hesitated, Malator read my mind.

"They're fine. *You're* fine, Lukien. Or you will be when you wake up. Now trust me. This is something you should see."

So I stepped into the hallway, and instantly it came to life. I had walked into another world entirely, back in time to a place so ripe in my memory that the sight of it paralyzed me. Suddenly my ears came alive with the noise—the rush of people, the clang of metal, the bawdy voices of men. The smell, that unmistakable coal smoke of the braziers, the kind that burned night and day and stained the old tapestries upon the gray brick walls. Maybe my mouth fell open, or maybe my eye popped out of my head, but Malator was laughing suddenly, giddy at my reaction to the phantasms he'd resurrected. He leaned over and kissed my cheek, like he'd given me a gift.

"Welcome home, Lukien."

Home. I was *home*. Back in Liiria, back in the castle where I'd grown to manhood. Back with friends I knew but who, for some reason, paid me no notice. There I was, just in trousers, my bare chest bandaged and standing there like a mute, and all around me rushed my past. Liirians I hadn't seen in decades, some who'd died in battle and some who'd later called me a traitor, laughing, celebrating, twirling pretty girls to the music of lutes from the other side of the hall. Servants moved through the crowd, passing out food from silver platters and sloshing beer from great big mugs. A teenaged boy hurried past me, brushing me aside, unseen. When I saw his face I remembered where I was . . . and when. I shouted out his name.

"Akeela!"

Of course he couldn't hear me. Thirteen again and this was his party. He ran, dodging the men and women his father had invited, chased by . . .

I waited, not breathing, knowing I would see myself bursting from the crowd. And there I came, the perfect happy memory, shoving past a flustered maid. The sight of my own, younger self seized my heart. I glanced at Malator, but the Akari said nothing, smiling serenely as he watched the other ghosts. I gazed at myself, my wonderful, younger self, my face bright with both my eyes and free of scars, laughing as I chased Akeela through the hall. I had teased him, I suddenly remembered, about a girl he'd fallen for but wouldn't admit. It wasn't Cassandra, though. It wouldn't be Cassandra yet for years.

"Nymira."

I whispered the name as I watched myself disappear. Malator shoved me into the hall.

"Go after them," he chided.

So I did. With the air of a ghost I passed through the crowd, running easily after the boys, knowing exactly where I'd find them. Malator kept up with me as I traced the route from memory, thrilling at seeing the castle again and studying the happy faces of men who'd one day be my mentors and women who'd be my conquests. I found the drawing room where I'd cornered Akeela and found us wrestling on the floor, a moment away from toppling the vase.

I thought of jumping forward, of moving the table before Akeela kicked it over or catching the vase before it shattered. But I was a ghost. No matter what, the vase would fall. My younger self pinned Akeela to the carpet. He struggled with a cat-like shout, his foot shooting out toward the table. The vase tottered a long time, but neither boy noticed it until it crashed down next to them.

"Oh . . . !"

The cry was mine. I winced at the shock in Akeela's face. The younger me released Akeela and sat back, astonished. Akeela cursed.

"Damn it!" He picked up bits of alabaster, trying to puzzle them together again. "Why'd you chase me, Lukien? Look!"

But it wasn't my fault. I remembered what I'd said to him: "Why'd you run then? You're so clumsy. You can't beat me in wrestling or anything else!"

"This was my mother's!"

"So? Blame me for it. I don't care."

Akeela nodded, but I knew he wouldn't go for it. Even then I knew he wouldn't.

"I broke it," he sighed. "I'll tell my father."

Neither my younger self nor Akeela got up. I drifted closer, squatting down beside us. Akeela looked exquisitely beautiful. So logical. So resigned. And I—or the me I once was—gathered up the pieces of the vase.

"Anyone could have broken it," I said. "Or stolen it. Get back to the hall. I'll get rid of it."

"You can't. We'll take the pieces to my father."

"No, Akeela. It'll be a secret."

"You'll get blamed for it. You always do. Forget it." Akeela used his cape to collect the bits, holding it out for me to dump my own into. "Here."

"That's crazy. It's your birthday!"

"So? I'm supposed to lie, then? What are they teaching you in the Chargers? You're going to be a soldier soon, Lukien. Soldiers don't lie, not even to protect their friends."

"But friends keep secrets. Secrets make the friendship stronger."

Akeela stood there with his cape full of broken alabaster, holding it out like a basket. "Come on," he said, and walked back toward the hall.

"Loyal, your king," said Malator suddenly. "Honest."

I nodded. "He was always like that. I was the disloyal, dishonest one."

"You were his favorite soldier."

"I was his friend," I corrected. "Being his soldier came later. But yeah, I was his favorite."

"A king should be like that with his soldiers, don't you think? Loyal to them? People forget that. They think soldiers are the only ones who need to be loyal."

"Yeah . . ."

I knew from my time with the Akari that Akeela was alive somewhere; really alive, just as Cassandra was alive in her own death realm. I wondered if Akeela was still insane, or if becoming a spirit had healed him. But I had never asked that question, not of Minikin or Malator or anyone else.

"Why'd you show me this?" I asked. "Did you think I'd like seeing Akeela again? Because I don't, Malator. I don't need to be reminded about what I did to him. I don't need you prancing around playing soldier!"

The room was silent except for my angry voice. Malator smiled without looking hurt.

"What?" I pressed. "There's a lesson here? There's always more with you, Malator. Tell me what it is."

Malator shook his head. "I can't, Lukien. I can only guide you."

"You know everything, don't you? What *was* that monster? What's this all about?"

"First," said Malator, "I don't know everything. I've told you that already. That monster was a demon, not of this world. Ask questions, Lukien. Follow the answers."

"But you won't give me answers!" I raved. "All I get from you is horseshit!"

"Then ask someone else. Who would know about the monster? Who is pulling the strings here?"

I shrugged. All I wanted was to be back to sleep. "Fallon?"

"Fallon indeed. He knows more than he's telling."

"Yeah, all right, but what about all this?" I looked around the room. "None of this has to do with anything. I can't figure it out, Malator."

"Food for thought, then," said Malator with his cheerful grin.

I took a breath to clear my mind. Thinking was tough, though. My arm started to hurt. "I think I'm waking up," I said.

"It's almost dawn." Malator sighed. "I should take you back now."

"Wait, what about that other thing you said? About me crossing between the worlds?"

"Oh, you won't remember anything about that when you wake," said Malator. "That's not for now, Lukien. For now, just eat what's on your plate."

"But—"

"No," he said sharply. "I can take you back or I can show you more of this world. That's all. Do you want to see more?"

"No, no more," I said quickly. "Just . . . take me out of here. It's time to talk to Fallon."

15

I awoke that morning just before dawn, before Cricket even, sitting up in bed with a shout that made my servants come running into the room. There were two of them, a man and woman, both beautiful, both assigned to me by Anton Fallon. It was they who had dressed my wounds, I quickly learned. Their names were Karik and Adela. I remembered this as I woke up—really woke up this time—from my long and fretful sleep. I had a thousand questions for them, but Karik and Adela gently scolded me to silence, pointing out Cricket still asleep in the nearby bed.

"What happened?" I whispered.

As the pair helped me into my shirt, they explained how Marilius and Cricket had brought me back to the palace on horseback. Cricket, it turned out, had spent most of the time watching over me. No wonder she was so exhausted. As I listened, the encounter with the monster returned to my memory. My arm had been badly burned, yet both of them marveled at how quickly I'd healed. I flexed my arm within the linen shirt, feeling remarkably good. I had Malator to thank for that. As Karik guided me down to sit on the bed, I hefted the Sword of Angels. While Adela put on my boots, I gave Malator my silent thanks.

"You should eat," whispered Adela. "Come, and I will get you something."

I shook my head. "I want to see Fallon. Take me to him."

The pair shared a grimace. Karik helped me to my feet.

"Master Fallon is in the Great Hall," he said. "But now's not the best time to see him."

"Too bad for him."

As it turned out, Fallon's palace was full of "great halls," but the one where he was hiding was at the eastern end of his enormous home, far from the rooms he'd given me and Cricket. Like everything in the palace the hall was enormous, sparkling with marble tile and golden fixtures. Towering windows of painted glass flooded the hall with dawn light. At any other time the hall might have been a ballroom for a lavish party, but now it was choked with mercenaries. They stood shoulder to shoulder, so closely crammed they could barely move. At least two-hundred of them stood guard, some with weapons drawn, but most so sleep-deprived that they'd sheathed their swords or simply dropped them to the floor. They took almost no notice of me as Karik and Adela brought me into the hall, until one of them called out my name.

"Lukien."

Marilius made his way through the crowd, pushing the others aside to reach me. One look at his bloodshot eyes told me he'd been up all night, too. His fellow mercenaries gave me the once over. I dismissed Karik and Adela as Marilius reached me. He studied my face, then my arm, then laughed.

"Those wounds might have killed someone else, but I shouldn't be surprised to see you're fine!"

"What's with the army? Waiting for the monster to come back?"

"It was a quiet night," said Marilius with relief. "Thank the Fate."

"You do this every night? Gather around the hall like this?"

"There's not usually so many of us. Anton's been in a panic since . . ." Marilius stopped himself. "You know."

"Yeah. Since I got beaten." I gestured toward the doors at the end of the hall. "Is he awake?"

"Are you kidding? He doesn't sleep any more, Lukien."

Marilius parted the mercenaries easily, leading me through the throng. The men posted outside the chamber opened the doors at once. I had expected another one of Fallon's grand rooms, but was disappointed to see a shabby, windowless chamber. A fireplace, a few upholstered chairs, and a long wooden table were the only furnishings, as if everything else had been stripped away. Fallon himself was slumped over the table, sniffing at it. He jumped when we entered, and a puff of purplish dust erupted from the table top. He looked at me, embarrassed and angry.

"Well! My protector!" He wiped the purple stuff from under his nose with a dirty sleeve. "Up on your feet already. How fabulous."

He was barely recognizable, his expensive robe stained and wrinkled, his face sallow. Even the black tattoo on his forehead drooped. His wobbly eyes strained to see me. That's when I noticed the purple stuff, arranged on the table in sloppy little piles.

"What's that?" I moved passed Fallon and stuck my finger into it. The stuff felt smooth, like powder. I sniffed my finger, appalled at the smell. "Ugh! You're sniffing dung?"

"It's acana," he snapped. "It calms me."

"Never heard of it. What is it? A spice?"

"Like a wild ginger," said Fallon. "But different. Not as good as having a magic sword though."

"You're sweating."

"Of course I'm sweating!" Fallon fell into the nearest chair. "That thing is still alive out there! You were supposed to kill it, Sir Lukien."

"I tried, Fallon. The thing—"

He silenced me with a wave. "I know what happened. Marilius told me. Why do you think I have so many men out there?"

"But it didn't come last night, did it?"

"No, no thanks to you." Fallon slumped against the table, barely able to stay awake. "And if you expect me to pay you for that mission forget it. I'm already going broke."

He looked pathetic, more frightened than angry, rubbing the tattoo and fretting over his mounds of spice. I knew Marilius felt helpless, too. I was glad we three were alone.

"Where'd that monster come from, Fallon?"

Fallon didn't look up. "I told you. From Diriel."

"It's a demon," I said. "It isn't from Akyre or any other country. It's magical. And you knew that all along."

"Did I? Well, if you say it's a demon, Sir Lukien—"

"How'd it get here?"

"How should I know? Ask Diriel! He's the one who sent it here. He wants me dead!"

"That's a lie." I touched my sword pommel. "You forget, I have help. A spirit of my own, remember? So when you lie, I know it."

For a moment Fallon groped for an answer. He looked at Marilius, then back at me, then wilted. "Oh." He laid his forehead on the table and let out an enormous groan. "What's the difference? I'm dead already."

Marilius put a hand on his shoulder. "Lukien, you should go."

I was itching for an argument. "Stop protecting him, Marilius. Stop lying for him. Why'd you keep me from entering the dell? What are you hiding in there?"

"There's where the monster lives," said Marilius. "I told you that."

"And what else?"

"Nothing!"

Fallon managed to sit up. "Forget it, Marilius. Tell him and let him be on his way."

"Tell me," I demanded. "I need to know."

"I'm tired," Fallon whined. He stuck his nose into the powder again, but before he could take a sniff I bent over and wiped it off the table. I took hold of his robe and lifted him from the chair.

"You can smell your cow manure later," I said. "Tell me about the demon!"

Marilius grabbed my arm. "Let him go, Lukien."

So I dropped Fallon into his chair and grabbed Marilius instead, pulling him right into my face. "You brought me here to fight that monster, but you didn't care for a second that I might have been killed. You let me go in there blind!"

Marilius grit his teeth. "I saved your life. Twice! You couldn't wait to go after the monster. Just like you went after Wrestler. Without even thinking!"

I let go of him, but I wasn't leaving without an answer. "What is it?" I pressed. "How'd it get here?"

Marilius smoothed down his tunic. Fallon pointed at his tattoo. "See this? I know you have. I've caught you staring. It's the mark of that beast, whatever it is. This mark came right after I let the beast loose. My beautiful face, ruined . . ."

"So you did let it out. From where? How?" I took a good look at Fallon. "Are you some sort of wizard? I've heard about Zurans . . ."

Fallon scoffed. "Show me a wizard who lives like I do. I'm a merchant. I do whatever profit requires. Spices, Lukien. People pay a lot of money for spices." He ran his finger through the dust left by the purple stuff. "I didn't lie to you about Diriel. He does want me dead."

"The monster, Fallon. How'd it get here?"

"An accident. Have you ever heard of mummia?"

I was sure I hadn't. "Another spice?"

"Sometimes it's called mummy powder," Fallon said. "Very rare. And expensive. Only a king could afford it. And I'm the only man in this part of the world who can get it."

"What's it do?"

Fallon peered toward the door, making sure no one but the three of us could hear. "Your sword isn't the only way to make a man immortal, Lukien. That's what mummy powder does. That's what Diriel wanted."

Finally I had a piece of the puzzle. "The Legion of the Lost. Diriel's army . . ."

"He contracted for the mummia. Paid a fortune for it. It wasn't easy, but I found it. Not the useless tree resin some people peddle but the real thing, from the old tombs of Zura. That's what mummy powder is—dried mummy flesh. But you have to know how to use it. I never thought Diriel would be able to."

"So they weren't just stories," I said. "Soulless soldiers . . . You really did it."

"Not me." Fallon put up his ringed hands. "I just sell spices."

"Sure, you're innocent. What did you think he'd use it for? To sprinkle on his eggs?"

"How could I know he had the magic to use it? Diriel's a fool! Everyone who's met him says so."

"But an indestructible army would make things nice and simple for Diriel, wouldn't it? No problem taking over a nearby country, just march your soldiers right on in. Did you ever once stop to think about what Diriel would do with the mummia?"

"Do to his men? They're soldiers! Like you, Lukien. I just sold them a better weapon."

It was a giant insult. Marilius couldn't even look at me.

"Marilius? This is the man you came back for?" I said. "You're risking your life for *him*?"

Marilius shrugged. "We're trying to fix things."

"What about the monster?" I asked again. "You said you let it loose. How?"

Fallon tilted his head back, struggling to stay awake. "That was after," he said. "Once Diriel took over Kasse he wanted more mummia. Quickly. You can't just lay your hands on mummy powder. There's tomb raiders to pay, bribes . . . and it takes time. I wasn't even sure I could get more. Diriel didn't care about any of that. He had the crown jewels and gold from Kasse and was willing to pay."

"You're a snake, Fallon. What did you sell him? Not mummy powder. Not *real* mummy powder."

"It's ground up mummies! That's it! That's what he paid for, and that's what I gave him. No middle-men this time. I did the work myself." Fallon closed his eyes and made a sound like he was tasting something sweet. "Oh, the money. He had so much of it, like it didn't matter to him. All he wanted was the mummia."

"So?" I pressed. "Where'd it come from?"

"The Valley of Lords," said Fallon. "That dell you saw with Marilius. That's where the old kings of Akyre are buried."

"You sold him the remains of his own ancestors?" Disgusted, I turned toward Marilius. "That's why you didn't want us going into the dell—so I wouldn't see the tombs."

"That's where it came from," said Marilius, "though I didn't see it for myself."

"I went alone," said Fallon. "Marilius didn't know until later, when I needed his help. Now the three of us know."

"No one else?"

Fallon shook his head. "When I went into the tombs, I found a burial stone marked with this." He pointed to the tattoo on his forehead. "I didn't know what it meant. I still don't."

I took a closer look at the tattoo. "Looks like a symbol. But of what?"

"Some ancient Akyren language maybe," said Marilius. "Perhaps the mark of the monster."

"The Akyrens never buried anything valuable with their dead kings," Fallon went on. "Statues mostly. Worthless to me. I only found one mummy there, under the burial stone."

"Just one?" I asked.

"I only needed the one," said Fallon. "I dragged it out, threw it over a horse and rode away."

"By yourself?"

"A dried-out corpse is lighter than you might think. When I found a private spot I burned it. Not too hot—just enough to get the powder I needed. But when I got back to the palace and saw myself in the mirror," Fallon tapped the tattoo, "this was here."

"The monster came the following night," said Marilius. "At first it prowled around outside the palace. Like it was waiting for Anton. Then it started killing people from the town."

"Trying to lure me into a fight!" said Fallon.

"No chance of that, right? You're a ghoul, Fallon. A grave robber. Not to mention a coward. And you . . ." I turned to Marilius. "You were right to leave him. You should have kept on going. Instead you dragged me into this."

"I'm sorry," Marilius said. "But what now? It isn't just the monster. Diriel's after Anton, too. He wants that mummia, and he wants his payment back."

"So? Give it to him."

"I can't," Fallon confessed. "I spent it."

"Spent it? On what?"

Fallon pointed toward the doors. "On all those men out there. To protect me! Don't you see? As long as that monster is out there I can't move. My routes are shut down, my contacts, everything. I'm a prisoner. I have to get that creature off my back!"

He looked so panicked and pathetic I laughed. "You created the beast that's eating you, Fallon. Good! You deserve it. Once that demon gets what it wants it'll leave everyone else alone."

Fallon staggered to his feet. "What about Diriel? Do you think he's going to leave everyone alone? Even if I'm dead he'll march his legions in here."

"They'll kill everyone, Lukien," said Marilius. "That's what they did in Kasse. Diriel's a madman. His mind is gone. He doesn't care what he orders his army to do. Remember that boy we saw on the road?"

I remembered. I'd always remember. "Have you ever seen Diriel?" I asked.

"No," said Fallon. "Wrestler speaks for him."

"Wrestler's the one who delivered the payments," Marilius explained. "But the stories about Diriel are true. They say his throne is made of skulls."

Fallon turned white, gripping the edge of the table. "He wants me killed. He wants my trade routes, and he wants me out of the way." His breathing grew shallow. "I'm a dead man."

Really, it was hard to argue with him. He had a demon on his tail and a half-dead army practically knocking at his door. But I couldn't feel sorry for him.

"There's something else," sighed Marilius. "Diriel's men didn't become walking dead men at first—the first mummy powder we gave them did nothing, though they thought it did. Diriel's superstitious, they say. His men easily crushed Kasse."

"So? I don't understand."

"After that, Diriel wanted more mummy powder," said Fallon.

"You told me that already. What's your point?"

"It was the mummia from the Akyren tomb that turned them soulless," said Fallon "The tomb with the monster."

"So they're connected? How?"

Marilius shook his head. "I don't know. Mummy powder's a myth. Men who take it believe it makes them stronger, so it does. But the stuff Anton made for them . . . well, it really worked."

"And woke the beast!" moaned Fallon.

"You did this," I sneered. "It's your own fault, all of it. I won't be part of it anymore."

"There's nowhere to go, Lukien," said Marilius. "You can't go to Akyre, and Diriel's taken over all the territories. Or will soon."

"I'll head home, then. Back to Jador."

"With Cricket?" pressed Marilius. "Do you think she'll be happy about that, after coming all this way to find out who she is?"

"We'll I'm not staying here!"

"Let him go," groaned Fallon. He sat down again, miserable. "He's useless."

"You're right, Fallon." I went over and patted him on the shoulder. "You *are* a dead man."

I was done with both of them. All I wanted was to leave. I headed for the doors, flung them open, and made my way through the crowd of mercenaries. That's when Marilius caught up to me.

"Lukien, wait!"

He grabbed my arm. I shook it off and kept walking.

"Get our horses ready," I told him. "Cricket and I are leaving."

Marilius stayed on my heels. "Where? Back to Jador? If you leave us we're doomed, Lukien. It's not just that monster. Didn't you hear what I said about Diriel?"

"I heard."

"We need you!"

I pushed through the hall, pretending not to care. "Sure. Let the man who can't die fight your battles for you. Forget it."

"Then why'd you come here?" Marilius took my arm more forcefully, spinning me around. "Because I saved your life? Or maybe you just wanted to prove yourself. Well you haven't yet. You lost against Wrestler and you lost against the monster, and now you're running away."

"You lied to me, Marilius. I thought I owed you for saving me, but that's over. You're as bad as Fallon. You don't give a damn about me, or about those men Diriel enslaved. They're *men,* Marilius."

"I didn't know what would happen to them, Lukien. Anton didn't either. Mummy powder! Who could ever think that would work? If I had known—"

"You would have done nothing." I poked my finger in his chest. "You're a swindler, Marilius. Just like your beloved Fallon. You think he cares about you? A snake like that cares only about money. You're smart enough to know that. But you're hiding in this palace because you're not man enough to face the real world."

Marilius stood his ground. "I'm not the one who's running this time. This time I'm staying to fight."

"Fine." I turned and continued on my way. "Then you'll get the death you deserve."

16

Maybe I was harder on Marilius than I should have been. Maybe I knew that and didn't want to face it. I admit I was angry, but I admired him, too. He really was a dead man for staying with Fallon. Only I didn't care so much if Fallon died. If there was a villain in this all, it was Fallon. Men like him didn't get rich by caring what happened to others. Fallon knew what Diriel would do with the mummia, or at least what he would try to do. He just didn't care. And all those deaths, and all those refugees—they were on his head. He was as guilty as Diriel.

But Marilius was different. Part of him was wily, like Fallon, but part of him had the heart of a soldier. He was loyal to Fallon, and loyalty is never really a flaw. Marilius had found what he was looking for in Isowon—a leader to love and a land to call his own. He had a mission now. I was sure it would kill him, but I envied him for it. Until I remembered that I had a mission, too.

My mission's name was Cricket. Only now, I didn't know how to save her.

It was still early by the time I returned to our chambers, so I wasn't surprised to find her still asleep. The servants had left her a breakfast of jam and bread, an appropriate favorite of a girl who was, in too many ways, still a child. Along with a decanter of milk and a bowl of bright, unrecognizable fruit, her food waited for her untouched on a sunlit table by the window. I paused from my tiptoeing to watch her sleep, undoing my sword belt and laying my weapon against my own bed. As I did, Malator's voice jumped out at me.

Where will we go now?

I strode over to the chair by the window and sat down facing Cricket. I didn't have an answer, but Malator knew that already, surely. Perhaps I should have been tired, but I wasn't. I was alive after beating at death's door again, and as awake and aware as ever. I stared at Cricket, admiring the way that sleep erased all the worry from her gentle face. She had stopped dreaming and now looked angelic, a beautiful reminder of why I had brought her with me.

Will you wake her? asked Malator. *If we're going soon she should know.*

"There's time," I said softly. "Let me think."

In my mind I heard Malator sigh, saw him stretching back as if relaxing by a campfire. I had gotten some answers from Fallon, but still couldn't shake the dread. The monster was his problem, but it was mine as well. It was stalking us all.

But why?

"You know why I brought her with me?" I whispered. "Look at her. You know why? You didn't want me to, but it wasn't because I needed a friend. It wasn't so I could save her. She saves *me,* Malator. She reminds me of the good in the world. Because I forget."

In my mind, I saw Malator nod. Then he said, *You remind people of the good in the world too, Lukien.*

That made me laugh. "Is that why they use me? Is that why I'm so trusting? How many men has Diriel turned into slaves? Hundreds? Thousands?" A thousand men like me. A thousand soulless soldiers. The thought haunted me. Was I a slave too?

What will you tell her?

"Everything. She needs to know the truth about Marilius. He betrayed us. He lured us here to fight."

Do you want to fight?

"You're in my mind," I whispered. "You know my heart."

But he asked me again. *Do you want to fight?*

"I want to fight. Yes! What else am I? I'm a fighter."

Cricket opened her mouth as she started to waken.

I stopped talking and spoke to Malator only in my mind. *I came here to do good. So let me!* I closed my good eye, focusing on him. *Tell me what to do. You know the answer. You know what I should do. Please . . .*

He shook his head. *Impossible.*

Then help me decide!

I have tried. His young face smiled at me. *Remember? You're a soldier, Lukien.*

So? Yes, I'm a soldier . . . I struggled with his riddle. *Soldiers do good. I want to do good.*

Loyal, he reminded me. *A king should be loyal.*

To his men . . .

Was Diriel loyal to his men?

Of course not. He betrayed them.

And who can help them?

I opened my eye in surprise. "Me?"

Cricket awoke as I blurted out the word. She smiled sleepily when she saw it was me. "Lukien."

I got out of the chair and went to her bedside. "Sorry to wake you."

She reached out her hand and touched my face. "I was afraid. You're all right?"

Lukien, interrupted Malator, *don't let her distract you. You were on to something.*

"Yeah," I told him. "Just a moment."

Cricket frowned. "What?"

"Nothing. Talking to Malator."

"Oh." She stretched with a yawn. "What's he want?"

I looked at her seriously as I considered Malator's idea. "He wants us to go to Akyre, I think."

Cricket brightened. "Finally."

"It'll be dangerous," I warned her. "Are you game, Squire?"

Cricket didn't have to think more than a second. That's the way she was—loyal. She tossed off her blankets as her bare feet hit the floor.

"Let me dress," she said quickly. "You can tell me more on the way."

In truth, I had two reasons for going to Akyre. I wanted to do some good, to see if I could end this war before it started and somehow save Diriel's men. But I still needed answers about the monster, and Akyre seemed the best place to find them. Of course I couldn't explain any of that to Marilius or Fallon. I couldn't even tell Cricket my reasons, or at least not all of them. She still had no idea the monster was after her as well.

When I told Fallon we were leaving he was as petulant as ever, refusing to say good-bye or wish us luck. He remained holed up in his parlor, sure that the monster would soon return. Marilius, however, did see us off, providing us with enough food and water for the journey north. He watched me mount my horse, then hugged Cricket before helping her onto her pony. The courtyard outside Anton's palace was nearly empty, but a handful of his soldiers watched us from the balconies. I wondered if they thought us cowards, or if secretly they wished they were leaving with us.

"It's a vendetta, Lukien," said Marilius. He spoke up just before we rode off. "You're going just to settle up with Wrestler. But you have a score to settle here, with the creature. Think on that while you're running away."

"You're wrong!" Cricket snapped. "Lukien's going to help them. You're the one who should be coming with us, Marilius. You're the one who turned those men into monsters."

The way she came to my rescue almost embarrassed me.

"Diriel's the monster," said Marilius. "You'll see what I mean when you get there." He spoke to Cricket like an older brother. "Look after yourself in Akyre. Stay close to Lukien." His voice got soft. "I hope you find what you're looking for."

Cricket gave Marilius her assurance that she'd be the one looking after me, then turned her pony toward the road.

"Ready, Lukien?" she asked. "Let's make some tracks." And she led us out of Isowon.

So I followed. With a nod to Marilius I let the girl I called my squire herald me away from Anton Fallon's gleaming palace, through the streets of his amazing city, and toward the ugliness of Akyre. We had the whole day and hours of sunlight ahead of us. Once we left the city behind the land grew dull and barren again, and there were no distractions, and no place to hide from Cricket's inquiries. I told her everything—about the demon and how Anton Fallon had released it, and how he'd hoodwinked King Diriel, selling him useless mummy powder at first, and then grounding up Diriel's own ancestor to make more—and that batch had worked. Somehow.

And then I told her about Marilius. By then we were more than an hour out of Isowon, and she had figured out his involvement already. But Cricket liked Marilius, I knew. She trusted him, and so I was gentle in my judgment. I brushed at the road dust on my cape, pretending that my words hardly mattered.

"It's what happens sometimes to a man," I said. "Soldiers most of all. Some would follow their leaders right off a cliff. Even mercenaries like Marilius."

"Marilius loves Fallon," Cricket observed. "That's why he did it. To protect him. That's why he went back to him. That's why he's staying."

"You're not angry?"

"Why should I be? He didn't lie to us, Lukien. Not really. He told us his friend needed help. We didn't have to go with him."

I laughed. "I want to be like you, Cricket! Really, I wish the whole world had your heart. Marilius didn't lie? But he didn't tell us about the monster, did he? Or that it's a demon, or that his lover was the one who let it loose. Not to mention the mummia."

Cricket shrugged. "You can be like me, Lukien. Just don't be so angry all the time. You know it makes you stupid. You said it yourself—that's what happened with Wrestler."

"Yeah, about that . . . we'll be seeing him in Akyre."

"If he touches me again I'll bite his hand off," she hissed.

"Tell you what—you control yourself, and I will too. Deal?"

"Deal," she agreed. But as we rode on her expression got thoughtful "Do you think Diriel will listen to you, Lukien? If he's as bad as they say . . ."

"No one's ever as bad as they say, Cricket. All my life I've been hearing about evil men. When I was young they sent me to war against Raxor of Reec. Why? Because they told me he was evil. Turned out they thought *I* was the evil one. It's the way people think when they're afraid. They make men into monsters."

"I don't remember Diriel at all. His name isn't familiar, and I don't remember what kind of king he is . . ." Cricket's eyes lost focus on the road, clouding over with amnesia. "I'm from Akyre. I'm from Akyre. I know it! I'll remember when we get there."

"You remember the Falls," I reminded her. "That's something."

"We'll be close to it. Marilius told me. I dreamed about it again."

"I saw you dreaming," I told her. "Last night. I woke up and saw you. Seemed more like a nightmare to me."

"Oh, no," said Cricket with a weird smile. "It was beautiful. I was a little girl in the dream. I was swimming. So happy!"

"Really?" I asked. "Happy? Were you alone?"

She bit her lower lip, thinking or pretending to think. "Hmm. I can't remember."

"I haven't forgotten my promise," I told her. "By tonight we'll make it to the bend in the river. Tomorrow, if you want, we can head east a bit, try to find Sky Falls."

"No," she said. "We have a mission first."

"It's on our way. If you think it'll help you remember . . ."

"I'm your squire, Lukien." She turned to look at me. "A squire doesn't tell her master where to go. The mission first, all right? Then we can go to Sky Falls."

"Cricket . . ." I squinted at her. "Is this you being strong?"

She straightened up high. "I'm not afraid, Lukien. Besides, we came here to find Akyre. Now we have a real reason to go."

But I was already doubting the mission. What seemed like a good idea just that morning now felt remarkably stupid. How would I free those men from the curse Diriel had conjured?

I didn't talk about it, and Cricket didn't ask me. She had faith in me. She was young and foolish and believed in me, and that meant I had to do my best.

We rode and rode, and I pretended to forget our troubles. We had all the food and water we needed, strong horses to carry us, and a perfect sun to light our way. Even at the height of afternoon the sun was merciful, warm enough to cheer us without burning our noses. We were far from Isowon by then, its beaches replaced by plains of grass and rugged hills. I listened to Cricket sing as we rode, stopping in the middle of her songs to share whatever tidbits popped into her mind. The solitude had loosened her tongue, and I was glad to listen, nodding at each observation she made, each childlike confession. She told me about missing Minikin, and how she feared Gilwyn would send her away once Minikin died, how she screamed sometimes just so people wouldn't ignore her, and how jealous she was of White-Eye, even though White-Eye was blind. When I asked why, she gave me the only reason that made sense for such a young woman.

"Because she's beautiful. Don't you think she's beautiful, Lukien?"

"White-Eye is very beautiful," I agreed. "But so are you, Cricket."

"C'mon." She rode on without looking at me. "I'm plain. Like this place where I was born." She sighed and took in our brown surroundings. "I've seen how men look at White-Eye, Lukien. Even you."

I shook my head. "Not me. Never."

"Yes, you. You just don't realize it. Don't feel bad about it."

"I have a woman, Cricket. I don't need another."

"Who, Cassandra?" She turned toward me. "Lukien, she's dead."

"She's alive. Just not where we can see her. But I talked to her. I told you—in the Story Garden. She's waiting for me there."

"She's gonna have a long wait as long as you carry that sword."

"You're changing the subject. You are beautiful, Cricket. You're becoming a lovely young woman."

"No."

Now I was puzzled. One thing I know about women—they like being complimented. And it doesn't matter their age. Once they're old enough to look in a mirror, flattery gets them smiling. Except Cricket wasn't smiling at all. She'd gone from happy to gloomy in just a few seconds.

"I'm confused," I confessed. "You're jealous of White-Eye because she's pretty, but you don't want me to think you're pretty too. Why not?"

"You're just lying to me, Lukien." She pulled the cape I'd made her close around her shoulders. "I'm plain and that's how I want to be. I'm not like White-Eye. Is White-Eye out here in the middle of nowhere?"

"She's in Jador. I'm still not getting it, Cricket."

"That's right, she's safe in her palace. Let her be beautiful there. She doesn't have to worry."

"Worry about what?"

"Anything. She doesn't have to worry about anything, Lukien. She knows who she is, where she belongs, who her mother was . . ." Cricket stopped herself. "What's that?"

"What?"

"That." She pointed on ahead of us. "A meadow?"

I'd been so flustered I hadn't even noticed. But there it was, blocking our way, spread out between the hills and dotted with a hundred colors: a meadow of wildflowers. Lit by the sun, I could see the bees darting through the blooms. The breeze carried the perfume.

"Now *that's* beautiful," I said. "See? You weren't born in such an ugly place after all."

Cricket's bad mood broke like a fever. "Can we ride through it?" she asked excitedly.

"No choice. We can rest there. The horses need a break, and you must be hungry."

"You too, right?"

I hardly ever got hungry any more, but I nodded. The truth is the sword gave me almost all the strength I needed. I let Cricket lead us deep into the flowers, marveling at the colors of heather and daisies. The blooms shot knee-high to our horses, rippling like water as we made a wake through them. We were in an ocean, with great, nodding sunflowers and tiny buttercups alive with lady bugs. The sweet smell reminded me of Jadori honey. Cricket laughed, driving her pony farther through the blooms, until she pronounced the perfect spot.

"Here," she declared, and dismounted. Flowers tickled her legs and her skin reflected the yellow sun. I looked at her and thought, yes, this girl is beautiful.

We took the blankets from our horses, laying them along the ground to make a camp for ourselves. I showed Cricket how to water a horse out of a canteen, and once our mounts were taken care of we broke out the provisions Marilius had given us. As Cricket wedged her bread and meat together, I stretched out to stare at the blue sky. Before long, Cricket nestled down beside me.

"No clouds," she remarked, disappointed. "I like seeing the shapes."

The sky was almost too bright. I closed my eye and watched the shapes appearing on my eyelid instead. I heard Cricket sigh, and I wondered again why she had argued about being pretty. Surely she knew what she looked liked. Surely she'd noticed boys watching her.

"Oh . . ."

"What?" she nudged.

I understood, but couldn't say so. I wanted to tell her I'd protect her, that she didn't have to worry about another letch like Wrestler. But the truth was I couldn't do that forever. She was my mission—for now—but one day she'd be a woman in a man's world. So I lied.

"Nothing. I was thinking about Malator."

"What about him?"

"Just talking to him."

"In your head, you mean." Cricket made a grumbling noise. "That bothers me sometimes."

I turned my head to look at her. "It bothers you when I talk to Malator?"

"Sometimes," said Cricket. She kept staring into the blue sky, like she was afraid of my reaction. "You talk to him but I can't hear it. Just feel left out sometimes. I wish I could see him too."

"I know, but it's impossible, Cricket. An Akari can only appear to his host. No one can talk to Malator but me."

That's not true.

Malator's voice startled me. "Huh?"

Cricket grimaced. "You're talking to him now, aren't you?"

"Yeah, he . . . huh?"

You said: I can't appear to anyone but you, Lukien. That's not true.

"What's not true?" I sat up, seeing Malator in my mind.

I never said I can't appear to anyone else, said Malator. *I said no one else can see me.*

"What? What's the difference?"

My choice, obviously.

"Lukien, could you two talk quietly?" asked Cricket. "I'm trying to rest. Do that thing in your head, okay?"

I was rattled. None of the Inhumans—not even Minikin—had ever shown me their Akari. I got to my feet as though facing Malator.

"Are you telling me you can make yourself visible? Cricket can see you?"

Malator smiled. *That's right.*

"You mean in her head, right?" I pressed. "Not really see you. Not the way real people see each other."

I don't just live inside that sword you wear, Lukien. I'm a being! I'm alive. And I told you—I'm more powerful than you think. If Cricket wants to see me, she can.

I stepped back, looked down at Cricket, and caught her confused gaze. "What is it?" she asked.

"Do you want to see Malator?" I held out my hand for her.

"Really?" She let me pull her to her feet.

I shrugged. "I don't know. He says you can see him!" Stunned, I crossed my arms. "All right, Malator. Show me."

The air before me shimmered. Like a ghost—like always—he appeared. Only this time, when I glanced at Cricket, her mouth dropped open. Malator winked to mock me, then floated to stand before Cricket, his Akari cape catching an unseen breeze. His handsome face, unmarked by all the battles he'd fought, shined like a copper penny. He put out a hand in greeting, stretching his smoky fingers toward her.

"I am Malator," he said in a perfectly clear voice. "And I am pleased to meet you, Cricket."

Cricket held her breath as she put out her own hand. I watched, surprised that Malator could seem so substantial, as their fingers met. Cricket's eyebrow's shot up.

"Oh! Cold."

Like the grave, I wanted to say. Malator had never revealed himself to anyone else, and I was already jealous of Cricket's admiration. Her eyes twinkled, encouraging him. Malator bent and kissed her hand.

"You're Lukien's brave squire," he said. "I'm honored to know you."

Cricket's hand fell away slowly. "Thank you. You're not the way I thought you'd be. You're so young looking. I thought you were a soldier."

"Soldier, sorcerer, lover, and voyager," said Malator. "I am an Akari, after all. You should know more about us after living with Inhumans so long. Lukien should tell you."

"I do tell her," I said. "And look who's keeping secrets! You never told me you could appear to others! Since when?"

"Lukien, I'm not just any Akari," said Malator. "When will you understand that? I'm not here just to keep you alive—I'm here to make you into something special. Like me!"

"But you never told me—"

"You never asked. You assumed I could not. But I'm not limited by your thinking, Lukien. Now I have to get you to open your mind. Does seeing me like this help you see the possibilities?"

I was just too stunned to answer. All along Malator had been telling me I was special. He was grooming me for something, but I still didn't know his purpose. And why were we even talking about this in front of Cricket?

"All right," I relented. "I'm sure that you told me only I could see you, but all right. So you're powerful. You see the future, you can make fire with your hands and little stick figures come to life. What's it all got to do with me? Or Cricket, even."

"Because we're on this mission together," said Malator. "Wherever it leads."

"But you know where it leads?" asked Cricket. "You can already tell?"

"Ha! He won't answer that," I laughed. "Don't ask him a direct question, Cricket. You can stick Malator with a dagger and pull out a corkscrew."

Malator reared back. "Untrue!" He lowered himself to face Cricket. "You have questions for me?"

"I have nothing but questions," sighed Cricket. "Can you help me remember who I am? Do you know?"

"I do not," said Malator. "If I were your Akari I could help you, perhaps. Whatever memories are locked in your mind would be mine to share. But I belong to Lukien."

Cricket grumbled, "Minikin wouldn't let me have an Akari. Why not, if she knew it would help me?"

"An Akari can make the blind see and the crippled walk," answered Malator. "Without an Akari these things are impossible. But you can remember without my help. Minikin knew that."

"But I can't!" said Cricket. "I try and try, but I can't remember! Just little things, little pictures of things like the waterfall. If you have magic, you can help me, Malator. Could I borrow you from Lukien? Just for a bit?"

I tried not to laugh. "It would be nice to be rid of you for awhile, Malator."

"I'm not joking," said Cricket desperately. "I'm going mad trying to remember. I need help."

Malator put on his serious face. "We will help you," he said. "Lukien and I together. And you, too. We'll find out who you are, Cricket. Before this journey is done, you'll remember everything."

I nodded, but when I turned to see Cricket her face was ashen. "What is it?" I asked.

She shrugged. "I guess I'm afraid." She studied Malator. "Should I be afraid, Malator?"

All I could think of was what he'd just told me—how sometimes he lies to protect me. But Malator smiled so sweetly at Cricket that it seemed no harm would ever befall her.

"You have Lukien, and Lukien has me," he declared. "And even death cannot stop me."

17

We reached the Dovra river that first afternoon, traveling north along its bank until nightfall, where we camped and fell asleep to the sound of rushing water. All that day the landscape shifted, changing constantly from rugged hills to flowered plains. Our horses drank thirstily at the river, and I was glad to finally have a landmark to follow. The Dovra would take us nearly all the way to Diriel's castle in the mountains of Akyre. That night as we slept by the river, I dreamed I was alone on a boat on the Dovra, being stalked in the water by Fallon's monster. I tried and tried to outrun the thing, crashing the boat as its tentacles dragged me under.

I awoke with a gasp. Cricket was sleeping soundly next to me. The moon was high and morning was hours away, but I did not sleep again.

When day finally broke I was happy to be moving again. By now Cricket had grown accustomed to Malator's voice in her head, and she spoke to him as if he were riding next to her, asking him questions about the life he had before he died, why the Akari helped the Inhumans, and all the other mysteries that I'd spent years trying to unravel. But Malator did not make himself visible while we rode. Instead he remained inside both our heads, sharing his voice with the two of us. When I half-jokingly asked him to conjure up a horse so he could ride with us, he sniffed at the notion.

"What if someone saw me?" he asked.

A fair answer, I supposed.

Nevertheless we were an odd threesome—me in my bronze armor, Cricket on her pony, and Malator, a disembodied voice popping in and out of our heads. But no one questioned us because no one saw us, even on that second day as we reached the mountains. Except for some abandoned homesteads, the road along the river was empty, a soulless highway leading, it felt, to nowhere. Though the day started out cheerfully, we all lost our smiles when we saw the black mountains.

Akyre. The flawed jewel of the Bitter Kingdoms.

I slowed my horse. Diriel's castle lay in the mountains. The river would take us to him. I studied the river, shocked to see the way it forked both north and east, crashing against the rocks in a churning tangle. I had never seen the like before. Cricket guided her pony toward the bank, up to the very edge of the tumult. Her lips trembled as her mind searched for something. Then suddenly, she sighed its name.

"The Bloody Knot." She nodded to herself. "That's what it's called."

I'd never heard those words, nor had I ever seen Cricket recognize a place before. I rode closer. "How do you know that?"

"I remember," she said. "This place where the rivers meet—it's called the Bloody Knot." She pointed east. "Kasse is that way. And behind us is Drin. This is where they border Akyre."

"That's good. You see? Coming here has helped your memory. Can you think of anything else?"

Her lips flattened into a thin smile as she strained to remember. She closed her eyes and held her breath. "I'm trying . . ."

"You must have come here once," I suggested. "Or someone told you about it. Your parents, maybe?"

"Maybe." Cricket grunted in frustration. "I can't think of it!"

"You will," I said gently. "But this is good. It's a start."

She nodded as she stared into the river. "The water. That's what makes me remember. Like the waterfall."

"Water?"

"Lukien, when we're done with Diriel, you'll take me there, won't you? I have to see it! I know it will help me remember."

"I told you, Cricket, I could have taken you to Sky Falls yesterday."

"I know, but it's different now. I'm really starting to remember things, see?"

"I'm glad for that," I told her. "Really, I am. I promise—if everything goes all right with Diriel."

"No! That's not what you said! You said you'd take me to Sky Falls when we're done. That was our deal."

"And I will," I said sternly, "if I can. Don't forget, Cricket, that you're the one who insisted we see Diriel first. Our mission and all that. You're the squire, and I'm the knight, remember?"

Cricket looked contrite. "I remember." She pointed her pony back toward the road. "We should go."

"You're trying to make me feel guilty," I said. "I won't. Not this time. This is important to me, Cricket."

"I know. Come on."

"Damn it!" I rode up hard and cut off her pony, making her look at me. "You can't act like this. We're riding into the teeth of the tiger, and I can't have a squire who just dabbles at the job. Think about the mission. Think about something besides yourself. Think about me for a change!"

Those last words slipped out before I could stop them. Cricket looked aghast, then hurt.

"Huh?"

"Are you brave? Or is it just an act? If you don't have the stomach for this job you should have told me so back in Isowon."

"What? No . . ."

"I told you we'd go to Sky Falls when we can. I told you I'd try. But right now I have to go to Akyre. Not just so you can get your memories back. Not just for those condemned soldiers either."

"Lukien, I'm sorry—"

"Just shut up and listen," I snapped. It was all coming out of me now, and I didn't want to stop. "This mission, this is my chance to do something good. That's what knights-errant are supposed to do, right? But so far all I've done is get my neck broken and be tricked into helping Fallon fight his monster. But this is something big. Maybe Diriel will kill us on sight. But maybe he won't. Maybe he'll listen, and I can make peace for a change instead of war. Just once I want to be a diplomat instead of a soldier."

Cricket said nothing. I couldn't tell if she was embarrassed or shocked. Malator was quiet too. At that moment I would have gladly left them both behind.

"I won't leave you here, but I won't turn back, either," I told Cricket. "I'm going to Akyre. Right now. If you turn back that's your choice. But don't tell folks I sent you away."

Here's how Cricket reminded me how young she was: She

didn't cry but struggled against her tears. She didn't argue or curse me. She just looked at me, helpless.

"I don't want to leave," she said, as her voice cracked. "I want to go with you."

"And we can talk about Sky Falls after this is done?"

She nodded and wiped her cheeks with her palms. *This is where I usually give in to her,* I thought. *Where I tell her I'm sorry.* But not this time.

"Good," I said. "Now follow me. From now on I take the lead."

We rode for nearly an hour more, until the mountains cast their shade upon us. The river bent eastward but the road bade us north, so we parted with the water and drove deeper into a sparse forest of stunted trees and rubble. With Cricket following and Malator silent, I studied the mountains looming ahead of us, watching as the road wound up the granite face toward Diriel's castle. Yet there was no town to greet us, no hint of anyone along the way, and I began to doubt we were really in Akyre at all. Until at last I saw the flag.

My one good eye is sharper than a hawk's. I noticed the flapping bit of green long before Cricket did. Halfway up the mountain, upon what I realized now was a turret built into the stone, waved the flag of Akyre. A squint brought the castle into relief.

"I see it," I announced, pointing the way. "There."

Cricket looked harder, finally noticing the flag. "Yeah. You think they see us?"

"Maybe not yet, but they will." Except for the thin trees, we were out in the open. "We don't want to hide anyway. Make them think we're friends."

I didn't ask Cricket if the castle looked familiar, or even if she was afraid. None of that mattered now. We rode straight and steady for the castle, each step drawing us higher as the road began sloping upwards. Now I could see the pitted walls of the place bulging out from the rock, the broken ramparts crenellated like old teeth. Two watchtowers stood at either end of the castle, one oddly shorter than the other and both caked with moss. A bridge connected the main gate to the road, a narrow passage of planks and ropes spanning a lethal gorge.

"We have to cross *that*?" asked Cricket.

Even from a distance, the bridge made her blanch. I pretended not to be bothered.

"It just looks small from here," I said. "It has to be safe."

"That place is crumbling, Lukien. Look at it."

"They get across somehow, Cricket. If they're not afraid of it, neither will we be."

Cricket gave a groan but kept on following, up and up on the serpentine road. Finally the road leveled, spitting us onto a ledge high above the whistling gorge. Ahead waited the bridge, and beyond that Diriel's castle. Now we could clearly see figures along the walls and watchtowers, armed men, mostly, staring at us. In the courtyard—if you could call it that—women toiled in a shriveled garden, their knees bloodied from the hardscrabble earth. A dozen naked men shoveled stones from an enormous ditch, each one chained by the neck to his neighbor. A one-armed sentry with a whip watched over the prisoners. At his feet a child drank from a water-filled hole.

One look at the place, and I knew I'd made a mistake.

"Cricket," I said softly. "I want you to stay close to me. Don't wander off, don't say a word."

Cricket barely nodded. I guided her toward the bridge. On the other side a man waved a burning torch, shouting of our coming. The women and prisoners looked up. Cricket and I paused at the very edge of the bridge, taking one regrettable look down. Had the road really brought us up so high?

"Lukien, if this thing breaks . . . we'll never survive!"

Well, you won't, I thought.

More soldiers gathered along the crumbling walls, but all I could hear was the wind and the wild ululation of the man with the torch. I wasn't sure if he was warning us off or inviting us across. But none of the soldiers moved to stop us. Sure the bridge would hold our horses, I urged Zephyr onto the span, then saw a figure scramble across the courtyard. A small, bizarre-looking thing, I thought at first it was a boy, running toward the bridge. He was dressed like a nobleman in a velvet cloak that didn't fit him properly and a chain of office around his neck. His outrageous red hair reminded me of candy, but despite his clearly aged face he was barely taller than a toddler. He grabbed the ropes on the other side of the bridge, swung onto it like a monkey and stuck his face out.

"Who are you?" he cried.

Cricket peered at him in shock. "What is that? A man?"

I'd spent too long with the Inhumans to be surprised—or offended—by any aspect of the human condition. "Respect," I cautioned. "Remember, Minikin was small."

"Minikin was a friend, Lukien. That one looks like a lunatic."

"I am Lukien," I called back. "From Liiria. May we come ahead?"

"From the continent?" The man bounded onto the bridge, shaking it with his bouncing. "Yes, come across! The master will be happy and pleased! Most happy and pleased! Come! Don't be afraid!"

"Ask him if the bridge will hold us," said Cricket.

"And offend him? Don't you think that's implied by the invitation?"

"Fine," said Cricket. "You first then."

I had thought about surviving the fall. But I really didn't think I could, not even with Malator's help. Still, Zephyr didn't blink at my order, putting one hoof in front of the other as I ordered him onto the bridge. The midget at the other end waved to encourage us.

"This bridge is over a hundred years old!" he declared.

"He's bragging?" quipped Cricket. Halfway across, she hurried me by bumping the butt of my horse. I urged Zephyr a little more, eager to get across. The midget sent to greet us made way, taking the reins of my mount and looking overjoyed.

"I'm Grecht," he said. "Lukien! Oh, I've heard of *you*. Yes I have! The Bronze Knight comes to Akyre! So lovely, lovely . . ."

His babbling made me think Cricket was right. Insane. And starved by the look of him. All bones and skin and yellow eyes. Bands of cloth kept the velvet cloak he wore from tumbling down his legs and arms. I took a breath and tasted dust. The skeletal prisoners looked my way, wondering who'd wandered into their hell, barely able to carry themselves under the weight of their shared chain. Up along the battlements, the soldiers watched without blinking. Each wore an elaborate uniform of gray and crimson, some studded with ribbon, others threadbare and torn, their faces painted a skull-like white.

Cricket and I dismounted. The tiny man took my sleeve and pulled.

"Master knows you're here," he said excitedly. "No one ever comes here from the continent!"

"Your name is Grecht?" I asked. "What happened here, Grecht?"

The midget acted puzzled. "I don't take your meaning. Is something wrong?"

"This is Akyre, isn't it?" asked Cricket. "This is where the king lives?"

Grecht beamed. "Emperor! This is Diriel's palace."

I gestured toward the prisoners. "And those men over there?"

"Kassens." Grecht spit on the ground. "Slaves now."

Sariyah had told us Kasse had fallen to Akyre. "Are there many?"

"All of Kasse are our slaves now!" said Grecht proudly. "Working to rebuild Akyre after what they've done. Do not even look at them, Sir Lukien. Why should a nobleman soil his sight with shit?" He looked at Cricket. "My pardon, young lady. Who is your companion, Sir Lukien?"

"My name is Cricket."

"Cricket?" Grecht tittered. "From Liiria as well?"

"No," replied Cricket.

"But from the continent? Master craves news from the continent. He awaits! Please come." He dragged at my sleeve. "This way, please."

"Our horses."

"Yes, yes."

Grecht howled to the women in the pathetic garden. A pair of them dashed forward, brushing the dirt from their tattered dresses. The older one took the reins of my horse without even a glance, but the younger one, a few years older than Cricket maybe, locked eyes with her, her mouth falling open as she studied Cricket's shiny hair.

"Move!" barked Grecht and gave the girl a slap.

"Hey!" hissed Cricket. "Don't touch her!"

Grecht reared back. "Girl?"

"This is my squire," I said quickly. "Too quick to anger, but she belongs to me." I handed Cricket's pony to the young one from the garden. "Take care of the animals. Hay and water if you have it. Grecht, please let us see your master now."

Grecht pulled up his flapping sleeves. He nodded anxiously and led us through the courtyard toward the lopsided gate, hanging open on its rusted hinges. The ancient place looked every bit its age, with moss climbing up the walls and slimy water trickling down. The crooked turrets that had somehow been blasted out of the mountain's dour face suffocated the sunlight and flaked dust onto our heads. Once past the gate, the oily interior of the castle warmed us with fiery torches. Dogs and filthy children crowded us. Grecht kicked them aside. The walls of the cavernous hall still had outlines where tapestries and paintings had once hung. Now weapons clung to the bricks, mostly morning stars and blood-stained axes.

And there were soldiers, lining the way to the open chamber at the end of the hall. Now I knew what had spooked that refugee boy. Now I knew why Sariyah had called them soulless.

The Legion of the Lost.

Their dead eyes watched us as we passed, their faces smeared with paint, their fingernails pale as they clutched their pikes and flails. White hair drooped beneath their battered helmets. No breath drew from their half-alive bodies, but there was sentience in their features still, some remaining spark of humanity that kept them in this world.

Malator, are they alive? I asked.

Their bodies live, replied the Akari. *But their souls dwell elsewhere.*

These were the men I'd come to save, and suddenly the folly of my mission came clear. Akyre was no longer a kingdom. Something—maybe war, maybe famine, maybe both—had eaten away its civilized self. This is what Cricket had fled: the tons and tons of sorrow that buried her memory. I could barely stand myself suddenly. I had dragged Cricket to *this*? The sight was barely fit for a grown man's eyes. Surely a girl could only be scarred by it.

I dreaded reaching the end of the hall, and when we did I stopped to let Grecht enter the chamber. Inside were more of the soulless fighting men and slaves, the soldiers at blind attention, the slaves naked and piled one atop the other in some feat of grotesque sculpture. Muffled cries came from the human mound as children poked at it with sticks. Another pile, this one of skulls, crowded around the wooden throne, as though the man atop it had used the bones for stepping stones. King Diriel sipped from a goblet, his bloodshot eyes watching us over its rim. He listened as Grecht announced us. At his side stood the man who'd broken my neck.

"Master, this is Lukien of Liiria!" chittered Grecht. He bent all the way down to the base of the skulls, his little palms on the floor. "He's from the continent, Unrivaled. He came all that way to glorify you!"

Diriel placed his goblet on the arm of his great chair. He wore no shirt, just a red robe open over his torso so the world could see his ribs. A crown of jewels capped his long, dark hair, but he wore no other gems or gold. Scuffed boots, the kind a military man would wear, slowly tapped the floor as he considered us. When he grinned, a mouthful of filed teeth displayed, pointed like a badger's.

I wanted to flee, not out of fear but out of sheer revulsion. I had seen madmen before, but not like this one. Even Akeela at the worst of his madness—a madness I myself had driven him to—hadn't compared to this. Diriel radiated lunacy. He leaned over and whispered to Wrestler, and the two of them gazed at Cricket. Wrestler nodded his bald head and folded his arms snake-like over his huge chest. He was exactly as he had been that day in Arad, shirtless, his stance full of challenge, and when he looked at me the grin he gave told me how satisfied he'd felt to break my neck, the way a man might feel when copulating.

"Come closer, Liirian," said Diriel. "The girl, too."

His voice was a syrupy lisp, the result of his self-sharpened teeth, I supposed. I made sure Cricket was right beside me before moving. My hand was ready for my sword. Grecht scurried away as we approached the throne, nearly tripping on a rolling skull. Wrestler kept his eyes on Cricket. His tongue poked out to lick his bottom lip.

"Great King, my name is Lukien," I said. "But you already know this. May I ask how you know my name?"

I didn't bow or avert my eyes. I looked right at Diriel instead. The king sniffed at my etiquette.

"The girl," said Diriel. "What is her name?"

"Cricket!" answered Grecht.

"Did I ask you, dwarf? Let her speak!"

"Cricket is my name," replied Cricket stiffly. "I'm Lukien's squire."

"Squire?" Diriel laughed, turning to share the joke with Wrestler. "What sort of knight chooses a girl for his squire? Unless you mean she takes care of your other sword."

"She is my squire, and I am her protector," I said calmly, but anger made my face hot. Diriel wasn't a king—he was a creature, and being polite took all my will. "She's come to help me in my mission, my lord, at great peril to herself."

"What peril?" asked Diriel. "If you mean my bodyguard, yes, he has an appetite for youngsters. He's already told me of your meeting. He offered a price for her and you refused."

"That's right, and I'll refuse it again," I said. "We've no slaves where I come from, my lord. It's not our way. For me to barter her would be immoral."

"The morality of the continent. Dog shit." Diriel shifted and the crown on his head tipped forward. "You asked how I know you. I know you because I know everything, Lukien of Liiria. I know you're in the employ of that sodomite Anton Fallon. I even know that Wrestler snapped your neck like a chicken bone before you ever reached Isowon. Wrestler doesn't lie to me, so I ask myself how it's possible for you to be standing here."

"Then you don't know everything, my lord."

"But I believe in miracles. Seeing you makes me believe, Sir Lukien. I hear from Isowon that you are immortal." Diriel shrugged. "So it must be true. Now I ask myself, why does Anton Fallon think to threaten me with an immortal soldier, when I have so many of my own? Unless you come to plead for him. Have you? I see no repayment for the money he stole from me."

"We're not in his employ," I said. "Not any longer."

"No?" Diriel got out of his chair with a great big frown. "I have an army barely a day's march from Isowon. Does he know this? I will have the mummy powder he promised and the money he stole from me! And yet he sends no one to plead for mercy?"

"I do come to plead, mighty Diriel, but not for Anton Fallon."

"Ah, so you want something!" Diriel's deduction made him grin. "You come to barter after all. I will pay a good price for the girl. We won't call it slavery if it offends you. A gift, let's say."

"Let me say it clearly. The girl is under my protection. She's not for sale or gift, and if anyone dares touch her they will be dead before they hit the ground." I looked right at Wrestler. "That means you. Don't put me to the test."

Diriel clapped with pleasure. "I would pay to see that if I had any money left." He dropped back into his throne. "I have none, you see. That goat-fucking swindler took it all, but it doesn't matter. My army will get back what is mine. You can tell Anton Fallon that for me."

"No, my lord, I can't do that. My business with Fallon is done. I'm here to—"

"Stop," bade Diriel. "You will do this for me. It is the only reason I allowed you to cross the bridge."

"You're a messenger boy," snorted Wrestler. "How do you like that?"

"Do you think I give a shit why you're here?" spat Diriel. "Did my peanut-brained midget tell you I'd be happy to see you just because you're from the continent? I wipe my ass with your courts and courtesies, Liirian. The last travelers who came here from the continent wound up with their organs on my dinner plate. The Liirians and Reecians should pray to their dead gods that I don't march my legion across the desert to conquer them next."

Wrestler grimaced with laughter. The mound of slaves whimpered. One of the children—a boy—moved from tormenting them to sit on the skulls at Diriel's feet. Another simply picked his nose. I could feel Cricket bridling next to me, just wanting to get out of there. I wanted to go too, but there was the mission, and as stupid as it seemed I was going to speak my piece.

"Your legions are the reason I've come, my lord. I had to see them for myself, and now I know that they are slaves too, just like these wretches you make entertain you. I ask myself, what kind of king would steal the souls of loyal soldiers? Anton Fallon is no friend of mine. Indeed he is a dog for selling you such an evil potion as mummia. But you can still truly be great, King Diriel. You can free these men and give them back their souls."

Diriel blinked his bloodshot eyes, pretended to give weight to my words, then shook with laughter—uncontrollable laughter that made him knock over his goblet and cry real tears. His jolliness spread like a contagion, first to Wrestler and then to Grecht and the filthy children. Only the slaves and soldiers were silent.

"You came all this way to ask me to free my men from the mummy powder?" chortled Diriel. He choked on his laughter, then spat a wad of mucus toward Grecht. He stood and picked his way down the pile of skulls to face me. "Help me figure this out," he said. "When did nations of the continent decide they were so much better than the rest of us? You don't come and ask me favors, Liirian. I am an Emperor!" He placed his palm on his naked chest. "My men love me. They *love* me. They're not my slaves. They're my children. They would do anything for me."

"How can they love you?" I asked. "When they can't even think for themselves? Do you want an army of mindless creatures, King Diriel, or men with the heart to choose their loyalties?"

Diriel smirked as though he'd been waiting for his chance. "Zursas," he said with a snap of his fingers. "Come here."

From out of the line of soldiers stepped a single legionnaire. White-haired like the rest of them, I knew from his pallid skin that he couldn't be more than thirty years old. The silence of the grave followed him as he moved, his worn-out boots impossibly quiet against the sooty floor. I fought for a glimpse of his dead gaze, looking for any spark of life.

"Zursas," said Diriel, "show these outlanders how much you love me."

It happened so fast I didn't have time to cover Cricket's eyes. The soldier's dagger flashed from his belt to his very naked throat, and with one deep and instant gash he sliced it. Blood sheeted down his neck. Cricket screamed and the soldier crumbled. The slaves in their sculpture began to squirm and wail, and the children scampered from the pooling blood. But Diriel didn't move. He stood there as the blood seeped around his boots, looking at me.

"Now, don't you wish your squire here was as loyal as that? This is what you're asking me to forsake. I need more men like this, not fewer. I bargained for them in good faith with Anton Fallon. He owes me the mummia, but that won't be enough to save him. He stole from me. An Emperor! Not even that monster will save him from me."

I froze.

"That's right, I know about the monster," said Diriel. "He hired you to help him kill it, didn't he? But it's still alive, yes?"

I nodded, unsure how much to reveal. Diriel already knew far more than I suspected. Cricket stepped back from the pooling blood, pulling me with her. I wanted to kill Diriel for making her witness such horror.

"The monster is Fallon's problem," I lied. "I'm here to talk about your soldiers."

"You have my answer about my soldiers," said Diriel. "Did you fight the monster? They say it's not of this world."

"Who says that?" I asked, eager to learn all I could about the creature.

"The scum I employ to tell me such things. They say it comes from the world of the dead. The same world where the souls of my soldiers live. You're a man of that world, too, Sir Lukien. An undead warrior. A forever knight! But even you couldn't destroy it, could you?"

I tried to ignore the dead man at my feet. Cricket held her ground without looking down. "You see things very clearly, King Diriel," I said. "I'm a stranger here. I know nothing of Akyre's lore. The monster's a mystery to me. You seem to know more about it than I do."

"Are we testing each other? I don't like contests, so let me tell you plainly—I do not know this monster or where it comes from. I only know it has power, and power is what I need. You faced the creature and survived. That intrigues me. If you could bring the beast to me, that would be worth something."

"That thing is uncontrollable," said Cricket. "It's not a pet."

"Or a weapon," I added. "I know what you're asking, King Diriel, and what you're asking is impossible."

Diriel stepped out of the blood, then wiped his boots on the dais around his throne. Wrestler came down to stand next to him. When I braced myself Diriel chuckled.

"You want to go," he observed. "You want to take the girl out of here because you fear for her. You're right to be afraid. Wrestler isn't as loyal as my legionnaires, but I tell you this in truth—you are safe in this castle, much more safe then you will be once you leave. You're under my protection here. Both of you. Stay. For the night."

My insides clenched. "I came to see your soldiers and talk sense to you, my lord. But maybe we're already done here."

Diriel picked up one of the skulls around his throne. "A Kassen," he pronounced. "Worthless. You should be glad they've been wiped away, but you're appalled because you're so moral and stupid." He dropped the skull to the floor. "You came to haggle with me. We're not done."

"Are we back to bargaining for the girl or the monster?" I asked.

"The monster, of course. The girl is safe for as long as you remain in my castle. Outside these walls I have no control over Wrestler. Stay. Think of a way to get me that monster. If you do, I will consider sparing Anton Fallon."

"Not a chance."

"Then think of something else you want. The lives of the people of Isowon, perhaps. If I have the monster I will consider Fallon's debt to me paid. Otherwise . . ." Diriel shrugged. "Who can say what will happen to them?"

We were in a trap. When I couldn't think of what to say, Malator spoke to calm me.

Agree with him. Remain here for the night. That'll give us time to plan something.

Cricket?

She'll be safe.

I had no choice but to believe him. "All right," I agreed. "We'll stay the night. If you'd make a place for us."

"What?" cried Cricket. She pointed at Wrestler. "So he can rape me while I sleep?"

Diriel seemed offended. "Child, haven't you heard me? This is where you are safe, not out there. Outside these walls you're a deer to be hunted. Inside you belong to me, and no one touches what is mine."

I looked at Wrestler. "Listen good, shit-eater. I don't need sleep. I'm going to be up all night standing guard over her. You're fast with your hands, I'll give you that, but it won't be a fair fight next time. You come after her, you'll lose your head. Understand?"

Wrestler winked to mock me.

"Gargoyle, I asked if you understand me."

"I understand."

Grecht hurried forward and took Cricket's hand, trying to lead her out of the throne room. She pulled free of him, glaring as though I'd betrayed her.

"Go with him," I ordered. "I'll be along."

Pleased, Diriel relaxed as he watched Cricket taken from the chamber. "Think hard tonight, Sir Lukien," he advised. "If you can get me the monster, we can part ways happy men."

"And you'll guarantee Cricket's safety?" I asked.

"For as long as you're here," agreed the king. "After that, I guarantee nothing."

18

I didn't sleep at all that night.

We spent the first half of it arguing—me, Cricket, and Malator. Cricket was angrier than I'd ever seen her, blaming me for risking her life and dragging us all to Diriel's hellhole in the first place. There was nothing I could do to defend myself. My mission was folly. I knew that the first moment I set eyes on Diriel. Now I had trapped us in a castle of horrors, where our host was a cannibal, and his henchman planned to hunt us the moment we left the grounds. Worse, I had learned almost nothing about the monster. I tried to apologize to Cricket but my words were stale. Up till now Cricket had always believed me, but this time I had truly blundered, and I knew that she wished she had never come with me to Akyre or ever agreed to be my squire.

We didn't eat that night either. Grecht brought food to our dismal little room, a tray of gray meat, hard bread, and some fruit that wasn't even ripe yet. Cricket and I took one look at the indistinguishable meat and wondered what, or who, it had come from. Food didn't matter anyway. Cricket was too afraid to eat, and I couldn't think about anything other than finding a way out. I stared out of the single dingy window, watching night collapse on the courtyard below. The tiny room felt like a prison cell. Malator stood by the door, fully visible to both me and Cricket, scratching his non-existent beard as he considered things. Cricket stretched out on one of the two hard beds, staring up at the ceiling, refusing to look at me.

"We're going back to Isowon," I said finally. This was after an hour of arguing, with no good suggestions from anyone.

"Why?" asked Cricket. "Didn't you already burn that bridge?"

"We have to warn them," I said. "Marilius was right about Diriel. He was right about everything. Diriel's insane. He's going after Isowon no matter what he says."

"He wants the monster," said Malator. "Maybe if he thinks you'll get it for him, it'll buy Isowon some time."

I turned away from the window to look at him. "Tell me right now: is that possible? A straight answer, Malator. Can that thing be controlled? Can it hear what we say to it? Can it think?"

"I don't know, Lukien, truly," said Malator. He didn't bother lowering his voice; the castle was so empty no one was listening. "You should have found out more about it from Diriel. He knows things."

"He doesn't know Fallon tore up his ancestors' graves for it," Cricket snorted.

"The creature comes from an Akyren tomb," said Malator. "But it's not some dead king. And it's not a spirit, either. It's something more powerful."

"A demon, you said."

"There are all sorts of demons, Lukien. All sorts of hells. But there is one thing I can tell you for sure: Diriel can't bargain with you for the souls of those men. Those men are gone."

"Gone where?"

"To whatever hell they believe in here. To the same realm the creature comes from, maybe. Remember what Marilius told you—the mummia only worked once the monster came."

"How many of those legionnaires does Diriel have, you suppose? I counted at least twenty in his throne room."

"More than that, surely," said Malator. "If he's planning on attacking Anton Fallon, he'll need far more than that."

"Well, we know they can die," I said. "That's something at least."

Cricket sat up with a groan. "Why do you care, Lukien?" She rolled to the side of the bed. "You don't know these people. You don't owe them anything. Malator's right—there's nothing you can do for them. Let's just get out of here."

"Back to Isowon?" Malator asked.

"Right."

"What about Sky Falls?" asked Cricket. "What about your promise, Lukien? I'm just starting to remember stuff. If I can just see the Falls again, maybe it'll all come back to me."

"And maybe it won't," I said sharply. "Has coming here helped your memory at all? You haven't said."

"No, but why would it? I'm sure I never came here before. No one could forget this place!"

"You forgot your mother and father. You forgot your family's name."

"I remembered the Bloody Knot."

"And nothing else. We've been traveling for days, and that's the only thing you remember." I lowered my voice. "We'll go to Sky Falls when we can, if we're lucky and no one follows us out of here. We'll see."

Cricket scowled but said nothing. She flopped back on the bed.

"Diriel will want his answer in the morning," said Malator. "What are you going to tell him, Lukien?"

Every option seemed dismal. "I need to think," I sighed and went back to staring out the window.

Cricket slept, and I watched over her as I'd promised, tipping back on the legs of my chair with the Sword of Angels in my lap and no one to keep me company. Malator had disappeared back into the blade. I could feel him within it, as though he were far away. Outside my dingy window I watched the moon rise and fall, watched the rats skitter across the colonnade. I listened to the wind, like it was crying, wondered if the Kassen slaves were still piled atop each other, and closed my eyes just long enough to picture that man who'd slit his throat the way another might cut a cake. No one came to our room that night, not even Grecht. When the sun finally came up, I welcomed the light until I realized nothing outside my window had changed.

Cricket woke up looking for breakfast, but there wasn't any, just the untouched tray of inedibles we'd been given the night before. She didn't apologize, but she didn't antagonize me anymore, either. She washed her face in a basin of gray water, waiting for me to tell her what kind of plan I'd come up with.

"So?" She dried herself with the inside of her cape. "What'd you decide?"

I was about to answer "Nothing," when a knock at the door startled us both. Grecht pushed the door aside and peeked in his oversized head. "Sir Lukien? Good morning! Are you ready?"

"For what?"

"Oh, I thought it was clear. King Diriel wishes to speak to you. Right at this moment, please."

I finally got out of my chair and sheathed my sword. "Our horses ready?"

"In the courtyard. Both fed and rested." Grecht opened the door wider and stepped aside for us. "Come now."

Grecht's smile seemed genuine. Was Diriel really letting us go?

"Let us get our things together," I said, even though we had almost nothing. Cricket draped her cape around her shoulders and shot me a look of mistrust. All I could do was shrug.

"Where is he?" I asked.

"In the cloister, waiting for you," said Grecht. "He's eager for your answer."

"Take us there," I ordered. Only I didn't have an answer. Not really. I spent the night trying to think of one, but Diriel wasn't going to be reasonable. He'd left reason behind a long time ago.

I followed Grecht into the hallway, keeping Cricket close beside me. The hall was as empty as the night before, and we didn't pass a single soul until we descended the stairs down to the ground level. The castle was even emptier than the day before. I supposed everyone was sleeping. Shafts of dusty light sliced through the hall from the slender arrow-loops. The hall led us out into daylight, into the arched colonnade I'd watched from our chamber. I took a deep breath to clear the smell of the castle from my lungs, grateful just to be outside again. The colonnade circled the back of the castle, away from the front courtyard and the wind of the mountains. The peace disarmed me. There were no slaves, no skulls, no half-dead soldiers, just old stones, grass, a few struggling trees. Wonderfully boring things. I began to relax.

Until a cry knifed through the silence.

Cricket stopped with a gasp. "What was *that*?"

When the noise came again I listened closely. "An animal?"

"Oh, that damn noise," grunted Grecht. "Come. Don't worry. Come."

Maybe a cat, I thought, remembering the way I'd heard them scream with heat in the streets of Koth. The silence of the morning made the cry seem ten times louder. Yet, my heartbeat calmed and we followed Grecht down the colonnade until we reached a lawn of overgrown grass and dead flowers. Out in the center of the scrubby lawn squatted Diriel, smack in the sunlight, petting a big, regal-looking peacock. The sight so stunned me, I went mute. Cricket peered at him, then declared him completely mindless.

"Now we know, huh?" she scoffed. "As though we doubted it."

He looked like a child, his knees smudged with dirt, his fingers gentle over the feathers. A big, insane child. He didn't even notice us watching him. The bird let out another of its piercing cries, and Diriel soothed it, talking to it like a baby and stroking its back. Grecht nervously cleared his throat before stepping on to the lawn.

"Unrivaled?" he called. "He's here."

Diriel didn't even stand up but waved me over like a playmate. "Come over here," he shouted.

"He means you, Sir Lukien," said Grecht. "Just you. Not the girl."

"Why? What's the problem? I keep telling him—"

"No, it's all right," said Cricket. "I'm fine. I'll wait here." She glared at Grecht. "Is that okay with you?"

Grecht held up his little hands. "He's the ruler not me."

"All right, just stay where I can see you," I told Cricket. "Let me get this over with so we can leave. Grecht, where's Wrestler?"

"Somewhere else. King Diriel only comes here himself. The cloister is forbidden to Wrestler."

I stooped all the way down, face to face with him. "If you're lying to me, Grecht, you should know I have no conscience about killing midgets."

Grecht raised his chin at me, then pointed with his flapping sleeve to Diriel. "Go."

He wasn't afraid of me. No one here was. I walked across the grass to where Diriel was waiting, digging in to a sack at his belt for feed for the peacock. He scattered the seeds or whatever they were on the ground, then stood to meet me.

"Have you made your decision?" he asked.

I stalled, because I hadn't. "Is that a pet?"

"No," said Diriel. "A prize. I wanted you to see it. Have you seen a peacock before? They used to be all over this part of the Bitter Kingdoms. No more though."

I knew he wanted me to ask, so I did. "Why? What happened to them?"

"War happened. The same thing that happened to all the people. Siege. Starvation. You must have wondered, yes? I saw you sitting by the window all night. You must have been thinking about something."

"You were down in the yard?"

"I wasn't spying, if that's what you're thinking. I walk every night through the yards."

"Bad dreams?" I asked. "I wonder why."

Diriel wiped the seed from his palms. He squatted down next to the peacock and ran his fingers over its long, back feathers. "People think this is a tail, but it isn't. It's called a covert. He doesn't always raise it up like this, but he's looking for a mate."

"Like a cat," I said. "That noise he makes."

"He won't find one, though. Not in Akyre. They're all dead. Haven't you noticed how quiet it is here? When you were on the road here, did you see peacocks? Or anything?"

I thought about it but couldn't recall seeing even a flock of starlings. The landscape was a rugged one, but even deserts had animals in them. "You said starvation. You ate them?"

"Everything that could walk, crawl, or fly through the sky," said Diriel. "And then anything else." He looked up at me with his pointed teeth. "The Kassens started it. You should know that. Always wanting war. Drin, too. They went along like lap dogs. They love to burn things, the Kassens. The farms were gone in a month. This castle was where they made their siege. We held them, though. They never made it across the bridge. It took almost a year, but eventually they gave up. Retreated back to Kasse. We had so many dead we tossed them into the ravine by the hundreds."

"When did you start . . ."

I stopped. I just couldn't say it. But I really didn't have to. Diriel took my meaning. He took my hand in his own claw-like fingers and guided them to the peacock.

"Like this," he said, directing my hand as we stroked the beautiful bird. When he let go I kept stroking, understanding instantly his connection with the creature, the only thing of any beauty for miles. I was in for a story whether I liked it or not, and petting the peacock somehow made it more bearable.

"When the siege broke we realized the Kassens had taken or destroyed everything. Anyone who didn't make it into the castle had scattered. The land was burned. Useless. They call these lands the Bitter Kingdoms for a reason. Even good years here have droughts, blight, every curse the gods know how to give. The year I was born, they tell me there were so many locusts you couldn't even see the sky. Those bastard bugs ate everything that year, but even then we didn't eat people."

Diriel prodded me suddenly with his finger.

"You getting what I'm saying, Liirian? You imagining how bad things were?" He pointed at his sharpened teeth. "You see these? I was the first. I filed them down and sucked the meat off the first Kassen's bones I could get my lips around, just to show my people I wasn't afraid. Scared the livin' shit out of the Kassens. Told them we were coming for them."

I kept petting the bird as calmly as I could. Just past Diriel I saw Cricket in the colonnade, puzzling over what we were saying.

"Is that when you asked Fallon for the mummia?"

"Not at first. At first I didn't need it. My legionnaires were starved but hungry for revenge. We broke over the border like a wave! And when those Kassen pigs saw us, all screaming and bloody, they ran. So we went after them. That's when I remembered. The old Akyren kings knew about magic. They called upon the powers of the dead. That's my bloodline. It's my right! I gave everything I had left to that skunk Anton Fallon. And you know why he took it? Because he doesn't care about anything but money. He didn't lift a pinky finger to stop the slaughter in Akyre. Just kept right on selling his spices from Zura, silks for his fancy-boy friends, everything."

"That sounds like Fallon all right."

"Sounds like a Liirian, too," spat Diriel. "I sent emissaries to Liiria. And to Reec and Norvor. Do you know what I heard back? Nothing. I told them how the Kassens were murdering us. I sent them a cloth from my own daughter's dress with a note about how she starved to death. You have some cold-hearted kings on the continent, Sir Lukien. They could've helped us. But they didn't. So piss on all of them!"

Slowly, I stood to face him. For a moment I'd thought his madness had passed, but now it was all over him again. Cricket looked nervous. I shook my head to ease her worry.

"They call you 'the Unrivaled' here," I said. "Your men are obviously loyal. They follow you because you saved them. You've already proven yourself, my lord. You've already beaten Kasse. You don't have to keep on fighting."

"There's Drin," said Diriel. "And Isowon. All the old lands of the empire. I'm intent on them. That's the only way to protect ourselves. No more *Bitter Kingdoms*. We'll be an empire again."

"And what about the people? The Kassens you haven't killed yet. What about Drin? You plan to kill them all?"

"Yes," said Diriel firmly. "Or make them slaves."

"And you'll be the emperor?"

"I *am* the emperor."

I looked down at his treasured peacock. "You know, I've been playing for time here, wondering how to tell you my decision. You already have an army of monsters. Why would you need one more?"

"The people of Isowon didn't help us, but they didn't make war on us either. You can spare them the fate of the Kassens, Sir Lukien, just by getting me that creature. It's my right to rule that beast. My privilege as emperor. But wait." He took my shoulder. "Before you decide, let me show you something."

Diriel urged me back toward the colonnade, where Cricket waited and Grecht stood with a stupid smile. Cricket looked excited, hoping we were finally leaving. I moved in a fog, wondering what last atrocity Diriel had to show us.

"Lukien?" asked Cricket as we approached. "Are we going?"

"Yes." Whether Diriel allowed it or not, we were going.

Diriel led the way, back through the colonnade, into the deserted castle and toward the gate where we'd first entered the day before. I caught sight of Wrestler, standing at the threshold with a wicked smile. Just ahead of him stood Zephyr and Cricket's pony, refreshed and rested, just like Grecht had promised. A flame of hope flickered inside me. But like a stiff wind, what I saw next extinguished it.

All across the battlements and catwalks, lined up along the castle wall and crowding the yard, stood a silent army, a phalanx of dead-eyed legionnaires, unmoving, armed with swords and spears and war scythes. I came through the gate and saw a hundred of them. Then hundreds more. An impossible number that made my bones freeze. All I heard was Wrestler laughing, loving my shock. The soldiers stretched beyond the courtyard, even around the castle's twin turrets. Dressed in their ragged uniforms and cast-offs, it seemed that every able man in Akyre had been turned into one of Diriel's soulless slaves.

"They've been called here," said Diriel. "From Kasse and the Drin border, mostly. Regular soldiers, too. Just so you see what Fallon would be up against. I thought you should know." He smiled in a way that made his lips twist. "Don't put me to the test, Sir Lukien. All of Akyre will be mine again, but you can save the folk of Isowon from the worst of it. Now tell me, what you have decided?"

I couldn't hide my contempt. "You have me," I confessed. "But I can't make promises. I don't know if I can control the creature. Maybe no one can."

"Don't worry, Bronze Knight," jeered Wrestler. "If you die trying, you can always try again."

"One week," said Diriel. "After that my army marches for Isowon. Tell Anton Fallon this. Warn him of our coming. We'll see if he's man enough to stand his ground or if he runs back to Zura."

"He's got an army of his own," said Cricket. "He'll fight you."

"He'll lose," said Diriel. "Be a friend to Isowon, girl. Help your master Lukien get me the creature."

Wrestler winked at Cricket.

"What about him?" I asked. "You'll call him off? That's got to be part of the bargain."

"One week," Diriel repeated. "After that, you and the girl are fair game. Isowon, too."

I nodded and pushed Cricket toward her pony. "You hear that, Wrestler?" I asked him. "Seven days. After that, you're fair game to *me*."

19

I couldn't get Cricket to speak. She simply wouldn't talk to me.

At first I barely noticed her silence. We were too busy riding out of Akyre to pay much attention to anything, and I kept worrying that Diriel was already sending his soldiers after us. I let Cricket take the lead again, confident she'd find us the fastest path south. We rode like that for over two hours, until our mounts were exhausted, and I was confident we weren't being followed. Finally, when I called for Cricket to stop, I thought she didn't hear me. She just kept right on galloping away.

"Hey!" I shouted. "Stop now!"

She jerked back the reins of her pony. The animal halted but Cricket didn't turn around. I'd already lost patience with her. I was tired, hungry, and more than a little afraid. I should have seen what was happening to her.

"We're gonna kill these horses if we don't slow down," I said, catching up to her. "The river's close. We'll find it and rest there. Nice and easy now."

Cricket didn't even nod. She rode off at a slow saunter. I kept back a few paces, taking the time to clear my head. To be honest I was grateful for the quiet. Malator must have sensed that, because he didn't bother me either. My mind kept tripping over what I'd seen: the legion of the lost, that mad midget Grecht, even the peacock. I tried to remember everything Diriel had told me. I needed sleep. But we were on a dirt road, out in the open, and more than anything we needed shelter.

So we were going back to Isowon. Not just to warn them, but

because I needed a place to hide Cricket. Wrestler was coming for her; I'd seen it in his eyes. Some sick kind of lust. Some men see a thing and have to have it. They get obsessed. Whatever it was, I knew Cricket wouldn't be safe until we were far away from the Bitter Kingdoms or Wrestler was dead. I'd already made my choice, and it wasn't to run away. I wanted to fight, not just Wrestler but the monster, too. I was making mistakes and knew it.

I let Cricket ride ahead of me for a while longer, hoping she'd calm down. In time she'd forgive me, I figured. She was owed an apology for being taken to Akyre, but I can't abide being ignored. I'd never regretted taking Cricket with me or making her my squire until right then.

"If she were a boy she'd be less moody," I grumbled. I dug into my saddlebag and took out an apple, one of the last Marilius had given us. Thinking it a good peace offering, I called out to Cricket. "You hungry?"

She rode on, swaying on her pony with her back to me.

"You haven't eaten a thing today." I held out the apple, hoping she'd turn around. "Here."

When she didn't answer me, I almost threw it at her.

"All right, enough," I snapped. "Now you're just acting like a child. What is it? Sky Falls? Or are you mad about Akyre?"

At last she muttered something, but I couldn't make it out.

"You're afraid. I know, but you don't have to be," I said. "We've got a week before they come. That'll give us time to help Fallon plan a defense. No one's going to hurt you, Cricket, I promise."

That's what set me off—making that promise and being ignored. I tossed the apple to the ground.

"We can run if that's what you want," I shouted. "Is it? But you won't get your memories back. They're *here*, not back in Jador. I'm not going to help Diriel get that monster. You know that. But we can't just walk away from Marilius and the others. They're innocent. They'll be slaughtered. I don't think that's what you want, is it Cricket?"

At last she turned around to face me. "It's just fine, Lukien."

She smiled, an empty, blank smile. Like she didn't know why. Like she wasn't even seeing me. I'd seen that look before—vacant, lost. In battle we call it "the stare." My guts seized.

"Yeah?" I asked carefully. "You're all right?"

"Fine," she sang. "*Fine!*"

She turned, spiked her heels against her pony, and drove the creature madly down the road. I sputtered before urging Zephyr after her, hearing her broken laughter as she sped away. She kept on singing and laughing, even screaming, bouncing on the pony's back, about to be thrown over. Zephyr dug into the road. We closed the gap, and I saw Cricket's gritty face, determined to outrun me. Then suddenly she let go of the reins and raised her hands to the sky.

"Catch me, Lukien!"

She was laughing. I reached for the reins, trying to bring her pony to a stop without spilling her over its head. When I finally got the beast to heel Cricket dumped herself from its back. She just fell off and hit the ground.

"Cricket!"

Slowly she lifted her bloodied face out of the dirt. She didn't say a word. At least she'd stopped laughing. I got down from my horse and bent over her. She blinked up at me through the dust and blood.

"Lukien," she whispered, "why did you take me there?"

I really had no answer. Cricket started shaking.

"I saw those things—now I can't stop. Why'd you let me see them?"

"It was a horror," I said. "I'm sorry. I am, Cricket. I'm sorry."

"That man cut his throat. His own throat. Those slaves . . ." Cricket pushed her face into mine. "They eat people!"

"I know, it's impossible," I fumbled for words. "You should never have seen it. I should never have taken you."

"But why did you? Why, Lukien?" She grabbed my breastplate. "You're supposed to protect me. We came here for *me*. You can't die, but I can! And now it's all inside me!"

I let her shake me until the tears came, until she drew back and crumpled. That's when I knew what I'd done. Why hadn't I seen it? She'd been brave in Diriel's hell-hole. Even when that legionnaire slit his own throat. She'd buried it, the way soldiers do. Now it was breaking lose.

I rocked back on my heels. All I could do was let her purge herself.

"Cricket," I said gently, "I'm a hard man. I've seen too much. It's all poisoned me." My mind was full of ghosts, the dead of my battlefields. Diriel's castle had merely sickened me. A lifetime of death had made me impervious to shock. But Cricket, her mind was virgin. No more, though. "Malator was right," I said. "I shouldn't have brought you here. No one could have been ready for what we saw. Just me."

Cricket swallowed her sobs. She laid herself down in the middle of the road, her cheek kissing the dirt. Her hand turned to a claw and raked her face, trailing it with red streaks.

"When will I remember?" she begged.

She wasn't asking me. Her question was for heaven.

"Rest," I told her. "Sleep if you can."

I rearranged her rass-skin cape, covering her with it like a blanket. Her breathing steadied, but she never closed her eyes. I sat down next to her with the Sword of Angels on my lap. Nothing would disturb her, I determined. Not a wolf, not a man, not even a bad dream. Whatever came down the road to harm her, I swore an oath to kill it.

I built a fire at the side of the road. Not a single rider appeared or even the hint of one in the distance. As the sun went down I listened for animals but they never came, and I remembered what Diriel had said about how they'd all been eaten. It was like we were in the desert again. Only the stars seemed alive. I made myself comfortable by the fire, leaning against my bedroll and tossing scrub brush into the flames. It had taken hours for Cricket to fall asleep. She refused food and drink. I wondered if she had a concussion from her fall. The cut on her forehead had stopped bleeding, though. I cleaned her up while she lay there, lost in her own mind. Sleep would help her, I thought.

I'd pushed us both too hard. Despite the strength the sword gave me I needed sleep, too. I closed my eyes from time to time, drifting in and out of slumber, determined to stay awake. I doubted anyone would come, but just in case.

Once I thought I saw Wrestler coming. He appeared more giant than ever, a monster emerging from the darkness. I shouted, waking myself. I cursed and ran my fingers through my filthy hair. My eye twitched. I was desperate for a bath. Suddenly Fallon's gilded castle seemed like paradise.

Soon, I told myself. *Just have to hold on.*

"Malator?" I whispered. "Where are you?"

He hadn't come to me for hours. I could only barely feel him.

I'm here, he said inside my mind. He sounded tired.

"I need strength."

You need sleep.

"Can't. Just help me."

I gripped the sword, waiting for the energy to fill me. It came but in a trickle.

"More."

There's no one to fight here, Lukien. That's enough. I need strength too, you know.

"Keep me company, then," I said. "Can you do that? I need to talk. I don't want to be alone."

I heard him laugh. *Ah, so you don't want to be rid of me anymore!*

"Not just yet. Come be with me."

He appeared at my left, shimmering into view in the firelight, sitting comfortably in the dirt like he'd been there all along. His handsome face bore none of the signs of his weariness. Malator just seemed eternally young. I envied him. Even though I was barely aging, I felt old. Malator studied Cricket as she slept. He turned back to me with a sigh.

"If only I could get into her head," he lamented. "I wonder what I'd find there."

"Something awful," I said. "That's all they have in this part of the world—awful things."

"You made your apologies," said Malator. "It's up to her to accept it or not."

"An apology can't change what she saw." I picked up the longest stick I could from my pile and poked it into the flames. "I gave her memories, all right. I'll bet she'll remember *those*." The heat burned my hand. "You were right, Malator. I shouldn't have taken her here. I should have listened to you, but I was too damn stubborn. Everything I touch turns to shit."

"Now you're feeling sorry for yourself. That won't help Cricket."

"I don't know how to help her! I thought taking her to Akyre would help. I thought making her my squire would. But everything's just getting worse." I looked suspiciously at Malator. "Is that what you thought would happen? Did you foresee this?"

Malator grew circumspect. "I did warn you, Lukien."

"Yes, and that's all you did," I said bitterly. "I need to know more, Malator. I need you to be specific!"

"Your decisions are your own, Lukien. Even what little I've told you might have been too much! You have a path to follow. But it's the monster that matters here, Lukien. Remember that."

Why was everything about the monster? The creature dominated me, not just my thoughts but my actions. Even Diriel wanted it. The monster was the key—but to what? To Cricket? Me?

"I can't bring it to Diriel," I whispered. "Even if I could control it. He'd be unstoppable with a creature like that in his army."

"Your lie bought us time," said Malator. "We have a week to get Fallon and his men ready."

"Six days," I corrected. Just sitting there was wasting time. The fire mesmerized me, bringing back Diriel's words. "Diriel said his ancestors knew magic. Maybe he knows about the monster. Maybe he thinks *he* can control it. You said it's a demon, right? Could the kings of Akyre control demons?"

Malator shrugged. "We're far from my expertise here, Lukien. Where I come from spirits were part of life. Maybe it's the same in Akyre."

"The monster came out of a tomb. Fallon said he woke it." I laid the puzzle out as best I could. "Is that why it's after him? It marked him, but he doesn't seem to know anything about it."

"Or he's lying. You know what kind of man he is."

"I do." I tossed my stick all the way into the fire and watched the sparks fly. "It galls me to be going back there. To help him, of all people. And what about the creature? If you can't tell me what it's after, can you tell me how to stop it?"

"The tomb. Remember? Marilius didn't want you to see it. If that's where the creature came from, there'll be clues."

I thought about it, liking the idea. "It wouldn't waste much time," I agreed. "Just a short detour, less than half a day. We'd have to enter in the daylight, though. I wouldn't want to face the creature with Cricket there."

Malator nodded but never got the chance to answer. All the while I thought Cricket had been sleeping. I jumped when she spoke.

"Face the creature?" she said suddenly.

She looked bleary-eyed, half-asleep. She leaned on her palms to keep herself upright.

"We're just trying to find out what is it," I told her. "We have to go."

"Like we had to go to Akyre?"

"It's all connected, Cricket," I said. "The monster, Diriel's legion, even you. I'll go in the tomb by myself, but I *am* going. We'll get you safely to Isowon after that."

She looked disinterested. She nodded, tried to smile, then closed her eyes and went back to sleep. Maybe she'd been dreaming, just talking in her sleep. I didn't know, but I remember thinking she wouldn't be the same any more. As it turned out, I was right.

20

When I finally awoke the next morning, it was Cricket who was standing guard.

My sleep had been so deep, so complete, that I couldn't even remember dreaming. Though I'd struggled to stay awake, I had finally succumbed at some point in the night, opening my eye to the sight of Cricket beside our readied horses. She'd already packed our things and doused the fire I'd built in the road. She stood with her back toward me, looking southward and considering the sky. The Sword of Angels lay at my side, but all my other belongings had been strapped to Zephyr. I looked at the sun and realized it was hours past dawn.

"You should have woken me," I grumbled. I wobbled to my feet then remembered the night before. "You all right?"

Cricket nodded but didn't smile. "My head hurts a little. I let you sleep because you needed it."

I looked around, toward the hills and up and down the barren road. "See anything?"

"It's been quiet." Cricket came toward me, picking my sheathed sword from the ground and handing it to me. "Here. We should go. It's at least a full day to the valley."

"You mean the tomb?"

"That's where we're going, aren't we?"

"We are."

She thrust the sword at me. "Then we should go. You can eat on the road."

I took the sword and began belting it around my waist. Cricket walked toward her pony. I watched her movements, looking for a trace of dizziness, any hint of a concussion. She was arrow-straight as she walked. Even her mood seemed fine. Maybe a little icy but nothing like the night before.

"Good that you rested," I said. "You seem better."

"Better?" She turned to look at me. "Better than what?"

"Than yesterday," I said. "Than last night."

"What happened last night?"

I was about to laugh until I realized she wasn't joking. The bruise on her head suddenly looked a lot bigger. "You fell off your horse. We were arguing. Don't you remember? You said your head hurt."

She probed her forehead, wincing when she touched it. "I do remember falling . . . kind of. Last night, we talked about going to the tomb. Malator was there."

"That's right." I went to her and studied her bruise in the sunlight, taking her chin in my hand. "Do you remember what you said to me?"

"I was angry?"

"You don't remember?"

"Just parts," she answered. She bit her lip. "Oh, my memory's getting worse!"

"You remember where we are, don't you? Do you remember Diriel's—"

I stopped myself. Cricket blinked at me. "What?"

Had she forgotten? I was afraid to ask. Part of me hoped the trauma of the castle had been wiped away, pushed out of her mind like the memories of her childhood. "We were in Akyre," I said.

She nodded. "I know." Then, blankness. I could almost see it, like a curtain coming down. "We should go, Lukien," she said in a hurry. "We're too out in the open here. I don't like it." She spun back toward her pony. "Let's make it to the river at least. We can follow it till it's dark. We'll get to the valley by tomorrow noon that way."

She mounted her horse, waiting for me to do the same. Zephyr looked perfect. She'd even brushed him.

"You don't mind going to the tomb?" I asked.

"I'm your squire, Lukien," she answered. "It's not my decision, it's yours. I'm not afraid. I know you'll protect me."

I smiled at her. My squire. She'd cleaned the horses and the camp but hadn't even brushed her hair. She had no idea how strange she looked sitting there on her pony, oblivious, her face still smudged with ash. She broke my heart.

"Good," I said, faking confidence. I got on my horse and told her to lead the way south. "We should sing something," I said as we trotted off. "Anything. No one'll hear us. Just any song you can remember."

We camped that night by the river, near a stand of withered olive trees strangled with vines. With Akyre behind us and the thought of Anton's palace ahead, we relaxed beside the burbling water, passing the time by finding pictures in the stars. All that day, Cricket had said nothing more about Diriel's castle or her strange behavior, occasionally falling into long silences while we rode. The day had been a good one, and I was happy to have Cricket acting herself again. I pointed out all the constellations I could recall from my life in Liiria, remembering how Akeela had taught them to me when we were boys. Cricket leaned against me, sharing the tree trunk and staring up through its bare branches.

"That one is called Kolervas," I said. "The sculptor. He lived a long, long time ago in old Liiria." I traced the star pattern with my outstretched finger. "He's chiseling. If you look closely you can tell."

Cricket tried very hard. "I don't see it," she sighed. "None of them really look like anything."

"You have to use your imagination," I told her. We'd kept our campfire small so we could see the stars. "There . . . there's a good one." I moved my finger west and down toward the horizon. "See that big star? That's Adreana. That's her head."

"Who's Adreana?"

"The Chained Lady." I smiled when I said it. "She was a princess. She was captured by King Lekara. When she refused to marry him, Lekara chained Adreana to an olive tree. Like these olive trees."

"Why?"

"To feed her to a giant raven."

"What?" Cricket sat up. "So, what happened?"

"The raven came and broke her chains and carried her back to her homeland. After that Lekara's country went to war with Adreana's. Those stories are called 'The Tales of the Reecian Wars.' I read about them when I was young. Mostly just legends. Fun, though."

"No giant ravens?"

"I don't think so." I leaned back and stared at the constellation. "Cassandra told me that story about Adreana. Akeela taught me all the other constellations, but Cassandra showed me Adreana. She told me she felt like Adreana, chained to the tree. Being here with these olive trees reminds me of her."

Cricket leaned back next to me. "She felt like a prisoner?"

"She was a prisoner. Akeela kept her in his castle for years. No one was allowed to look at her, not even Akeela himself."

"Because of the amulet?"

"That's right. The Eye of God that Gilwyn wears now. It kept Cassandra alive. She had a cancer."

Cricket listened, wanting me to go on. My past was still mostly a mystery to her. "You don't talk about Cassandra much since we left Jador," she remarked. "I like when you talk about her." She grinned. "It's a love story."

"I did love her," I sighed. "I still do. She's still out there, waiting for me. I just have to die to be with her."

"You promised Gilwyn you wouldn't."

"What? Let myself die?" I shook my head. "Not yet. Someday, though. I told Cassandra that in the Story Garden. She told me it wasn't my time yet to be with her but one day I will. One day when I've done enough. I've got a lot of bad things to make right."

"Is that why you're helping me?" Cricket asked.

Something about the starlight gave me a burst of honesty. "I guess it is," I admitted. "I couldn't save Cassandra. Once I looked at her again, I broke the amulet's spell. The cancer killed her instantly. But I always believed she was alive somewhere. I could feel her. Minikin used to tell me that nobody ever really dies, so I knew all I had to do was find her. Then I found the Story Garden." The memory chilled me. "She was alive. Just like Minikin said."

Cricket's eyes got big. She was quiet for a moment, thoughtful. She put her head against me sleepily. "That's how I feel sometimes. Like Cassandra. Like a prisoner."

"Because you can't remember?"

"Yes," she whispered.

She felt warm against me. Not a lover's warmth, but a child's. I put my arm around her. "Do you remember what I told you when we started out?" I said. "Your memories are here. Somewhere. Just like me finding Cassandra. I knew she was there, so I kept looking. That's what we're going to do—keep looking. We'll find them."

"I thought so too at first. But now . . ." She shrugged. "I don't know."

"We will," I said confidently.

"We only have a week."

"No," I said in a hush. "Plenty of time. You're young, and I've got all the time in the world."

She didn't laugh at my dark joke. She just rested in the crux of my arm. I laid there against the tree, unmoving, studying the constellations until she fell asleep.

All the next morning we followed the river. The sunlight had broken our melancholy moods, and we stopped for a time to watch fish jumping in the chop. It was a remarkably beautiful day for the Bitter Kingdoms, the first one I could remember since laying eyes on Isowon. Once again the landscape was changing, shifting from the bleakness of Akyre to southern greenery. We were less than a full day's ride to Fallon's palace, and only an hour or so from the dell where the tomb lay. The river meandered toward the valley where we'd first encountered the monster.

When we saw the valley, each of us fell silent.

It was Cricket who first sniffed the air. Once, then again, deeper. I did the same, but couldn't catch a whiff of the pile of bones and flesh that had greeted us last time. Cricket, who'd already seen her share of horrors, braced for another. This time, though, we'd prepared ourselves. My mind touched Malator as he stretched out over the dell, looking for the creature. Through his eyes I saw him racing through the trees and around the rocky enclaves, like a wild bird set loose from a cage. This time, we were determined to find the monster first.

It's nowhere, said Malator. His frustration grew. *I don't sense it anywhere.*

"It's daytime," I said. "It must be here."

Just because it kills at night doesn't mean it won't move about in the day. It's a spirit, Lukien, not an owl.

"Check the tomb," I said as I continued riding toward it. "Do you see it?"

It's just ahead. But I don't feel the monster. I would if it were here.

Perplexed, I turned to Cricket. "It's not here," I said. "Malator can't sense it."

"He's sure?" she asked.

"Seems to be."

I am, Malator replied. *It was unmistakable last time.*

"Then where is it?"

"Maybe eating," suggested Cricket. "We saw all those bones last time. Like they were licked clean."

"Malator, do demons eat?"

Maybe. If they get hungry.

"Quit joking," I snapped.

I'm not. This creature isn't like me, Lukien. It's here in your realm as flesh. It shouldn't be, but it is. Maybe it gets hungry, cold . . .

"Lonely?" I scoffed. "Maybe we should sing to it."

Malator suddenly flashed out of my mind. The next second he was standing in front of me, glaring and frightening my horse.

"Are you an expert on the realms of the dead?" he asked. He folded his arms over his shimmering self. "We're here to learn about this creature, aren't we?"

I nodded. "Yes."

Malator glowered at Cricket. "You?"

Cricket just looked overwhelmed to see him. "Uh-huh."

"Then do as I say. Get down from your horses. We'll go on foot from here."

I was uncomfortable but trusted Malator. The two of us dismounted, then reined the animals to a nearby tree. We were at the edge of the dell, but coming at it from the north this time. I could see the river cutting across the valley, disappearing in places amongst the evergreens. We walked downhill, skidding over loose rocks until we came to the river again, moving sluggishly toward a hillside where it disappeared into a cave.

"That's the tomb," said Malator, pointing toward it.

The way the river cut through the hill surprised me. The cave was open to anyone who dared enter. I supposed the river came out the other side somewhere.

"It'll be dark in there," said Cricket. "The sun won't help much."

"Leave that to me," said Malator. "Stay close."

We were in his hands now, so we did as he asked, following him toward the mouth of the cave, the rocks like teeth rimming a jaw. Cricket walked rigidly beside him, determined not to bolt. I still didn't know if the knock on her head had helped or harmed her. Her eyes were steely and alert. Malator paused right at the edge of the cave, his feet disappearing into the water without disturbing the river at all. He peered inside in an oddly human way, as he himself didn't trust his Akari instincts. Then he let out a breath.

"All right," he said. "It's clear. I'm sure of it."

I unsheathed my sword anyway. "Go."

Once the darkness touched him, Malator's body began to glow. His figure was like a torch inside the cave, shedding its soft light on the damp walls and gravel. He turned up his palm and lit a flame in it with his mind, the way I'd seen him do before. Then he turned to Cricket.

"Take this," he told her.

Cricket took the flame without hesitation, marveling as it flared in her hand. "It's not hot," she remarked. "Almost cool."

I remembered the sensation myself. Malator was full of tricks these days. But I didn't want a flame of my own, just my sword. I pointed ahead with it. "Look."

Through the gloom I saw the river rounding a bend in the cavern. Where it turned was a gash in the wall of the cave, like a doorway. Slabs of rock had been moved away from the opening, discarded into the river.

"Fallon," I whispered. "He must have used horses to move the slabs."

Cricket leaned forward with a squint. "That opening is barely wide enough for a person. How'd the monster get out?"

I wondered about that myself. "Somehow it squeezed itself into those bones," I remembered. "It changes itself, maybe."

"We can get through," said Malator. "Me first."

He floated over the river where the slabs lay like tombstones, then slipped easily through the crack. His iridescent body appeared on the other side, lighting up a vast chamber beyond.

"Lukien, Cricket." He turned and smiled at us through the portal. "You have to see this."

Cricket stomped anxiously through the river. She barely had to turn sidewise to make it through the opening. When she did, she gasped.

"Whoa!"

I felt like an explorer. I sheathed my sword in a hurry and squeezed myself through the gash in the rocky wall, scraping my nose and breastplate. Fallon had obviously rushed his excavation. But once inside, every sense of tightness fled. Suddenly I was in a vast chamber with a sky-high ceiling and a finger of the river running through it. A hundred stone eyes watched me, the glorious work of long-dead sculptors, awash in Malator's magic light. Cricket held up her flame for us to see. I saw dozens of sculptures, all of them animals, cut into the walls of the tomb or built up high on pedestals, like a lush jungle of wild cats and birds. Faded paintings in gold and scarlet decorated the walls, depicting battles and forests, a landscape of an Akyre that no longer existed. The entire chamber was filled with vases and urns, their contents turned to dust. Another chamber echoed to our left. The little tributary disappeared into its darkness.

"Lukien," whispered Cricket. "Look."

She walked toward the center of the chamber, where a large stone coffin stood, raised up on a marble pedestal chiseled with words. The slab that had once covered the coffin lay to the side, a reminder of Fallon's grave-robbing. Atop the slab was another sculpture, this one of a bird. Cricket ignored the coffin and looked at the bird instead.

"It's empty," said Malator as he floated over the coffin.

"Of course. Fallon got what he needed. Whoever it was has been turned into mummy powder."

Malator moved his hand over the words inscribed on the pedestal. They were foreign to me, like runes. "Can you read it?" I asked.

"No," said Malator. "It's probably some old Akyren language."

"His name was Atarkin," said Cricket. I turned and saw her reading the words, holding out her flaming palm as she knelt near the slab. "He was the last Emperor of Akyre."

"How do you know that?" I asked. "Not even Malator knows that."

"The words," said Cricket. "I can understand them."

"Well, now we know you're definitely from Akyre," joked Malator.

"How can you remember that?" I asked "How can you remember a whole language when you can't remember who you are?"

Cricket pondered that, as confused as I was. "I don't know. It's like remembering how to talk I guess."

"What else does it say?"

She leaned in and read some more. "He was called 'the Nightingale.' That's what the people called him."

"The bird," said Malator, noting the sculpture on his slab.

"The Nightingale? Strange thing to call a tyrant."

"Maybe he wasn't a tyrant," said Cricket. "Maybe he was a good king."

I knew she wanted to believe that. "Maybe." I touched the coffin, noticing for the first time the stone flowers carved into it. "Roses," I whispered. "Nightingales and roses." I looked around the tomb, struck by all the beautiful paintings and statues. "Was this Akyre? Is this what it was like?"

Cricket went on studying the words. "He was the master of the dead. Huh."

"Huh?"

"That's what it says, Master of the Dead." She pointed to show me. "What's that mean, Malator?"

Malator thought for a moment. "Master of the Dead." He looked around the chamber. He stroked his chin with his glowing hand. "Emperor. Master of the Dead. What did Diriel say to you, Lukien? About magic?"

"He said the old kings called on the powers of the dead," I recalled. "Whatever that means."

"Master of the Dead," Malator repeated. "*Master*." He tipped his head over the empty coffin and looked inside. "Atarkin's body. You can't just grind up any old mummy and expect to make men immortal from it. Something about Atarkin was special."

"His bloodline maybe?" said Cricket.

"That's what Diriel said," I pointed out. "He said it was his right to control the monster."

"It's a puzzle," sighed Malator. I could feel his frustration. "The monster came from here. From right here in this chamber." He turned toward the darker part of the tomb, where the tributary flowed. "From there."

Cricket and I both froze as we watched Malator drift along the side of the water, gradually illuminating a tunnel of stone. The monster wasn't here—I believed Malator about that. So why was I so anxious? I helped Cricket up and walked with her after Malator, following him into a dark antechamber. The flame still burned in Cricket's hand. She held it up, revealing the opposite wall. Jagged rock, like all the others, the wall was painted with an enormous mural depicting a place I'd never seen before, a twisted landscape with blighted trees and burning mountains, peopled with tormented ghosts. In the center of the world stood a multi-armed, multi-headed beast, its long tongue roped around a naked woman, its tails rimmed with bloody thorns. It had the face of a human and a goat and a bird and a pig, and it was the goat's tongue that held the woman, about to devour her. Above the painting was chiseled more of the Akyren letters.

"Gahoreth," said Cricket. She turned to Malator. "What's that?"

But Malator didn't answer. He was looking down at the ribbon of water. "Look at the river."

I'd been so struck by the painting I hadn't noticed the river at all. It didn't wind off into the darkness as I'd supposed, but disappeared directly into the wall. I peered closer, not sure what I was seeing. The river was there, right at my feet, and then it wasn't. It didn't pool at the wall like a dam. It just flowed right into it, into the painted world.

"Gahoreth," said Malator. "One of the realms of the dead. A hell. That's where our monster comes from."

Cricket's white face filled with awe. She shifted her magical flame from one palm to the other, then reached out to touch the wall. But her hand didn't go through it the way the water did. She looked oddly surprised. She dipped her fingers into the water, then touched the wall again.

"It's real," she gasped. "But where's it going?"

"Into Gahoreth," said Malator.

"How's that possible?" I was neither awestruck nor afraid. All I felt was baffled. "You know this place Gahoreth? You've heard of it?"

"It's a place where souls go after life," said Malator.

"I thought souls go to their own death place. That's what Minikin taught me. You said so, too. Like Cassandra in the apple orchard. You never said anything about them going to hell."

"Not hell," said Malator. "Like a hell. That's the best word for it. The souls trapped in Gahoreth aren't in their resting places. They've been stolen. Taken to Gahoreth."

"How?"

"I don't know." Malator turned back to the painting. "The monster perhaps."

Cricket was busy studying the picture. She traced her finger over a bit of writing beneath the image of the beast. Her lips moved while she read.

"Cricket? What's it say?"

"It's name. It's name is Crezil."

"Crezil?" I looked closer at the writing. "All those words for that? What else?"

"I don't really understand it, Lukien. It says Kasdeyi Orioc. Or Oriox. Something like that. The words don't mean anything though. They mean like . . . Guardian Slave. Kasdeyi is an old Akyren word for a guardian or even a lighthouse. Oriox means slave." Cricket read again, stringing the whole thing together, "I am Crezil the guardian slave. I'm sorry, Lukien. That's the best I can figure."

"Malator?" I called. "What do you think?"

Malator didn't answer. He cocked his translucent head, examining the creature in the painting. It didn't look like the one we'd seen, but something made me sure this was it. A guardian. A slave. I tried to unravel it.

"It guards the tomb," I suggested. "The Akyren kings summoned it, maybe."

"Or they thought they summoned it," said Malator.

"What's that mean?"

"A creature like this Crezil doesn't guard a tomb. It doesn't even belong in this world." Malator pointed at the painting. "It belongs there. That's its world. Gahoreth."

"Then it's the guardian of Gahoreth," said Cricket. "You think so?"

"A guardian *and* a slave," I said. "But a slave to who? Or what?"

"The ruler of Gahoreth, presumably," said Malator.

"That doesn't help. Who's the ruler of Gahoreth, then?"

Malator didn't answer.

"We're just guessing," I grumbled. "We're wasting time. Diriel's army is on its way. We need to get to Isowon."

I turned to go, but neither Malator nor Cricket followed. Both were still enthralled by the painting and the disappearing river.

"They're all clues," said Cricket. She looked up at Malator. "Right, Malator?"

"Pieces to the puzzle, Cricket," he agreed. "The monster came through here—through this wall. Like the river. It crossed between worlds." He grinned at me. "Hear that, Lukien?"

"We know that already," I said. "What else?"

Malator crossed the chamber to face me. "We learned a lot," he insisted. "The name of the monster, the fact that it's from Gahoreth . . ."

"And none of us has any idea what that means," I said. "Fallon set that monster free when he stole Atarkin's body. But why? What's it looking for? Revenge? Souls? Do you know, either of you?"

Cricket looked away. Malator seethed but didn't say a word.

"I didn't think so. Well, enough now." I trudged my way into the main chamber, splashing through the water. "I'm done with riddles and clues. I'm done with running and hiding. It's time to fight."

"Oh," said Cricket, "now I see. You're mad because you didn't learn anything helpful to kill it. That's what you want, isn't it? To fight it. To kill it."

"That's right." I turned on her. "You want to know? I'm mad because the damn thing isn't here. But I'm going to find it, and when I do I'm going to kill it. And then I'm going to find Wrestler and I'm going to kill him, too. That's what I do, Cricket. I'm a killer." It felt so good to finally admit it! Like chains had been broken. I couldn't get to Isowon fast enough. "We're done here," I told them. "Let's go."

"We just started looking!" argued Malator. "There's time. We have the whole tomb to explore."

"Malator . . ." I struggled to control myself. "You've taken me astray. Remember when we set out? I told you I was in charge. You're *my* Akari. But then I let you show me visions, get my head all turned around. Look at us. We're in a tomb! Like grave robbers. Like that scoundrel Anton Fallon. Well, no more." I pulled my sword a few inches out of its sheath. "Time for you to go home."

Malator eyed the blade. "You're making a mistake."

"Go on, get in there," I coaxed. "I'll call you when I need you."

"I'm not a slave—"

"Yes, Malator, you are! That's the price you pay for keeping me alive. For keeping me away from Cassandra and everything that makes sense to me! I say where we go from here. Not you. Not anyone else. Now, get in the sword."

He contested me with a long, hard stare, but he couldn't win. Malator hated to admit it, but I owned him. In a puff of light, he disappeared. Out went the flame in Cricket's hand. Darkness swallowed us instantly.

"Uh, Lukien?"

"Don't worry. I can see."

I still had the miracle of Malator's powers. I took Cricket's hand and guided us along the river, out of the tomb, and out of the cave, picking our way carefully and wordlessly over the rocks. When the sunlight finally touched us, I saw the worry on Cricket's face.

She's afraid of me, I thought.

Maybe that was a good thing. We found our horses where we left them. I mounted up, told Cricket to hurry, and rode south for Isowon.

21

Crezil.

The word kept going through my mind.

All that morning and into the afternoon we rode south for Isowon. Cricket spent her time talking about frivolous things, trying to draw me out of my sour mood, and avoiding any discussion of what we found in the cave. She bounced along behind me, commenting about the trees and how lovely the day was for riding, and how pleased Marilius would be to see us again, but she never once mentioned the monster or her ability to read the writings in Atarkin's tomb. I never mentioned it either. I was sick of her memory lapse, sick of her not even trying to remember.

And I was suspicious. For the first time, I feared all her lost memories were nothing but a lie. Yet I knew there was nothing to be done for it. We had our hands full with Diriel's army and the promise I'd made him to deliver up the monster, and now that I knew the creature's name, I pondered ways to beat it.

Crezil.

To know it's name almost put a face on it. I imagined Gahoreth, the hell it called home. In Liiria we had no hell. We had only the Fate, and I didn't believe in it. Minikin and the Inhumans had cured me of that fairy tale, showing me a world beyond our own, beyond death even, and when she died Malator had taken up my tutoring. But still, it all befuddled me. Every new bit of knowledge called into question the bits I'd learned before.

I pulled my water skin from Zephyr's side, opened it with my teeth and took a drink. Behind me Cricket started talking to herself, realizing at last that I wasn't listening. The bruise on her head had turned a dullish blue, and whatever her fall had knocked loose in her skull was still rattling around in there. She might have been on the brink of a breakthrough or an utter collapse; I could no longer tell the difference. All I wanted was to get to Isowon.

We rode on past noon, past the time when Fallon took his midday meal naked by the pool. I looked up at the sun and thought about the last time I'd seen him, balled up like a baby and sniffing that awful smelling spice. For a moment I regretted returning, until I thought of Isowon. Glorious Isowon was a company town; Fallon built it and owned every stick of it, but its people were innocent. I couldn't abide their slaughter.

"Cricket?"

She snapped out of her daze. "Yeah?"

"My father smoked a pipe."

"Huh?"

"My father. You're always asking about my past. He smoked a pipe made of black bronze. Heavy goddamn thing."

She rode up beside me with a wondering smile. "Oh, yeah?"

"These are the kind of things you remember. Sometimes I can't even picture his face. I try and try, but I can't. I have to sneak up on the memory. But that pipe . . . that's what I remember. Him lighting it, puffing on it. That smell, like old leather. He used to blow the smoke into my eyes."

"Why'd he do that?"

"Because he was a bastard. Some people are born bastards. And their children become bastards. They can't help it. It's just what happens." I looked at her and felt like crying. "You get me?"

Cricket took my words to heart, thinking on them. She said, "People can change. That's what I believe."

"That's what young people believe. That's what gives them hope." I looked ahead of us, desperate to see Isowon. "It's changing other people that's hard."

An hour later we were finally in Isowon, riding through the city's tree-lined streets. I'd expected to be greeted by soldiers and to see the citizens and merchants out in the sunshine, but instead the streets were deserted. I peered into the homes and saw boarded-up windows and chains on the doors, as if the townsfolk already knew Diriel's army was coming. Except for the distant churn of the ocean and the stray notes of songbirds, all was a hush. Cricket rode out ahead of me, swiveling her head around at all the locked shops and houses. Fountains still spouted along the avenues, but no children gathered to watch them. Cricket reached into a tree and plucked off a fruit. Never having seen the fruit before, I warned her not to eat it.

"Not gonna," she said, then tossed it hard at the nearest home, squarely hitting the door. A rustle came from inside the house, then a shadow at the window. Someone peered out from a slit in the boards.

"Hey," shouted Cricket, "where is everyone? Why you all hiding?"

There was a long, unmoving silence. Then, "Get off the street," warned a voice. "Get to the palace if you're soldiers."

"Why?" I called back. I trotted to the edge of the road. "What happened?"

"Are you stupid? The monster! Now go! I don't want to talk!"

The shadow left the window. I glanced around the street, but saw no sign of the monster, or even an attack. I could feel eyes watching us from the buildings, but no one echoed the man's warning. I wheeled Zephyr about.

"The palace."

Cricket was already ahead of me, racing her pony over the cobblestones. I tucked in after her, studying the towers Fallon had built around his home. As we drew nearer I noticed them crowded with soldiers. A contingent milled inside the gate, coming to life as they heard us. They signaled our approach, but not a single bowman tilted toward us. I heard my name above the din, then a cry to let us enter. The shocked faces of the soldiers greeted us as we stopped to let the giant gates swing wide.

"Lukien!" cried a man who took my horse. Another grabbed my hand. Cricket jostled her pony through the swarm. Not only soldiers crammed the palace but townsfolk and their children, too.

"What's happening?" I asked. I looked around for a friendly face, but they were all strangers to me. "Where's Marilius?"

A one-handed man with a dented helmet pushed toward me through the crowd. "You're back too late! It's done and over!"

"What is?"

"You had hours! You come *now*?"

I dismounted, jumping down in front of him. "Was it the monster?"

"Yes! *Your* monster, Liirian. The one you were supposed to kill!"

"Mine?" I pushed the man so hard he tumbled. "Where's Marilius? Someone bloody tell me!"

The noise stopped, and all their ghastly faces stared at me. Cricket got down from her pony to stand beside me.

"What's wrong with you all?" I shouted. "You're all struck stupid suddenly?"

"Lukien."

A man came toward us from the edge of the yard. It took a moment for me to realize it was Marilius. He was almost staggering, favoring a bandaged leg and supporting himself with a homemade cane. Blood spattered his arms and cape, even his face. The breath he took rattled from his lungs. Cricket raced to help him.

"Marilius!" She wrapped herself around his arm. "What happened?"

"Last night," said Marilius. He could barely catch his breath. "In the hall."

"Fallon?" I asked.

"Alive."

I couldn't tell if he was relieved or disgusted. He let Cricket help him back toward the palace entrance, wincing with every step. "It was almost dawn by the time it came. Half of us were asleep. The gate, the towers . . . bloody useless. No one even saw it until it was near the hall."

"What'd it look like, Marilius?"

Marilius shook his head. "I can't even describe it. Like a sack of old skins. Animals, people . . . it wasn't bones this time. Just skins, like it was wearing them."

"Mother-whore. But it didn't reach Fallon?"

"A damn miracle," said Marilius. "The men tossed themselves at it. We couldn't get out of the hall. We were trapped. You need to see for yourself."

We walked into the palace, past all the shocked soldiers and shopkeepers and confused little kids, deep into the wing where I'd last seen Fallon. Another group of soldiers stood guard just outside the great hall. Marilius waved them away. The noise of the crowds dropped off behind us as we rounded the corner and the hall echoed before us. Sunlight gushed in from the towering windows, touching the golden pillars and alabaster tiles and human wreckage.

Cricket gasped.

"Oh, Fate . . ." I stepped around to block her way. "Marilius, take her out of here."

Cricket pushed me off. "No!"

"I don't want you here," I said, but it was too late anyway. She'd already seen it.

The hall looked like a battlefield, the kind I'd seen a hundred times. Dozens of corpses spread out along the floor, some with horror-stricken faces, others with their heads caved in. Men with sliced bellies and missing limbs lay atop each other, oozing stomach juices across the polished tiles. Blood trickled down the walls and dripped from the ceiling. A pair of arms hung from a chandelier, the dead fingers still clutching the wrought iron. A shattered fountain in the center of the hall spread water and dead goldfish over the tiles. Every gentle statue had been toppled. Down at my feet an eyeball sloshed. I kicked it aside before Cricket could see it.

It was an image of hell, worse than the painting of Gahoreth. Next to me, Marilius made a whimpering noise. Amazingly, Cricket found the guts to put her arm around him. She didn't even look away.

Guts, I thought proudly.

"They didn't break," said Marilius. "They stayed. All the way until the sun came up."

"What happened to it, Marilius?" I asked. I'd hoped to see the monster laying dead among the mercenaries. "Did you wound it at least? How'd you drive it off?"

Marilius pointed to the giant windows. "The sun drove it off, not us. Once the light came it ran."

"Ran? Where?"

"How should I know? We didn't go after it! Fuck, Lukien, look around! It's unstoppable!"

"But it stopped," I mused. I looked back down the hall. No one had tried to keep it from escaping. I turned to see the other end of the hall where Fallon's private chamber waited. The door was open, but I was sure it had been locked up tight last night. "So you were trapped in here, guarding *him*. Is he in there?"

"He won't come out," said Marilius. "I can't even get him to talk to me."

"He has to talk," I said. "Now."

I trekked straight through the hall, over the pools of blood and stinking entrails, heading for Fallon. Marilius called at me to stop.

"Forget it," I snapped. "He's got more troubles then he knows."

I reached the chamber and peered inside. The room was just the same as I'd left it days ago. Only now Fallon looked worse. He'd obviously sniffed up all his purple spice, because only the residue of it stained the table. Fallon had his head down and his arms spread out across the tabletop. I thought he was asleep until he turned his bloodshot eyes to face me. He'd been weeping. Trails of dried tears streaked his dirty face. I pictured him cowering in his sanctuary while his men were ripped to shreds just beyond the door. Surprisingly, I pitied him.

"You came back," he whispered. He smiled without a trace of joy. "What does it want, Lukien? Why won't it leave me alone?"

"I'm not sure yet," I said.

"Did you go to Diriel?"

I nodded. "Yeah."

"I was right about him, wasn't I?"

"You were right," I admitted. "All of Akyre's an asylum." Cricket and Marilius finally came up behind me in the threshold. I stepped into Fallon's sanctuary. "He's coming after you, Anton," I said. "He's got an army. The Legion of the Lost. He gave us seven days to make ready. That was three days ago."

Fallon didn't bother lifting his cheek off the dirty table. "I don't have his money."

"He knows that," I said. "It's not the money he wants. It's you. And he wants the monster. He thinks I can get it for him. I told him I would, to buy some time. You need to get ready, get your men ready."

Marilius asked, "Lukien, are you bloody blind? We can't fight an army!"

"You are an army!" I shouted back. "You're soldiers. It's time to fight—men this time, not monsters."

"Men that *are* monsters, you mean," said Marilius. "You saw them yourself. They're not human anymore."

"They can be killed, and we're going to kill them," I argued. "So they have no souls, so what? They have bodies and bodies can die."

"It's hopeless," groaned Fallon. "We can't fight them. We don't have enough men."

I went and stooped down to face him. "Anton, listen to me. Diriel doesn't have a regular army, not the way a country does. They're a mismatched group of soldiers and sheep herders, and not all of them have used the mummia. His country's a wasteland. He can't even feed an army. They get one shot at this. We drive them back, and they're finished."

Fallon managed to lift himself up. "A hundred men are dead out there," he said as he pointed to the hall. "Can't you smell that? That blood? Maybe more than a hundred. I can't even tell because they're in pieces!"

"Find more men, then. Buy them, bribe them—do whatever you have to but get them here. Get them here now."

"How can I pay for them? I told you, Lukien—I'm finished! I can't even pay back Diriel."

"No one's going to come here now anyway, no matter how much he pays them," said Marilius. "Not after what happened. Even the men we have won't stay. Many have left and others are talking about it."

"What about Drin?" asked Cricket.

We all blinked at her innocent question. "Drin?" I asked.

"They're fighting Diriel too, right? That's what I keep hearing. Maybe they can help."

"But I can't pay them!" roared Fallon.

"No, no, she's right," I said. "What about that, Marilius? The Drin are fighting, right? What if they came here to join us? This is their last chance—if Isowon falls they're finished. They must know that."

Marilius thought about it. "I don't know," he shrugged. "Maybe."

"How many men do they have? Are they a big army?"

"No, they can't be," said Marilius. "Some of the other mercenaries come from Drin, but it's a small country. There's been some fighting, I know that. But Diriel was after Kasse."

"Yes, Kasse first," I said. "But Diriel's not going to stop. The Drin are on his supper plate, too. If we can bring them here, get them to listen—"

"Hey," barked Fallon, banging on the table. "Are you forgetting something? The monster? I told you, we can't fight with that thing on top of us!"

"He's right," said Marilius. "How can we build a defense? We can't even leave the palace."

"Marilius, bring the men into the hall," I said. "As many as you can. I want to talk to them."

"Why?"

"Because they need to hear me. Go. Get them into the hall. I want them to take a good look at what happened to their friends."

Marilius shook his head as he shuffled out of the chamber. Fallon looked confused.

"Anton, stand up," I said.

"Are you going to hit me?"

I grabbed his arm and pulled him to his feet. "You're filthy," I said, smoothing down his shirt. "Wipe your face. You look like you've had your head in a bucket of mud. Cricket, can you do something with his hair?"

"Huh?"

"Use your fingers or something. Try to make him look presentable."

"What is this?" Fallon complained.

"Your men aren't going to follow you unless they believe in you. They may be mercenaries but they're soldiers too, and soldiers won't respect a man who doesn't respect himself. I'm going to talk to them, but you're the one they're going to see."

Cricket went to work, reaching up and combing his tangled hair with her fingers. "What are you going to say, Lukien?"

"You'll see. Bring him into the hall when he's ready."

I left them behind in the shabby little room, stepping back out into the desecrated hall. Marilius rounded the corner with a couple dozen men behind him and more on the way. I climbed onto the remains of the broken fountain so everyone could see. The mercenaries muttered and pointed, still shocked by the horrors in the hall. Some bent to touch their fallen friends. I saw Cricket and Fallon appear and waved them closer. Fallon looked about to faint. Marilius stepped forward, leaning painfully on his cane. I heard the hope in his voice. "We're listening, Lukien."

"Then listen well," I said loudly. "And look around. Look at your dead companions! Because this whole town is going to wind up like this if you turn tail and run. There's an army coming. In a few days it'll be here. You all know what I'm talking about. Diriel's legion isn't a myth. I've seen it. You think you've seen death? You're all hard men? You think you've seen rape? You haven't seen shit. All of Isowon is going to look like this hall—unless we stop them."

"How?" cried one of the men. He pushed past Marilius, almost knocking him over. "You got one good eye—*you* look around! Why should we end up slaughtered? Not me! I'm going."

He snorted as he spun on his heels. A few of his comrades did the same.

"You leave, and I'll kill you," I said.

The man stopped dead. "Eh?"

"You think I'm joking?" I pulled out the Sword of Angels and jumped down from the fountain. "Any man who walks out of this hall before I have my say gets a blade though his belly. You want to cut and run after I'm through with you, go ahead. But know this: Diriel's not going to stop. After Isowon it'll be Drin. And after Drin he'll be on the march to your towns. I saw it in his eyes. Now, I know none of you are cowards. If you were, you would have left already. We've got a chance to stop Diriel right here, right now. This is the only chance—there won't be another."

"Lukien, what about the monster?" asked Marilius. "We can't kill it."

"That's right you can't," I said. "You can't kill it, because I'm going to kill it."

"What?" Cricket blurted. "You're not!"

I tried to ignore her. "Marilius, take some men and ride for Drin. Tell them this is where to make their stand. Tell them to get here as fast as possible. There'll be food and water waiting for them when they get here. We need everyone, not just a token. You ride and tell them that."

Cricket clawed my shirt. "Damn you, Lukien, no! If you go after that thing it'll kill you! For sure this time!"

"What if they won't listen?" asked Marilius.

"How am I going to pay for this?" shrieked Fallon.

"Beg them, threaten them, anything you have to do," I told Marilius. "Just get them here, all right? You *have* to, Marilius. The rest of you," I climbed back onto the broken fountain, "listen to me—you'll be safe from the monster. It's not coming back. I'll see to that."

"Why should we stay?" asked another man. He was a big fellow, a Norvan from the cut of his cape, the skin on his face carved up from battle. "What are you going to pay us with?"

"You'll be paid," I promised. "You'll get paid double for staying and seeing this through."

"What?" Fallon screeched. "How can I afford that? I told you, I'm broke!"

"You want your trade routes open again?" I asked. "Then you'll pay these men double for saving you. Otherwise you won't just be out of business, Fallon, you'll be dead."

"Lukien . . ." Cricket's brooding face caught me through all the noise. She couldn't finish speaking. Around us the room erupted in arguments. Fallon was still screaming at me. Cricket shook her head and turned away.

"Cricket, wait."

"I'm not listening," she said. "You've been lying to me all this time. You promised to take me to Sky Falls. You promised to help me."

"I will, Cricket, I will!" I grabbed her arm to keep her from leaving the hall. "But I can't do anything yet. Not until I beat this monster. Who else can do it? Only I can kill it. I have to!"

"Why?"

"Because it will kill you if I don't!"

"It won't!" she railed. "You'll protect me! Just stay here with me, please!"

"Cricket, no!" Though I knew I would bungle it, I tried to explain. "I saw Crezil when we were still in Jador. Malator drew a picture of it in the sand. And when my neck was broken I saw it again. Malator told me not to bring you here. He warned me! I have to kill this thing before it can hurt you, Cricket. I have to go. Now!"

My artless explanation stunned her. A face as young as hers should never show so much contempt. "This whole time?" She shook her head, disgusted. "Go, then. Go and get yourself killed. I'm not gonna help you anymore. I'm not gonna be your squire."

She stormed away before I could catch her, weaving through the mercenaries and the dead until all I saw was her rass skin cape disappearing in the crowd. Marilius almost went after her, but I stopped him.

"Let her go," I told him. "There's no time. Marilius, you need to leave for Drin."

Marilius nodded. "I'll go, but I'm not sure they'll listen."

"Make them listen," I urged. "Bring them here no matter what."

"What about Cricket?" he asked.

I looked into the crowd. Cricket was already long gone.

"There's nowhere for her to go," I said. "She just needs to cool off."

I was sure I was right—Cricket just needed time. That's what I convinced myself to believe.

22

For hundreds of miles I'd ridden with a companion at my side. Now, I was alone again.

There'd been no time to argue with Cricket. She'd made her feelings plain, and there were too many places for her to hide in Fallon's palace for me to go chasing her. She was young and a girl, and now that I was alone I realized the folly of making her my squire. After all, she was at that *age*. Argumentative. Bullheaded. I was pretty sure a boy would have been no better. Even if Cricket was a boy, I wouldn't have taken her with me to hunt the monster this time, not after what I'd seen in the hall. I was sure she'd be better when I returned.

If I returned.

I was immortal, or very nearly so, but I knew the monster could best me. To die—and to stay dead—didn't frighten me. Cassandra was waiting for me on the other side. But the thought of being bested gnawed at me, and I was anxious to find the beast before nightfall.

I wasn't a tracker, though. I was a city boy, born and bred, and though I'd spent my share of time outdoors, it was mostly on battlefields. Hunting had never come easy to me, even when tracking rass, and having one eye didn't help. If I were tracking a bear I might have looked for its den. Or water. Or scat, even. But the creature I was pursuing didn't even belong in this world. I needed something else to track.

*   *   *

I stopped at the edge of a field, near a ridge of fig trees leading to a canyon. Tall mountains surrounded me. I'd left the palace behind more than two hours ago, and just when I'd thought the trail was cold I saw a scrap of flesh hanging from the tine of a branch. It almost looked like a misshaped fig, but when I reached for it I realized the ghastly fruit was a human ear.

"Fate Almighty."

A trail of blood and body parts had brought me this far. I didn't need both eyes to follow it. From the pools in the Great Hall to the puddles in the courtyard, the remnants of Crezil's victims had fallen like rain. At first it was impossible to go even a few yards without seeing a smear of blood or tattered bit of flesh. But as the hours went by and the landscape changed, the clues became fewer. I touched the branch where the ear dangled and bent it toward me. The ear hadn't been chewed, just ripped off its owner's face. I looked down at the ground, saw a few drops of blood, then inspected the rest of the tree. Snapped branches told me which way the thing had gone.

I studied the canyon. A grassy valley cut through it like a ribbon, dotted with buttercups and shadowed by the mountains. The creature hated sunlight, but I still didn't know why. I wondered if there were caves in the canyon, or if the beast was still plodding toward its lair. Did it know I was after it? Would it even care?

"Malator."

At first he ignored me. I felt him inside me and yet also far away, moving grudgingly as I called his name. We hadn't spoken since the tomb.

"Malator!"

His sigh was petulant. *What?*

"Do you sense it?"

He took his time answering. *Yes.*

"So it's near?" I looked ahead. "In the canyon?"

Yes.

"Great. How long were you going to wait to tell me?"

Until you asked me. You told me not to bother you any more, Lukien. You were very clear on that.

"What do you want me to say? That I need your help? Obviously, I do. Not just to fight it, but to find it."

Are you worried I'll let you die?

"Actually, yes."

He laughed inside my head. *It could happen!*

"Are you going to help me, damn it?"

You know I will. I have plans for you, Lukien.

"Fuck your games," I hissed. I grew anxious as we trotted into the canyon. The grass and buttercups rose up around Zephyr's legs, moving in the breeze. I looked up into the craggy mountains, spying nesting birds, but no monster. "Where is it?"

It's here. Ahead a little. Malator focused his concentration. *It's watching you.*

That unnerved me. "If I can't surprise it," I whispered, "I won't bother trying."

With a jab of my heels I galloped deeper into the valley, jangling in my bronze armor and sending birds flying from the grass. Finally I spun my horse to a stop and pulled out the Sword of Angels.

"Demon!" I cried, raising high the sword. "I am Lukien! Come out!"

How did one call a demon? I looked around the mountains, listened for its approach. The remnants of my cry echoed off the rocks.

"Where is it, Malator?" I demanded. He answered in a calm, almost fatherly voice.

Turn around.

When I spun back it was there, waiting in the flowers, blocking the way I'd come. Twelve feet tall, a mismatch of skins, it had changed from the last time when it was all just bones. Now it covered itself in the flesh of its victims, animating their torn-off limbs and wearing their scalps like hats. It stood hunched on three legs, each a different size and color, all of them bloodied and knit together. It had no head of its own, just the blinking eyes of its prey, and I could not tell if it used them to see or just to frighten me. Mouths moved in silent screams. The blonde hair of a woman sprouted from its back. Five arms erupted from its torso, two of them armored and three of them naked. I looked for a face, a thing that was its own, but saw nothing real among the borrowed parts.

When it was bones it was monstrous. Now it was a horror, all the gore and viscera I'd seen in the hall brought to grisly life. Zephyr roiled beneath me. I fought to keep him steady. The creature moved closer, out of the shadows until the sun struck its body. I half expected the light to burn it, but the sun had no effect at all. It had no weapons, no horns or thorns or sharpened nails. Yet somehow it had shredded Anton's men.

"Malator," I asked. "How do I beat this brute?"

Run.

"Stop joking and help me!"

Why haven't you figured this out yet? It's a creature from the realm of the dead. It's here for something, and it won't leave until it gets what it wants.

To me that sounded like a coward's answer. "I won't let it take Anton," I said.

Then fight it.

"Help me kill it!"

I'll help you. But we can't kill it.

"You know something Malator?" I snorted. "You're useless."

At that moment I counted more on my horse than I did my Akari. I patted Zephyr's neck, then trotted slowly toward the monster. Its many eyes turned to watch me and the purple lips along its body parted, showing human teeth. Bloody fingers twitched on its stolen hands. Somewhere beneath its quivering flesh hid the real demon, or at least I supposed so. If I could pierce it, if it had a heart or brain or any real substance of its own, I could kill it. I brought my horse to a stop about twenty feet from it and held out my weapon.

"This is the Sword of Angels," I declared. "The sword of the Akari, Malator. The sword that slayed the demon Kahldris. *My* sword, monster. The sword that's going to kill you."

The monster's five arms punched at the air and the mouths opened in soundless screams. Its biggest, tree-trunk leg pounded the ground. I reared back in surprise.

"You hear me? Can you understand me . . . *Crezil*?"

The creature stopped moving. The dead eyes blinked.

"Crezil," I repeated. "That's your name?"

I got no answer except the telling silence.

"All right," I said. "I know what you are. Kasdeyi Orioc. The Guardian-Slave. You're from Gahoreth. You don't belong here. What is it? You want Fallon?" I pointed to my forehead. "The man with the tattoo. Is that your mark?"

Maybe it was thinking. I glanced past it, toward the entrance to the valley and up into the hills. I saw an outcropping of rock in the shadows that reminded me of a cave. Where was the monster under all those skins?

"You're hiding," I realized. "Why?" I groped for reasons. "You're not afraid of the sun. You're afraid of the *light*. Malator, could that be it?" I didn't give him time to answer. "Crezil," I said, "are you afraid?"

The monster—Crezil—backed away. It wasn't much, hardly a full step. But I knew now it understood me.

"You want to go home," I guessed. "Then go. Go back to Gahoreth. I give you leave." Now it was my turn to step back. I circled Zephyr back a length, then watched for the thing's reaction. "Go," I ordered. "We can end our quarrel here."

For a long moment the demon didn't move. Then it raised one of its dead hands and marked one of its dead foreheads, just the way it had seen me do. I understood immediately.

"No," I said. "That man you marked is a bastard and a cheat, but even he doesn't deserve what you've got planned. You leave with one life today—your own."

Crezil took a step forward. Zephyr bucked.

"No!" I insisted. "You're done feasting on humans, demon. No more."

It won't yield, Lukien, said Malator. *It wants Fallon. It won't leave without him.*

"Why?" I yelled to it. "Why Fallon? For waking you? For vengeance? You've punished him enough." I raised my sword just high enough to threaten. "If you make me champion him I will."

Part of me hoped Crezil would turn and slither away. But another part of me—the very part that drove me here—wanted this fight. Cricket had always been right about me. So had Gilwyn and Malator. I needed to prove myself or die trying. Just then I remembered the pledge I'd made to Gilwyn, to return in time for the birth of his baby. As Crezil rushed toward me, I wasn't sure I'd keep that promise.

It came like a bull, charging on its three legs, ridiculously fast. I jerked Zephyr away from its five flailing arms. All along its body the mouths opened wide, the hands became claws, the muscles ripened with blood. I had no new weapon, no new strategy to try. All I had different this time was experience, and as I aimed for Crezil I braced myself for the shock.

"Malator!"

The monster charged, my horse twirled, and the Sword of Angels whistled through the air. This time I caught one of the arms, slicing it off. I raced past Crezil, saw the stump of the arm I'd severed, and couldn't believe I was still on horseback. There was no surge of pain, no burning heat to shock me unconscious. I spun around for another go.

"Malator . . . how?"

That wasn't Crezil, he explained. *Just flesh.*

I steeled myself. To kill Crezil, I'd have to find it under all that skin. The monster came again, unconcerned by its stump, not even bleeding. It turned one of its heads sideways and lashed a bloated tongue at me.

"Then I'll cut them all off!" I swore. "And peel it like an orange."

Crezil readied itself but didn't charge. Its remaining arms stretched and writhed. The nails of its many hands enlarged, curling out of its fingertips into crusty claws. I had to avoid them, keep my distance I decided. One by one I'd sever them all. A flood of strength filled me as Malator gave me his magic. I cocked the sword, picked a limb, and charged again.

Spittle flew from my horse as I spurred it forward. The monster's putrid eyes watched me. I steered for its flank, threw my shoulder toward it, and swung my sword. I caught another arm, easily slicing it, thrilling as the appendage twisted skyward. But Crezil moved fast, immune to pain, and with three more arms took hold of Zephyr and pulled him out from under me. I went headlong over my mount, flying out over the grass and crashing to the ground. As I shook my rattled head, I watched Crezil lift my braying Zephyr by his hind legs and fling him over its body, smashing him and killing him against the rocks. His neck snapped, his chest collapsed. The whole big, beautiful creature just popped like a balloon.

"Bitch!" I screamed. I staggered to my feet. "That was a horse! My horse!" Rage gushed out of me. "That was a beautiful animal! Innocent! Oh, Malator . . . let me kill this bloody beast!"

I'd tried to talk, but damn it all . . . Crezil needed to die, and I wanted to be the one. I forgot about pain and fear and promises. I dove for Crezil like a madman. With my sword held like a dagger I went for its heart, to stab it, to kill it and piss on its corpse. The thing was like a mountain, though, and when I jumped, Crezil didn't move. I screamed and plunged the sword. It pierced a searching eye, going deep, popping it, spewing on me, but I held on. An arm grabbed me, wrapped me, but I pushed on that sword until I felt the hellish heart of the thing beating.

And then, like before, my insides fried. The most intense burning sizzled up my arms and deep into my bowels. Not like fire, though. I could have plunged my face into a fire and not felt nearly such pain. This was *hellfire.*

"Malator!"

I screamed like a child. It must have startled Crezil because it let me go, pitching me aside. I rolled through the air and landed on my back, and for a moment couldn't breathe at all. Everything inside me seized. An inferno seared my brains. I tried to raise myself, then realized the sword was gone. When I lifted my head I saw the blade, still stuck inside Crezil's oozing eye.

Slowly the pain began to ebb. I mustered myself, getting up on my elbows. Crezil stalked toward me, blocking out the sun. Somehow, it pushed the sword out of its body, letting it clang to the ground beside me. I reached for it, gasping, wrapping my fingers around its solace. Then I looked up at Crezil and smelled its rotting flesh.

I was pinned, but I had the sword, and I took every bit of strength it gave me. "Kill me," I rasped. "You'll have to. I'm not giving up. I'll keep coming after you unless you kill me now."

I felt the heat rising off its bloody skins. It brought up its arms, making fists of the hands and swelling them like hammers. I closed my eye and waited.

When it hit my leg I shrieked. My *leg*! I opened my eye, wailing, and saw in amazement Crezil leaving, galloping away through the valley, using all its remaining limbs to propel it through the grass. My leg was shattered. I couldn't even crawl.

"Whore! Come back here!" I swore, clutching at both the sword and my thigh. "You come back here and finish me!"

Malator was already at work. *Stop moving!*

The armor around my leg was crushed, and I knew the bone beneath it was, too. The healing magic flooded through me. I closed my eye against the pain.

"It's gone," I gasped. "It got away."

Malator didn't bother answering me. He had his hands full—again. I laid back in the grass and looked up into the sky. I remembering thinking what a beautiful day it was.

I guess I passed out, because when I opened my eye again the pain was almost gone. The sword remained within my grip. A stormy looking cloud obscured the sun. I didn't know how long I'd been there and I didn't much care. Crezil was gone. Worse, we were both still alive. Malator floated just above my thoughts. I could feel him reading them. I felt his pity.

"Why'd it spare me?" I asked. The cloud above me was so big I wanted to reach up and grab it. If it rained on me, maybe I would drown.

Your leg—it's almost healed, said Malator. *You'll be all right, Lukien.*

"Of course I will. That's the curse. Why'd it spare me, Malator? Why didn't it kill me? You know the answer. I can feel it."

Malator tried to sound comforting. *The creature takes souls,* he said.

I pondered that. "Yes." I nodded. Maybe I was too afraid to figure it out. "So?"

Your soul is spoken for, Lukien.

"Spoken . . . ? Huh?"

You have me. I keep you alive in this world. The creature saw no soul in you to take.

I began to panic. "Malator . . . where is my soul?"

Gone, Lukien. It's been gone since Gilwyn gave you the amulet to keep you alive. It's been gone since the day you died.

23

The rain began falling just after I left the canyon.

It had taken me two hours to reach the canyon on horseback. Without a mount, I knew I wouldn't make Isowon before nightfall. I'd waited as long as I could for Malator to knit my fractured femur together, until it was strong enough for me to use. At first I was wobbly, still dazed over Zephyr and the news of my vanished soul. I even briefly considered continuing my hunt for Crezil. A stupid idea, since it would have taken days to reach its lair on foot. I'd have to return to the palace, I knew, and face Anton's mercenaries. Once again, I'd have to tell them how I'd failed.

The rain only added to my misery, falling in fat drops from the clouds that appeared from nowhere. By then the horizon was filled with them, threatening a long, muddy slog home. A cool breeze struck me as I emerged from the canyon. I shivered in my battered armor. Crezil had crushed the bronze cuisse along my thigh I doubted even a blacksmith could fix it. Rain water soaked my eye patch, making the empty socket beneath it itch. In my lungs I could still feel the touch of Crezil's fire, like a bad sunburn when I breathed. But I just kept walking, mindless, barely aware of my surroundings. Half a mile later, I paused in the middle of a field. I looked up, saw a flash of lightning, and couldn't stop the question screaming from my lips.

"Where is it!"

A rumble of thunder was my only reply. Even Malator was silent.

"It can't be gone," I cried. "That's impossible!" I pounded my breastplate. "I have a soul! I feel it. How can I be alive without one?"

My knees weakened, and I slumped to the dirt. But I kept my face skyward, hoping that heaven was up there, hiding my soul from me.

"What am I? Without a soul, am I alive? Dead? Someone tell me!"

You're alive, Lukien. Weep for your soul but have no doubt about your life.

"I doubt!" I screamed. I raked my hands across my cheeks just to feel the blood. "I'm flesh alone!"

Living flesh! Alive!

"You've taken my soul, made me a puppet! Damn you, Malator. Damn all you Akari!"

I staggered up again, took a step or two, and tripped over my feet. My face hit the mud. Then I started laughing. "I should have known I didn't have one! No man with a soul could do the things I've done!"

My laugh was demented, the worst kind of self pity. I rolled onto my back and imagined spitting in Malator's face. I felt him inside me, right next to me, like he was putting an arm around my shoulder.

"Let go of me," I seethed. "Your touch makes me sick."

He held on to me with his invisible arm. His voice spoke gently to me. *A soul is not all there is to being alive, Lukien. It is only half.*

"The important half!"

No. Just the immortal half. It is the soul that keeps a person alive. When you died fighting Trager, you lost yours. Amaraz kept you alive. Then it was my turn.

Amaraz. The great Akari god. He was Gilwyn's protector now. But the Eye had been mine first, before I ever passed the curse of immortality to Gilwyn.

"Does Gilwyn have a soul?" I wondered.

Gilwyn never died. You gave him the Eye of God before his soul fled. Trager killed you when you fought him. The Eye brought you back just in time. Too late for your soul, though. Do you remember when White-Eye lost her Akari?

I nodded. I wasn't in Jador when that happened but knew the story well.

That's how it was with your soul. White-Eye's Akari vanished forever.

Even souls can die, Lukien. They disappear. Yours is gone. It can never come back.

"What if I die? Here in this world, I mean? Will I be gone forever?"

Yes.

I sighed. "Then I can never be with Cassandra. All that time spent hoping to die . . . just a waste of time. Why didn't you ever tell me that, Malator? How dare you keep such secrets?"

Because you don't trust me, Lukien.

"No, don't do that! Don't make this my fault!"

When we left Jador I told you I would be the only friend you need, and that you were meant for something special. All I've asked for in return is your trust, yet you won't give it to me.

"I want my soul back."

It is gone. Mourn for it if you must, but do not expect to get it back.

The rain pelted my face. All I could think of was Cassandra. Death had always been my great release. I could die in battle or just walk away from Malator and his accursed sword and then be with Cassandra. No more, though. I wasn't just mortal now, I was something less than alive. Like one of Diriel's dead men.

"I was wrong when I called you a slave, Malator," I said. "I'm the slave. *Your* slave."

Lukien . . .

"First it was Amaraz, now you. The Akari—"

Hush! Someone's coming.

I didn't know if I should roll over or just lie there. Finally I whispered, "Where?"

Across the field, from the north. Five riders.

From the north. I twirled like a crocodile onto my belly. The weeds and rain obscured me, I hoped, enough for me to chance lifting my head. Across the field I saw them, five like Malator said, four of them dressed in soldiering clothes. They rode at an angle to my hiding spot, trotting closer on their miserable horses. I parted the grass with my hands for a better look. The dark uniforms made them easy to recognize.

"Akyrens."

They came a bit closer. Now I could see the man in front. A giant, burly man with a bald head and unmistakable face. My stomach clenched.

Wrestler.

Already he was hunting us. Hunting Cricket, more precisely. My whole body tensed.

Don't, warned Malator.

"That's Wrestler!"

They don't see you. Let them go.

"I can kill them."

You can't. You're weak. Shut up and get down.

I knew he was right, but I didn't lower my head. I just stared at Wrestler through the grass, sizing him up. Maybe the others would kill me, but I'd get to Wrestler first. I'd cut off his conceited head before they even saw me. They came closer, their only purpose to escape the rain. One of the group pointed to the canyon, seeking shelter I supposed. Wrestler shook his head and kept right on riding. He looked enormous, a black cloak around him, the kind an abbot might wear. His horse was enormous too, an ugly, snorting stallion with an arrogant gait.

How I wanted to kill him!

There'll be another time, Lukien. You'll get your chance.

I had my hand so tight around the sword my knuckles hurt. "Promise me that," I whispered. "Just once, look into the future for me. Promise me I'll get the chance to kill him."

You will. I swear it.

His answer was so sure, so swift, I had to believe him. Gradually I lowered my head, hiding myself in the grass. I didn't look up at all as I heard them approach. The hoof beats of their horses echoed through the ground. My heart thumped louder and louder as they neared. I listened, waited, even hoping a little that they'd find me. And then . . .

They passed. I hesitated a moment before sneaking a glance, and saw the backsides of their horses. The breath leeched out of me as I watched Wrestler ride away.

"Malator," I said. "I'm going to hold you to that promise."

Let them move off a bit, he replied. *We've got a long walk ahead of us.*

The journey back to Isowon took the rest of the afternoon and a good part of the evening. I had no food, but plenty of rain water to drink, and took the strength I needed from Malator to go without stopping. My recently broken leg wasn't a problem at all. If anything, it seemed to strengthen as I walked, propelling me easily across the miles of dirt roads and open fields. I kept my eye on the horizon, looking for any sign of Wrestler and his scouts, but they did not appear again. Crezil, I supposed, was gone as well, back to its lair in the Akyren tombs. Except for Malator, I was all alone, and the Akari did nothing to interrupt my thoughts. By the time I reached the outskirts of Isowon I was beyond famished. Food was suddenly foremost on my mind.

I headed straight for the palace. By now it was well past the supper hour. The streets were dark, and as empty as they were that morning when I'd arrived with Cricket. I glanced at the locked homes and shops, saw a few candles burning in the windows, but no one offered me a greeting, much less a scrap of food. The rain had slackened to a drizzle and puddles ran through the spotless streets. I reached the palace, going through all the nonsense I'd endured twice before. This time, though, the mercenaries recognized me. To my surprise, the gates were already open. There were fewer men, too, and an uncomfortable chaos in the air. Obviously, they were all still reeling from the slaughter the night before. As I stomped through the courtyard, a group of mercenaries swarmed around me, asking about the monster.

"Did you find it?" one asked.

"Did you kill it?" asked another.

"What happened to your horse?"

I waved off all their questions, demanding to know where Fallon was. None of them knew, but once inside the palace I found Adela, the servant who'd looked after me and Cricket our first night in the palace. She was carrying a bucket of bloody water and her pretty hands were covered in grime. Her face looked sallow, haunted. I realized at once that she'd been cleaning the great hall—and the remnants of the morning's massacre. She looked surprised to see me. She stood there with her bucket, blinking and vacant. When I asked where I could find Fallon, she gestured down the hall with her chin.

"By his pool," she said. She thought for a moment, then added, "Isn't that absurd?"

No one could see the things she'd seen and not be shocked by them. "Yes," I told her. "It's all absurd."

She glanced into her bucket. A finger floated atop the dirty water. She stared at it.

"Lukien, did you kill it?"

"No," I said softly. "But I will."

Adela nodded. "You have to kill it, all right? I won't be able to live if you don't kill it."

That seemed like such an apt thing to say. The kind of thing I felt, too.

"I have to get back now," said Adela.

I wanted to take the bucket from her, to pluck out the offending finger and help her forget the things she'd seen. Instead I let her go. She shuffled off with the heavy bucket, sloshing water over the sides, and I turned and went the other way. The chamber with the pool was on the other side of the palace, but no one challenged me as I hurried through the hallways. When I arrived the doors were already partly open, waiting for me. Moonlight flooded in, lighting the pool. I could smell the surf of the ocean. There at the table sat Fallon, pouring himself tea from a silver urn. He wore a robe of emerald silk, and his hair was slicked back on his head, wet from one of his extravagant baths. Servants stood off to the side. Between me and Fallon stood a phalanx of mercenaries.

"Fallon," I called, pushing past the doors. "Back to normal for you, I see."

He seemed frightened to see me. And the wall of soldiers didn't part as I'd expected.

"Let him in," said Fallon. He stirred his tea with a dainty spoon. I knew I was in for bad news, but the table was cramped with food and wine, and I didn't really care about anything else.

"Have to eat," I grumbled as I shouldered past his guards. I pulled out one of the metal chairs and fell into it, clawing up an entire loaf of bread and tearing into it with my teeth. My other hand grabbed a roasted bird and waved at a servant to pour me wine. A short-skirted girl quickly obliged, filling a nearby goblet to the rim. Fallon watched as I washed down my mouthful of bread, guzzling and spilling the wine down my chin. His mercenaries circled closer.

"Where's Marilius?" I burped. "Did he leave for Drin?"

"He did."

"How are his wounds? Better?"

"Better, yes."

"What do you think of his chances?"

Fallon shrugged. "I don't know. Lukien—did you find the monster?"

I put down the goblet and waved at the mercenaries. "Well, gather 'round closer so you can all hear. You're all wondering the same thing. No, I did not kill Crezil. I found it, and I fought it, but I didn't kill it."

There was silence for a moment. Then the youngest of the soldiers broke. "I knew it. We're dead!"

"Shut up," growled Fallon. He watched me go on eating. I observed him as I stuffed myself. More than just the monster was on his mind. "So?" he asked. "What happened?"

I swallowed a painful lump of meat and leaned back. "I followed it to some mountains about two hours ride from here. I tried to talk to it. It understood my words. When I told it I couldn't let it go on killing, we fought."

"But it's still alive. So are you."

"Almost not," I admitted. "It left me for dead in a canyon before getting away."

I didn't tell Fallon how the creature had searched for my soul and not found one. How could I? I was ashamed enough for letting it escape. His men shifted on their feet, glancing at each other without a word. Fallon pushed aside his tea cup like he was about to vomit.

"I'll find it, Anton," I promised. "I know where it lives, I know it's name . . . I just have to figure out how to beat it."

He nodded, barely listening. Plainly, he was terrified.

"I'll leave in an hour," I told him. "Just give me a horse and a bit of rest. I'll ride out to its lair, catch it while it's sleeping maybe. Let me just see Cricket first, straighten things out with her."

That's when Anton turned white. His gaze flicked toward his men. The servants suddenly backed away. The most horrible thought popped into my mind.

"Anton . . . where's Cricket?"

"Gone," he said. His hands started shaking. "She rode off, Lukien. She asked some of the men about Sky Falls, told them you'd be taking her there when you returned. She wanted to know where it was."

I pushed back my chair. I looked at the men around me. "And you thought they would save you from me?"

I flipped up the table, exploding, sending all the food and tea cups flying. I was on Fallon in a second, grabbing hold of his robe and pulling him out of the chair. My other hand released the sword as I dragged Fallon toward the pool. The men stalked after us, but the sword and my wrath kept them from rushing.

"Any one of you tries to help him, any or all of you dies!"

Fallon was blubbering, shrieking for me not to kill him. I took his hair and hauled him to the edge of the water. His men stayed back, too afraid to help. But I wasn't going to kill him. Even in my rage, I knew I never would. I yanked him forward, sending him tumbling into the pool. He bobbed up with a scream.

"Stop!"

I lowered my sword. "You brainless, useless fop! How could you let her go? How could you be so stupid?"

"I didn't!" Fallon pleaded. "I didn't know, I swear! She just stole her pony from the stable and went!"

"When?"

"Hours ago," he gasped. "After you left." He didn't climb out of the pool, or come even an inch closer. "Lukien, it was chaos here. We were cleaning up the hall, burying the dead. We were trying to keep the monster out, not keep people inside!"

His words made no sense to me. Nothing did. Cricket was gone! My knees turned to water. I leaned on my sword, trying to think what to do. Suddenly the monster meant nothing to me.

"Get me a horse," I barked at the men. "Now!"

All five of them scrambled. Fallon waded cautiously out of the water.

"Lukien, I'm sorry," he said. "I'm sorry! Tell me what I can do."

Suddenly I wished Marilius was around. I needed help. A friend. Anyone.

"There's nothing you can do, Fallon," I said. "Just tell me the quickest way to Sky Falls."

24

Fallon gave me the speediest horse in his stable, a hot-blooded Ganjeese barb with a shining black coat and a clipped, silver mane. It was the kind of horse Zuran princes raced, he told me, worth ten times my faithful Zephyr. I tacked the horse with a saddle and blanket, stripped off my own bruised armor, and took just enough food and water for a lean, fast journey. I needed to move quickly, and that meant traveling alone, and at night. Though there were no shortages of volunteers to help me find Sky Falls, I took only a hastily drawn map with me and a warning from Fallon to be careful.

The clouds had blacked out the moon entirely. The streets of Isowon and the horizon beyond slept in utter darkness. There was no way another man could have kept up with me. But my horse didn't hesitate, trusting my sure hand and the magical vision Malator provided my one good eye. Luckily the rain had stopped, and as I thundered through the streets a plume of water jetted up behind me, soaking the back of my shirt. My hunger, my weariness—both had fled, replaced by the most ghastly thoughts. Cricket was almost a full day's ride ahead of me, heading north toward Akyre, where girls were scarcer than diamonds. And Wrestler was out there, too. By now he'd be long gone from the canyon, I suspected, and probably asleep somewhere. The odds of his finding Cricket were powerfully slim. I hoped.

So I rode fast and hard, taking only the breaks my horse really needed and following the scribbled map past all the hastily jotted landmarks. Sky Falls, it turned out, was near Akyre's border with Kasse, which made sense since Cricket had seen the Falls before.

But it was a no man's land, an oasis in a blighted hellhole. I tried not to think of Cricket being captured by bandits or slavers. I did my best to bury the guilt. I'd broken my promise to take her to the Falls. I should have seen how fragile she was, but I never supposed she'd ride off alone.

Guts. That's the word that made me smile. She was as brave as any man, braver than any of Fallon's mercs. She deserved better from life.

I rode and rode, pushing my horse miles too far, letting him rest only minutes at a time. He wouldn't make it back alive, I knew; you couldn't ride a horse that hard without killing it. I patted the beast's neck and whispered in its ear, encouraging it, challenging it to go faster. Its stout heart answered, and by dawn we were more than halfway to Sky Falls. That's when I saw the camp.

The flatlands of the Bitter Kingdoms had one good aspect—I could see for miles ahead of me, even in the dark. As dawn approached I caught a glimpse of fires smoldering in the distance. With no one on the road to discover me, I turned my horse toward the camp and saw the green flags of Akyre waving in the blackness. A company of soldiers had bedded for the night. I counted up the tents and horses as best I could. Maybe two hundred soldiers, making ready for their southward march. I couldn't tell if they were legionnaires or just unlucky conscripts, but I knew Diriel was keeping his promise. Our seven days were running out.

I continued north, taking the long way around the camp, getting as much distance as I could from it before sun-up, and when the sun finally rose, the sky was clear again. My desperate horse brayed for water. I emptied my water skin into his mouth, then tossed the skin aside.

"Make it," I pleaded, rubbing his muzzle. "Not for me. For Cricket."

My own thirst hardly mattered. Soon we'd reach the river. I'd let the horse rest there, I promised him. But first we had to get there.

The river drawn on my map was part of the same waterway that led south to Isowon. It was also the same water that bisected Akyre and Kasse, and had sparked the genocidal feud between them. The river started way up in the mountains south of Norvor, an impenetrable range of peaks that never lost their snowy caps, not even in summer. The mountains were called the Quarrels, and had been inked on my map as a big black line, a clear indication that there was no going further. The Quarrels had kept the wars of the Bitter Kingdoms isolated from the rest of the continent, so that Norvor and Liiria and Reec could have their own wars.

By the time we made it to the nameless river my horse was near collapse. I could barely feel my tongue. I plunged my head into the water, drinking all my stomach could hold, letting the barb slake its thirst next to me. He was breathing hard, his black coat lathered. His brown eye watched me as we drank beside each other. I knelt down near him on the muddy shore and pulled the map from my pocket.

"Here," I showed him. I traced the river with my finger. "That's where we are." Then I moved upward to where the Falls were drawn. "And that's where we're going. Sky Falls. Just a little farther. You can do it. You can."

I'd spent my life around horses. In Liiria, as a Royal Charger, I'd seen all manner of horses, but this one was special. I'd ridden him hard through the blackest of nights, then all morning through scrub land. I'd starved him of food and rest and jabbed my heels in his flanks just to get more speed, and still he was upright. His eye blinked at me but didn't look away.

"You're a marvel," I told him. "If there's a heaven for horses, that's where you'll go."

I started to think he might not die at all. I reached out and scratched the side of his neck. But I didn't want to love him.

"Don't be my friend," I warned. I glanced down at my sword. "I'm only allowed one, it seems."

Malator had been almost completely quiet the entire journey. I didn't know if he was afraid for Cricket or just staying out of my way. His mood was difficult to read. Why was he so distant? Instead of summoning him I studied the map. The man who'd drawn it—a Marnan named Pellin—said Sky Falls was part of a fork in the river, one of many I'd encountered so far. I was to look for a group of black rock hills surrounded by a forest, but that didn't help much either. From the way he'd drawn the map I couldn't really tell how close I was, or where the border with Kasse began. For all I knew I had already crossed it.

I folded the map and looked up river. To me, all the hills looked black. A patchwork of trees sprouted from the landscape. I was about to mount up when a flash of movement caught my eye. I stiffened, listened, and watched as an animal emerged from behind a ten-foot rock. A small horse, without a rider. Just a pony, really.

I should have recognized it instantly but for some reason just stared. That's how it is when you see something out of place. When the truth finally hit me, I froze.

The pony knew me at once. The empty saddle where Cricket once rode hung lopsided on its back. Slowly it trotted toward me.

"Cricket!" I called, running past her horse, hoping she was just beyond the rock. But when I rounded it all I saw was the river. "Cricket!" I shouted, again and again, walking in circles and looking for clues. I went to the pony and asked in a panic, "Where is she?"

It just looked at me stupidly.

"Malator! Where's Cricket?"

Malator kept his distance. I knew he wanted to answer me, but in my mind he shook his head. *Ride, Lukien,* he said.

"Why?" I pressed. "Do you see her?"

You are close to so many things, he replied. *Don't ask me. Go.*

I had no time for riddles and resented Malator for speaking them. "Sorry, boy," I told my horse as I climbed into the saddle. "This time we don't stop until we find her."

There was nothing I could do for the pony. It was too small for me to ride and bringing it would only have slowed me down. Maybe it would find its way to Isowon, or maybe a friendly farmer would find it. I gave it one last look, then wheeled my stallion northward and galloped away. I forswore the map, riding by instinct alone, frantically searching the land as it passed me. My mind was a blur, every bit of me focused on finding Sky Falls. But maybe she hadn't made it there. Or maybe the pony had wandered for hours, stranding her somewhere far from the Falls. I called out for her as I rode, afraid that someone else might hear me. But now it didn't matter—I was ready to kill anyone who tried to stop me.

I rode that horse through the mud and rocks of the riverbank, giving no concern at all for the brave beast. He might have easily snapped a leg or lost his footing on the slimy shore, but I drove him cruelly, uncaringly, thinking only of Cricket. The dark thoughts that had plagued me all day were freed, filling my head with the worst of predictions. By the time I sighted the black hills, the barb was frothing. I could feel his heart pumping wildly in his breast, about to burst. The guilt of one more dead horse overwhelmed me.

"Enough!"

I reined back, cursing. White foam dripped from his mouth. I leaned forward, rubbing his neck.

"Enough . . ."

Ahead of me lay the hills. Maybe Cricket, too. But I couldn't kill the noble barb, not even for her. I looked up river, following the ribbon toward the forested hills. If there was a fork ahead, it was hidden in trees. Gently I nudged the horse forward, calling out for again for Cricket. Birds shot out of the branches, but no one answered.

I knew she was there, though. I could feel her.

The horse caught its breath as we entered the woods. The river moved more quickly now, running with an easy music. High branches filled with colored leaves shaded me. The harshness of the world fell away, and suddenly I was in a different place, a green cathedral of flowers and jumping fish. Trees sprouted from the rocky faces of the hills and dragonflies buzzed the shore. I gazed around, sheltered by the trees that held me like motherly arms. I jumped down from my horse, onto the pebbly bank. That's when I heard the Falls.

The sound was quiet at first; I had to cock my head to hear it. I left the horse behind and followed the sound until it was unmistakable. It grew into a rumble, like the growl of a dog, and suddenly I was running, hurrying toward it. I saw the fork where the river split, breaking west against the ancient rocks, then looked up into the stepped hills where the river tumbled down, falling and rolling over itself and crashing into foam.

I stopped. I think I even gasped. It must have been forty feet tall and the sun was right behind it, tossing rainbows into the spray. Birds nested in the moss-covered cliffs. I could hear their young chirping over the noise. The fallen water spread out into a lake, flooding the valley it had carved from the hills. Suddenly I realized why Cricket had remembered this place so vividly. In the midst of desolation, Sky Falls was a paradise.

"Cricket!" I shouted. "It's me—Lukien!"

If she could hear me, I couldn't tell over the din. I moved carefully toward the distant falls, studying the ground for clues, anything at all that might tell me if she'd been here. Amid the sheer hills there seemed a hundred places to hide, but when I saw hoof prints in the soft earth I knew I wasn't alone. They looked like the prints Cricket's pony might make, small and coming to a stop near the end of the river. I tracked them backwards to where they disappeared into the woods. That's when I noticed the other prints—dozens of them, deep impressions made by big horses with heavy riders. I discovered them yards from where I'd seen the pony's prints. Following them took me to the first real footprints. Human prints.

I stared down at them, not wanting to believe it. The prints weren't made by Cricket. Only a man could have made them. I shut my eye tight as sickness writhed inside me.

"Malator," I moaned. "Where is she?"

Look.

He directed my gaze toward the other side of the river, not far from where the water tumbled from its cliff. There, like a flag on a stick, hung the rass skin cape I'd made for Cricket, draped atop a branch plunged into the ground. I splashed toward it, fording the water up to my waist and calling out for her, shouting over the roar of the falls. I forged up the opposite shore, searching frantically as I snatched the cape from the stick. There was no blood on it; it wasn't even torn.

"Cricket! Where are you?"

A feeble voice answered from behind a rocky outcropping. First her hands, then her face crawled into view. She was almost unrecognizable from the bruises puffing her eyes. I dropped the cape and ran to her, saw her lying broken in the sand, her bare feet pushing to reach me. Her clothes had been ripped open, top and bottom, and her wrists were bound and bloodied, tied with rope. Dried blood crusted her broken lips. A patch of blood soaked the right side of her head. Not far away sat the stone used to crack her skull.

I sank down next to her and tried to keep the horror from my face. I had never in my life seen a person so brutalized. A girl! She looked at me and tried to talk. I put my hand to her cheek.

"Don't," I told her. I lowered my face to hers. "Don't move or say anything."

Cricket broke into sobs. "He found me, Lukien."

At first I thought she was the one who'd made the flag, but seeing her made me realize that was impossible. *He'd* stuck the cape there. He'd done it so I'd find her, so I'd see her like this. I slipped my hands beneath her battered body. She cried out as I cradled her. I could feel the lumps on her skin and the pulpy contusions through her tattered clothing. She felt cold but didn't shiver. Her dark eyes—swollen to slits—smiled at me.

"Did you get the monster?" she gurgled.

I shook my head. I pulled her feather-light body against my own. "No. I tried, Cricket, but I couldn't."

She strained to talk, coughed up a bubble of blood, then pointed to the water. "Take me there."

"In the water?"

She nodded, clutching me with her broken arms. Her request made no sense to me. Then I realized she'd been trying to reach the water all along. Carefully I stood up and carried her down the river bank and into the water, going deeper until I was up to my waist again. She let go her arms and floated there, looking up at Sky Falls with my hands beneath her back. A sigh of enormous pleasure peeled from her lips. Her body went limp in my palms.

"I'm sorry," I whispered, struggling. "I failed."

"No . . ." Her fingers curled around my shirt. "I remember."

Gently I lifted her dripping head from the water. Her dark hair spread out like ink on the surface. "Cricket? You remember?"

"Not Cricket," she said. "Lisea."

"Lisea." I cooed the name like she was a baby. "Your name is Lisea."

She gave a little nod. "Cricket was my sister."

That made me freeze. She locked eyes on me and wouldn't look away. Her newfound memories made her battered face slacken. She was waiting to unburden herself, and like a priest I gave her leave.

"Go on."

"Don't take me to shore. Keep me here in the water."

"I will, Lisea."

Her breath came in bursts. "Cricket drowned here," she said. "My father sent us here. To hide us."

I held her as still as I could. "All right," I whispered. "It's all right."

"I was the protector that time, Lukien." She laughed, then started to cry. "We ran. I couldn't save her . . ."

She started shaking. A line of red saliva trickled from the corner of her mouth. I didn't know if she and her sister had run from the war, or who her father was, or . . .

"She was just a baby!" Cricket wailed. "And I . . . I . . . I . . . dropped . . . her!"

Then she screamed so loud it nearly drowned out the waterfall. Her hands curled into claws and her whole body stiffened, and there was nothing I could do to stop her enormous grief. Suddenly

I was screaming too, cursing the Fate and the Akari and all creation. Cricket—*Lisea*—was dying. It might have been merciful, but I couldn't bear it.

"Malator!" I cried. "Help her!"

My sword vibrated with his sorrow. I felt him inside me, watching Cricket through my own sight.

I cannot.

"You can! Do it! I command it!"

No.

"You black-hearted jackal . . ."

She's dying, Lukien. Don't let your curses be the last thing she hears.

In my arms Cricket went on screaming, her whole body a spasm of pain. I lifted her out of the water completely and hugged her to my breast. I put her wet head to my lips and spoke softly in her ear.

"I love you, Lisea," I said. "I love you, and you're going to a better place."

She stopped her cries. She held her breath. Her muscles tightened, and she rubbed against my cheek, the only reply she could marshal. I could feel her heart struggling inside her, beating wildly and weakly, losing its battle. Her hair smelled young and girlish. I kissed her, I rocked her, I did the only things I knew to do. Her last breath came in a rush, pushing past her lips to warm my face.

And then she was gone.

I held on to her for long minutes, standing with her in the river with the spray and roar of the Falls all around me. Malator hovered somewhere in the distance. A fish brushed past my leg. I waited, and when the anguish came I crushed it down, deep down. I had work to do first. So I waded to shore with Cricket in my arms and looked for a place to bury her.

25

I chose a spot far enough from the river so that she wouldn't be disturbed, yet close enough for her to see the waterfall. A wise-looking tree stood guard over the spot, giving her shade and a place for her spirit to sit and remember the better life she'd had before war and madness touched her world. I had no shovel, so I used my hands to dig out the soft earth enough to cover her slight remains. I worked in a fog, alone, cutting my fingers on rocks and ignoring the blood. This was her death place, and I wanted to make it beautiful.

Ten at a time I carried armloads of stones from the river banks, choosing the largest and prettiest ones I could find. I stacked them neatly atop her grave, saying nothing as I worked, oblivious to the hours slipping away. I suppose I was exhausted. I really can't remember. Those hours are like broken glass in my memory, almost impossible to piece together. Malator did not come to me nor speak to me, nor offer any apology for letting her die. I wrote her name in smaller stones at the foot of the grave.

L I S E A

To me, she was Cricket. I'd call her that forever. But she had a name before she'd taken her sister's, a name given by a mother and father, and I meant to honor that. I looked at her name and said it softly to myself. I touched the stones that made it. And I realized I never really knew her. Over and over I heard her cries in my mind. Her screams reminded me of someone else I'd lost.

"Lukien?"

I turned from the grave and saw Malator standing behind me

near the river bank. His long face looked as if he'd been weeping, but I knew that wasn't possible. He looked at me cautiously, reminding me that time was wasting. He took two shimmering steps forward then stopped. His vaporous feet made no marks in the sand at all. I remained kneeling over Cricket's grave.

"Cassandra died screaming, too," I said softly. "She died like Cricket died. With me. Because of me."

Malator glided closer. "Cricket didn't die because of you, Lukien."

"She did. And you knew she would. You warned me." I turned to look at his glowing face. "You never wanted her to come with me. You saw this, didn't you?"

Of course, Malator didn't answer that.

"I thought it would be the monster," I said. "I thought it would be Crezil. Why'd you let me believe that?"

"Did I ever tell you that? No, I did not. I warned you not to bring her, and that was all I ever said."

"I let her get between us. Is that why you wouldn't save her?"

"Are you angry with me for not saving her?" he asked.

I thought about that. "At first," I replied. "But not anymore. Not with you. But I am angry."

My fury burgeoned like a thunderhead. I could barely check it. And now I didn't have to. I got off my knees and went to the place where the rass skin cape still hung upon the stick. Malator floated after me without a word.

"He followed her here," I said. "To try and get to me."

"He must have thought she was going north to meet you," agreed Malator.

"I could have stopped him. I could have killed him when I saw him." I bent and picked up the cape. Weeks of wear had made the rass skin supple like velvet. "Must I live with that now? That and everything else, every day of my life?"

"How could you know?"

"I didn't know! I shouldn't have cared! I just should have ended him, right there!"

"And be killed yourself by the others."

"But I would have spared her this." I put the cape against my face. The smell of her overwhelmed me. "She was fourteen, Malator. He raped her."

"A child," nodded Malator. "Wrestler is a beast beyond compare. Worse than Crezil."

I unsheathed the sword, holding it out in my palms and dropping to my knees. "Help me, Malator," I pleaded. "Only blood can avenge this crime. Give me the magic of life and death. Grant me the power to grind them to dust!"

Malator floated closer, looking down at me with a sober expression. "Vengeance is just, but you must know what you're asking, Lukien."

"Give me the power to damn them!"

"Understand me," he insisted. "I can give you the might to match your fury, but it will change you. There's no turning back from what you ask."

"Do it!" I demanded. I slammed the sword point-down in the dirt. "I'll pay your price. I'll follow my fate. Just let me destroy them!"

Malator put his hand over my eyes. Though his fingers were translucent, I was suddenly blind. "Hold on to the sword. Do not let go."

I reached in front of me to where the Sword of Angels stood speared into the ground. My fingers burned as they wrapped around the leather hilt. The bones in my hands fused, unable to move as the blade's fire entered me.

"Give it to me," I gasped. Sweat gushed from my skin. A glorious pain boiled my blood. "Make me strong. Make me unstoppable!"

"Feel it," commanded Malator. "That is the fire of the Akari. The forge of life! No man will stand against you. You are reborn, Lukien. Forever!"

The magic engulfed me, immolating me. I tried to scream but couldn't. My mind saw my body blazing, kneeling in the sand. And there stood Malator, like a duke of hell, touching me with his ghostly hands. I felt my bones melt, then mend themselves. Every scar burned away. Memories of my long life wailed inside my rattling skull, of Cassandra young and beautiful, of Akeela old and mad. I opened my mouth and a tongue of flame spat out.

"Help me . . . !"

This was hell, I thought. This was Crezil's Gahoreth. But I kept hold of that sword. I didn't care if Malator turned me to ash or a spirit like himself. I wanted my revenge, and I knew he alone could give it to me. Finally, when all my strength had fled, I heard Malator's voice again.

"One day," he said, "you will know why I agreed."

The flames enveloping me died. A cool breeze touched my skin. Malator pulled his hand away. Slowly my fingers unwrapped from the sword. Then, as weak as a newborn, I toppled over into the sand. Malator hung over me, but offered no help. I glanced up and saw him cock his head, then smile. My whole body was soaked with sweat. My hands shook, but when I looked at them they seemed different, like they weren't mine. I took half a breath. Something more than air filled my lungs.

"How do you feel?" asked Malator.

"How do I look?" I croaked.

Malator's flashed his familiar grin. "Go to the river."

I dragged myself to the bank of the river. The water moved quickly, but as I hung my face over it the water suddenly stilled like a mirror. What I saw chilled me.

"Is that *me*?"

My hair was yellow again. No fading, no gray at all, just the wheaty gold of my youth. I'd lost the lines of age and my skin was tight again. I peered down further, touching my cheeks, feeling the skin with my soft fingertips. Even my teeth seemed straighter, whiter. I was as I'd been when Cassandra loved me, when I'd first met her years before.

"What did you do to me?" I asked. "I'm young again!"

"You are as old as you ever were," he assured me. "But stronger. More whole." He reached down toward my face, gently plucking off my eye patch. I jerked back, surprised and annoyed by the intrusion, then realized an eyeball had replaced the dead, white flesh. "Look at the world now, Lukien."

Around me everything was clear and beautiful. Deep, the way it hadn't been in years. I stood up, wobbly at first, flexing my fingers and then my arms. I stomped my feet and felt the strong bones inside my legs. Fresh air swelled my chest. I hardly recognized myself! Malator glided over to where the sword stood in the dirt and pulled it free. He returned and handed it to me. I hesitated.

"Do I still need this?" I asked. "Can I not live without it?"

"We are bound, still and always," said Malator. "Until the day you decide to discard me, we are together."

"Then I accept you," I said and sheathed the sword. "Now we make Diriel's end."

"And Wrestler's," added Malator.

"Oh, yes." I had a special end in mind for him. "Wrestler will not die a man's death."

"There's an army to fight too, Lukien. You need to be ready. Those men you tried to save—Diriel's legionnaires—they won't stop. You'll have to kill them."

"They are forfeit," I declared. "Every mother's son of 'em."

I meant to have them all—not just Diriel and Wrestler, but all the filth that followed them. Everyone pledged to that demented cannibal would be slaughtered. They were the ones who made me this way, I told myself. They deserved the coming storm. But first I needed to find them. I went back to where I'd left the horse, the majestic Ganjeese barb that had brought me all this way. He was standing on the other side of the river, watching me, waiting. I hadn't even tied him. The stallion's brown eyes noticed the change in me approvingly.

"You are a prince of horses," I told him. I patted his barrel, feeling his powerful rib cage. "I have never seen your like or equal. Will you ride with me? Battle with me? We'll see many bloody days."

Horses understand. They really do. This one knew exactly what I meant and didn't buck or complain.

"You'll need a name," I told him. "I don't know what Fallon calls you, and I don't care. I'm going to name you for myself." I took his muzzle in my hand and looked into his eyes. "From now on you'll be called Venger."

I climbed up onto his broad back, feeling like a Royal Charger again. Malator looked up at me with approval, then disappeared into the sword. I took a long moment to say goodbye to Cricket, trotting Venger over to her grave and trying not to weep. It was just a body, I told myself. Her spirit—her soul—had already left it. Realizing that, I glanced around the serene setting that was her death place, knowing that she was here, in this very spot. I just couldn't see her.

"Goodbye, Lisea," I whispered. "I'll kiss Gilwyn's baby for you."

Venger turned from the grave, then led me back down and out of the river valley. I wasn't sure where I was going—maybe south, maybe east. Just for now, I needed to ride. And to think. I needed to plan the bloodiest doom possible for Diriel and his puppets.

26

Southeast was the direction I chose. With Diriel's army directly south and more of his men probably on the march, I decided to evade them, crossing over the river into Kasse and following one of its many branches south and east toward Drin. The landscape was less dreary here, with fewer mountains and plenty of trees to hide me as I rode. But like all the Bitter Kingdoms, Drin was nearly abandoned now, its people scattered by the threat of war, its farms overgrown or fallow. There were good roads, though, built during more peaceful times, and I moved quickly all that first day. Once I saw some figures watching me from the window of a distant farmhouse, but when I waved they quickly disappeared. I stopped and watered Venger from a trough of rain water, hoping they'd come out to greet me, but they never did.

So I moved on, south and east, sometimes following the river and sometimes following the road, and did my best to forget what I'd seen just hours before. Cricket's screams were too fresh in my mind to examine head-on; I could only approach them sideways, like a crab, and tell myself I did the best I could. If I'd been faster, or listened more, if I'd taken her to Sky Falls or never taken her with me, she'd still be alive. But none of those things happened, so she was dead. I could only blame myself. And I would, but not today. Not until Diriel and Wrestler both were dead.

As the sun sank behind me I continued on, riding into the sound of crickets. The river reappeared alongside me, fat and sluggish, wider than I'd seen it in some time. Mosquitoes bloomed out of the dusk to feed on me. I thought how strange that was: that

Malator had made me nearly immortal, but insects could still abuse me. I had hardly gotten used to having my eye back! Everything seemed clearer to me. I could ride with ease through the darkness. Was this how a hawk felt, I wondered? Or a bat? The night made my senses tingle, tuning them like an instrument. I took a deep breath and smelled the dampness of a coming rain. Looking up revealed clouds gathering around the moon, and when I breathed again I smelled smoke in the air.

"Ho," I said softly, reining Venger back. He stopped, perking up his ears at the noise ahead.

Voices.

Another camp, I supposed, but I was too far south now to turn around, and my newfound strengths made me brash. I eased Venger forward, guiding him around the bends in the river and weaving in and out of the pine trees. Firelight glowed up ahead. The voices gradually grew louder. When I finally slipped out of the cover I saw what looked like a raft on the river, almost empty and tied to the shore by lines of rope. Scores of men stood on the shore, some of them carrying torches, others holding swords across their chests. I drew back at once, not recognizing the standard that waved above them. From the shadows I spied the boat's cargo—a man-shaped parcel wrapped in grayish cloth, like one of Anton's mummies.

"A funeral," I whispered, bending down to speak in Venger's ear. "Hold back."

At least two hundred men stood along the bank. Far behind them hid a village, veiled by trees, composed of modest homes and a single cobblestone avenue. People from the village had gathered with the soldiers, mostly women and children, their faces gaunt with sorrow. The soldiers stood nearly silent as a young man stepped out from among them, wading knee-deep into the water. He dressed as the others dressed, in a long, black leather coat with armored shoulders and brass buttons running down his left breast. Articulated gauntlets rode up his forearms. When he bent to touch the raft, his long hair tickled the water. Then he kissed the edge of the raft and spoke a farewell I couldn't quite hear. I don't know what made him turn in my direction, but as he trudged ashore he caught a glimpse of me in the shadows.

His eyes met mine, but there was no fear in his young face. Really just a boy, he called toward me. "You—who are you?"

His gathered soldiers turned to see me. I trotted out of the shadows. "My name is Lukien," I declared. "I'm heading south."

I didn't expect anyone to know me, or my name. I certainly didn't think to hear a familiar voice. So when I did, I started.

"Lukien?"

The voice was incredulous. I looked around, unable to place it until a figure pushed through the throng. And there was Marilius, aghast to see me, looking wholly out of place in mismatched garb. Marilius! He leaned forward, blinking in the torchlight. The boy soldier glanced between us.

"Marilius?" I called back. "Really?"

"Is that you, Lukien?" he asked. He took a few steps forward as I rode closer. "You look . . . what happened to you?"

"This is Lukien?" asked the boy. Now he was incredulous too. "Truly?"

My luck astonished me. I dismounted Venger and led the horse toward Marilius. "Cricket's dead," I blurted. "They killed her at Sky Falls."

Marilius turned the color of milk. "Who?" he gasped.

"Wrestler. Others too, I guess. It doesn't matter. They called down the storm and now they're going to face it."

"Your eye." Marilius inspected my face. "What happened? You look so young!"

"Malator did it," I said. "So I could beat them." I glanced around and discovered the soldiers staring at me. A few of the older ones, men of rank, encircled the boy. "Your Drinmen, I take it?"

"We are," answered the boy.

"Then I need to speak to someone important."

Marilius took my arm. "Lukien—this is a funeral."

I looked at the boy, then at the raft, then came to my senses. I'd ridden so hard I'd forgotten myself. "I'm sorry," I said. "I just came from a funeral. Forgive a stupid man for being tired."

"Lukien, this is Kiryk," said Marilius, presenting me to the boy. "Son of King Lutobor."

"Lutobor?" I remembered the name suddenly. I looked at the raft again and my heart sank. "The body on the raft—your father?"

"He died this morning," answered Kiryk. Despite his grief he kept his head high. "Killed by raiders from Akyre. They were on their way south to war with you in Isowon."

"So Marilius told you, then," I nodded. "This village is Drin?"

"It's called Jelah," said Kiryk. "But this is borderland. Diriel's men have been up and down this area for months."

"Taking men, stealing food and supplies, anything they can get to use against Isowon," Marilius explained. "Lutobor told me all about it."

I had a thousand questions but knew they'd have to wait. "I'm sorry for your father," I told Kiryk. "Let me stay and pay him homage with you. Then if you'll listen, we can talk."

Kiryk nodded with half interest, then turned back to his men. I led Venger up the riverbank, through the throngs of men, waiting for a chance to get some answers. That's when I saw the other corpses. They were piled up at the edge of the village, waiting to be buried or burned. Most were Drinmen in their black uniforms, but others were unmistakably Diriel's. Quickly I made an accounting of the bodies, putting the dead easily past a hundred. Marilius followed my gaze toward the village.

"That's only part of it," he sighed. "Lutobor's men have been fighting off Diriel's raids for weeks."

"He told you that himself?"

"It took me time to find him. I rode for his castle in Prang first, then on to Akja where he was camped. They'd already been chewed to pieces by the Akyrens. Lutobor let me ride with him here to Jelah."

That surprised me. "You fought with them?"

He nodded. "I did."

"The legionnaires?"

Marilius turned away, but I knew that look. He gestured to the villagers. "See their faces?"

They were mute. Filled with fear. A girl grasping her mother's hand stared straight back at me. I almost smiled, then noticed the fresh scar jutting down her cheek. The others looked the same—vacant, joyless, unable to speak. A handful of men stood with them, mostly old, sickly ones.

"Tell me what they were like," I said to Marilius. "How were they in battle?"

A sharp hushing from one of Kiryk's men silenced me. I nodded an apology, then watched as Lutobor's son took a bow and a single arrow from the eldest of his soldiers. He turned to the raft bearing his dead father, then signaled to another nearby man.

"Cut him loose."

The man pulled a dagger from his belt, trudged down to the ropes, and one by one sliced them, freeing the raft. The current took it slowly down river, and as it drifted away each soldier stood and waited silently. There were no prayers for the dead king, no wailing from the women on shore. A torch bearer stepped forward. Kiryk nocked his arrow, then bent the tip into the torch, setting it alight. He took his time, drawing a careful bead on the raft as it drifted into the darkness. He took so long I thought he'd miss the craft entirely. But he didn't. He let the arrow fly and struck that raft dead-eyed perfect. It went up like an inferno, nearly exploding. Whatever they'd used to soak it brought daylight to the shore and a huge spiral of black smoke. I watched as Kiryk lowered the bow and moved his lips in a wordless goodbye. The raft burned and sputtered as it drifted down river. Then, as if the crazy gods of the Bitter Kingdoms had held off long enough, it began to rain.

We met in a house near the center of the village, sitting around a rickety table while thunder shook the window. It was nearly midnight, and we were all exhausted, but Kiryk had agreed to meet with me before retiring. Most of his soldiers had found beds for the night in the homes around the village, but three of them—all confidants of his dead father—sat beside him while Marilius and I made our plea. The house belonged to a woman named Ursilil, chosen for Kiryk because it could be easily guarded. Ursilil was newly widowed, the mother of the scarred child I'd seen at the funeral. As we settled in our chairs Ursilil brought us milk from the only cow in the village that had somehow escaped the Akyren raiders. I was beyond famished, and it was simply the most delicious milk I'd ever drunk.

After the funeral, I'd spent most of the night conferring with Marilius, listening to everything he knew about Lutobor and Drin and their war with Akyre. Kasse, it turned out, wasn't the only Bitter Kingdom to fall to Diriel. Large swathes of Drin had been taken as well, the lands ravaged and their men conscripted into Diriel's army. Lutobor's own army had slowly been decimated, until now there were only a few hundred soldiers. Most of these belonged to the Silver Dragons, the personal guard of the dead king, of which the three men sitting across the table were members. Each wore the insignia of the order on their leather coats, an embroidered firedrake coiling up the left side collar.

Many things had happened in the short time that Marilius and I had been separated, and much of it I could barely talk about. I told him of my battle with Crezil and how the monster had let me live, but I didn't tell him about my lost soul. That was still too great a burden for me to confess to anyone. Marilius had his own theories about why the beast had spared me but they were all nonsense. I knew the truth—because I was soulless. I just couldn't confess it.

And of course I told him about Cricket. Under a jutting roof with the rain falling around us I told him how she'd gone to Sky Falls without me, how Wrestler had tracked her there in hopes of finding me, and how he'd killed her. I described it all; it gushed out of me. He listened stoically to the tale of her rape, but I could tell his guts were turning to stone. Revenge began boiling in his eyes, and it remained there as we sat with Kiryk, drinking milk around the table.

I remained quiet while Kiryk conferred with his men. Their names were Sulimer, Jaracz, and Lenhart, and all of them looked like they'd been at war a very long time. They had the grizzled faces of men who'd spent their lives in the sun, training soldiers and leading them into battle, and Kiryk seemed out of place among them. But there was no smugness from the three, only desire to help the boy through an impossible task. Finally, Kiryk turned to the woman Ursilil, who'd been buzzing around the table filling our glasses.

"Thank you," he said. "Go to your daughter now. Make sure she's sleeping."

Ursilil seemed relieved to be dismissed. She was an attractive woman, or at least she had been before the raiders came. Losing her husband had given her face a glaze. She gave Kiryk a little bow, me a tiny scowl, and eagerly left the room. When she was gone Sulimer, the oldest of the soldiers, reached beneath the table and lifted up a sack he'd brought with him. He dropped it on the table with a thud.

"What's that?" I asked.

Sulimer smirked through his peppered beard and peeled down the wrapping, revealing a severed head. "From this morning," he said. "A friend from Akyre."

The head sat upright, facing me with its dead eyes. The horrible pallor of its skin told me at once it had been dead longer than just a day.

"A legionnaire."

I reached out and bounced my finger off its cheek. A chalky dust fell from the skin. He'd been a man about my age, with just about my hair color too. The eyes still had that empty look I'd seen in Diriel's castle—dead and alive at the same time. Marilius had told me there'd been at least twenty of them with the other Akyrens, sent in first like fodder for the Drin. Only the Drin hadn't cut them down so easily.

"Beheading them is the only way to stop them," Sulimer pronounced. "Nothing else will do it. Not cutting off an arm, not pumping them full of arrows, nothing. You have to get right up close and swing. You don't get a second chance."

"Swords?" I asked.

"Axes are better," answered Lenhart. He'd been the quiet one so far. "Swords weren't heavy enough for some. The legion started wearing leather bands around their necks once we discovered their weakness."

"What about just bashing their brains in?" asked Marilius.

Lenhart shrugged. "That should work if you can manage it."

"Marilius, I didn't see a lot of axmen with Fallon's mercs," I said. "What about that?"

"Axes aren't a problem. Anton can buy axes. It's men we need." Marilius looked at Kiryk seriously. "I pleaded with your father, now I'm pleading with you. Will you help us?"

Kiryk leaned back in his chair. The weight of his decision made his shoulders slump. "The soldiers in this village are almost all that's left of our army," he said. "Some are back in Prang, some are on patrol watching the north. That's maybe five hundred men."

"And not all of them professionals," said Sulimer. "Some are just farmers with scythes and forks. That's all who's left to defend Drin."

"Kiryk, forgive me for asking this, but I have to," I said. "Are you the king now? I'm all out of time, and I need to be talking to the right man. If it's these others who'll make the decision—"

"He is king," said Jaracz, the one sitting just to Kiryk's left. "The only question of that is in your mind, Liirian. He's the son of Lutobor. He has the blood."

"So you'll follow him?" I asked. "And the other Silver Dragons too?"

"*He has the blood,*" repeated Jaracz. "The decision is his alone. But he hasn't decided yet. There are still questions."

Kiryk said, "Only one that matters. Who'll defend Drin from Akyre if we leave here, Lukien? If we join you in Isowon, Drin will be wide open. What would stop Diriel from turning his men north again once he sees we're in the south?"

"He won't," I said, "because what he wants is in Isowon. Isowon is the prize."

"He wants Anton Fallon," added Marilius. "Not just for revenge but because of his spice routes."

"Anton Fallon is a merchant," said Jaracz. "Why should we give our blood to that pirate? He's a Zuran. I've heard he's not even a man."

Marilius shot back, "Not a man? What does that mean?"

Jaracz leaned forward. "He likes boys," he said, then made a kissing noise.

I put up my hand to calm Marilius. "What does it matter who he takes to his bed? You don't have to like Anton Fallon. No one does. But he's the one with the army. He's the only one with the forces to stop Diriel. Are you really going to let his choice of lovers stop you from fighting?"

Their silence acknowledged me. Sulimer, ever the serious one, asked, "How many men does he have?"

I looked to Marilius. "Be honest," I said. "What do you think?"

"Several hundred probably," said Marilius. "It depends. If he's convinced them to stay then at least that many. If they quit and ran off . . ." He shrugged. "Who knows?"

"Several hundred," I repeated. "Those are good enough odds, Kiryk. With your men and Fallon's fighting together, it'll be a nearly equal match."

"Equal?" Kiryk shook his head. "Diriel has twice that many. Maybe more."

His calculations surprised me. "Why do you say that? Diriel himself told me his forces were devastated by Kasse. Almost all of them starved. He put the number close to a thousand."

"A lie," said Lenhart. He reached for the severed head and pushed it aside for a better look at me. "Every man his soldiers snatch is enslaved by them, pressed into his army. Not just his own people but Kassens, too."

"Even Drinmen," admitted Kiryk darkly. "Diriel means to deceive you, Lukien. He won't show up in Isowon with an army that small."

"And even if he did, how many of them would be legionnaires?" asked Jaracz. "I've been asking this one the same questions since he got here." He pointed at Marilius. "He can't answer me. Can you answer me, Liirian? Can you tell me how we're supposed to beat an army of men who are half dead already?"

"Indeed I can." I picked up the head by its muddy blond hair and held it out like a lantern. "By doing this to every damn one of them! That's the way—the only way. You've already done it! If you come with us you'll have hundreds of men to help you. And you'll have me."

Kiryk looked at me without a word. No one spoke until Sulimer finally stood. "Lukien, Marilius tells us you're a man who can't be killed. You're like one of Diriel's soulless." He gestured to my sword. "That's your magic? That's what keeps you alive?"

"It's more than a sword," I said. "It's more than magic even." I lowered the head to the table and let it roll to a stop. "It's kept me alive through a broken neck and a battle with a demon. Now it's made me young and strong again just so I could make war on your enemies. This morning I had one eye. Now I have two. But Diriel and his horde could pluck them both out, and I wouldn't stop. I'm not going to stop until they're dead. That means Diriel and Wrestler and all his brood. Every damn one of them."

Marilius rose to stand beside me. "King Kiryk, you can stay here and let us carry the fight in Isowon, but it won't save you. If we lose, Diriel will be back for you all."

"You're brave men, but your fight isn't over," I told them. "Diriel won't stop until all the lands of the Bitter Kingdoms belong to Akyre again. Drin will be a country of ghosts. That's all that'll be left."

Kiryk stood, and then his trio did too. A flash of distant lightning lit his face, revealing how young he really was. "I'll think on it," he said. "I can't decide something this big so quickly."

"You have to," I said. "Because we're leaving in the morning with or without you, and Diriel's not waiting. Make your choice tonight, my lord. Before you leave this room. I'm giving you the chance to avenge your father. Take it now—you'll never get another."

Kiryk's eyes dropped to the severed head. "This is the one that killed my father," he said. "It was Lenhart who took this head, not me. The head I want now belongs to another. Will you promise me Diriel's head, Sir Lukien?"

"I can promise you his death," I said.

"His head," repeated Kiryk, "so I may show it off like a trophy. So that every child in Drin can see they've been avenged."

"Then I will get it for you," I pledged. "With pleasure."

Kiryk nodded, and that was all he had to do. Sulimer, Jaracz, and Lenhart all bent in a bow, then one by one took his hand and kissed it.

"You are the blood," said Lenhart as his lips brushed Kiryk's fingers. "You are our master."

Those words haunted me all that night, but I didn't figure out why until the morning.

27

Exactly two-hundred and eighty-two men left Jelah that morning, including Marilius and myself. The number was far less than we needed but more than I'd hoped for, comprised mostly of Silver Dragons but also of men from nearby villages who'd heard about the battle brewing in Isowon. The women and children of Jelah waved goodbye to us, piling grateful kisses on their young king and blessing him with strips of cloth torn from their dresses. Kiryk, embarrassed by the attention, made the bold promise that he'd be returning soon with Diriel's head, a pledge that made the women cheer.

Of course there were too few horses, forcing a full third of the men to march their way to Isowon. Not only would that slow us down, it also meant they'd be exhausted when battle came. But we had enough supplies for the journey—barely—given us by the women of Jelah, who'd hidden whatever they could from the Akyren hordes. I promised the Drinmen that Anton Fallon had more than enough to fill their bellies, and that when we finally reached Isowon they'd all be fed well. Still, it would be days until we made it that far south, days I didn't have. Diriel's army had already marched south. To my reckoning, the seven days he'd granted me to bring him Crezil were almost over. With so many of us on foot, I knew we wouldn't make it on time.

The rain continued all that night and into the morning, turning the road to mud. I rode near the head of the column with Marilius, the two of us staying just behind Kiryk and Sulimer. Our pace was slow—painfully so for me. I longed to jab my heels into Venger and sprint the long distance to Isowon. There were far too many of us to keep our trip secret, and once every hour or so men from surrounding villages caught up to our column, pleading with Kiryk to join us. No one was turned away, and I started to hope that maybe—just maybe—we'd have the numbers needed to face Diriel.

When we'd marched our first twenty miles, Kiryk called the troops to rest. I watched him move through his little army, seeing to the needs of his "infantry" and waiting till every man had food before taking any for himself. I even saw him order a limping man to remove his boots, so that Kiryk could examine his feet. That's when the similarity struck me. I smiled, tucked it away without saying anything, and continued watching Kiryk. I admired him, but it was hard for me to call him "king." Akeela had been that young once, too, and had been a similarly good and caring king—for awhile. My lust and betrayal had crushed that part of Akeela's spirit. I wondered if the same would one day happen to Kiryk.

I was drawn to him. He reminded me of the youth I'd lost and had magically regained in body, though not in spirit. When the column started moving again, I waited until he was done speaking with Sulimer and looked for a chance to talk to him alone. While Sulimer dropped back to be with the other lieutenants, I eased Venger to the front of the line. Kiryk looked surprised to see me. I could tell his thoughts were elsewhere. He nodded at me then looked up into the slackening rain.

"It's stopping," he remarked. "I don't want it dogging us all the way to Isowon."

"No," I agreed.

A moment passed. Kiryk regarded me. "Something on your mind, Lukien?"

"No," I said. "Well, yes. I've been watching you. You remind me of someone."

"How's that?"

"The way you are with your men. I had a king like you once. He was dear to me." I glanced over my shoulder. "You're dear to them. You've been king for only a day and already they love you. They're following you into hell."

"They loved my father," said Kiryk. "They hope to see him in me."

I nodded politely but didn't think that was it. "Bravery isn't passed on like blue eyes," I said.

"Then they follow me because I'm of the blood," said Kiryk. "My father's son, my grandfather's grandson."

"I've seen sons that were tyrants whose fathers were saints," I said. "We're not all like our fathers."

"We are," argued Kiryk. "Even when we don't want to be. I'm sure you're more like your father than you think. It's inescapable. But if you were royal, if you were of the blood, you wouldn't be able to escape that either. Neither would your people."

"Drin is different from other places, I think. Not everyone loves their kings and queens."

"It's not love," said Kiryk. "It's duty. Honor. It's . . . I don't know . . . of the blood."

"They call you their master," I said. "Last night. I heard Sulimer and the others call you that."

"That's right," said Kiryk, but I could tell the title didn't sit quite right with him yet. "It's not a choice. And it's not permanent. Sulimer is pledged to my father. Lenhart and Jaracz too. When they die they'll go to him again. They'll serve him forever in heaven."

I grinned but didn't laugh. "You believe that?"

"Of course. We are Drinmen. I'm their master for now, here on earth, but just for now. They'll die and serve my father. Someday I'll have men pledged to me that way." Kiryk looked behind him. "Some of these men, probably."

"Because you're of the blood?"

"Right." Kiryk smiled at me. "Why does that baffle you? Weren't you pledged to a king?"

"I was."

"So when you see him in heaven you will serve him again, yes?"

I never, ever thought of seeing Akeela again. I could barely answer. "Uh, I suppose so." But really something else was going through my mind, the threads of a riddle coming together. I looked at the terrain ahead then back at the men. They were moving so damn slowly, and suddenly I knew I couldn't wait. "King Kiryk," I said, "I have to ride ahead."

"To scout?"

"No. I'm sorry, I have to ride ahead." I called out behind me. "Marilius!"

My shout startled everyone. Marilius charged forward. "What is it?"

Right in front of Kiryk, I said, "I'm going on ahead. You stay with the others. Tell Anton I'll be there. Start getting our defense together."

"What?"

"I can't explain," I told him. "Just go and buy us whatever time you can. And I want you to give Diriel a message for me, all right?"

"You're blind-siding me, Lukien," said Marilius. "A message?"

"That's right. Tell him I'm going to bring him what he wants. Got that?"

"You want me to tell that to Diriel? What's it even mean?"

"The monster," I said. I didn't bother saying farewell. "I'll see you again."

I sped away, not sure when I'd return to Isowon but certain enough to know that I would. Kiryk's words had ignited my mind, burning away the fog that had been there for days. Now, at last, I had the plan I'd been searching for.

28

I mused on my strategy the whole way south, leaving Marilius and Kiryk and the others behind as I branched away from the river, looking for the straightest path to the Akyren tombs. My plan had its risks. Diriel might not take my bargain or might have already begun his invasion. Anton and his mercenaries might surrender without firing a single arrow. Or Crezil might just kill me. That was the kink that seemed most likely, but I reminded myself that I was soulless. I had so little to lose. So I pointed Venger toward the coast, and using the map I'd gotten in Isowon, called on my memory to fill in the rest. After all the travelling I'd done, the Bitter Kingdoms were feeling smaller to me now.

Meeting Kiryk and his Silver Dragons had shown me that not everyone in this part of the world was like Diriel or even like Anton Fallon. The Bitter Kingdoms had been plagued by every misfortune imaginable—war, starvation, even a demon—but good-hearted men and women still lived here and still struggled. If I could do some good myself, if I could help them, then I would. I would be for a moment the knight-errant I'd hoped.

So I rode, pushing myself ever farther, and drank from the river and ate from my saddle bags, and it was like those old days back in Jador, when I'd escape to the desert just for solitude. I feared nothing and plowed down the miles until day and night passed, and I was at last in the north part of the forest that hid the Akyren tombs and the lair of the beast.

I looked through the trees and into the valley and then up into the sky. It was afternoon, but the sun was cast with clouds and a breeze threatened rain. The woods rustled with the noise of animals. Birds chirped in the highest branches. Up ahead loomed the caves, barely visible through the foliage. The quiet and the daylight made me sure I'd find the monster there. Then I had another thought—what to do with Venger? I'd already lost a horse to Crezil. They were easy, tempting targets, and I could not bear another being killed. I dismounted and walked my new friend to the edge of the woods.

"I wish you were a person," I whispered. "Then I could send you away to come back for me."

Venger flicked his velvety ears. His brown eyes rolled toward me.

"You know I can't bring you in there with me," I told him, "but you need to hide. You need to trust me. I'll be back for you, all right?"

He didn't really nod; I just imagined that from the way he moved his muzzle. But I refused to tie him, either. If Crezil came after him—or if anyone did—I wanted him to be free to run.

"Wait for me, but if trouble comes then bolt," I said. "I'll find you again."

Venger turned slowly and trotted into the cover of the trees, where he suddenly stopped. Satisfied, I left him there as I descended into the valley, through the trees, following the tributary toward the creature's cave. Malator came to life at my side, humming inside the sword. I stalked toward the cavern, splashing through the stream and then peering inside the murky cavern. My eyes adjusted quickly, and I could hear insects crawling over the rocks. I went a little deeper, leaving the sunlight behind. The smell of rot and cadavers stung my nose. When I reached the stone blocking the entrance to the tomb, I suddenly stopped.

Malator, I said silently, *where is it?*

I don't know, he answered. *I don't feel it. I don't think it's here.*

That's impossible. It's daylight.

Malator stretched himself across the chamber, spreading out like smoke. I could feel him searching, taking my mind along.

"I can't see well," I said finally. "Can you help?"

Hold out your hand.

I did as he asked, and a puff of fire appeared in my palm. I felt like a wizard! Now I could see the tomb clearly, bathed in the orange glow. I squeezed past the stone guarding the tomb, casting the chamber beyond with light. There stood the coffin that once held

Atarkin. The silent sculptures of all the animals watched me. I knew as soon as I entered that Crezil had gone. But where?

"It's daytime," I grumbled. "Why isn't it here?"

Maybe it's gone to Isowon, said Malator.

"Don't say that. Don't say we're too late."

For my plan to work, I needed to face the creature. I sat myself down in the dust and waited, amusing myself by casting giant shadows of the animal sculptures upon the rocky walls.

I feel asleep dreaming of Gilwyn's baby. In my dream the baby was a boy and looked like his father, small and mousey, with a hook for a hand. Compared to a clubbed foot, I told Gilwyn in my dream, a hook for a hand wasn't such a bad thing. At least he could run when he grew up. At least he wasn't blind like his mother. The Gilwyn in my dream smiled and agreed with me and cooed when the hook grabbed his finger. He called me Uncle Lukien.

When I awoke I realized I was crying, my shirt wet with snot and tears. I ran a forearm under my nose and forced myself to stop, but couldn't get the image of that little hooked hand out of my brain. My bladder burned, begging for a piss, and I realized I'd been asleep for hours. The tomb was even darker than I'd found it. Outside, night had fallen—I felt it in my bones. I was wasting time and angry with myself, and the little flame Malator had given me had gone out. But I didn't ask for another. Instead I groped like a blind man for a corner, unbuttoned my trousers and pissed on the wall. The smell of it in the airless tomb made me sick. I finished fast, shuffled to the other side of the chamber and sat down again, lost in my own black thoughts.

All of my life had been plagued by dreams. Nightmares, really. I never dreamed of good things, and as I sat there waiting for the monster I wondered at the turns that had brought me to this place. At night, when sleep evades, all your mistakes come haunting. I wanted to be drunk suddenly, to drown myself in wine or bury myself in a woman's thighs—anything to take the pain away. The aloneness strangled me. The darkness played tricks on me. I could easily make out Cricket in the shadows, or Cassandra, or Akeela, or any of the others my love had murdered. I sat back and let them dance before my drooping eyes, somehow keeping my tears at bay as I drifted to sleep again.

When I awoke, hours later, the little flame was once again alive in my hand. I smiled at it, thanking Malator for the gift. I took the flame from my palm and lit a stone with it, giving me just enough light to move around the chamber. I studied each of the sculptures, marveling at the grace of the leopard and workmanship of the eagle's feathers. I wondered if Malator could bring them to life for me, the way he'd drawn the monster in the dirt all those weeks ago.

The Sword of Angels rested in my lap. I caressed it as I thought of Cricket. First I smiled, then I laughed as I remembered her. How she could badger me! Malator noticed my mirth and popped into my mind.

What? he probed.

"I was thinking of Cricket," I said. "All she ever wanted was to talk, remember? About anything. Even when she fell into a mood, she wanted to talk."

About you, mostly.

I nodded. "Yeah."

In the darkness of the tomb, with death and eternity all around me, I wondered: I never really understood her curiosity about me or mine for her. I never answered the question for myself. Had I wanted to be her friend? Her father? Was I looking for a squire or something more? I had forever to face myself, but I didn't want to look. All I knew for sure was that I loved Cricket. And I missed her.

"She was a child," I whispered. "Not even a woman yet. But she would have been a splendid woman. A brave woman."

Lukien, you will avenge her, said Malator. *Remember, I promised you that.*

"I remember," I said but wondered if vengeance would ease me.

Lukien, said Malator, *we should go into the antechamber.*

I sighed. Malator always tried to change the subject to deflect my sour moods. "Why?"

Because the portal is there.

"So?"

Lukien, it's a gateway to another realm.

"A gateway to Gahoreth," I corrected. "To hell."

To a realm of the dead, he argued.

I didn't get his meaning, and I didn't care to. "Why are you pushing me? We were talking about Cricket. If you want to cheer me up, come up with something better than a visit to hell."

I was about to set aside the sword when suddenly Malator spoke.

Lukien . . . it's back.

I knew at once what he meant. I *felt* it. Slowly I got to my feet, letting the sword dangle in my hand. I stared at the stone blocking the door and held my breath, listening to the noise of its approach growing ever louder. Then, it suddenly stopped.

It knows, said Malator.

I waited, tensing, my mind going blank. If it knew I was here why didn't it come? I thought of calling out to it but didn't. I took a small step forward then paused. The light Malator gave me still flickered atop the stone.

"It wants darkness," I whispered. "Malator . . ."

The light instantly extinguished. And my eyes, having grown accustomed to it, went blind. I stood there in the blackness, frozen, my heart noisily thumping, and turned my ear toward the crack I'd come through. Beyond the slab I heard the sound again, like something dragging closer. I had trapped myself, I realized. Not too loudly, I called out the demon's name.

"Crezil."

The dragging stopped. Silence. But only for a moment. Next came the shocking noise of the slab being pulled—ripped—away from the tomb. It tumbled sideways, rolling and crushing the rocks beneath it, finally crashing to the ground. I backed away, peering through the dust, looking desperately for Crezil. A crumb of light from the far-off entrance outlined the creature. I was twelve feet away from it, and yet could barely see it. But Crezil saw me clearly. I knew it did, putting one appendage forward and pulling itself nearer. Slowly my eyes adjusted to the horrible view.

It was as I'd seen it in the painting of Gahoreth, many-limbed and huge, man-shaped but disfigured, with tails for arms that wriggled over its bulbous head. Now it was exposed, without the bones and skins to hide it. I stood my ground, using my enchanted eyes to see. There was no stench from it, nor any sound at all, but Crezil had not returned alone. Dragging behind it, held by a claw-like hand, were the bodies of a man and a woman. Both were naked and badly bruised, with the man being pulled by an ankle and the woman by her long, bloodied hair. Before I knew what was happening, Crezil lifted them off the ground, letting them dangle before me like a string of fish.

"I see them," I said. I sheathed my sword and put up my hands. "I'm not here to fight you."

Crezil tossed the bodies at me. They landed hard and rolled to my feet. Shocked, I knelt to examine them, to be certain they were dead. Not a strip of clothing remained on either of them. I wondered if Crezil had killed them in lovemaking. When I put my fingers to the woman's neck, all I felt was a chill. I looked up at Crezil in disgust.

"Are you giving these to me?" I asked. "Why?"

Malator spoke up. *A peace offering, perhaps.*

I rose slowly to face the beast. "What shall I do with them?" I asked it. "Eat them? I'm not like you, Crezil. I'm not a demon. I'm a man."

There was no answer from the monster. It hovered there on its bony limbs, watching me through the darkness.

"Did you know I'd be here?" I asked. I gestured to the bodies. "Did you kill them for me?"

Again, no reply. Yet I knew the thing could understand me.

"No more killing," I said. "We stop now. I don't want to hunt you. Do you see?"

Crezil either couldn't or wouldn't speak. Instead it took a single step backward. Its shining eyes watched for my next move.

"All right," I said carefully. "Now listen to me. I know you want to go back to Gahoreth. *Gahoreth*. Your home. Yes? I don't want to stop you. I want to help you."

It seemed intrigued. Its tails or arms or whatever they were wrapped around its pulsing body.

It's listening, Lukien, urged Malator. *Go on.*

"I'm going to get you what you want so you can go home," I told Crezil. "But you have to help me, too. No more attacks on Isowon. *No more*. You stay here. You wait for me to come back. Do that, and I'll bring you what you want."

I kept my voice calm, like talking to a dog. Crezil responded with silence.

"I can't kill you, and you can't kill me," I continued. "We're immortal now, both of us. I have no soul for you to steal. But we can both get what we want. You can hide here so no one sees you, and in a few days I'll return." I carefully stepped over the bodies of the man and the woman. "Will you make this peace with me?"

Crezil moved back into the shadows, shrouding its massive body. But was that an answer?

"You can go home," I said. "And then I can go home, too. Agreed? If not, tell me so now or let me walk out of here freely. If you don't try and stop me, I'll know we have a bargain."

I took another step. This time Crezil didn't move. There was just enough space for me to walk past it. I eased myself forward, careful not to look at Crezil as I groped through the darkness, focusing on the distant sunlight. As I brushed past the creature, I felt its cold, inhuman breath. It could have easily lopped my head off, yet it did not. Two more steps, and I was past it.

I kept on walking, just a little faster. Behind me Crezil moved into its tomb, ready, I supposed, to feast on the dead lovers.

29

The way west was harder than I remembered. The sky was clear and the road was good, and I had gotten enough sleep in the tomb to last me a week. Yet I could not ride fast enough to suit me and pushed Venger more and more to reach Isowon on time. By now I'd lost count of the seven days Diriel had granted me. It had been morning when I left Crezil's lair, and all that day I followed the sun's movements west, finally reaching the road to Zura. Fallon himself had come across the road as a teenager, even younger than Cricket, he'd told me, and made a fortune looting spices from his homeland. Now, though, the road was quiet, tottering between sandy coastline and sparse forests.

I needed no map to find my way back, and so spent my hours planning Isowon's defense and daydreaming of my vengeance. By now Marilius and Kiryk had reached the palace, I supposed, and Fallon had no doubt bolstered his defenses. So far, Fallon had been a disappointment. I doubted he'd be much help in the coming battle. But that hardly mattered. All I really needed from him was his gold and a promise to pay his mercenaries on time. Given the odds against us, I was sure many of the mercenaries had already fled, but with Kiryk's men to strengthen us and enough of Anton's own remaining, maybe we had a chance.

If I was lucky and reached Isowon by nightfall, I told myself, I could meet with Anton and the others. We could council and make plans. There were so many questions going through my mind. How many men had Diriel brought with him? How many of them were legionnaires? Had Marilius made it back yet? I could barely keep my mind together. Questions flew through me like arrows.

"Enough!" I shouted.

The birds scattered from the treetops. I took a breath to calm myself, then heard a surprising reply.

"Someone?"

The call came from far ahead, buried from view and muffled by trees. Venger's ears perked up. I listened, eased Venger ahead, then heard the noise of riders. I rounded the bend and saw them ahead of me—a dozen men, all on horseback, each horse the deepest black I'd ever seen. The men wore fur-lined helmets of riveted iron, with leather and animal skins cloaking their bodies. Long arrows fletched with white feathers stuck from the quivers on their backs, and some carried spears in their hands. A skirt of metal-rings draped around their legs, falling down to their ankles. Each had a sword as well, a curved scimitar that bounced inside its dangling sheath.

These were men riding to war. Even their horses were armed, shielded with plates and iron spikes. Red and yellow ribbons flowed from their bridles. The man in the lead paused when he saw me, bringing his companions to a halt. His dark eyes stared at me from a face of bronze. He had turned the company around to find me, and now just seemed confused. Or was he delighted?

"Luck upon your journey," he called to me.

I had never heard that greeting before. "To you as well," I offered.

He and his men looked at me and at my horse. Their own mounts were spectacular. Clearly they knew horseflesh, and appreciated Venger. With no reason to fear them, I trotted closer, raising my hand.

"I ride for Isowon," I said. "From Drin territory."

The man's face brightened. "We ride for Isowon! We ride from Zura." He poked a thumb to his breast. "We are Zurans. *Bogati*."

"'Bogati'? I do not know that word," I said. "But Zura I know. You're far from home."

"Bogati always hear the call of war," he said. This time he touched his ear. "We follow the wind and listen. If it is just, we come. Do you ride to the war in Isowon?"

His accent made him hard to understand. "Yes," I answered. "I've been to Isowon—I know the man who leads there. Have you heard of Anton Fallon? He's a Zuran, like yourself."

The man laughed, then turned to his fellows and translated the joke. The man looked at me and said proudly, "I am the only one of us who speaks the western words. All Zurans know Anton Fallon! Fallon not Bogati, though. Fallon is . . ." His face scrunched as he searched for the word. "A soft man."

"And Bogati?" I asked. "Horsemen?"

His smile broadened to show his big teeth. "Ah, you know Bogati! None are horsemen like Bogati horsemen. We are twice other men. Three times." He studied my horse. "But you are horseman." He put his hand over his heart. "My greeting is sincere. No offending. You will ride with us to Isowon. We fight together."

"Why would you fight for Anton Fallon?" I asked. I still didn't know how the news from Isowon had reached them. "Because he's a Zuran?"

"No," said the man flatly. "Never for Anton Fallon. For the bronze man."

One of his companions spoke up. "Others come that way, too. All who have heard. Bogati, Zithras . . . all men from Zura come to see this man."

The leader quickly nodded. "You say you come from Isowon. Have you seen him?"

"Who?" I asked.

"The man of bronze. The one kissed by heaven. If you're from Isowon you must know him."

"I think I might," I said. I'd left my battered armor back in Isowon, but the reference was obvious. "You mean Lukien."

"Yes!" said the man, and all his companions nodded when they heard the name. "The Undying." He turned to the others, gesturing and grinning. The men with the spears shook them excitedly. They shared some words I couldn't understand before their leader looked back at me. "Have you fought with him? Will you tell us of him?"

"You're going to Isowon because of Lukien?" I asked.

"Yes, because of the stories," said the man. "We will join the siege at Isowon. We will join the man of bronze and fight with him." Suddenly he dropped down from his horse. "I am fool," he pronounced, bowing deeply with his hand across his heart. "My name is Chuluun. Of the Bogati. All of us. We ride with you, bring you luck and victory."

I dismounted to face Chuluun, not wanting to tell him the truth but not wanting to lie to him either. "Chuluun, you and your men ride to find Lukien?"

"We do." Chuluun straightened, waiting for me to give my name.

"To fight with him? He has need of many men, but the fighting is fierce in Isowon."

"We will leave blood and teeth across the sand," Chuluun promised. "We know of Diriel's sorcery. We are not afraid. When we see the bronze man we will prove that."

They were all looking at me now. Chuluun kept his dark eyes on mine, even when I reached for my sword. Very slowly I pulled it from its sheath, laying it out before me in my upturned palms.

"Have you ever heard of the Sword of Angels?" I asked.

Chuluun shook his head as he stared at my blade. "Is that what you call it?"

"It's the sword that keeps Lukien alive," I said. "Inside the sword is an ancient spirit. Do you believe in spirits?"

"All is spirits," said Chuluun. "The trees, the sky, the flowers. And swords?"

"This is the Sword of Angels, Chuluun. This is the sword Lukien carries. He's not made of bronze. He's a man, or at least he was a man." I held out the sword for him. "Touch it if you want."

Chuluun looked at me blankly. "You?"

I nodded. "The sword looks plain. So do I. But I'm Lukien, and I need all the men I can find to help me battle Diriel. If your men are up for it, I'll gladly ride with you to Isowon."

Chuluun lightly touched the sword, drawing back his fingers quickly. There was no disappointment on his face, only awe.

"I *am* Lukien," I told him. "Whether I'm kissed by heaven or cursed, I'm him. I'll set you straight on whatever else you've heard about me, but I'm in a hurry and can't waste time." I sheathed the sword and looked over their horses. "Can those beasts keep up?"

The Zuran snorted at my challenge. "Bogati means people of the wind," he said. "Ride with us and let us show you."

West we rode on the road from Zura, west toward the shore of distant Isowon, like a storm cloud rolling across the horizon. The black horses of the Bogati packed the road and stirred the dust with thunder, crushing the stones beneath their hooves and daring Venger to keep up. Singing to the odd music of their bouncing ring-mail skirts, Chuluun and his men made a show of riding, the ribbons on their tack and clothing spiraling out behind them. On occasion we slowed to rest the horses or to let them drink from one of the rivers we found on our way. At a farmhouse, a woman took one look at us and ran inside to bolt the door. We slaked ourselves with water from her well, and Chuluun put a silver coin on it to repay the "generosity." As we rode away from the farm, he explained that no act of kindness could go unacknowledged, not for a Bogati. It was the first of many Zuran rules I would learn from him.

Being with Chuluun and his men eased my memories of Cricket. It was good to be with men again, good to be riding toward a certain, bloody battle. But no matter how hard or fast we traveled, there was just no way to reach Isowon by nightfall; as the sun began to set our exhausted horses called an end to our ride. Famished and parched, we set to making camp in a stand of birch trees not far from the road. Chuluun and I tended to the horses while the others built a strange looking tent, a circular shelter of canvas and felt held up by wooden rods and ropes driven into the ground. Each of the Bogati horses carried a different part of the tent—some the stakes, some the rolled up lengths of fabric—and each man did his part with ease. As we fed the horses, Chuluun explained another in his long list of Bogati customs.

"It is called a kurelt," he said. He lifted the hoof of one of the horses, digging out the packed dirt with a knife. "A Bogati never sleeps under the sky. He must be covered, always."

I worked carefully on one of the black horses, gently removing the bit from its mouth. The men building the kurelt sang while they erected the tent. "Why? I like to watch the stars while I sleep."

Chuluun shook his head. "Tonight you sleep with us in the kurelt. The stars are for the gods."

"What about a fire?" I asked. "How can we cook?"

"We cook in the kurelt," said Chuluun. He looked at me oddly. "I see I have a lot to show you. Never mind. You tell me about how you cannot die, and I will teach you about being a Bogati."

By the time the sun was down the kurelt was up and all our horses were resting. Two of Chuluun's men waited outside the tent, guarding the horses and the rest of us while we took our ease inside the spacious kurelt. I leaned against the felt wall, going around the circle of men and practicing their exotic names. Nalinbaatar, Chuluun's brother, cooked our meal over a fire in the center of the kurelt, the smoke spiraling up and out of a circular cutout in the roof. He laughed, stirring his pots and correcting me, while I worked my tongue around the names.

"*Bahlochchur,*" he said.

Bahlochchur, one of the youngest of the warriors, grinned as I tried to pronounce his name, forcing the sound out of my throat to get the guttural sound just right.

"Bahlochchur," I said.

"Bahlochchur," Nalinbaatar corrected.

I tried again. "Bahlochchur."

Chuluun, who was sitting next to me, shook his head. "No. Bah . . ."

"Bah . . ."

"Lou-ak . . ."

"Loo-ak . . ."

Bahlochchur waved me off, feigning disgust. "*Oyuun ukhaan nandin.*"

Chuluun laughed. "He says you make baby talk."

I nodded and gave up. "Chuluun, your name is easy. You'll speak for me then."

Chuluun shook his head. "Not now. Now we eat."

It was another of their Bogati rules, I learned later: no talk of war or business over meals. Meals were sacred, Chuluun explained. I liked that. Eating their spicy food and laughing at jokes I didn't understand made me forget, and forgetting was the one thing I wanted more than anything. They fed me generously, like the desert folk of Ganjor, never letting my cup get dry or my plate too light. I ate as they did, using my knife to push my food from my plate to my mouth, the way men always eat when women aren't around.

And Chuluun was protective of me, almost jealous of my attention. When questions came my way he let only the most benign ones through, translating for his comrades their inquiries about my horse and the places I'd been and about my family and the children I didn't have. Never once did they ask me about my sword or how my eye had grown back or about my Akari, and I knew that was because Chuluun wouldn't let them. They were intensely curious about Isowon and what they would find there, but they didn't seem at all afraid, and I wasn't sure how much of what I answered actually got back to them, or how much Chuluun kept to himself.

Finally, when it was long past sundown and all of us had eaten and gotten drunk enough to sleep, Chuluun pulled gently at my sleeve. I had already fallen half asleep against him, my head lolling onto his shoulder. His voice whispered in my ear.

"Lukien, walk with me."

He got up, tiptoeing past his comrades toward the tent flap. I shook off my grogginess and followed. Bahlochchur opened one eye to watch me but didn't say a thing as he tracked my leaving, following Chuluun outside. The night air struck my face. It was fabulously dark, with only a few stars poking through the murky skies. The tribesmen who were still on guard looked at Chuluun from their places in the darkness. Chuluun nodded at them and whispered, and the two men gratefully retreated into the kurelt.

Was it our turn to stand guard? All I wanted was to sleep but didn't moan about it. Plainly Chuluun wanted to talk. He moved away from the kurelt, just out of earshot of his comrades inside. The darkness made his expression even more serious. He scratched at the scraggy hair that bearded his neck, kicked at the dirt, then dug into the pocket of his jacket. I expected a pipe to appear, or just some tobacco for chewing, so when I saw the silk scarf I was surprised.

"This is for you," he said. He turned to face me. "Put out your hands, please. Both please."

I did as he asked. "Why?"

"I know you are ignorant so I will teach you. This is a hahlag . . ." He placed the scarf into my palms. "For Zurans, it is a gift of respect and friendship. I brought this with me for you, Lukien, to ask your permission to fight with you."

I took the gift, not really understanding. It was soft and expensive looking, and blue from what I could tell. But it wasn't womanly, at least it didn't seem so coming from Chuluun. It obviously meant something, too, so I bowed to him, holding the scarf carefully, and smiled.

"A hahlag," I repeated. "What does that mean?"

"It means person," said Chuluun. "A person. A man . . ." He shrugged. "A friend. One of the tribe."

"Ah, thank you," I said. "So I am a Bogati now?"

Chuluun took the scarf and began tying it around my neck. "When Zurans see this, they will know you are one of us," he said. "There will be other Zurans in Isowon. More will come to fight. I can hear them."

"How do you know?"

"Because they are stirred," said Chuluun. He spun me around to look at the hahlag, approving of its appearance. "By you, Lukien."

"Chuluun, why are we speaking out here alone? Why do you

keep the others from speaking with me? We rode all day, and I know so little. I have questions. Your men have questions."

"I speak for them all," said Chuluun. "They must see no doubt in me. They must hear no fear."

"What were they asking me? What do they want to know? Tell me. I'll answer all their questions. And yours, my friend."

Chuluun smiled. He looked drunk. He gazed up at the stars. "The gods sleep, except for a few . . ." He pointed to the handful of visible stars, poking at them one by one. "They watch us."

I looked up and smiled, pretending to agree, not having the heart to tell him that there were no gods hiding behind the starlight.

"They chose you," said Chuluun. "Why?"

I thought about that. I'd always thought about that. Bad luck was the only answer I'd ever come up with. "I don't know," I confessed.

Chuluun looked down at the sword, my constant companion, belted to my waist. "The god that keeps you alive—what is its name?"

"Malator," I replied.

"Malator." Chuluun squatted down for a closer look. "Malator," he whispered, speaking to the blade.

"Do you want to see him?" I asked.

Chuluun's narrow eyes turned as round as walnuts. "You can see him?"

"Yes," I nodded. "He will show himself if I ask it. If you want me to I will."

The temptation made Chuluun shiver. He stood up and shook his head. "No," he said softly. "You have been kissed by heaven, Lukien. Not I. I have been chosen to follow you."

"Tell me about that." I took a few more paces away from the kurelt, giving Chuluun space to speak freely. He stayed beside me as we pretended to study the dark forest. "Tell me why you've come to fight Diriel. Many men wouldn't. Many have already fled. Why do you have it in your heart to make this fight?"

"Because Zuran men fight," said Chuluun with a little shrug. "We are born to it. In Zura there is too little war these days. Too many men like Anton Fallon. Rich men. You see? Bogati ways are old ways. Simple ways. Our hearts never change. I do not know if I can make you see."

"I understand fighting," I replied. "All my life has been fighting. But I want to stop. I want peace now."

"No," said Chuluun. "I do not see that in you."

"You barely know me."

"But I see clearly," he insisted. "Your eyes do not hide the truth. There is no peace in your eyes, Lukien. Only vengeance."

I laughed. "Oh, indeed there's that! I've been wronged, and I will have justice. My vengeance will be a rain of knives. I mean to kill them all, Chuluun, for what they've done. But when it's over . . ." I had to steady myself against the rage. "When it's over, I'm going home. I'll have my revenge, and then I'll have peace."

Chuluun sighed like he didn't believe me. "All right," he said. "Or, you can accept what you are and find *true* peace. Tell me: Why did you come here? You are Liirian. Liiria is far, far from here. No one would come to this place without reason. Why would you leave the home you say you must return to?"

I didn't like the way the conversation had turned. "Because I was restless," I admitted. "Because I was looking for answers. You asked me why I was chosen to live forever. But I don't know. That's why I came here—to find out. To try and do some good."

"With a sword," Chuluun pointed out. "Why not a spoon?"

"What?"

"Why not carry a spoon instead of a sword?"

"Because the sword keeps me alive."

"Huh." Chuluun smiled. "So it's not a spoon that keeps you alive."

"No, and it's not a fork or a hoe either. What's your point?"

"My point," said Chuluun, "is that a sword has always kept you alive." He yawned, then stretched, then turned back to the kurelt. "Will you watch over us, Lukien? I am tired and need sleep. You do not need rest. You only think you do."

And that's how he left me, alone and baffled, having put just enough doubt in my mind to keep me awake all night.

30

The next morning Chuluun and his men broke camp the way soldiers do—quickly and perfectly, like they'd done it a thousand times. They packed the kurelt, sharing the parts of it amongst their magnificent horses, buried the embers of our campfire, and pointed their mounts west again. I rode with my blue hahlag around my neck, proudly pretending to be a Bogati, smelling of their spices and eager to reach Isowon. The closer we came the more the land flattened and the air filled with brine from the ocean, and by the time we were mere miles away my heart had swelled with so much bloodlust I was very nearly drunk with it. The handful of days Diriel had granted me to bring him the monster had nearly passed, and I was certain he'd already marched his army to the city's outskirts. I doubted, though, that he'd done anything but threaten Anton. Diriel wanted Crezil, and only I could give him the monster. I had played my gambit and played it well, and was feeling better about myself than I had in months. Very soon, I told myself, I would have the revenge I needed so badly.

Isowon appeared: a shimmering mirage, perched serenely on the ocean like a daydreaming lover. Chuluun and his men cheered when we saw her, pointing and congratulating themselves and whooping over the coming war. The city was quiet, and from our great distance I could see the smoke of fires in the eastern hills, where Diriel's army was no doubt camped. The haze above the landscape helped me estimate their numbers, a vast sum that withered my confidence. They were barely a two-hour march from the shore. But they were still camped, I reminded myself, and that meant Isowon was safe.

For now.

"Lukien," called Chuluun, riding up alongside me. "The sky." He pointed with his regal nose.

"I see it."

The sight of the smoke thrilled Chuluun. "So many enemies. Heaven blesses us."

It was something a madman would say. Or a young man. Maybe Chuluun was both. "Blood and teeth," I reminded him. "We'll spare none of them."

Only madmen could win this fight, and I needed an army of them. Men like Chuluun, who thought the gods called them to slaughter. Or men like Kiryk, who'd lost so much they'd lost their fears as well. Men like me. Men too crazy to be afraid. We didn't slow our pace a bit when we saw the smoke. In fact we drove our horses harder, eager to reach Isowon, to swing our swords and throw our spears. It was nearly noontime, and the hot sun bore down on our lathered horses. I remembered the way the city looked in that perfect light. I had thought she was asleep, but as we finally reached her outskirts I saw the fighting men along her sandy streets and perched in her white towers, armed and silent like a pincushion of blades. A patrol of mercenaries stood guard just inside the city's main road, the very road that had led me and Cricket into Isowon that fateful first time.

Chuluun had never seen the likes of Isowon and, in awe of the sight, he slowed his horse. Finally, with the gleaming city growing in our vision, and at last bereft of words, his face slackened, startled by its splendor. He'd come from a world of steppes and campfires, where children played with bones and wealth was measured in wives and horses. And now . . . Isowon. So hard to describe, so achingly beautiful, that Chuluun and his men gasped. Up ahead, the mercenaries on the main road spotted us, turning their attention toward us with a shout. I raised my hand high and called out a greeting, then heard my name from the crowd. There were at least thirty men. But one in particular stood out from the rest, waving both hands over his head when he saw me.

"That's Marilius," I said with a smile. "The one I told you about, Chuluun."

Chuluun gestured to his men to ride abreast of us, forming an arrowhead with himself and me at the tip. He brushed the mane of his black horse with his fingertips, straightening up tall in his saddle as if about to meet a king. We watched as Marilius hurried to a horse, riding out quickly to greet us. Just the sight of him buoyed me. He had made it back safely, and that meant Kiryk's Drinmen were here as well, probably preparing for the coming battle. From what I could tell already, Isowon was working hard to prepare.

Marilius thundered up on a dapple gray, grinning wildly at my companions. We greeted each other like the friends we had never been, clasping arms and saying how pleased we were to see each other. Marilius looked surprisingly well rested, but also relieved to see me.

"When did you get back?" I asked. I spied past him toward the city. "Kiryk?"

"Two nights ago," said Marilius. "Kiryk's at the palace with his men. Anton's got the whole city jammed in there with us." He looked over Chuluun and his men. "But we've got room for more."

"Marilius, this is Chuluun, from Zura," I pronounced. "Leader of these men. I can't even tell you their names—bloody tough language—but they've come to fight."

"Bogati," said Marilius. He smiled warmly at Chuluun, then put his fist over his chest the way Chuluun had done when we'd met. "People of the wind."

Chuluun puffed up like a rooster. "You know of Bogati?" he asked.

"Only a little. Only what my employer has told me. We welcome you, Chuluun, and your men. Others have come from Zura already. They told us more would be on the way."

"Others?" I asked. "Really?"

"I tell you this, and you do not believe," laughed Chuluun. "Bogati do not run from a fight! We ride into its fangs."

"How many?" I asked Marilius.

"Forty at least. Fifty maybe. They keep coming! They come because of you, Lukien. You're all they talk about."

Chuluun gave a cocky snort. "He is one of us now," he said, pointing at my hahlag. "You see that? We are brothers in this battle. He rides like a Bogati. If you fight with us, man of Isowon, then we are brothers too."

I hadn't told Chuluun much about Marilius—certainly not about his "friendship" with Fallon. Now I was glad I hadn't. The look on Marilius's face was priceless.

"Call me brother then, Chuluun," he said. "We will fight together."

"And the Silver Dragons of Drin, too," I said, "and all the mercenaries who've stayed. How many have stayed, Marilius?"

Marilius smiled. "All of them, Lukien."

"All?" I was stunned. "Not *all*, surely."

"All and more. Everyone has come! Not just Zurans, but Drinmen and men from Kasse, too. And every one-armed, one-legged merc who can still swing a sword. The whole city's packed with them, just waiting."

"For Diriel?"

"For you, Lukien." Marilius's grin flattened. "They have nothing, most of them. They've lost everything. You should hear their stories. All their leaders are dead, except for Kiryk. He sent word north that anyone willing should join him here in Isowon. It's a last stand. He's the one that told them how you can't die. They believe that."

"It is true," said Chuluun. He pointed at my sword. "He has a god for his very own."

"I know," replied Marilius. "And now everyone knows it. That's why they've come."

The news overwhelmed me. "Mercenaries too? I know mercenaries, Marilius. They fight for money."

"That part you're right about," said Marilius. "That's Anton's doing. He's given them everything to stay and fight. The palace is stripped. He told each man to name his price, then told any of them who thought of running that you'd come after them. You did say you would, you know."

"I did," I recalled. "And meant it."

"I will slice off the ears of any man who tries to run now," swore Chuluun. "Or anyone who raises a hand to you, Lukien."

"But Anton? Really? I never met a man who loved money so much. I can't believe it."

"He could have run himself, but he didn't," said Marilius. "You should credit him for that, at least. He loves Isowon. It's his. He's not going to give it up."

"Then I'm glad to be wrong about him," I said. "If I am."

"I have heard no good things about Anton Fallon," said Chuluun. "In Zura he is talked of as a thief. We have not come to help him but to fight with Lukien."

Marilius looked sharply at Chuluun and said, "We all fight for our own reasons. Some for money and some for a grand crusade. Or for revenge, like the Drinmen. But make no mistake—you're in

Isowon now. This is Anton Fallon's city. If you won't respect that, turn yourselves around."

There was real steel in Marilius's voice. More than just loyalty. Love, maybe. He stared at the shocked Chuluun. I didn't get between them.

Chuluun was good-natured enough to let the threat pass. He shrugged and said, "Brothers fight. My brother Nalinbaatar . . ." He waved his brother closer, and Nalinbaatar rode up to join him. "Once he took a knife and stuck me in the backside with it. When he was just a boy! But we will fight together for Isowon. We will fight with you and Anton Fallon, Marilius."

Nalinbaatar, who couldn't understand a word being said, shoved his brother nearly out of his saddle. It was enough of an apology to give Marilius ease.

"There's room for all your men in the palace, Chuluun," said Marilius. "You should rest. There's plenty of food—we won't need to conserve it. This won't be a siege."

"Oh? Who made that decision?" I asked.

"Anton," replied Marilius. "And I agree with him. We need to beat them back, not let them push us out to sea. It's just us now, and whoever else shows up in the next day or so. We should go after them in the field, not in the city. Once they breach the city they won't stop."

"And Anton?" I asked. "Will he ride with us?"

Marilius frowned. "C'mon, Lukien . . . he's no good on a horse. He'll be killed before—"

I laughed. "You made the right decision, Marilius. We'll charge out to fight them. There . . ." I pointed to where the smoke of Diriel's camp defiled the sky. "Let Anton stay in the city. If he dies, the mercenaries won't get paid."

Marilius nodded, then gave me a look that meant he wanted to speak alone. I turned to Chuluun and said, "Ride ahead, my friend. Rest, eat . . . you'll be welcome. We'll speak tonight."

Chuluun rounded up Nalinbaatar and the others and trotted forward toward Isowon, leaving Marilius and me behind. Marilius waited until the Bogati were out of earshot before delivering the news.

"I gave Diriel your message, Lukien," he told me. "Soon as I arrived. He's waiting for you." He smirked. "But it doesn't look like you've kept your bargain."

"Did you expect me to?"

"Maybe. Diriel wants the monster, Lukien. That's the only reason he hasn't attacked yet. You'll have to tell him something."

"I'm back now," I said. "There was always going to be a fight, Marilius. Now it can begin."

Marilius looked disappointed. "So you're not going to tell me what happened? Where'd you go? Did you see the monster?"

"I bought us some time," I said. "We need to talk about Diriel's army. What's it look like? As big as we feared?"

"Anton wants a council. He said we'd meet to talk as soon as you arrived. Lukien, what about the monster? Diriel's expecting you to bring it to him."

I started Venger toward the city again. "Have Anton call his council tonight. I want Chuluun there, and Kiryk, and that old man he listens to. No more defending ourselves—now we go on the attack."

"What about Diriel? He'll want to hear something."

"Oh, he'll hear something," I promised. "A real skull-cracker."

Marilius spurred his horse to follow me. "Lukien, there's something else."

"What else?"

"Someone who says he knows you. He came three days ago, before I got back with Kiryk. He says he wants to speak with you."

"Who?" I asked. I was tired, perplexed, and annoyed by the demand. "What's his name?"

"He's a Ganjeese, Lukien," said Marilius. "He says his name is Sariyah."

I followed Marilius to the west side of the city, where avenues of modest homes stood among the fruit trees. We crossed through the abandoned market, the stalls empty of goods. Most of the people had gone to the palace, explained Marilius, but some had stayed in the west side because of the prayer tower. Isowon had no patron god and no one creed. Its people had come from across the region to trade or find work with the generous Anton Fallon, and had taken all their beliefs with them, mingling them in the city's single "church." The tower itself was easy to spot among the squat little homes. It rose up at the edge of the city, a cylinder of pearly brick overlooking the ocean. A colorful crowd had gathered around it, about thirty men and women anxious to offer prayers. But according to Marilius, Sariyah wasn't letting anyone inside.

We dismounted near the tower and handed our horses off to one of the mercenaries standing guard. The crowd was orderly, most of them just sat and waited, so there weren't many soldiers needed. The few present greeted their captain, relieved to see us both.

"Should I tell him you're here?" asked the Norvan who took our horses.

I shook my head. "No. Just go away. He's harmless."

I hadn't seen Sariyah or his sons since Arad, just before my tangle with Wrestler. I always imagined he'd made it to Zura, to start amassing that fortune he'd bragged about. But he'd come alone to Isowon, and that worried me. Marius said he'd come looking for me, and on foot. When they told him I was expected, he took his scimitar up to the prayer tower, threatened to kill anyone who came up after him, and waited.

"We would have dragged him out if he wasn't your friend, Lukien," said Marilius, looking up at the tower. "And he's piss drunk. At least let me go with you."

"No," I sighed. "Go back to the palace. Take your men with you. Tell Anton I'll be there soon. Have him make ready for our war council."

Marilius turned and got back on his horse, ordered the rest of his men to move off from the prayer tower, and left me in the middle of the orderly throng, wondering about my first move. The folks around me looked up in confusion. A young woman sitting at the steps of the tower took hold of my hand.

"Let him pray," she said. "Leave him. He'll come down when he has his answers."

Her compassion surprised me. Around her some others nodded. That's when I realized it was the mercenaries who wanted Sariyah down. The prayerful were content to wait.

"If he wants to stay, I won't force him down," I promised the woman. "But he's asking for me. I need to go."

"He rages at Vala," she said. She had deep brown eyes and a scarf around her head that might have been Ganjeese. "He mourns."

My fingers slipped out of her hand. My heart sank, but I didn't ask the obvious question. Maybe I was too afraid. Maybe I already knew. I shuddered as I entered the prayer tower, my breath suddenly loud within the echoing structure. An odd assortment of religious icons lined the circular walls. Burnt out incense hung in silver sconces. A winding stairway of alabaster twisted toward the top of the tower, but the candles along its way had all long since gone out. I paused at the bottom of the stairs, listening, but heard only silence from above.

"Sariyah," I called up the stairway. "It's Lukien. Can you hear me?"

There was a long gap of silence. I put my foot on the first alabaster step and heard a voice call back to me.

"Shalafein."

That was a name I never heard anymore. Instantly it carried me home.

"*Azizi,*" I answered. The Ganjeese word for friend. "I'm coming up."

The turning staircase enveloped me in windowless darkness as I journeyed upward, higher and higher past the dead sconces, using my enchanted eyes to see the glorious frescoes painted on the walls. Gods and animals bade me up the tower, the endless tail of some intelligent looking dragon pointing my way, like a rope to follow to heaven. When at last I reached the top, my eyes flooded with sudden sunlight, streaming in from the many archways and balconies. A pure breeze straight off the ocean stirred through the tower, filling my nose with brine. There, beneath one of the arches, sat Sariyah, his back against the wall, two empty glass bottles strewn beside him. His enormous scimitar rested on his lap. His eyes met me through the shadows of his filthy hair.

"You came." His voice was a rasp, scratchy from shouting, I supposed. Or maybe from days of thirst. His cheeks were parched and blistered, his clothes soiled from travel. His jet black mustache had overgrown his mouth. I could smell the stink of him even over the ocean breeze. The odor of liquor reached me from across the chamber. He was alone, just as Marilius said he'd be, and he wore his aloneness like chains.

"Of course I came," I answered. I moved toward him, unafraid. He was still enormous, but had left a good bit of himself somewhere on the road. He looked starved but totally disinterested in food. I knew that look. I'd seen it in mirrors. "They tell me you've been asking for me," I said.

I dropped down to one knee before him. He reached for his scimitar and set it aside.

"You look different." His finger rose to trace my face. "Your eye. What happened? You look so . . . young now."

"I will tell you," I sighed, "but a lot has happened since Arad, my friend."

He looked at me with dread. “Where is your girl?”

I bit my lip. I couldn’t answer. Sariyah dropped his head back against the wall.

“No, tell me not. I told you this was no place for a girl. Dead?”

Seeing him made all the sorrow unbearable again. “Cricket’s gone, Sariyah. They killed her.”

He didn’t look away. “Then you and I have our vengeances to settle, Shalafein. They took my boys. My beautiful boys.”

“What happened?”

“We were on the road. To Zura, remember? We left Arad and kept moving quickly, but Diriel—his men are everywhere now. They made my boys join them. Their death army! We fought them, but . . .”

His face just sort of crumbled.

“Two of my boys are dead,” he said. “But they took Asadel, and I don’t know where he is. I don’t know where he is, Lukien!”

“They take men for their army, Sariyah. It’s happened all over the Bitter Kingdoms.”

“They turn them into monsters. They take their souls.”

“We don’t know that. We don’t know what happened to Asadel.”

Sariyah tried smiling. “I heard you were here with Anton Fallon, Lukien. I begged to make my way here. I want to fight alongside you. I want to kill them, and I want Diriel’s head.”

“There’s a lot of people who want Diriel’s head,” I said. “And one man in particular who’s been promised that prize. But we will kill them, Sariyah.” I rose to stand over him. “I’m not the man you left in Arad. I’m not a man at all anymore. I have no soul to lose and no mercy in my heart. I will kill them for you and avenge your sons, but you need to rest. You’ll die out there if you fight like this. You need to survive and go home to your wife and daughters.”

Sariyah stood to face me. Even starved, he’d lost none of his powers of intimidation. “Shall I go and tell my wife her sons are dead? A Ganjeese man never returns home with such news, not without the hide of his enemy. You ask me to shame her.”

“No, Sariyah, I don’t—”

“You do but do not know it. Listen to me, Shalafein: my life is yours now. Use me as a spear to throw against our enemies. Use me as a shield, and I will take the arrows. I will find this King Diriel, and I will break him in two pieces over my knee. And if Asadel has been turned into one of his slaves, I will cut off his head to give him peace." Sariyah stepped forward and pushed his giant chest against my own, bumping me backward. "But nothing will keep me from the battle. Not even you. Do not test your immortality against me."

I saw nothing but purpose in his eyes. I wondered if that's what I looked like now.

"Sariyah," I said softly, "This is the only moment in my life when I've known exactly what I was doing. There's no more doubt in me." I stooped to pick up his scimitar, holding its golden hilt carefully and handing it to him. "Tonight we call a war council. Tonight we decide how best to skin Diriel and his snakes. You'll sit with me, Sariyah, and ride with me—right beside me—when we take the battle to them."

31

I had taken time to eat and clean myself and had even slept a few hours before arriving for the council. The chamber was already filled to bursting when I got there. A long banquet table took up most of the floor, and everyone was already seated, drinking and talking amongst themselves as they waited for the council to begin. Anton sat at the head of the table with Marilius on his right, while behind them hung a large, roughly-drawn map, stretched against the wall. Anton's many mercenaries filled most of the chairs on his side of the table, while Zurans and Drinmen sat around the other half. My empty seat sat directly opposite Anton across the lengthy table, a glass of wine already poured for me and waiting. Sariyah sat to my immediate right, in the chair next to my own. Chuluun and his brother Nalinbaatar sat to his right, Kiryk and his advisors to my left. They watched me as I entered, but only Sariyah stood.

We met that night in the very same hall where Crezil had massacred Anton's men.

The room grew quiet. The laughing and clanking glasses ceased. I wasn't a king, but I felt like one suddenly. My face felt hot.

"We didn't start yet," said Anton from across the room. Like Sariyah, he stood. "You didn't miss anything, just some drinking."

I hadn't seen Anton since leaving to rescue Cricket. He hadn't seen me, either. He looked me over curiously, grinning at the reappearance of my long lost eye.

"Lukien, you are a miracle," he said. "I cannot believe what I am seeing."

Chuluun rose to greet me. "He is kissed by heaven."

"He is Shalafein," said Sariyah.

"He's late," muttered Sulimer. Against his chair rested an enormous battle-axe, his favorite tool for taking Akyren heads. He looked older than usual, his face grooved with worry lines. His young king, Kiryk, put a hand on his arm.

"It's enough that he's here now," said Kiryk, and he rose to greet me, too. With a genuine smile he said, "We've waited, and now we're ready to kill our enemies, Sir Lukien. Lead us."

I bid them all to sit, then stood behind my chair for a moment. "We've all come for the same reason," I said. "Before another word is spoken, thank you. Thank you for not running away. Thank you for helping me."

"We all want to save ourselves, Lukien," said Anton. On the floor beside him rested two chests, their lids closed to hide their contents. "We can only do that by fighting together."

"We want justice," said Kiryk, "for all those Diriel has murdered."

"We want vengeance," said one of Anton's mercenaries. "For all our brothers murdered in this room by Diriel's monster."

Anton and Marilius both flushed at his statement. Their men still thought Diriel had sent Crezil against them.

"Forget the monster," I told them. "The monster won't come again. Your enemies are out there, just beyond this city."

"So you've beaten the monster, then?" asked Anton. "We should at least speak about it."

"The monster's not the problem. I've dealt with it," I said.

I didn't like putting Anton in his place, not in front of all his men, and not in his own home. He'd impressed me by keeping his mercenaries together, and I could already tell by the bare walls of his palace that he'd given up a good part of his fortune to keep his men paid. I stood behind my chair, the entire chamber staring at me. Even the servants stopped pouring to hear my words. I felt lost suddenly, but when I thought about Cricket I knew what to say.

"We're all outsiders here," I began. "Especially me. I look around this room, and I see faces from different corners of the world. Even you, Anton. You came from somewhere else. You built this place and now someone wants to take it from you."

"That's right," Anton nodded.

"Everyone in this room has lost something," I went on. "Friends or brothers. Family." I glanced at Sariyah. "Sons." I looked around the room at all the diverse faces. "I barely knew the Bitter Kingdoms before I came here. I was warned not to come. A very good and wise friend of mine tried to stop me."

Inside me I felt a little tremor from Malator. No gloating. Just sadness.

"Pride's my downfall, you see. It always has been. Some of you think I'm blessed. I've not found a thing yet that can kill me. The spirit inside my sword tells me I have no soul any more, and I know he's right because I can't feel it. The only thing I feel now is the need for revenge."

"Then let that be enough," said Kiryk's man Lenhart. "It's enough for me. It's enough for us all."

Chuluun said, "In Zura we know of Diriel. We know he will come one day for our lands. So my brothers and I claim vengeance against his intentions." He and Nalinbaatar both nodded. "It is enough for us, too."

They all nodded, in fact. Every man around the table, so many of them strangers to me. Sariyah kicked out my chair for me.

"Sit, Lukien," he offered.

I took my seat. "Marilius?"

Marilius stood, clearing his throat and taming his nerves. He had a riding crop in his hand that he used to point at the map. All heads turned toward him anxiously. Anton shifted aside a bit, giving his man room.

"Diriel's army is camped in a place called the Sklar Valley," said Marilius. He made a circle around the valley with his riding crop, in an area just to the north and west of Isowon. "That's barely two miles from here, and between Isowon and Sklar there's nothing but flat ground. It's barren. Mostly sand. Some trees and brush, but no hills, no caves. Nowhere for them to hide."

"Flat ground is good," considered Chuluun. "Good for horses."

"That's our one advantage," said Marilius. "They have horses, but not as many as we do."

"That's because they ate them all," I said.

"And because I brought in as many as I could," said Anton. "Horses are good business around here."

"They don't expect us to come after them," continued Marilius. "They expect us to hold up here in Isowon."

"We're not doing that," said Anton quickly. He looked around the table where the teams I'd brought to the fight were gathered. "I've already explained this to my men. There won't be a siege of Isowon. I won't have it. There'll either be a victory or a massacre."

"We signed up for either," said Kiryk. "My Drinmen came to fight, not hide. We're ready to go right now."

"Good," said Marilius, "because I only bought us a bit of time. A day and a half ago I rode out to see Diriel. That was at your request, Lukien. I gave him your message."

The faces around the table looked puzzled. "Go on," I told Marilius.

Marilius parried nicely. "I saw his camp, and I saw how strong they are. He's cocky, and he's out of his mind. He has no intention of backing away."

"Tell them what Diriel said to you," urged Anton. "Tell them word for word."

Marilius hesitated. "He said everyone of us would be disemboweled. Even the children, he said."

The girl near me dropped her pitcher. The crystal shattered into bits. She looked down at what she'd done and almost fainted. Two more of Anton's servants rushed to help her.

"Go, get her out of here," said Anton. He flicked his wrist at all his servants. "All of you, get out."

Leaving the broken glass and wine strewn across the floor, the servants fled the chamber. But not a man around the table flinched at Diriel's threat.

"We'll feed him his own intestines," said Chuluun. "To threaten little ones . . ."

"He's not lying," said Kiryk. "We've already seen his handiwork."

"Numbers, Marilius." I leaned forward. "What's he got?"

"Two-thousand," he estimated. "Maybe twenty-five hundred. Maybe a bit more."

"And us?"

"A thousand counting everything. A bit less probably. That's a few hundred mercenaries, a few hundred Drinmen, men from here in Isowon, some men from Kasse . . ."

"How many from Zura?" asked Chuluun anxiously.

Marilius replied, "Ninety or so. That's just a guess."

Chuluun translated the news for his brother, and the two of them shared a grimace. "There would be more if there was more time," said Chuluun. "They will come. But by then . . ."

"Ninety is enough," I announced loudly. "Ninety Zuran horsemen are worth a thousand Akyren goat fuckers. Kiryk, you were right. Diriel lied to me about his numbers. So what? We all knew we'd be outnumbered."

"How many legionnaires?" asked a helmeted merc.

Marilius shrugged. "I don't know. I couldn't tell, and Diriel wouldn't say. But he's got his conscripts too. And he's got dogs."

"Dogs?" said Lenhart. "They didn't use dogs in Drin."

"Well, they have them now," said Marilius. "Scores of them, chained up and starved mad."

"They'll send those dogs in first," guessed Jaracz. He spoke softly, as if talking only to his king. "Which is why you'll need to stay in the rear, Kiryk."

"No," said Kiryk. "I'm a Silver Dragon. I lead tomorrow." He turned to look at me. "The battle starts tomorrow, Lukien, yes? We're all ready."

I didn't know how to answer, so I looked to Marilius. "Are we ready, Marilius?"

Marilius put down his riding crop. "Anton has spent everything he has to keep his men paid. The men at this table and the others that follow them aren't going to run. Yes, I think we're ready."

"Anton?" I looked at him across the table. "It's your city. I'll be in charge of the battle but you're Isowon's leader. Tomorrow?"

"You were the last piece of the puzzle, Lukien," said Anton. He mustered a smile on his golden face. "If this doesn't work I'll be ruined."

"You'll be dead!" joked Lenhart.

The room broke with laughter. Only Sariyah, ever stone-faced, didn't grin.

"Anton?" I looked at him from across the table. "It's your decision."

He couldn't hide his fear, but he didn't hesitate either. "Tomorrow we make war," he said. "Unless the Akyrens attack before then."

"They won't," I said. "Diriel wants his monster, and only I can give it to him. I still have time, and Diriel will honor our bargain."

Anton nodded. "Tomorrow, then."

I pushed back my chair and stood. "Tomorrow."

"Tomorrow!" cried the men, all of them standing to echo me.

"Tomorrow," said Sulimer, and took his big axe and smashed it flat side against the table. The table bounced, shattering glasses and spilling food and wine. "Remember your axes," he chided. "Remember to take their heads!"

"And remember that Diriel's head is mine," said Kiryk.

Anton said, "I think I should have that trophy for my own."

"Kiryk has claimed it, Anton," I called. "But if you want, I can cut off his balls for you."

The men laughed again, even Anton, and raised the remaining glasses. Only Sariyah remained seated. I didn't know how many of the men knew what had happened to him, or to his son Asadel. The only one I'd told was Marilius, who took pity on Sariyah from across the chamber, lowering his glass and meeting Sariyah's sad gaze with encouragement. I put my hand on Sariyah's shoulder and bending to his ear said, "We carry your wounds inside us, my friend."

Sariyah nodded, then stood, then pounded a fist on the table as heavily as Sulimer's axe. "Listen to me, all of you," he boomed. "My son Asadel is out there with Diriel. Taken from me. If you see him tomorrow on the battlefield, spare him." He gazed into every face. "I beg you to see he is not your enemy. But if he has lost his soul—if now he's a mindless one—then I beg you to destroy him."

Young Kiryk, who didn't have a glass to raise because his trusted Sulimer had shattered it, put up a hand to speak. "My father's name was Lutobor, King of Drin. He was taken from me, and none of my tears have returned him. In his name I swear: if your Asadel lives, we Drinmen will find him for you. And if he only half lives," Kiryk's hand fell to his heart, "we will end his misery, friend Sariyah."

"We will," said Lenhart.

"We will," said Jaracz.

Sulimer, oldest of the Drinmen, dragged his axe from the table. "I will," he swore.

His words chilled me. I knew he meant to die tomorrow and drag a thousand souls to hell. Sulimer had reached his own valley in life, a place few ever reach, where a person has no fear at all. He had his mission of vengeance and needed nothing else. He was why we could win tomorrow, I told myself. He and all the men like him, who had nothing else to lose, could change such terrible odds. Sariyah gave the Drinmen his thanks and sat back down again. One by one the men around the table all returned to their seats. The servants scrambled back into the room, and the chatter rose around the table, about archers and strategy and how it felt to lose one's soul. I kept myself out of this talk, drinking and watching Anton and Marilius field the questions. Both had done remarkably well. Marilius had become a leader almost overnight, and Anton . . .

Well, I still disliked him to be sure, but he was less of a snake than I'd thought.

We went for hours, long into the night, loosening our fears with Anton's good wines and admiring the curves of his servant girls. The captains gave orders to their underlings to make ready their troops, each a tiny army under my supreme command. We decided our assault would not come at dawn—there was no sense in that, not when sleep would be so precious. The men outside the council chamber would drill and organize and make all the preparations, but the men here, in this bawdy chamber, would drink themselves mad and sleep late enough to regain their senses.

But none of them had my stamina, and one by one the men around the table took their ease, Sariyah first among them. Then came Nalinbaatar, sick from foods he had no taste for, and then the mercenaries. Kiryk and his Drinmen surprised me with bottomless stomachs, but even they succumbed eventually, and left the chamber as a drunken herd. By then Chuluun had moved into Sariyah's vacant seat. He'd stopped drinking long ago but refused to leave my side. When at last Marilius said his good-nights, there was only Chuluun and myself, and Anton Fallon on the other side of the table, looking tired and oddly content, resplendent in his robes and womanly hair, a silver bowl of some unknown spice at his fingertips that he snuffed up his nose. He offered it out to me from across the table, and when I shook my head he looked at Chuluun.

"What about you, Bogati?" he bade. "Alwani spice. It will give you courage for the battle tomorrow."

Chuluun smirked at his fellow Zuran. "I am unafraid, Anton Fallon."

Seeing them together made me realize how different they were, and how vast Zura must be. Where Chuluun was savage, Anton was regal. I could tell they didn't much like each other, only tolerating each other for my sake. Anton shrugged, pinched up more of the spice and sucked it up his nose. I realized suddenly how he'd managed to stay so awake. I had my sword to keep me vital, and Anton had his spices.

"Chuluun, will you leave us?" asked Anton politely.

"If Lukien wills it," Chuluun replied.

"Go on, get some sleep," I told Chuluun. I knew Anton had something to ask me. I even knew what it was. "I'll see you in the morning."

Chuluun gave Anton a courteous bow, then bent down as if to whisper to me. Instead he kissed the top of my head.

"Sleep well," he said softly. "Dream of victory."

He staggered out of the chamber, drunk on his feet, watched with surprise by Anton, who seemed almost jealous of the attention. We were just two, now. He had dismissed the servants long ago. For the first time in our long night, I noticed the blood stains still on the chamber's ceiling. I reached out for my goblet then remembered it was empty. Anton clicked shut his silver spice case. He'd managed to stay awake with me, but his eyes were bloodshot and cried for sleep. Beside him still rested the large, unopened treasure chest.

"Is that the money you owe me?" I joked.

Anton turned his chair, stretching out his legs and resting his feet on the chest. "Did you kill the monster like you were supposed to?"

I shook my head. "No."

"You told Diriel you'd bring the monster to him. Why'd you tell him that if you didn't mean to kill it?"

"To buy us time. I needed to tell him something."

"You're lying, Lukien. I've made my living selling lies so I know one when I hear it. Besides that, you're no good at it." Anton's voice slurred as he spoke. He reached for a dirty, nearly empty glass of wine, tipping drops from it to his outstretched tongue.

"Go easy now," I warned. "We've got a fight tomorrow. Between the wine and that spice of yours you won't be able to stand."

"It's the only thing that gives me courage," said Anton. "They think I'm a coward, but I'm not. All my men—they think I have a flower in my chest instead of a heart. I'm not like that, you know."

"I know, Anton," I said. "I see that now."

He smiled. "You called me Anton."

"Yeah."

"Don't betray me, Lukien," he sighed. "Don't give me to Diriel."

"Is that what you think I've planned?"

Anton wiped his mouth. "I dunno. You told Marilius you were going to give Diriel what he wants. I thought that was the monster. But here you are, empty-handed as usual." He pointed at my face. "Except for that new eye. I like that eye."

"Anton, you're drunk. Why don't you go to sleep now?"

"Can't. First you have to promise me. Promise me you won't give me over to Diriel, Lukien. I figured it out. That's the only way you can save yourself."

"I don't want to save myself, Anton. The last thing I want in this bleak world is to save myself."

"Why?" He got out of his chair and shambled toward me. "Look at you—you're young again! Beautiful, like me! You made a bargain with that thing inside your sword, didn't you?"

"Only to have my vengeance. Do you believe me, Anton?"

He sat down on the table with a slump. "I suppose I have to. I'm sorry about the girl. Marilius told me what happened to her. It is right that your heart breaks for her, Lukien. But I did warn you of Diriel's horrors."

"You did," I admitted. "But I never listen, you see. I'm the one who got her killed. Tomorrow I'll make everything right."

"All right," he whispered. "If that's the best answer I'm going to get . . ." He pushed himself from the table, wobbling back to the big chest. He waved me closer. "Come. I have something for you."

I was curious as I got out of my chair. The room swam a bit around my head, but I straightened and swallowed my nausea. The one thing Malator couldn't cure was a hangover, it seemed. Anton stepped aside when I reached him, gesturing to the chest. There was no lock on it, just a latch keeping it closed.

"Open it," he proffered.

I did and had to shut my eyes at the brightness of the contents. Gold, I thought at first, a whole chest of it! But when my sight adjusted and my thinking cleared, I recognized the shining helmet staring back at me, the very perfection of handmade armor. It was my own, bronze and beautiful, better than new, and it blinded me with its glittering. I must have said something, because I remember my mouth falling open in awe.

"You like?"

I touched the helmet, then the gleaming breastplate beneath. I'd last seen it ruined, first by weeks of dusty travel, then by Crezil's brutal battering. I'd left it in Isowon, dented and forgotten. But here it was again, reborn, more like gold than bronze, a suit of shining precious metal.

"Anton," I lifted the helmet out of the chest, "how?"

"I like shiny things, Lukien. I have many smiths and jewelers here in Isowon to make my world pretty. Fixing your armor wasn't easy. The monster left it quite a mess. It's amazing what real craftsmen can do, no?"

"It is," I agreed. "Almost perfect."

I was tempted to try the helmet but didn't. I just stared at my reflection in its surface, the way the finish distorted my face, and saw my giant smile. My armor was new again, like me. I wondered if Anton knew how great a gift he'd given me.

"Any debts you owe me are paid," I told him. "This is better payment than anything else you could offer."

"Good," said Anton, "because I can't afford anything else. Even if we win tomorrow, I will have to rebuild."

"But you'll still have Isowon. You'll have a home."

"You can stay if you wish, Lukien. After the battle, I mean."

"No, Anton, thank you. If I live tomorrow I'll return to Jador."

"And if you die at least you'll be well dressed!" he laughed. "You should go to heaven looking your best."

I put the helmet down slowly. "I can't go to heaven, Anton, remember? I have no soul. No heaven would take me."

Anton thought about that for a while. He blinked a few times, then said, "I am very drunk."

"Yes, you are."

"I should sleep."

"We should both sleep."

He staggered toward the open doors, taking the last bit of merriment with him. But before he exited he paused one last time to comfort me.

"Don't worry about heaven, Lukien," he slurred. "You can't die."

The logic of a drunken man. "Thank you, Anton," I said. I picked up my helmet again. "And thank you for this."

He waved and mumbled something and then was gone. A manservant appeared suddenly in the doorway, peering inside the chamber.

"Sir Lukien? Can I help you to your room?"

"Thank you," I answered. "I think that would be best."

"I'll have your armor brought up to you," said the man. "It will be waiting for you when you wake."

A sad thought crashed my brain. "I'll need help with it tomorrow," I said. "To dress for battle. I've lost my squire."

The servant smiled with pity. "Yes, sir. I'm very sorry."

"I loved her."

"Yes," said the man. He came to me and took my arm. "I'm sure she knew that."

I looked at him. It was the wine, I knew, but nothing made sense to me suddenly. "Do you think so? I want to believe that. How can I be sure?"

He got me on my feet, smoothed down my wrinkled shirt, and said, "I'm sure you told her so, sir, even if you never said a word."

Then he pointed me toward the doors, gave me a gentle nudge, and followed me all the way to my private chamber, where the softest bed in the world lulled me instantly to sleep.

32

I slept a drunkard's sleep, deep and troubled, my mind far from the world where my body lay in soft, expensive sheets. I'd once had a fever when I was a boy, sleeping in the streets of Koth beneath a blacksmith's shop; a fever in which every monster my mind could conjure visited and chased me in my sleep, and every time my eyes opened I screamed, because the sickness was so thick in my body I could not stay awake. The next morning, when the fever finally broke, the monsters left me, but the terror of that night always remained.

That was the kind of night I had before the battle. Only it wasn't monsters that found me sleeping in Anton's palace, and it wasn't Crezil that called my nightmares. A long parade of dead friends came to me instead. Or, rather, it was I who went to them, like a troubadour.

I visited each of their death places. In my dreams I saw Akeela, my beloved brother, my king, one of the only people I ever truly loved. I dreamed of him so infrequently over the years that it startled me to see him. We spoke, but his words were foreign to me, so twisted by rage as to be incomprehensible, and when I left him he was crying after me. Screaming, I think.

Next I saw Minikin, my old mentor, and she spoke to me about love, and about how powerful she'd been in life, and how I was now even more powerful than that. I think she pitied me. So I left her quickly, and one by one visited a gallery of past friends and enemies. There was Figgis the Librarian and Trager, my nemesis, and nameless men I'd slain on battlefields. I saw Meriel, who'd loved me, who I'd spurned into the arms of a madman, and then I saw the madman himself, Baron Glass. Together they spoke to me of the burning that had taken Meriel's life and the peaceful world of the dead, and when I told them I had no soul they wept for me.

That's when I grew tired of the dream. I tried to awaken. I pushed myself, but somehow I could not, and so I went in search of Cassandra but could not find her. Nor could I find Cricket. I felt myself panicking, lost in my dreamworld, trapped like that little, fevered boy. I had the terrible thought that I wasn't dreaming at all . . . and that's when my eyes finally opened.

Not wide, though. Just slivers, just enough to see that I was still in my bed in the palace. I fought to stay awake, to sit up and wait for morning, and that's when I saw Malator seated at my bedside. He was dressed for battle in his splendid Akari armor, perched patiently on a plain wooden chair that I knew had been in my chamber earlier. I looked at him as I laid there, reassured to see him but unable to fully awaken. He smiled at me.

"Is this a trick?" I asked softly.

The room was so quiet, so like a tomb, that I would have thought myself dead if not for my cursed life. I could see the Sword of Angels where I'd left it, propped near my bed, and the boots the servant man had pulled off my feet. I could see the window and the darkness beyond it, telling me that morning was still far off. Yet I could hear nothing, not even my heartbeat.

"Do you think I'm tricking you?" Malator asked.

"Why can't I wake up? Am I sick? Or is this just another one of your illusions?"

"Nothing I've never shown you has been an illusion. Nothing I've ever said has been a lie."

"Why are we talking now, then? Why won't you let me sleep in peace?"

"You're moving through the worlds of the dead, Lukien. Those aren't dreams you're having."

I lay very still. "Am I still in those worlds? This feels unreal to me. What time is it?"

"You have time, don't worry. It's hours yet until morning."

"Hours? That can't be. I've been dreaming all night."

Malator shook his head. "Only a little while."

"But I've seen so many people . . ." I studied his face for treachery. "So, they're real? Akeela—was that him? Where is he?"

"In the realm of the dead. I told you, Lukien, you are special. Wait. You'll soon understand."

"No." I somehow managed to prop myself up. "Tomorrow is the end for me, Malator. Even if they don't manage to kill me. If I survive I'm leaving here. I'm going home to Jador. There's no more time for your puzzles. Tell me why I'm special. Tell me now."

"You will wait," said Malator gently. He was like a father at my bedside, and I felt like the sick child, frightened and impatient. "You will not die tomorrow, Lukien. Remember? I promised you your vengeance."

I nodded. "And I gave my soul for it."

"You lost your soul long before that."

"Is that why I can move through the death realms? Because I have no soul?"

"Partly." Malator grinned. "You're getting it, Lukien."

"Then tell me the rest. Or let me sleep. A real sleep. I don't want to see any more phantoms. Why'd you want me to come here, Malator? Why didn't you want Cricket to come with me?"

He smirked at me. "Lukien, that bit is obvious. It was too dangerous for Cricket. Did I not warn you? You need no other friend on this journey. Just me. If you trusted me . . ."

He stopped himself. He looked down at his lap. But I knew what he meant.

"Cricket's dying is my fault. I know that. And tomorrow I'll make Wrestler pay for it. I'll make them all pay. That was our bargain, Malator. Don't renege."

"Renege? I have given you everything you need to be unstoppable. You are a living weapon now, Lukien. Tomorrow you may occasion as much carnage as you crave. Tomorrow you will be the end of the world to your enemies. I have dressed for it! Let hell's gates swing wide for them."

"Then answer me, Malator: What has all this been? A lesson? A test?"

"Training," replied Malator.

"Training? For what?" I was indignant. "What's the point of all this misery?"

"Not yet." Malator's voice was soothing. Suddenly my eyes began to close again. "Soon."

"No . . ."

I clutched for him, but my world quickly darkened.

"Sleep, Lukien," he whispered. "Grow strong. Tomorrow you will be at your glorious best."

I dreamt no more that night. Whatever enchantment Malator had put on me sent me to the most peace I'd known in ages. And the next day, when I awakened, I felt like a giant.

33

I slept past the morning, through breakfast, almost till noontime. No one dared to wake me, but when my eyes snapped open Malator was still in my room, bathed in the bright light of the sun pouring through my window. At the foot of my bed sat the chest holding my bronze armor, its lid open wide, its contents gleaming. Malator was stone-faced. My body roiled with an energy I'd never known. I remembered the dream I'd had, the promise he had made me. I flexed my fingers to test their strength and knew I could crush a rock with them.

"Rise," commanded Malator.

I did as he said, standing before him in his own resplendent, spiked Akari armor, my feet naked on the carpet.

"A squire needs to help you prepare," he said. "Since you have lost yours, I will dress you."

I didn't ask what time it was. Malator's manner told me everything was ready. My chamber was quiet, but outside in the courtyard I could hear the commotion of men riding forth, joining the ranks of their battle-ready brethren. The day had started, but not the war. Not without me. I held up my arms and let Malator pull my old shirt over my head. Next came the trousers, and when I was naked he turned silently to my fresh garments, waiting for me near my newborn armor. He dressed me like a father would; I could feel the warmth of his pride. He seemed hardly a spirit at all, so real that I could touch him, and for the first time, probably the first time ever, I wanted to embrace him and thank him for his gifts.

But I did not. I was a warrior now, and no thoughts of love

could sway me. I wanted no tenderness in me today, no humanity to stay my sword. Some men pray before a battle, but I was never one of those. I had no gods. But if I could have found a patron devil, I would have prayed to have my mercy stripped away, to turn me to stone. In that moment I saw what I had ever been, what I would always be—a fighting man.

Slowly, lovingly, Malator encased me in bronze. Not a word passed between us. We shared a single mind now. His thoughts were as open to me as the sea. I felt his placid calm, he felt my boundless vengeance. One by one he closed the bindings on my legs and arms, taking his time with the ritual. When I held out my hands, he slipped my fingers into my golden gauntlets. The sunlight bounced off me like a kaleidoscope, splashing prisms of color across the walls. Malator stepped back to eye his work and finally allowed himself to smile.

"Your helmet," he said, then stooped to hand it to me. I put the golden helm in the crux of my arm.

"Your sword."

Malator reached for my battered, blood-stained blade. In his fist he held it out for me, and my own fist closed around it. Together we held it, sharing its power, our eyes seeing straight into each others' minds.

"This is the Sword of Angels," whispered Malator. "It lay dormant for years until you found it. And I slept within it, alone and lonely until you came for me, Lukien."

His confession surprised me. "If it's a debt you feel you owe me, Malator," I said, "you've already repaid it."

"Not quite yet," said Malator. "But I will. On the other side of this day."

I said nothing, just let him speak his riddle. All I wanted from Malator was the strength to have my revenge, and he'd already given me that. He let go of the sword, his hand disappearing as his fingers uncoiled, and soon his whole arm was gone, and then his whole body. But I wasn't alone in the room. He was with me, inside the sword and inside my entire being. So I belted the sword around my waist and went to find Marilius.

I found Marilius in the courtyard of the palace, waiting for me. Nearby, surrounded by mercenaries, was Anton, speaking frantically, waving his arms about, pointing at different areas of his city.

The courtyard was filled with soldiers and horses, all of them ready to march through the gates.

Three men stood apart from the crowd, watching me as I emerged. Sariyah, Chuluun, and Kiryk were dressed for battle, each in the garb of their varied lands, each of their horses decorated differently. The buzz in the yard quieted as I entered, the heads turning to see me in my resplendent armor. Even Anton quit his ranting. He turned to face me, his eyebrows shooting up in wonder. The sun was high above my head, and the anxious faces of the soldiers told me they'd been waiting long for my arrival. I stopped myself a few paces into the yard and looked at them.

"I slept," I declared. "But no ordinary sleep. I will make your wait worth it."

Even my voice sounded different, not just from the bronze helm but from the magic coursing through me. The men nodded and looked toward their leaders, my unlikely generals. Young Kiryk, King of the Drinmen, clenched a fist at his side, Chuluun bowed his dark head, and Sariyah took a single, silent step forward. Marilius called out to his mercenaries.

"To your places!" he cried, and the mercenaries in the yard broke rank, riding for the gate. Kiryk gave the order too, and then Chuluun, and the Drinmen and Bogati rode forth, kicking up dust as they rode for Sklar Valley. Only a handful of men and horses remained behind, including Venger, who'd been prepared for me with armor the color of my own and Bogati ribbons in his jet mane. Another gift from Anton, I supposed. He smiled when I noticed it, but I could tell he was terrified of the battle ahead.

"Anton," I said, "you'll stay here in Isowon, but not out in the open like this. Guard yourself inside. Diriel might have assassins come for you."

"I'll be protected," said Anton, gesturing at the ring of mercs who'd stayed behind. "Lukien, before you go, I want to know about the monster."

I shook my head. "I can't. Just trust me on this one."

Anton pointed at his forehead. "I'm the one that bears the mark! It's not Diriel's assassins I'm worried about. If I stay behind, these few men can't help me against Crezil."

"But you're not going to run," I said. I went to Venger and patted his side, glad to see my beautiful horse. "Thank you for this," I told Anton. "I'll ride him with me to the battle, but I'll need another horse for the fight."

"Another?" asked Marilius. "Why?"

"Any good warhorse will do," I said. "Venger will stay in the rear until I need him." I waved at Sariyah and the others. "Gather," I said.

They huddled around me, Sariyah jealously taking my right, Chuluun my left. Kiryk stood slightly apart from the rest, attentive nevertheless. I looked at Marilius.

"You're not a captain anymore," I told him. "None of you are. You're all generals now. Congratulations."

Chuluun smirked. "Is that good?"

"It means you're a leader," Kiryk explained.

"That's right," I said. "Each of you will report to me directly. And each of you is in charge of your men, like we planned. Marilius, is everything in place?"

"Just as we planned," he said. "Diriel's waiting. I sent him a messenger two hours ago like you asked. He's expecting you."

"Maybe he doesn't want to fight," said Anton. "He could have attacked by now but hasn't."

"Don't hope that, Fallon," warned Kiryk. "Don't even think it. Diriel lives to destroy. He's just savoring Isowon like a good meal."

"Everything he wants is here," I agreed. "Except for one thing."

"Crezil," said Marilius. "That's why he's waiting for Lukien. And since I don't see Crezil anywhere . . ."

"Just buying time," I said. "That's all it ever was. Just a ploy. What about that horse?"

Marilius called to one of the remaining mercenaries. "Bring him another." He turned back to me peevishly. "We can't really spare horses this way, Lukien. Most of the men are already on foot. Venger's perfectly suited for fighting. What's the problem?"

Kiryk cleared his throat. "I should go. My men are waiting."

Chuluun turned to his brother, Nalinbaatar, who was holding his horse. "We will see you on the field, Lukien."

I turned to Sariyah. "What about you?"

"I will not leave your side," said Sariyah. "To protect you."

"Protect me? You might have that backwards, my friend."

Sariyah replied, "You are our only hope, Lukien. If you fall we all will surely lose. Consider me like your shadow—inseparable." He went to his horse, a burly beast with two battleaxes tied to its haunches, one on each side. On any other day one would be enough, but Sariyah meant to take many heads. He mounted up and followed Kiryk and the Bogati to the courtyard gate, where he waited for me while the others trotted off. The man Marilius had dispatched returned with another horse for me, not nearly as splendid or well-armed as Venger. He handed the reins to me almost apologetically.

"The best I could find," he said.

"Good enough. Now, protect your master Fallon. Don't be tempted to ride out to join us. Whatever happens, you make sure your master lives."

The mercenary nodded, mostly because he remembered my threat to kill any of them who abandoned Isowon. "Good luck to you, Sir Lukien."

"Anton." I turned to the man who'd brought me here to slay his unbeatable monster. He looked pale, and I could see a trace of some unknown spice staining the flesh beneath his nose. "No more of that false courage," I said. "You're stronger than you think. You stayed alive this long, after all."

His eyes flicked toward Marilius. "Bring him home safe," he whispered to me.

Marilius shifted. "Anton . . ."

"Don't be embarrassed by your love," I said. "Remember what I told you, Marilius? There's no shame in loving each other." I turned to Sariyah and said, "Ride ahead for me."

"I will not leave you, Lukien."

"Just to the edge of the city. I need to speak with Marilius."

He agreed grudgingly, and when he was far enough ahead I called to Marilius, "Come along. It's time."

He hurried to his horse and sped the beast to where I was waiting. Anton gathered his bodyguards and disappeared into the palace. Suddenly the yard was deserted. The street ahead was nearly empty as well. I could see Sariyah trotting through Isowon, looking forlorn among the fountains and hanging gardens, and ahead of him rode Kiryk and Chuluun. It was a fair distance to Sklar Valley, but the time it took to get there would be the last peace we'd know for days. My plain brown horse clip-clopped down the street. Marilius checked his gear as we rode.

"You look anxious," I said. "Are you?"

"Anxious. Terrified." Marilius put his hand on his sword. "Why shouldn't I be?"

"You checked your sword already. Leave it. Remember what I told you when we faced Crezil—when the time comes, you'll know what to do."

"This isn't like that, though."

"No," I agreed. "It's much worse than that."

Marilius laughed nervously. "How come you're not afraid, then?"

I thought for a moment. I searched myself for fear. Maybe it was because I had no soul. Or maybe I wanted to die. "You're right. I'm not afraid," I said. "But I wish I could be. The only fearless people I've ever known have all been madmen. Maybe I'm one of them now."

"Maybe it'll come back when this is over," said Marilius.

"What? My soul?" I shook my head. "That's gone for good."

"Your sanity, then. Maybe when you finally get home, it'll be there waiting for you."

I smiled beneath my bronze helmet. "I like that. I'll remember it."

"Why are you bringing two horses, Lukien?" asked Marilius. "I know you don't have much luck keeping them alive, but still . . ."

"I have a plan. Don't ask me to tell you what it is, because I won't."

"You're asking all of us to trust you, but you don't trust us. I have to say, I'm not inspired."

"Marilius, if this is going to work you need to stop thinking so much. Worry less about what I'm doing out there and more about what you're doing. Use your wits to keep your men alive, not to untangle my motives."

"All right," he grunted. "But I'm going with you when you ride out to see Diriel."

"I want you all there," I said. "Kiryk, Chuluun, and Sariyah too. I want the Akyrens to see what they're up against."

"Why? Diriel won't care. He already knows."

"Fuck Diriel. I want his men to see us."

A horde.

That's what I saw when I reached the battlefield.

Horses and dogs. Archers and infantry. Dirty conscripts, dead-eyed Akyrens, pikes pointed skyward, flaccid banners of a ruined country. Eager, soaring buzzards. A vast, badly stitched quilt of legionnaires and starved slaves, of Drinmen and Kassens in chains, of swords and hammers, of wagons, of war sleds, of terror and disillusionment. Bringers of death. Bringers of worse than death. Made whole by the whips of madmen, and a king on a chariot adorned with peacock feathers.

From a berm in the sand I watched with the wind in my face. Diriel had rolled out from his horde when he saw me on the hill. He drove his chariot through his front line of dogs and conscripts. My own men—my four tiny armies—waited in perfect formation, facing the black wave from Akyre. In front were Marilius's mercenaries, lined up in three tight rows of infantry and horsemen. Kiryk and his Silver Dragons held the north flank, bolstered by other Drinmen who'd heard the call. A contingent of Zurans and Bogati horsemen secured the south flank to my left, not really under the command of anyone. There was no way to hold them back, I knew, so I'd given them no orders at all. Once the fighting started, they'd fly into battle.

We were outnumbered in every way I'd feared, except for horses, where we had the advantage. We were also better rested and better fed. But we were half as many as our enemies. Even with all our horses and all our axes, I still didn't know how we'd take so many heads. The conscripts posed no threat at all. But the legionnaires . . .

I spied them from the berm, counting and sizing them up. There were at least as many as I'd seen at Diriel's castle. They wore collars now to protect their necks, thick leather bands they'd started using after their brief war with Drin. I knew they wouldn't stop the Sword of Angels, but I worried about the battle-axes. Sariyah, who sat next to me upon his horse, rested his big axe on his shoulder and scanned the field for Asadel. Chuluun galloped out from the Bogati, and Marilius called up from the bottom of the berm.

"That's Diriel," he said, pointing at the approaching chariot.

"I see him," I replied, then guided my nameless horse slowly down the sandhill, leaving Venger in the care of a young servant boy. His name was Cern, and he promised to protect Venger with his life. It was the kind of loyalty I didn't expect from one of Isowon's puffy young men. I believed him enough to trust him, and he'd be far enough from the fighting to keep himself alive.

I reached the bottom of the berm—my sandy command post—and didn't say a word as Chuluun and Marilius wheeled their horses to flank me. Sariyah came after me, equally silent, and as we trotted forward, Kiryk broke away from his men to join us. Our troops watched silently as we rode out together toward Diriel, whose own contingent gathered around his chariot. We had agreed to meet in the spot between our facing armies. Amazingly, Diriel had brought Grecht, the midget from his castle, the one who'd greeted me and Cricket at the bridge. He bounced out in front of Diriel's chariot like a weird little herald, carrying an already tattered flag and, I think, whistling.

"Who is that?" whispered Chuluun when he saw Grecht. He rode slowly at my side, scimitar sheathed, unable to take his eyes off the midget.

"If only they were all that size!" said Kiryk.

I took the point, letting the others fan out behind me, matching Diriel's deliberate speed. Four legionnaires came with him on horseback, the only four with perfect uniforms, I supposed, each of them pale and expressionless. And, as I'd hoped, Wrestler was with them. His bald head caught my eye at once, gleaming and helmetless, with a sword at his side and his loose black clothes draping his uncanny body. He smiled, a grin I felt more than saw, a laughing, contemptuous leer aimed right at me. He almost looked like he'd grown since our fight, his arms more apelike, his chest even more like a beer keg. Finally, I'd be close enough to kill him.

At last Diriel's chariot came to a stop, and the king himself dropped the reins of his twin horses and stepped down on the battlefield. Grecht performed what looked like a curtsy, then stepped aside for Diriel to pass. I jerked my horse to a halt just a few paces in front of him. His legionnaires remained in the rear, but Wrestler rode up to protect him. Diriel's vulnerability was meant to calm me, I knew, but I couldn't help thinking how stupid he was. He held apart his empty hands in greeting.

"Why don't I see the creature with you?" he asked.

"It's sleeping," I replied.

"I've waited, Lukien. You promised to bring it to me."

"If you believed that, you're even dumber than I thought." I glanced at Wrestler and said, "Get yourself an advisor with some brains, Diriel. Maybe you'd make better decisions."

"I see you brought your sword this time," taunted Wrestler. He pushed back his robe to reveal his own. "I'll toss mine away if you want to go again, Liirian. I'd love the chance to snap your neck again."

"Not just my neck." I pointed at my eye. "See? Magic."

"Then take a good look, Sir Lukien," advised Diriel. "You're outnumbered. Even you can't beat all of them. Does Anton Fallon know you're throwing his life away?"

"Anton Fallon has a message for you," chimed Marilius. "Isowon is his. He built it, he rules it, and he's not given it over to you.

Lukien speaks for us all. If you want Anton, you'll have to kill us all first."

Diriel looked up at Marilius, flashing his sharpened teeth. "Why doom yourself, boy? Run back and tell your master I'll spare him if he surrenders to me. But I want the monster, too. I want what was agreed upon."

I laughed in his face. "Idiot. The monster was never going to be yours. I told you that to buy us time, to build this army!" I leaned over my horse to look at him. "If you want the monster, go get it!"

"Where is it?" demanded Wrestler.

"In its lair," I said. "In the crypts of the old Akyren kings." I heard Marilius shift with surprise at my admission. "That's where the mummy powder came from, Diriel—from your dead ancestors! Anton Fallon dug up your mothers and fathers. He ground them into dust and let you feed them to your men!" I took great glee in my taunt, and in the shock on Diriel's face. "He played you like a fool, and you know why? Because you are one! Did you really think I'd ever hand over a weapon like Crezil to you? Are you so deluded to believe I'd let you take control of it? Crezil belongs to *me*!"

Diriel was so unbalanced by his rage he could barely speak. His eyelids fluttered and his fingers clenched, and he looked up at Marilius and seethed, "Imagine the worst death you can for yourself, boy. I will flay you. I will boil you for what your master has done!"

"You'll do nothing," I spat. "Because you'll be dead. And then Crezil will be mine. Anton Fallon will take over Akyre, and together we'll drink beer until our bladders are bursting and piss on the graves of your ancestors. But they'll be empty, because Anton dug them up and turned them into fairy dust."

Truly, I thought Wrestler's bald head would explode.

"Death!" he screamed, his hand flying to his sword. "Sweet Diriel, let me kill this foreign pig," he pleaded. "Let me pull out his intestines, I beg you!"

"Then I'll just come back," I sneered. "An eye, a neck—haven't you figured it out yet? I am forever! And you, you demented child raper—you'll be dangling at the end of my sword soon."

Wrestler was about to pull his blade. Chuluun nearly pulled his own. But Diriel wasn't stupid enough to end things yet. He regained his composure, ignoring everyone but me.

"One more chance," he warned. "Behold, Sir!" He swept his arm toward his warriors. "Think. The monster and Anton Fallon, and you ride back to Liiria with everything you had."

"Not everything," I said.

Wrestler took my meaning. "No, not everything," he agreed. He licked his lips. "Not your pretty squire. She fought a little with her little girl fists, but she loved me on top of her. I showed her some of my best wrestling holds."

"Demon," hissed Sariyah. "She was a child."

"She was candy," crooned Wrestler.

I could barely keep myself together. I could have—should have—leapt off my horse and torn his throat out. But I remembered why I'd come, and somehow steeled myself. Behind Diriel waited his army, with the dogs and conscripts at the front. The conscripts seemed little more than slaves, starved-looking and in rags, poorly armed with whatever throw-away weapons the real Akyrens didn't want. There were hundreds of them, too, some still in the chains that had dragged them to battle. The only expression on their gaunt faces was dread. I spurred my horse away from my men, past Diriel and knocking past Wrestler.

"Hear me!" I cried to the conscripts. "We are free men in Isowon! We do not bow to evil! Be free and join us!"

Sariyah hurried to my side. The legionnaires surrounded us both. Diriel laughed.

"They won't join you," he said. "I have broken them. They're mine."

"They will join us," I answered. "When they see your heads rolling in the sand, they will."

I could see Kiryk's hand twitching on his sword and Chuluun was just dying to fight. I turned one more time toward the horde, raising up a defiant fist toward his enslaved soldiers.

"Watch how free people fight!" I cried. "Watch and grow strong!"

Diriel made his way back to his chariot, waving off his legionnaires. "Sir Lukien," he said, "you should never have come here."

"On that, we agree," I replied. "If you have a devil, Diriel, make your peace with him. By tomorrow you'll be in hell."

Then I spat onto the ground between us, spun my horse around, and led my men back toward our army, turning my back on Wrestler and his king in one final act of contempt. I didn't look back—I pretended not to care. I just kept on riding as Marilius caught up to me.

"Lukien!" he said insistently. "Why'd you do that? Why'd you tell Diriel about the mummy powder?"

"To kick a hornet's nest," I said. "Why do you think?"

34

I had barely reached the berm with Sariyah when I heard the arrows overhead. Up on the dune, Cern pointed skyward with a shout of alarm. A peculiar buzzing filled the air, and when I spun my horse around, the sky was black with missiles. My men held their places in the field while their commanders rode and cried out orders. I shouted up to the top of the berm where Cern stood.

"Cover yourself! And protect that horse!"

Cern couldn't really do both so scrambled to guard Venger with his own unarmored body. The arrows wouldn't last long, I knew—maybe one or two volleys. Diriel was too impatient for archers. Kiryk's Silver Dragons raised their shields as the arrows arched, and the mercenaries with armor crossed their arms over their chests. The Zurans jeered at the arrows, daring them to strike, and Marilius rode furiously at the front of the army, rallying them all to stand fast.

I meant to climb the berm but didn't. I should have commanded from there, at least for a while, but Wrestler's taunts still rang in my brain, and all I wanted was the chance to fight. I wouldn't be a general who, from a place of safety, ordered men to die. And I had trophies of my own to take. Out sprang the Sword of Angels, to my lips came a curse, and I rode out screaming for the arrows to strike me. Like a heavy rain they fell, around me, pelting me, bouncing from my armor, and pounding on my helmet. Men cried and dropped about me. I galloped through them, willing the arrows to catch me, snapping them off as they pierced my bronze armor. I turned my face toward them, howling, and Chuluun picked up my wolf-cry. Soon a chorus of howls erupted from his Bogati, even as the arrows pounded them.

"Steady!" cried Marilius.

"Hold!" hollered Kiryk.

Sariyah thundered up behind me. "I am with you, Lukien! Let us ride!"

"Wait," I said, then heard the drop of chains across the field. Another volley filled the sky. A few mercs with bows answered it. Diriel could have picked at us all day, but the sound of chains told me he wouldn't. He set his dogs on us instead.

And then they came, heralded by the arrows, slobbering and grunting, their bodies welted and emaciated. Their heads looked enormous, nothing but jaws, their legs pumping as they scrambled toward us. I heard the horses whinny and the men gasp and the arrows land amongst us. I watched a dog sight me with his wild eyes and run to make a meal of me. Up went my sword, and my horse bolted toward it, ready when it leapt for me. I caught it easily in my left hand, my fingers closing instantly around its throat and crushing its windpipe.

I think I tossed it over my shoulder. I can't even remember, it was so effortless. My body burned with Malator's power, an overwhelming, magical inferno. And if the arrows cut me I didn't know it. I felt nothing, least of all pain, just the enchanted strength of my patron Akari.

"Malator!" I cried. "Give me my vengeance! Today is my day!"

He didn't respond. He didn't need words. He *was* me now. All around me snapped the dogs, pulling at my legs and climbing up my horse, who kicked and shattered their bones and carried me across the battlefield. Chuluun's men broke formation, slicing at the dogs, while the Silver Dragons held their position, and Marilius's mercs held back the worst, defending the poorly armed civilians behind them. Sariyah swung his axe, gutting one of the big, feral monsters and spraying me with its blood. I hacked and pulled them from me, slaughtering them, crushing them and wishing they were men. An arrow struck my head, bouncing off my helmet. Another felled a dog. But when I looked up again the sky had cleared, and my army gave a cheer.

Next were the conscripts. And this I didn't want.

Shouting for my men to hold, I rode out with Sariyah to the front of our lines, through the dogfight and the Bogati. Up ahead, Diriel's generals were urging their first wave of men onto the battlefield. Sariyah blanched as he looked at them, wondering where among them was his son. Kiryk rode out from the Dragons to join us. Lenhart and Jaracz followed.

"We'll find him if we can," I told Sariyah. "I remember what he looks like. We'll get him out of here."

Sariyah raised his axe. "Or I will die here with him."

They were a terrible lot, those conscripts, those scores of enslaved. Hundreds of them in rags and broken armor, stolen from their own armies and homes and beaten into submission to fight for Diriel. They looked mindless now, stripped of their humanity, and I knew when I saw them my words hadn't reached them. So I rode out to try again.

"Hear me!" I cried. "Join us! Asadel, hear me! Be free again!"

Far away on his chariot, Diriel gave his order. His generals echoed it, the whips behind the conscripts cracked, and that sorry horde of slaves came at us, running headlong into death.

"I don't want this," I told Sariyah. "They're not Akyrens."

Sariyah bumped his horse against mine. "Don't lose this battle because of my son! They're enemies now."

"They didn't kill Cricket," I said. "Gods, I'm not a murderer!"

They were running straight for us, but Sariyah turned his back on them to shout at me. "They joined Diriel! They could have died with honor like my sons!"

"But Asadel—"

"Is dead, then! Now fight, Lukien! Fight!"

There was barely time to give the order. Already the Zurans were galloping forwarding, slicing past the dogs to meet their human foes. The conscripts came in a wave, screams tearing from their throats, the swords and hammers and spears held high. Kiryk held back his Silver Dragons as planned, but Marilius looked at me for my sign. Dread-filled, I gave it.

"Attack," I cried half-heartedly. Then, under Sariyah's stare, I shouted, "Attack!"

Marilius dropped his sword, and a hundred freelance horsemen charged. In moments they were around me, then past me toward the conscripts. I forced myself to join them, riding hard to catch up to Marilius. When the conscripts were just a few yards out, I raised my sword to defend myself.

On another day, the clash might have been even. In another world more just than mine, the conscripts would have been fed and willing and capable, but today they were neither, and I've seen infantry fall like they do. So easily, so quickly my horsemen trampled them. Like dead grass their bodies crumbled, their weapons barely glancing the mercenaries. I hurried into the fray, swooped over one of the men to grab up his collar, and lifted him off his feet like a child.

"Get to the rear!" I shouted at him. "Take safety with us!"

His eyes barely saw me. He tore at me, dropping his sword and using his fingernails instead. I shook him, then smashed the pommel of my sword against his cheek.

"Do you hear me?" I asked. "Go! Leave the field!"

I dropped him and he tumbled, and when I turned I saw Sariyah near me—but he wasn't swinging his axe. He too searched the faces on the field, looking for Asadel. The horsemen stopped their charge, whirling to hack down the conscripts around them. A handful of unlucky ones were pulled from their mounts. Others saw my lead and stayed their hands, using their horses like plows to push the conscripts out of the way.

"To our lines!" I cried. That glimmer of an idea had given me hope. "Push them toward us!"

Some listened, others didn't. I rode out to where Marilius was, pushing past the soldiers attacking me but refusing to cut my path. When I reached Marilius he had somehow been surrounded. He hacked down one of the conscripts, then another, then instinctively pushed back the others with his horse. One of the soldier-slaves dropped his sword, staring up at Marilius.

That's when I knew we'd broken through.

"To the rear!" I yelled. "Gather your comrades and retreat to our lines. Let Diriel see you are free!"

The man did as asked, grabbing at everyone around him and shouting at them to lay down their weapons. Marilius broke away from his attackers and galloped out to circle his troops.

"Push them back!" he shouted. "Back to our lines!"

With a moment to breathe I glanced toward the Akyren lines. Dogs and conscripts still wrestled around me, but I knew Diriel's first wave had failed. It was easy, and I took no joy in it. He still had hundreds of slaves left to throw at us, and not all of them would come to our side.

"Malator, remember Diriel," I huffed.

I am watching him, the Akari replied.

Diriel wouldn't leave the battle soon. Not until I turned the tide.

But he *would* leave eventually, I was sure of it. His greed was too predictable.

A dog came at me from the chaos, jumping for my throat. But I was like a stone wall, and the impact of the beast barely moved me. My arm locked around it, my elbow flexed, and I broke its skull so easily it frightened me. It dropped to the field with blood gushing from its ears.

I was invincible. I was now everything Malator had promised. I refused to fight the conscripts, letting them hack at me instead, their blows so weak they felt like nothing.

"What have you done to me Malator?" I whispered.

I wheeled my horse around to face Diriel's forces. There were still more dogs to kill, more slaves to endure. I braced myself, wishing Diriel would send me his vaunted legion.

We took as many conscripts into our lines as would join us, and the men from Isowon took them to the rear of our army to care for them. They were all brainsick from their time with Diriel, shocked by the things they had seen and mistrusting of anyone with a weapon, but they did not rise against us once they surrendered. I galloped back and forth between the battle and our "prisoners," hoping to convince them to take up arms and help us. The men of Isowon did the same, and in fact a handful of them did join us, though the rest were too afraid. Some even escaped into the valley, where I was sure they wouldn't last the night.

The other conscripts sent against us fought like madmen. They were not quite the rabble of the first wave, and I had no doubt that the "Emperor" had threatened them with the worst possible torture should they lay down their arms. None of them seemed to care about the battle, but none of them thought Diriel would lose, either, and so they threw themselves against our swords and axes, mindlessly sacrificing themselves. Sariyah searched for Asadel, of course, but his son never appeared. He might have been among the dead for all I knew, for the dead were piling high now on the field, and the sand was thick with blood.

Of all our forces, only the men from Isowon and the Drinmen held back. We would need the Silver Dragons against the legionnaires, and I saw no need yet to call upon civilians. I would spare them what I could, I decided, and took upon myself the role of slaughterer, slashing down the conscripts who wouldn't join us and tossing them aside, piling them like cord wood as they came at me upon my horse. The butchery was easy for me, vile even, and not once did a sword or spear harm me. Malator's magic had turned me to metal, it seemed, making me impervious. But the real test was yet to come, and as I glanced out to where Diriel stood upon his chariot I realized his legions were at last preparing to ride.

"Marilius, Sariyah, Chuluun—to me!" I cried and galloped through the combat to gather them around me. One by one they fought their way toward me, knocking aside the slaves and hacking at those that wouldn't yield.

"Look," I said, pointing toward the Akyrens. "The legionnaires."

Chuluun let out a giant gasp. His brother Nalinbaatar thundered up behind him. "Good!" he cried. "We Zurans await them."

"Marilius, tell Kiryk it's time," I told him. He was covered from head to toe with blood and sweat, but had managed to keep himself alive so far. "And bring up the men from Isowon now. Remember, all of you, keep a look out for Asadel."

"What about the legion?" asked Marilius, wiping his brow with his palm.

"No mercy," I said. It was the moment I'd been craving. "Kill them all."

35

The legion of Akyre didn't bolt out into the battlefield but moved like a deliberate hand, slowly spreading out its gray fingers. First came the infantry, hundreds strong, marching out onto the battlefield and trampling the dead beneath their boots. Behind them rode the cavalry, trotting in a freakish parade, their lances and pikes poised for a charge that never came. Like a machine they came, their feet and hooves beating out a dreadful music. In the distance of the Sklar Valley, Diriel still stood upon his chariot, anticipating his victory. He was firing his best bolt at us now, the biggest weapon in his quiver, and I saw my men wilt a little at the sight of it.

How long had we fought? I'd lost all sense of time. The mercenaries were bloodied and exhausted, and the Zurans had already taken surprising losses, their numbers too small to overcome Diriel's throngs of slaves. They had started with ninety horsemen, and from what I could tell they'd lost a third of them so far. Even as the legion approached, one more of Chuluun's men passed me on the field, being dragged by a boot caught in his stirrup. I thought almost nothing of the sight until I realized the dead man was Nalinbaatar.

But Chuluun spared no time to mourn his brother. He was steely eyed upon his steed, the very picture of Bogati pride. With his bloody scimitar he pointed at the legion, rallying his men and being the first to charge. As though shamed by Chuluun's bravado, Kiryk cried out to his Drinmen.

"For Drin!"

A soldier blew a trumpet, and suddenly Kiryk and his Dragons were racing into the legion's lances. Lenhart and Sulimer followed, their swords cocked back to strike. Jaracz stayed just behind them, leading their footmen who sang out as they charged, beating their chests like wild men and cutting through the swamp of conscripts. The defenders from Isowon poured out after them, and suddenly both sides had emptied their armies onto the field. I glanced at the berm where Cern waited with Venger. I watched as the prisoners we'd taken struggled with their choices. I heard a voice in my head urging me to kill everything that moved. I even said a prayer to Cricket. Then I snapped down my bronze visor and stormed into the fray.

I found my first legionnaire, the closest one to me, surrounded by his dead-eyed brothers and armed with a spear. He raised his weapon, threw it, struck me . . . and I kept on riding, right into him, pushing the Sword of Angels straight through his head. His skull exploded at the impact, and when I turned three more heads were bobbing around me. I struck them all—one, two, three—and could not believe the ease with which they shattered. A glamour was upon me, not from heaven but from hell. I plowed my willing war horse through them, cutting of their heads like fruits.

"Blood for Malator!" I bellowed. "And bloody vengeance for his host!"

I could have flayed them, I realized. I didn't even need my sword. My strength was everything Malator had promised me, and I released myself to it, to all the rage that had built within me, and I made that sword sing! I forgot the world around me, forgot my men and duties. I even forgot good Sariyah fighting right beside me. To me the world was a smear of crimson. I feasted on the legion, hacking them down, spilling their entrails and squashing their brains so that the dark magic animating them was snuffed. My horse slowed beneath me, and I realized his hooves were buried in body parts and smothered with gore.

"Around!" I shouted, spurring the beast free. The tide of legionnaires kept coming, relentless, but their endless numbers only fed my fury. Their weapons smashed and dented me, their lifeless fingers clawed my armor, and I cut them all away from me, sending their heads spiraling from their shoulders.

"Wrestler!" I cried. "I'm coming for you!"

There was no way he could hear me. I could barely hear myself over the clash. Soldiers speak of ground-shaking battles, and the ground shook today. The air shook too, not just with screams but with death rattles. I had lost everyone in the chaos; I was completely surrounded in a noose of soulless fighters. If Sariyah was still with me, he was somewhere in the mêlée dueling for his life. Someone called out that the horsemen were upon us.

Finally, I felt something. Not quite pain, but something nonetheless. A single pale-faced legionnaire had homed on me, knocking against my horse with his own armored beast and smashing his pike into my ribs. I should have fallen, but I didn't. My armor split and blood sprayed from my side, but the blow that should have been mortal merely panged me. I grabbed the pike, yanked it from its wielder, and spun the blunt end through his eye, sawing it back and forth to wrench the brains from the hole I'd made. Yet the man-thing didn't die. It grabbed up its sword, swiping at me even as I held it at bay with its own impaled weapon.

"Die, jackal!" I screamed. "Die and be in hell!"

I released the pike, swung my own sword, and sliced down from head to heart, watching in detachment as his body opened and fell from his horse. I was like Crezil in Anton's hall, I thought. Merciless. Insatiable for blood. And nothing in the human arsenal could stop me.

I fought like this through the afternoon, the tide of bodies swelling around me, carrying my horse and me across the battlefield as I slayed them one by one. Sometimes I caught glimpses of Marilius, sometimes of Chuluun, and I knew that on the north side of the field Kiryk's Drinmen held their line. I should have been exhausted. I should have been dead! But the fire Malator had lit in me knew no end, and though my armor was battered and cracked the Sword of Angels kept its magical edge, undulled and unsated by the scores it slaughtered.

Finally I broke away from the mass of Akyrens, driving my horse to a tiny patch of blood-soaked sand in the center of the battle. I spied the berm where, amazingly, Cern still waited with Venger. They were alone on the dune, protected now only the by the conscripts we had rescued from the field. These men had at least gotten to their feet, raising their weapons once again as if to hold the horde from Isowon. I looked for Marilius, so he could lead the conscripts into the fight. Sariyah was far from me now, his axe rising and falling on the heads of his attackers. The spell of bloodlust released me for a moment, clearing my mind enough to really *see* the battlefield. So astonished was I by the sight, that I nearly dropped my sword.

The mass of men who had faced each other just hours earlier had dwindled, both sides diminished to a third of their numbers. Corpses covered every grain of sand. A thunderhead of buzzards blocked the sky above, the smell of death drawing them for miles. The ground sucked at the hooves of my mount, saturated with blood, and hundreds of bruised and severed heads littered the earth, laying in their own gore or kicked along like playthings by battling horses. Limbs were everywhere. Prayers rose to heaven. I looked back and saw the path I'd cut and could not believe the carnage I'd made.

I couldn't say how many legionnaires were left. Hundreds, certainly. But the conscripts who'd stayed to fight for Diriel were mostly dead, lifeless on the field or crawling over the bodies of men and dogs and horses. My own men were among them, heaped atop them with their own screams and missing limbs. The Bogati had all but disappeared, and I could not find Chuluun in the chaos. The mercenaries had fared only slightly better, and only because their numbers had been so many more. Now they fought in little pockets, exhaustedly swinging at the throats of the legionnaires, desperate to remove their heads. I swung my horse north toward the Drinmen, spotted Kiryk in the tumult and realized he was all alone. Neither Sulimer nor Lenhart nor Jaracz were beside him, just a handful of Silver Dragons.

I made the bloody calculations and realized we were losing.

"Marilius!" I shouted, throwing myself once more into the battle. I needed to reach him, to find him and rally him, but a wall of soldiers blocked my way. I cut at them, stabbing and trampling into the heart of the fray, calling out to the mercenaries to help me find Marilius. At last I found him, still alive, still atop his wounded horse. A band of mercenaries fought alongside him, encircled by legionnaires. I watched, amazed, as Marilius hacked at them, his helmet knocked from his head, his face scarlet. He looked nothing like the youngster who'd brought me to Isowon. That fellow was gone, replaced by a berserker.

"Here, devils!" I cried, luring the legionnaires to me. They turned at once, sighting me and raising their weapons, some on foot, others on horses so damaged now they could barely stand. Marilius and his gang pressed with new vigor, fighting their way out of the noose as he we swatted a path to each other.

"Lukien, get to the front!" cried Marilius as our steeds met. "Get to Diriel before they push us back!"

"We can use the conscripts," I shouted. "Get to them. Get them out here to fight."

"Them?" Marilius glanced over his shoulder toward the rear of our broken ranks. "They can't fight, Lukien."

"They're ready," I swore. "Rally them! Tell them we can win!"

"Lukien, you can win! Fight your way to Diriel and kill him. We'll ride with you!"

"Go!" I ordered. Killing Diriel wasn't my plan. "Bring them into the fight. Drag them out there if you have to!"

"He won't have to," cried one of the mercs. "Look!"

Together we turned toward the sand dunes. A wave of men came pouring onto the field, ragged, exhausted, but holding high their weapons and shrieking like madmen. The charge of the conscripts fed our army's spirit. The mercs cheered when they saw them, and the Drinmen picked up the cry. The men of Isowon joined their brothers, and suddenly we were moving again, pushing hard against the Akyren wall, exploiting every tiny crack.

"Malator, where's Sariyah?" I asked. I searched the field, but in the madness saw no sign of him. "I have to get to him. I have to protect him."

Suddenly Malator burst into my mind. *Lukien! Diriel!*

Suddenly the cue I'd waited for all day had come. At once I whipped my horse around, sitting up high and riding out to see. And there was Diriel's chariot, turning at last from the battlefield.

A thrill shot through me. Now I needed speed.

"Marilius, take the front!" I shouted.

Marilius looked stunned to see me riding the wrong way. "What? Where are you going?"

"Trust me, remember? You're in command now. Don't give them an inch! Push until your heart bursts. Push and push until they're dead!"

"Damn it, Lukien, you can't leave us! Tell me where you're going!"

"To save Anton," I shouted. "To kill Diriel!"

I heard his curses follow me as I raced toward the berm, where my swift-footed Venger waited.

36

Venger was the kind of horse that would literally run until he died. He had that kind of rare heart, so I knew that what I asked of him that night was not impossible. It was nearly dusk by the time we left the Sklar Valley, but I didn't notice the sun until the battlefield was far behind us. I pointed Venger east, following the coast, choosing the quickest route I knew to the tombs of the Kings of Akyre. I doubted Diriel or anyone had seen my escape, but I knew that the madman himself would be close behind me. There was only one thing he wanted enough to make him leave the battle, I knew, and I suppose he thought his generals could take care of the rabble he was leaving behind. I didn't know how well Marilius would fare, if he'd be dead when I returned or if Isowon would be overrun by legionnaires. I had but one plan in mind to end my enemies, and it all depended on Venger.

And on Crezil.

So we rode, through the forest and through riverbanks, and through the night when it finally came. I used the eyesight Malator had given me to navigate the hazards on our way, and Venger trusted me completely, never flagging even as the road grew rocky. It was nearly a full day's journey to the tombs, a treacherous trip in darkness, and yet Venger seemed as enchanted as I was, as though he too gleaned power from the sword. Malator remained silent inside me, hidden from me, but I could still feel the enormous strength of him coursing through me. My armor and the flesh beneath it had been battered. Pieces of my golden suit hung from rivets. I had bathed in blood and smelled of every human stink, and I knew I looked like a carcass as I rode, finally stopping at a river to rest my horse and wash myself. The moon rose above me. I stopped splashing and knelt by the river to listen to the silence. Venger lapped the water next to me. Insects made their noises. But there were no screams, no clash of swords. Slowly, I felt my humanity creeping back.

How could that be, I wondered? I had no soul, yet still had a conscience. I regretted nothing of what I'd done, the heads I'd taken. And yet . . .

Washing myself had turned the river scarlet. It looked black in the moonlight. I saw my stricken face in the water.

"I'm broken," I whispered. "I need to fix myself."

But not yet. I still had vengeance to meet out.

The valley of the tombs was suitably deathlike when I finally reached it. With hours left until morning, the moon waned over the dark land, barely touching the valley with its light. By now poor Venger had given me all he could. I dismounted and led him by foot between the hills and toward the ribbon of water leading to Crezil's tomb. The place was deserted, of course, but I knew Diriel wouldn't be far behind me. He would take enough horses with him to expire as many as he needed, but he wouldn't reach the tomb until sunrise. That gave me time to rest and plan. More importantly, it let me seek out Crezil for myself.

As if awakened by the valley, Malator suddenly stirred within my mind. I picked up a broken branch, held it out in my hand, and asked the Akari to light it for me. At once a soft, heatless glow engulfed the stick, lighting the river rocks around me. Crezil's cave lay just ahead, the great, silent maw of it menacing me. I glanced around, looking for fresh victims, piles of bone, anything to tell me whether Crezil had fed. The area was eerily bare.

"Malator," I whispered, "is it in there?"

Yes, said Malator.

"Is it awake?"

Yes. And it knows we're here.

I approached the entrance to the tomb, sensing the monster within it. Through Malator's eyes I saw it deep within its lair, waiting near the portal to its own, hellish world. Crezil felt curious to me, almost impatient. I thought of going to speak to it, but stopped myself.

"Wait," I said, trying to impart my thoughts to the creature. "Soon. Soon we'll make our bargain."

If the beast could hear me or sense my words, it made no move to say so. It merely waited, and in the cloudy vision of Malator's sight I saw it looking back at me with its many eyes. It had changed again, I realized. Divested of bones and human flesh, it was naked now, like it had been when Anton had first pulled it through the portal. Even in the darkness it was enormously vile. I shut my mind to it, shuddering, and stepped back from the entrance.

"Will it wait?" I asked Malator.

For a time, I think, he replied. *But not much past morning.*

"It won't have to wait past morning," I said confidently.

I no longer felt immortal. The battle had drained me, or maybe it was seeing so many, many dead. Slowly I stripped off my ruined armor, examining each damaged piece as I laid it aside. The vambraces were cracked, and the breastplate was so badly dented that it pushed against my chest. I had cuts and bruises I didn't even realize were there until I peeled the armor off. Finally, when that was done, I stripped off the torn and bloodied shirt beneath. I made a filthy pile of the lot until all I wore were my trousers and boots and the blue hahlag Chuluun had given me.

Then, afraid to sleep, I settled myself down at the edge of the river with the Sword of Angels in my lap and waited for the sun.

Crezil did not come out of its lair that night. It remained true to the bargain we'd struck, waiting patiently for me to deliver on my promise. When the sun finally came up over the valley, I realized I had nodded off, and looked around my peaceful spot for any signs of Diriel. I did not have long to wait.

Like me, they had ridden through the night, but unlike me they didn't have Venger or a pair of magical eyes. I don't know if they expected to see me or not, but when they finally rounded the hill and saw me by the river, they reined in their horses with contempt. Diriel looked exhausted, his face more wild than I'd ever seen. He had taken three bodyguards with him, all legionnaires and all as dead-eyed as the others, dressed in gray and crimson and staring soundlessly at me. And of course, Wrestler had come. He rode his horse the closest to me, splashing into the river and grinning triumphantly when he saw me.

"Have you come to protect your monster?" he taunted. "Good! Fight us for it and lose!"

Diriel trotted closer. "Sir Lukien, will you honor our bargain and give me the monster? We will kill you for it if we must."

"You still make that boast?" I said. "After you've seen what I can do?" I rose to my feet with my sword still sheathed. "How many of your men do you need me to slaughter, Diriel?"

"Your men fought better than I ever imagined," Diriel admitted, "but they haven't won yet."

"How do you know? You ran away once your slaves revolted."

"Because the battle is as good as mine. Don't you see? All of this belongs to me! This is my empire! Even that monster is my slave. Now, stand aside."

"Truly, you are mad," I sighed. "I could kill you with a breath yet you don't see that." I looked at Wrestler. "What about you, gargoyle? Still think you can beat me?"

"Put down your sword and let me try," replied Wrestler. "Fight like a real man."

"I want the monster," Diriel said again. He'd ridden all night and had lost all patience. "Give it to me."

"Believe it or not, that's why I'm here," I relented. "I am a Knight of Liiria, and a knight keeps his word." I strapped the sword around my waist again. "The monster Crezil is there." I pointed toward the cave. "That's its lair."

Diriel went white. "The tomb of my fathers . . ."

"Anton Fallon woke it when he desecrated your ancestors," I said. "He pulled it from its world into this one."

"That's why it's hunting him," said Diriel with delight. "Revenge!"

I didn't bother correcting him. "It's lost here," I said. "It needs a master to guide it. I promised I'd give it to you, Diriel. If you want it, it's yours."

"At what price?" challenged Wrestler. "We've already won Isowon!"

"You haven't yet," I shot back. "But that's not the bargain. You're my price, Wrestler. After I give Crezil to Diriel, you wait here for me. You don't run or hide. You face me and die."

"Put down your sword, and we'll fight now," spat Wrestler. "Don't wait, coward."

"I want the creature!" cried Diriel. "Give it to me, Sir Lukien. Now!"

I looked only at Wrestler. "Do we have a deal?"

"We do!"

I stepped aside for Diriel. "Follow me, then. Just you."

Diriel dismounted and approached me. "If this is a trick, you should know I will be unmerciful to you, Sir Lukien, and to every child in Isowon."

"No more threats, Diriel," I said. "I'm sick of hearing them. Come and get your monster."

Wrestler and the trio of legionnaires dismounted but did not follow us as I led Diriel toward the cave. With the sun coming up the entrance looked less forbidding, and Diriel was so out of his mind that he seemed not to care. I led him past the slab guarding the tomb, scraping past the crack in the rock. He gasped as we crossed the threshold, just as Cricket and I had done when we first entered the tomb. I held up my flaming stick so he could behold the ancient glories. The paintings and sculptures jumped to life. The eyes of the stone animals gazed on us. Diriel pursed his lips like a child, taking it all in.

"Magnificent."

"This is the tomb of Atarkin," I said. "The last emperor of Akyre."

"And now I am the first again," he said, awed by his own words. He went to the stone coffin that had once held Atarkin's mummied corpse. He ran his fingers over it, grimacing with his sharp teeth.

"You've given your loyalty to a criminal," he said. "Anton Fallon must pay for desecrating this place. Do not expect me to spare him. I cannot."

"We came for your monster," I reminded him. "This is where it sleeps."

"It's sleeping?" asked Diriel. He splashed into the stream running through the cave. "Can you waken it?"

"It's waiting for you," I said. I was actually getting nervous, and could hear the quaver in my voice. "It knows you're coming."

"It knows I am Emperor," said Diriel madly. "It will bow to me when it sees me."

"It needs you," I said, trying to sound calm. And nothing I'd said so far was a lie. I'd figured it out—the whole riddle of the beast. "Soon you'll both have what you want."

"And you'll be dead," said Diriel sadly. "Wrestler will kill you, you know. Without your sword, you cannot beat him."

"Just keep your bargain and make sure he doesn't try to run."

I held up the flaming stick, lighting the way to the chamber where I knew Crezil was waiting—the portal chamber. "This way," I told Diriel.

For the first time, Diriel hesitated. He peered down the narrow corridor of rock. "Where are we going?"

"To see your monster," I said. I looked at him. "Are you afraid?"

He was. His mask of madness cracked just enough for me to see it. "I have never been afraid," he said. "Continue."

With the flame lighting my way, I stepped into the rocky corridor. I could feel the unmistakable presence of the beast up ahead, calmly crouching in the darkness. My eyes scanned the gloom. I went deeper, leading Diriel onward, and finally saw the source of the river, still flowing magically into the wall. The portal flared with light suddenly, revealing Crezil's hellish world. Diriel shielded his eyes from the flare, squinting to see, and when he opened them again he saw the monster emerging from the dark.

I stood very still, not moving forward but not backing away either. Crezil rose up on its sinewy legs, its pink eyes blinking, its naked body pulsing like the throat of a frog. It was enormous, made more so by the smallness of the space, its many heads lowered on its necks. No bones or stolen flesh hid it this time. Now I could see it all, the same, repulsive creature revealed by the painting just behind it over the portal. A human face stared back at me. A bird face clicked its beak. The goat head shook its bloody horns and the pig's jowls dripped blood. Fleshy tongues darted in and out like tentacles.

"Crezil," I pronounced. "I have brought you your master."

Diriel was like stone beside me, his mouth hanging open and his eyes wide. He stared at the creature in disbelief. I knew I had to speak fast.

"This is your master," I told Crezil. "Not Anton Fallon. Not the one who woke you. This is the last King of Akyre. He is of the blood!"

"Yes!" crowed Diriel. "I am your master, beast! The blood of a hundred Akyren kings runs in my veins!"

"Not Anton, Crezil. Not Anton. Do you understand?" I pointed at Diriel. "Him!" I looked at Diriel, waiting for the sign to tell me I'd done right. "He is your master, Crezil," I insisted. "He's the one you're looking for. Take him!"

"Yes!" nodded Diriel. "I am . . ." He glanced at me. "What?"

"Take him!" I shouted.

As he looked at me, stunned, the mark of the monster appeared on Diriel's forehead. I smiled with more contentment than I'd ever felt in my life.

"It's yours, Diriel," I hissed. "Kasdeyi Orioc! The Guardian-Slave of Gahoreth. You'll be Crezil's master, but not in this world." I turned toward the creature. "Take him home, Crezil. You can go now. You've got what I promised. You're free!"

"What?" cried Diriel. "No, here! Here in this world!" He looked up into Crezil's monstrous faces. "I am your master. Obey me!"

"It came here because Fallon called it by desecrating these tombs," I said. "Your ancestors bound this thing to themselves for protection. But they didn't realize they weren't just protecting this tomb. It's been looking for its master ever since it got here. It needs to take you with it." I stopped smiling. I almost pitied him. "Don't run, Diriel. Don't bother."

But Diriel tried. He turned and took quick steps before a snake-like tongue shot out and seized him, wrapping around his neck. Another grabbed his waist, and another his ankles. Soon he was hovering, carried up by the monster and being dragged backward. He screamed, his face puffing for air, the black tattoo on his forehead flaring to life as he got closer to the portal. Crezil ignored me. It had what it wanted, and our bargain was done. If it was glad for it I couldn't tell. I watched as it stepped into the living painting, dragging the screaming Diriel into Gahoreth.

The glow from the painting vanished, and all was darkness again. Diriel's cries echoed down the cave and then were gone, disappearing like the man who'd made them. He wasn't dead, though. He was just in the realm of the dead. I suppose he still had his soul, and that irked me. A man like that . . . it seemed so unfair.

37

I took my time leaving the tomb. For awhile I stared at the place where the portal had been, wondering at the kind of world Diriel would find there. It seemed perfect for a cruel lunatic like him. I had, in fact, kept my promise to him. I had given him what he wanted: his monster. Let Gahoreth deal with him, I figured. This world, *my* world, was better off without him.

In the last two days I had killed more men than I could count. Their blood crusted my fingernails. But I still had one more execution to carry out. I lingered by the dead portal a few moments more, then sauntered out of the chamber and through the corridors of the tomb without the aid of my fire stick. I didn't suppose that Wrestler had run off. In some ways he was as insane as Diriel and still thought he could best me. When at last I emerged from the cave, Wrestler was waiting for me, standing in the river, stripped to the waist. He had removed his sword as well, tossing it to the riverbank where his horse waited. The three legionnaires lay dead in the mud.

At first I thought Wrestler had killed them. He was completely unbothered by their corpses, stretching his enormous back and contorting his arms into impossible shapes as he prepared for our fight. He paused as he saw me come out of the cave, and didn't seem surprised I was alone.

"You killed him," sighed Wrestler. "I knew it the moment these clods dropped dead. Diriel was a fool to trust you."

"No, I didn't," I said. "Your master got what he wanted. The monster took him to hell." I stepped out to the bank of the river, spying the dead legionnaires. If they had died when Diriel left, maybe the other legionnaires did, too. That was part of the plan I hadn't counted on, but it thrilled me. Isowon was safe, then. "You should have run," I told Wrestler. "I would have found you eventually, but as least you'd have had a chance."

Wrestler threaded his fingers together, raised his hands over his bald head, and stretched his body until his spine popped. He bent almost all the way backwards, then stood upright again, grabbed his right leg, and touched his ankle to his chin. I had never seen anything like it.

"Do you know how hard it is for me to find an opponent worth fighting? Maybe you'll be it this time. You certainly weren't last time." He gestured to my sword. "Will you be a man and toss that away?"

I thought of taking his head off with a stroke. He knew I could have, but knew I wouldn't. I undid the Sword of Angels from my waist and laid it down in the mud of the river bank. I expected Malator to scream at me, to chide my foolishness, but he didn't. Instead he whispered vengeance in my ear.

Make him suffer.

I pulled off my boots and lay them by my sword. I had wrestled like this as a boy, half-naked and brutal, just to prove myself. It felt oddly familiar when my bare feet hit the mud. I strode out into the river, charged with Malator's power. Wrestler seemed to be growing by the moment. His giant chest swelled out as he stretched, his ropey arms flexing. The veins in his head pulsed and turned his face scarlet.

"Something went wrong in this part of the world," I lamented as I watched him. "Butchers for kings, freaks for subjects. I won't miss this place at all."

Wrestler stopped stretching and made his stance, bending his knees to pounce. "She said her name was Lisea," he taunted. "Have you ever been with so young a girl?"

Why, I wondered, had she told him that? Had she remembered her name when he was raping her? But there was nothing he could say to goad me. "She was better than this world," I replied. "She's in a better place. Not where you're going, by the way."

I saw no remorse in him at all. "You loved her."

"I loved her," I admitted. "But with humanity. You're an animal, Wrestler."

We'd both crawled out of slums, I realized. Wrestler became a beast. I became . . . whatever I was. I didn't move, waiting for him to come. When he did he came flying. His big body left the ground, his arms out and reaching, spanning the yards between us like a stallion. His speed shocked me, and though I spun to avoid him he hooked me somehow with his fingers, grabbing my ankle as he crashed to the ground and twisted me off my feet. My face hit the rocks; I felt a sudden pain as he wrenched my leg upward. Just as he'd done in Arad, he wrapped himself around me like tentacles, forcing me into his hold.

I barely resisted.

His legs wrapped around my chest and squeezed. The air seeped from my lungs. I closed my eyes and summoned the strength of Malator, concentrating only on my pinned right arm. Wrestler put all his might into crushing me. I felt my bones constrict under his assault. I could smell his sweat as it dripped on me. Slowly, bit by bit, I tugged my arm out of his hold. He cursed as he felt me slipping away, tried to flip me onto my back. That one fatal move loosened his grip. Out came my arm, my fingers like arrows shooting into his skull, bursting one of his eyes. Wrestler screamed, letting go of me and spinning away, but now I was the hunter. I snaked my arm around his neck, used my other arm for leverage, and dragged him backward. He fell against me, choking, gurgling, his legs flailing and his eye socket sluicing blood.

"Wait, wait," I whispered in his ear. "Don't die yet."

His iron fingers worked to wedge themselves under my hold. I tightened just enough to threaten him. Saliva dripped from his mouth, but his screams were nearly silent, more like a screech.

"Now you know what it's like to be helpless," I said, wrenching him back each time he struggled. "Now you know what it's like to be a little girl, afraid, with no one around to help you!"

He cursed and kicked but couldn't free himself. I delighted in his antics. Like a cruel child I wanted to torture him, to make him suffer as Cricket had suffered, but I knew there was no bringing her back. There was only this brutal kind of justice.

"Good-bye, Wrestler," I sneered. "Let's see how you do with a broken neck."

I jerked back, flexed my arm, and snapped him like a toy, twisting his head around as the last breath gurgled from his lips. He died instantly, falling against me, then into the river. I leaned back and watched the water wash through his ruined eye, and I remembered how much losing an eye had hurt. It was so much worse than when my neck broke. I was glad Wrestler had experienced both.

His horse nibbled at the grass by the riverbank. The horses of the three dead legionnaires wandered aimlessly around their corpses. I stood up in the river, and when I did Venger came to me, splashing through the water to reach me. It took a moment for me to realize it was over. I rubbed Venger's eager nose, my mind strangely blank. With the legionnaires dead, surely Isowon was safe now. There was almost no reason for me to return there.

Almost no reason. There was still the matter of friendship.

38

The next afternoon, I returned to Sklar Valley.

I rode like a savage onto the bloodied sands, half-naked, my ruined shirt left behind at the tombs. I had even left my bronze armor there. I supposed it could have been repaired again, but I didn't feel like the "Bronze Knight" any longer. I wasn't sure who I was now. Without a soul I wasn't really human. Humans weren't immortal. Gods were, I supposed, but I certainly wasn't one of those. Mostly I felt lost, and very, very anxious to go home to Jador.

Finding the valley was simple enough. I merely followed the cloud of buzzards. The roar of battle had fled, but people still moved among the dead in the field. Mostly these were folk from Isowon, men and women who'd come out from the city to look for survivors and start burying the countless dead. A stench had already started rising from the corpses. Buzzards and other beasties pulled at fallen flesh. I rode Venger into the heart of the field, going mostly unnoticed by the soldiers and civilians. At once I saw the bodies of legionnaires scattered in the human wreckage. Like their brothers at the tomb they had collapsed when Diriel left. It was a mystery even Malator couldn't quite explain—something about his being the one who called them. I reined in Venger over one of the figures, looking into his white face. He'd already been dead, long before yesterday.

"Are you with Diriel in Gahoreth now?" I wondered out loud.

"Lukien!"

I turned at the sound of my name, seeing Kiryk striding up to me through the carnage. He had a huge gash down his face, still unbandaged, and had not even cleaned off his blood-soaked uniform. He looked exhausted, too, barely recognizable. Worse than that, he was all alone. My head swiveled to scan the field, and I did see a handful of Drinmen, but none of the proud trio that always accompanied the young king. Kiryk stopped just in front of my horse, looking up at me in shock, immediately asking the question I knew he would.

"Why'd you leave us?"

I tossed my leg over Venger's back, dropping down to face him. "I had to. It was the only way. Diriel's gone, Kiryk."

"You could have killed him on the battlefield. You could have done it easily."

"I had other business." I kicked at the dead legionnaire with my boot. "They fell like dolls. All I had to do was cut the strings." I glanced around the grim scene. "Lenhart?"

"Dead," said Kiryk.

"Jaracz?"

"Dead. Sulimer too."

I hesitated. "Sariyah?"

Kiryk's face caved with sadness. "He found his son. They're both dead, Lukien."

"How?" I asked softly.

Kiryk unbuttoned the top of his uniform and sighed. "Asadel wasn't a conscript. He'd been given the powder, Lukien. He was one of Diriel's. When the rest of them fell, so did he. They just kind of dropped where they were standing. And then . . ." He shrugged. "Then it was over. It was just over." He looked around, still trying to make sense of the horror. "Over."

We stood like that for awhile, together and alive in a sea of heads and body parts. A good many mercenaries were among the fallen. Zurans, too. I thought of Chuluun, my friend for so brief a time, and how anxious he'd been to fight with me. I still wore the hahlag he'd given me around my neck, only now it was splattered with blood. Where was he in this slaughter, I wondered?

"We buried Sariyah with his son," said Kiryk. He pointed to the very sand dune where Cern had waited with Venger the day before. Now it was covered with men with shovels, burying the dead who'd been dragged to the berm.

"Not exactly a hero's grave," I sighed.

"My men are there too. Better than being food for vermin."

I nodded at that. So far, I'd been too afraid to ask my final question. "Kiryk," I said. "I see a whole lot of dead mercenaries."

"Yes."

"Did Marilius make it?"

At last, Kiryk cracked a grin. "He did."

"He did?"

"That's one lucky man," said Kiryk. "Lost a hand, though." He flexed his right hand. "This one. Lost it in the last charge. No more freelancing for him."

It was an unholy thing to smile in such a place, but I did. Of all the men who'd died here, Marilius had survived. That, at least, was something. I wanted to go to him, to tell him about Diriel and Wrestler and to see his missing hand.

First, though, there were bodies to bury.

Late that night I returned to Anton's palace with Kiryk. Instead of mercenaries, servants greeted us, hurrying us to Anton's lush baths and filling us with food and drink. The palace was less grand than I remembered—Anton had given most of his belongings to his mercenaries—yet there remained that sense of wonder to the place, and I let the bare-breasted serving girls pamper me, massaging my shoulders in the bath and feeding me newly plucked grapes. Kiryk dismissed himself quickly after that, anxious to be with his fellow Drinmen and make his way home. He left the very next day.

I remained in the palace for a week. Occasionally I visited Marilius in his sick bed and jibed him about his missing hand. Anton spared no expense for his dear captain's comfort, of course. Marilius had his own room and his own servants, even a musician who sometimes sang to him while he tried to sleep. The pain of his wounds was excruciating, but it would pass. Not only had he lost his right hand to a legionnaire, but he'd taken a sword to the side of his belly as well. He looked like a real man now, I told him. The father who had so easily disowned him would have been proud.

I healed, too. I spent my time looking at what was left of Anton's art collection. I swam in his pools and made love to his servant girls. I even sniffed some of his spices. I wanted to forget, but I couldn't. Cricket was always in the back of my mind, dying over and over again in my arms, and no amount of spice or lovemaking could make her go away.

Anton and I made peace, and I no longer blamed him for all that had happened. The tattoo of Crezil had vanished from his forehead, and he delighted at the story of Diriel's demise, insisting I tell it to him again and again. He'd lost so many men, but he would rebuild. He still had his spice routes, and he still had his guile. Each day he implored me to stay behind, to be his personal bodyguard or help rebuild his private army, and although Isowon was truly like paradise, I was never tempted by his offer. I had my own home and ached to see it again.

Finally, with Venger beneath me and fresh new clothes on my back, I left Isowon. I pointed us toward Arad, said my good-byes to the city on the sea, and rode for Jador. I had many days of travel ahead of me and no real hurry. Gilwyn and White-Eye's baby wasn't due for a while yet, and without Cricket I had no mission for myself. I wore the Sword of Angels, of course, but without my armor didn't think myself a knight-errant anymore. My time in the Bitter Kingdoms had cured me of that. Now it was back to the boredom of Jador, of hunting rass for sport and lying out in the desert to wonder at the stars.

I passed through all the towns I had passed with Cricket, retracing our steps so I could remember her perfectly. And when I finally reached Arad I went to the spot where Wrestler had broken my neck and where Marilius had saved me. Malator was my soul companion, and I spent long hours speaking to him while I rode. Sometimes he would appear beside me, sometimes only in my brain. We spoke of good things, mostly, and he told me stories about the way his life had been when he was alive. I made my own confessions, too, the secret things that Cricket could never pry out of me. I was happy, or at least mostly contented, but I still had questions for Malator. Too much had gone unsaid.

Two days after leaving Arad, we came to a nameless forest. With a stream and leaves falling into the water, I knew I had found the perfect place to rest and, perhaps, get some answers. I made camp in a tiny clearing, where a hole in the treetops let me see the sky, and built a fire to warm myself as the sun slowly went down. Venger drank from the stream as I ate supper from my saddle bags, and when the first stars appeared I settled down in front of the fire, lay the Sword of Angels in my lap, and called forth my Akari.

"Malator." I practically whispered his name. "It's time for answers."

It is.

He gave no argument, but materialized before me, sitting cross-legged like some shaman in the firelight. This time he didn't wear his military garb. He dressed himself in simple Akari clothing, like a man at leisure. I looked at him and smiled.

"I did as you asked," I said. "I have no friends but you. I gave myself to you, and you granted me vengeance. I'm grateful to you, Malator. But now I need to know—will you tell me without riddles? At last, will you please?"

"There are doors, Lukien," said Malator. "Like the portal Crezil came through. Ways for men to enter other realms as Diriel did. Only he was taken there against his will."

"Go on," I said softly.

Malator looked sad. "You think I've been harsh with you. But I tried to warn you about Cricket. I told you to go to the Bitter Kingdoms on your own. I wanted you to learn. What did you learn?"

I thought hard over that. "That there are monsters?" I ventured. "Other worlds. I knew that already though. I learned that I have no soul. I learned that I am special, or so you keep telling me. Only that's the part I don't understand, Malator. How can all of this been worth it? What did you want to teach me?"

"Not teach you," he corrected. His eyes shimmered. "Change you. And I have. You are not a simple man any longer, Lukien. You could have gone through that portal to Gahoreth as easily as Diriel, but without Crezil. No other man could have done that. No living man."

"You confuse me, Malator," I said. "Why would I want to go to Gahoreth?"

"Because you can," he said. "Because no other man alive can. Because Gahoreth is a world of the dead, and there are many such worlds. Without a soul, you are a walker between these worlds, Lukien. You can see things no man alive has seen." He leaned forward. "Even lost loves."

His words chilled me. I blinked but didn't speak. I couldn't bring myself to hope it. "What?"

"Cassandra, Lukien," said Malator. "You can be together with her, if you wish it. You can find the door to her death place and walk through it and back again. This is not death I speak of. Death would take you out of this world forever. I'm talking about you, alive, as you are now."

"Cassandra . . ." I spoke the name like a prayer. "If I find the doorway?"

"I can help you, Lukien. Together we will find it. And others too."

"How?" I asked. "When?"

"The same way we found Gahoreth—by following the clues. When?" Malator shrugged. "Whenever you wish it."

"This is your gift to me," I realized. "For all my suffering. A great gift." I sat back and spied the twinkling stars. "A walker between the worlds," I sighed. "Yes."